"I want you. Right here and now."

"So why are we still talking?" Annie asked.

"Because we both need to know what we're getting into."

"I won't read anything into this if you won't. Or are you telling me you've changed your mind?"

"Does it feel as if I have?" Sam's arms tightened around her. "I'm just trying to keep things straight."

"I'm tired of keeping things straight. For once I want to be absolutely reckless." She stared up at him. "You're supposed to grab me and jump me, McKade."

"I'm considering it," he said thickly.

Annie leaned into him, remembering every detail of his powerful body. *Could you ever go back?*

She found the buttons on his shirt. "Done considering yet?"

Sam's eyes darkened as he freed her skirt. "I was done two days ago."

Books by Christina Skye

CODE NAME: NANNY

HOT PURSUIT

MY SPY

GOING OVERBOARD

2000 KISSES

THE RUBY

COME THE NIGHT

COME THE DAWN

THE BLACK ROSE

MY SPY

Christina Skye

A Dell Book

MY SPY
A Dell Book

PUBLISHING HISTORY
A Dell Book / February 2002
Dell mass market special edition / August 2004

Published by
Bantam Dell
A Division of Random House, Inc.
New York, New York

This is a work of fiction. Names, characters, places, and incidents
either are the product of the author's imagination or are used fictitiously.
Any resemblance to actual persons, living or dead, events, or locales is
entirely coincidental.

ISBN 0-440-24249-5

Manufactured in the United States of America
Published simultaneously in Canada

OPM   10   9   8   7   6   5   4   3   2   1

MY SPY

Prologue

It was a good thing Sam McKade didn't believe in love.

He never had, not in all of his thirty-seven years. He was pretty sure he never would.

Standing on a polished yacht off the California coast, with one shoulder to the mast and the sun streaming down from the west, he looked toward the beach and a woman in a battered straw hat.

Something kept him motionless, watching her climb the sunlit dunes. Not her body, even though that had been remarkable. Not her smile, like clear sun on clean water.

He frowned.

No, it was the way she'd drawn him into her world with open arms, sharing everything she was and expecting nothing particular in return.

Her generosity, he thought. Her warm, open laughter. Those were the things that held him here.

Sam's hand tightened on the mast as he remembered how they'd spent last night, naked on the teak deck, looking up at the stars when they weren't wrapped around each other, driven by reckless hunger or caught in laughter like a pair of loony, irresponsible kids.

But Commander Sam McKade was no kid.

His gear was stowed below, coffee steamed in a thermos, and he'd laid in his position on the sat-nav. He was ready to go hunting.

Yet something held him in this sunny cove, curiously tense as he watched a lone woman cross the dunes, hat in hand.

She was probably humming. Probably had a handful of straggly flowers in her hand. Probably she'd forgotten him already.

That idea hurt more than it should.

He jammed a hand through his hair. He had no time for day-dreams. He had known what he wanted to do with his life since the moment he could say Navy SEALs, and that's exactly what he'd done. Now he had a mission to complete and a rendezvous in four days north of Puerto Vallarta.

Time to go.

He shaded his eyes, looking up the hillside. He saw her there, hat in hand, waving broadly. He answered, feeling a punch of regret when she turned and vanished over the hill.

What did he expect? Did he think that she'd ask him to stay?

Hell, he didn't believe in love. There was no possible reason for regret or delays. No need to wonder about why and when and what might have been.

Time to haul up anchor and raise sails. Time to steer back in harm's way, deep undercover as he skirted the Baja coast for a meet that was bound to turn ugly.

He had escaped death twice in the last three months. Now things were going to get even tougher. The net was closing, and his target was in sight. Not even a breathtaking, stubborn, amazing woman called Annie could get in the way of what lay ahead.

Sam McKade had a traitor to catch.

And he had to do it before the traitor caught him.

Week One

Chapter One

"There's a naked man in the swimming pool."

Annie O'Toole didn't turn her head.

Smiling, she watched her assistant bend closer to the telescope positioned by the broad glass windows of Summerwind Resort and Beach Club.

Every inch of it was hers, from the high flagstone terraces to the windswept beach. And as far as Annie was concerned, work outweighed any male body—naked or not.

"Trust me, Megan, he isn't naked."

Her assistant squinted harder. "Wait, I'm serious here. I can't tell if that's his butt or his—"

Annie reached across and covered the lens. "That's not a naked man, that's Mr. Harkowitz from room thirty-one. He always wears a flesh-colored suit for the shock value."

Annie's assistant gave up in disgust. "From what I saw, Mr. Harkowitz doesn't have a whole lot to shock with."

"The man's pushing ninety, so give him a break. And if the naked-body scare is over, maybe we could get back to work." Annie stared down the length of the table. Her staff was excellent, and she paid them well. Each one was experienced, fit, and enthusiastic. Annie knew she was lucky to have them.

But lately they made her feel . . .

Old.

Stupid, of course. Annie wasn't even thirty. There was no earthly reason she should feel as if her life were stuck on the pause button.

She cleared her throat. "We've got new arrivals in the Santa Barbara Suite. They'll need lavender salt glow scrub and our signature candles. Repeat guests in rooms twenty-two through thirty-five. Remember the daily flower arrangements. And put out edible chocolate body paint for the honeymooners in the Monterey Suite."

Ignoring an off-color comment, Annie shoved back a strand of cinnamon-colored hair, once again struck by the sense that life was passing her by.

She drove away the thought. "Heather, what about the new inversion equipment?"

"Up and running." Her Pilates trainer, a twenty-year-old with impossibly small thighs, snapped to attention. "They're fully booked."

Annie made a note in her book and moved on. "Zoe, what about the organic produce?"

Her chef shrugged. "The new beds are thriving. We'll have lettuce and baby carrots before the end of the month. But . . ."

Annie crossed another item off her list. "Is there a problem?"

"The new basil is ruined."

Annie's eyes narrowed. "Vandals?"

"Rabbits." The chef drummed her fingers on the country pine table. "Damned sneaking little things."

Annie fought back a smile. Somehow rabbits didn't seem like a particularly earthshaking threat. "Try more netting. I'll have Reynaldo take a look after lunch." She made another quick note, then moved on. "Marty, what about the problems with the new whirlpool overlooking the beach?"

Chairs creaked. Annie glanced up, searching for her chief engineer. "Where's Marty?"

Across the table Zoe cleared her throat. "Remember how he wanted to clear that brush near the garden?"

"Don't tell me the rabbits got him, too."

"Not rabbits, poison ivy. Full body. The man's blown up like a radioactive radish."

Annie blew out a breath and scribbled another reminder on her list. "I'll go see Marty as soon as we finish up. Meanwhile, we need that new whirlpool ready for evening treatments, and all the landscaping has to be in place." She stared out the window, watching a lone surfer tackle a pounding wave out beyond the cove.

For a moment she yearned to be there beside him, feeling the sun, face to the wind.

Or maybe on a sleek boat with sails unfurled.

No, she couldn't think about *that*. Not ever again.

She stared blindly at her leather notebook. "Let's phone the company in Monterey, Megan. See if they can send someone to check the whirlpool installation."

"Sure thing, boss."

Boss? The word had never bothered Annie before, but now she winced.

Could you have a midlife crisis at twenty-seven?

"Tell them to send more than one crew. Considering what we paid for that whirlpool and the new flagstone terrace, they should send three crews." Annie's eyes lit with mischief. "Tell them if the installation's not done by tomorrow, I'll have to cancel the order for new flagstone around the saltwater therapy pools."

"They'll go nuts," her assistant warned.

"I certainly hope so." Annie's smile grew. "Remember, no deadline, no flagstone."

Megan gave a thumbs-up. "I'm on it, boss."

Annie tried not to wince. After all, she *was* the boss.

As the manager of thirty-five glass-and-adobe guesthouses and a striking resort set on California's rugged coast, she was used to bearing heavy responsibility. Summerwind was a family legacy, and three generations of O'Tooles had lived above its magic beach.

Since Annie had taken over the management of the resort after her parents' deaths four years before, her flare for innovation had garnered a string of awards. She had turned Summerwind into an intimate but elegant home away from home, where harried guests could linger on a quiet beach and feel their stress melt away. Hollywood celebrities and sports stars made semiannual visits, knowing their privacy was assured. Annie was famous for her attention to details and her high standard of personal service, which resulted in a nine-month waiting list and a fanatic clientele.

All in all, life was good.

But sometimes she *did* wish she had a private life.

She suppressed a sigh as her summer receptionist burst into the conference room. "We've almost finished here, Liz."

"No, you have to come now. It's *him.*"

"Who?"

The receptionist, a third-year drama student at Berkeley, gestured outside. "I saw him on the television. When I saw what he was doing, I thought I would die. I mean absolutely *expire right in front of the television.*"

Annie rolled her shoulders. It was only 9:22. Why should she suddenly crave a king-size double cappuccino? "Sorry, Liz, I don't understand."

"You will. It's *him.* He's on a bus."

Annie sat back in her chair. "Who is on a bus?"

"That man, the one who was here last month. At least I think it's him."

Annie felt a sharp stab of pain. "You must be mistaken. Sam's down in Mexico."

"I don't think so. I just saw him on a bus full of schoolchildren." Liz gestured again, her big hoop earrings swaying madly. "Come see for yourself."

Annie heard the excited staccato of voices from the television out in her office. "Where is he?"

"D.C. The bus is zigzagging up Pennsylvania Avenue, four miles from the White House, completely out of control. The driver might have had a heart attack. Then *he* appeared—*poof!* It's like some kind of miracle."

With the rest of her staff, Annie raced for the television,

where an aerial news camera focused on a bus careening through crowded city streets.

A solitary figure crawled along the yellow roof.

"That's him," the receptionist whispered. "I'm sure he's your man from the beach. Sam."

Sam.

The word tore through Annie, reopening jagged memories. It couldn't be. Sam was in Mexico.

"He's almost at the front of the bus. If he can't get to the wheel, those kids are goners."

Annie sank into the nearest chair, mesmerized by the bus's wild swerving. She stiffened as she saw the man stretched out on the roof.

"They think he's Navy," the receptionist said.

"Navy?" Sam wasn't in the Navy. He was on a boat headed to Mexico.

It had to be a mistake. Why would her rich, charming drifter with a new yacht turn up on a school bus in Washington?

"He's in dress whites." Annie's chef bent closer to the television. "Definitely Navy, and the man knows what he's doing. In two more feet he'll be above the driver's window. I think he's trying to get inside and take the wheel. You didn't say Sam was in the Navy, Annie."

Because she hadn't known until that moment.

The receptionist pushed closer. "Why don't they just shoot out the tires?"

"Because the bus is going too fast. I used to work in a school cafeteria," the chef said tensely. "If that's a city school bus, it doesn't have seat belts, and those kids would be tossed around like human cannonballs."

Annie shuddered. A news helicopter flashed by, circling low to capture the strained features of the unknown man on the top of the bus. In the brutal clarity of a telephoto lens, Annie saw him look up.

Strained face.

Black hair.

Keen eyes somewhere between blue and gray.

A powerful jaw and a scar above his mouth.

"Oh, my God, it is Sam." Zoe locked her hands. "It really is your friend from the cove."

Annie couldn't seem to focus. She blinked and looked again, fighting disbelief.

Sam was supposed to be sailing somewhere off the coast of Mexico, enjoying a long vacation after selling his Internet company. He'd told her that very clearly.

But cameras didn't lie.

So what was going on?

She barely noticed her nails digging into her palm as the helicopter swung low for a tighter shot. Now there was no mistaking that lean face and hard jaw. The sexy stubble was gone, but it was definitely Sam fighting his way across the roof of the swerving bus.

"He's falling!" Annie shot to her feet.

Annie's chef squinted at the set. "No, he's going for the open window."

Suddenly the bus lurched sideways. Annie could barely watch as the man in the white uniform clung to the side of the bus and clawed his way forward.

The bus straightened abruptly, clearing a line of parked cars by mere inches. Without warning, all of the children vanished.

"What happened?" Annie pressed a hand against her chest, breathing hard. "Where did they go?"

"He must have told them to brace against their knees, the way you do before an airplane crash."

That made sense. Annie joined in the wild applause as the bus held steady, joined by a phalanx of D.C. police cars with sirens flashing.

But the chorus of cheers was cut short as the aerial news

camera panned north, where a wall of concrete cut across the highway.

Annie heard the reporter explain that all traffic was being detoured up the side ramp. Sam had to stop the bus fast. Otherwise . . .

Otherwise he and his young passengers were headed into a deadly blockade of cement and construction girders.

Annie closed her eyes, feeling faint.

Zoe squeezed her shoulder. "You want a glass of water or something?"

"I'll—be fine." Annie opened her eyes. "How far to the construction area?"

"About a mile. The police are stacking sandbags in case your friend can't stop the bus, but at the rate they're traveling . . ."

There was no need to finish.

Annie pressed a shaky hand to her chest as if she could hold off her terror. Suddenly the screen cut to a close-up. Sam was wedged inside the front window now, and he was pulling something from behind the driver's seat.

A hockey stick.

He was trying to reach the brake pedal, she realized.

The announcer was nearly drowned out by the shriek of sirens and the cries of bystanders lining the streets. "With less than a mile to go, the police are extremely concerned," he said grimly. "At its current rate of speed, I'm told the bus has about three minutes until impact."

So little time, Annie thought.

It would take a miracle to save Sam and those children.

"He's done it!" Coverage switched to a reporter in a news helicopter circling the scene. "The bus is finally starting to slow down. Ladies and gentlemen, I think we're watching a miracle take place here in Washington. A real miracle."

The bus lurched into its final turn.

The cement wall lay dead ahead.

"He's still going too fast," the reporter said shrilly.

Annie stood frozen, caught in a nightmare. She watched the hockey stick jerk free. With a desperate kick the man in the uniform jammed the stick down again. As he did, Annie got a good look at his face—and the bright stain covering his right arm.

"He's bleeding," she whispered.

Suddenly the bus lurched.

The big wheels dug in hard, laying skid marks against the gray roadbed. The bus bucked in a wild dance, its rusted body screaming as smoke poured from the engine. In a cloud of dust and smoke, it flashtailed sharply, then slammed to a halt with one tire wedged against the half-built wall of cement and girders.

The force of the impact threw the officer backward, shattering the side window. He flew into the air, tossed over the bus, his powerful body twisting as he fought to control the fall.

But there was no chance at any kind of control. He struck the edge of a girder, then slammed down onto a row of scattered sandbags, his arms at an unnatural angle.

Blood welled up, staining his face and covering his torn uniform. The news camera captured every detail.

"No," Annie whispered. "He's not moving."

No one spoke.

Don't be dead, Sam. Please, please open your eyes.

But the hero in the torn uniform didn't move.

"Is he alive?" she rasped.

Even the announcer was silent, stricken by the life-and-death struggle played out in grim detail.

"*Is* he?" she demanded, her whole body shaking.

She fought to breathe, but the air felt hot and thick. Then her legs went weak and the floor simply wasn't there.

Chapter Two

ANNIE OPENED HER EYES SLOWLY AND INHALED.

Why was she lying down in the middle of the day? And why was she stretched out on the couch with her staff crowded around her?

Her confusion grew as she tried to sit up. She heard voices, sirens, the drone of helicopters.

Suddenly she remembered.

She struggled to see the television. "What happened to Sam? Is he—"

"Calm down." Zoe held out a glass of water. "Drink this and take a deep breath. You're sheet white."

"*Tell me!*" Annie wobbled toward the television, where an ambulance raced through crowded streets, trailed by a full police motorcade. "*Is he alive?*"

"No one knows. At least they're not saying."

Swaying, Annie reached for the corner of the couch. "What about the children?"

Reynaldo, her maintenance chief, answered. "Upset, but all safe, thanks to that man in the white uniform." His eyes narrowed on Annie. "He is the one who was here before, but he never spoke of the Navy. Was he on leave?"

"I don't know, Reynaldo." Annie's eyes locked on the television. "*Someone* must know. What are the news people saying?"

"Not much. There's a complete blackout." Her chef frowned. "Why didn't Sam tell you he was in the Navy?"

Annie stared at the ambulance, her heart racing right along with the swift wheels.

She hadn't known Sam was in the Navy. She hadn't known

he was going to Washington. He'd said very little about himself, shifting the talk to his boat and the weather and the voyage ahead of him. Annie hadn't pressed for information, since it was clear he wasn't going to be staying long.

For two weeks they'd laughed and sailed and explored the cove.

For two weeks they'd toasted marshmallows on the beach and watched the stars through his big telescope. Annie had been busy, but she'd made time to slip away. One star-swept night she had leaned against his strong chest, tugged off his shirt, and pulled him down onto the teak deck.

Afterward, they'd kissed slowly, without words or regrets.

Both had been very careful not to talk about love.

Now he might be dying in a pool of blood at the back of an ambulance three thousand miles away.

Footsteps raced down the hall. The door to the office flew open.

"Where is she?" Annie's older sister surveyed the room, stunning in tight black trousers and a black silk blouse. Only Annie noticed the ink smudges on her wrist and palm, a dead giveaway that she'd been in the middle of editing a new book.

Annie sat up straighter. "What's wrong?"

"You are." Taylor O'Toole threw up her hands. "I was in the middle of a delicious murder of a very nasty villain when I got a call from your assistant saying that you'd fainted. You've been overworking again, haven't you? Missing meals, too, probably. Why didn't you tell me you needed help?"

Annie avoided her sister's anxious gaze. "I'm fine, Taylor. It was the bus." *The blood. Sam's blood.* She drew a strained breath. "All those children. It just took me by surprise."

"You and twenty million other Americans, who are glued to their TV sets even as we speak." Taylor sank down beside Annie on the couch. "You look like the walking dead. I'm calling Dr. Royland."

"I'm fine, Taylor. Don't overdramatize."

Her sister's eyes glinted. "One more word and I'll carry you out to the car myself."

Annie felt her sister's hands tremble and realized Taylor was terrified, but working hard to hide it. "I'll make an appointment next week, I promise. But not now. I'm too busy to be sick."

"Last time I checked you had a staff," her sister said acidly.

"A very fine one." Annie watched her anxious employees drift outside. "But they're overworked already," she added quietly.

"And *you* aren't?" Taylor barked. "You're getting me seriously pissed off." She glanced at the television, watching a replay of the miraculous rescue, ending in a tight shot of the fallen officer.

Taylor leaned closer, studying the man's features. "Wait a minute. Isn't that . . ." There was new understanding in her face when she turned and took Annie's arm.

"What are you doing?"

"Getting you up to the house. After that, I'm doing something I don't do often enough."

Annie's brow rose. "Giving up leather pants?"

"Very funny." Taylor opened the door. "I'm going to take care of my baby sister."

"I'm no baby." Annie took an irritated breath. "I told you I can't take time off right now."

Taylor examined the cuff of her silk shirt. "Too bad. As the co-owner of Summerwind, I would be bound to conclude that my manager needed a vacation. An *enforced* vacation."

Annie stiffened. "You wouldn't."

"Try me."

"That's cheap. No, that's rotten and low-down."

"Isn't it, though?" Taylor smiled coolly. "Now, are you coming or not?"

❖ ❖ ❖

"LET'S HAVE THE DETAILS."

Annie didn't turn as she searched for her house key. "About what?"

"About that gorgeous man on the school bus. He's the hunk who moored his boat in the cove last month. You told me he was sailing down to Mexico."

The key trembled in Annie's hand. She didn't want to re-member Sam's lazy grin or lean, tanned body. She didn't want to think about his first kiss or the moment it had raced out of control.

"Last month?" She tossed down her coat, kicked off her shoes, and headed for the bank of windows overlooking wind-blown trees and brooding coast. "It did look like Sam, didn't it?"

"Don't pretend it wasn't. I saw his face on the television and that's the man you described to me, the one who had just sold his company and was headed on a long, leisurely trip to Mex-ico and the Caribbean."

Annie opened one hand slowly on the cool glass. "Did I?"

"I'm your sister, not one of your staff, for God's sake. I was gone, remember? So give me the details." Taylor's eyes nar-rowed. "Were you lovers?"

Annie closed her eyes and let her forehead sink against the cold glass. "I told you most of it, Taylor. He said he was off the clock for the first time in five years, and he was going to savor every second."

"And?" Taylor prompted.

"He was nice and funny and we had fun together. I could see he was interested, but he didn't push things. When I had some problems with the new smoke detectors, he offered to take a look." Annie smiled. "You wouldn't believe how fast he diagnosed the problem. He helped Reynaldo fix the wall below the rose garden, and the next day he repaired Dad's old motor-boat in the cove. He was amazing."

"So the man was good with his hands." Taylor's eyes narrowed. "Did you sleep with him?"

Annie turned away from the twenty-mile panorama of wild sky and racing sea. "I'd rather not talk about it."

"Tough. I'm your sister and I want an answer."

Annie paced restlessly, avoiding Taylor's eyes. "He was off limits and I knew it. The man was in the middle of his dream voyage and I was swamped with work. We had a few pleasant strolls on the beach, traded a few tall tales and shared a few meals."

"What else?"

"Okay, we spent two nights together. He was ... incredible. That's the end of it."

Taylor's eyes narrowed. "I don't think so."

"Okay, I didn't *want* him to go." Annie's voice broke. "I didn't want it ever to end, but it had to, and I felt like a complete fool for letting myself in for a fall. I mean, how stupid can you get? He was on a boat, leaving in a matter of days. I—I fell for him like a misty-eyed teenager." She took a shaky breath. "But he never made any promises. Neither of us did. So that was that."

Taylor moved, blocking Annie's path. "Then why are you freezing? Why did you go bone white when you watched that replay?"

"I'm not allowed to care? He was covered in *blood,* Taylor." Annie sidestepped, hugging her chest. "Why is it so cold in here?"

"Sit down while I light the fire. After that, you're having my special tea spiked with whiskey."

Annie sank into her favorite cozy wing chair. For a long time she didn't speak. "It doesn't have to *mean* anything. It was just the shock of seeing him on the cement. Completely still." *Maybe dead.*

"Sure it doesn't mean anything," Taylor called from the kitchen.

Annie closed her eyes, trying not to think about Sam. Finally she shook her head. "I can't stand this. I'm calling Washington. The Navy must have an office there."

Taylor carried in a tray. "Of course they do."

"Then I'm calling."

Taylor poured Annie's tea and set the cup on the end table their father had carved for their mother thirty years before. "I'll make the call. Sit still and drink this."

Annie didn't hide her surprise. "I thought you'd be out the door by now. You hate being here at Summerwind. And your next book is due—"

"My book can wait," Taylor said flatly. "I don't like the resort, true enough. We both know this place has never been my thing. Even when I was twelve, I was tired of watching the rich, beautiful guests get all Mom's and Dad's attention." She shrugged. "I guess that makes me a bad-tempered brat, but there it is."

"You have your own interests, your own career. There's nothing to apologize for."

"Maybe." Taylor stood by the fire, stiff and slender and effortlessly elegant. "I should have helped you more, Annie. I should have been here, especially that winter when Mom and Dad . . ." The words trailed away, as gray as lost dreams, as heavy as broken promises. "Okay, I screwed up, I admit it." Taylor glared out the window at nothing in particular.

"No one said you screwed up."

"No one had to. It was on everyone's faces when I came back. I was the wild O'Toole, the one who broke all the rules and didn't even show up for her parents' funerals."

"That's not what people thought," Annie said quietly.

Taylor raised a manicured hand. "It's time for the truth. I couldn't face losing them any more than I could face coming back to Summerwind and the town where I've always been such a screw-up. But that's over now," she said tightly. "I'm here to help, even if the thought of pampering your trophy wives and overpaid sports heroes ranks right up with a double root canal." She took a deep breath. "I'll even manage to smile when I hand out the aromatherapy masks to the ladies who lunch."

Annie couldn't hide her surprise. "I thought you only rented that house on the cliffs for two weeks."

"I changed my mind." Now it was Taylor's turn to fidget. "I bought it last week. You're overworked and you're going to get a break, courtesy of your big sister. Right after I call Washington."

Annie was almost too surprised to answer. "I can call myself."

"But I can do it better." Taylor stared out at the dunes rolling down to the sea. "This place is so incredibly peaceful. How could I have forgotten?" She took a breath. "About Washington—I did a book tour there last year. There was a big shindig in Georgetown, and I met half a dozen diplomats and three or four admirals that night. Lucky for you, I always keep private phone numbers."

"You got their private numbers at a cocktail party?"

Taylor straightened her shoulders. "Of course. Having a direct line to an admiral or diplomat can come in very handy."

"In case of a hostile invasion?"

"You are such an innocent." Taylor sniffed. "Drink your whiskey and tea while I concentrate. Offering blatant flattery can be hard work."

For the next hour Annie watched her sister charm and cajole her way through the endless bureaucracy that protected all highly placed military figures in Washington. Taylor was shunted through the Pentagon before finally managing to track down the top admiral on her list. Friendly at first, he turned remote the instant Taylor brought up the wounded officer on the school bus.

No matter how Taylor finessed and flattered, the man wouldn't budge. No information was available about the status of the fallen officer. Not to *anyone*.

Irritated as much as disappointed, Taylor hung up. Her other calls to Washington proved equally unproductive.

On television, every major channel was replaying the bus footage, intercut with veteran commentators interviewing the relieved parents of the rescued children. But there was no news about the officer who had been carried, bloody and unmoving, aboard a Navy helicopter and airlifted from the scene.

In a haze of worry, Annie tried several Navy hospitals on the East Coast, only to be blocked by harried operators fending off similar calls. Clearly, all of America wanted to know what had happened to their newest hero.

Taylor finally left, promising to handle any problems at the resort. Both sisters were surprised when Annie didn't protest.

Tears pricked, but Annie shut them away, telling herself that modern medicine could work miracles. She knew Sam would be getting the finest possible care. He was probably in surgery at that very moment. Because there was nothing else to do, she began another round of phone calls, hitting the same dead ends.

As shadows gathered, she sat by the phone, praying for good news.

Where are you, Sam? Are you alive or dead?

But like the rest of America, she had to wait.

❖ ❖ ❖

Bethesda, Maryland

The surgical ward was closed down tight. Two senators and a presidential aide paced before the big green doors, glaring at the uniformed guard who patrolled the ward.

Nurses spoke in muted voices from the nursing station. Down the hall, past the double doors, came the muffled echo of voices mixed with the beeps and hums of advanced technology at work.

"What the hell's going on in there? It's been almost nine hours. How long can they operate, for God's sake?"

No one answered the presidential aide. Lean and tanned, he waved a coffee cup. "I need answers. The White House wants a photo op and a prime-time announcement about the recovery of America's newest hero." He slammed down his paper cup, cursing as his pager began to vibrate. "What the hell am I supposed to say?"

"Tell the commander in chief that the officer's still in surgery. That much is obvious." The senator from Montana was a red-faced man whose homely features hid a mind like a shredder. He leaned toward the doors, listening intently. "The equipment is still working. At least they haven't pulled life support."

The aide balanced a sleek palm-top device and punched in a text message. "What good is news if you can't stroke it or use it? We know as much as every other damned person in America who saw that live footage. Who the hell *was* that officer anyway?" He glanced at the senator from Montana. "You work military appropriations. Can't you find out?"

The senator moved closer, his voice falling. "I know that already. The man's military record would fill a book—if it weren't all classified." He stared at the big green doors, where his colleague was pacing. "But we may have a bigger problem."

The aide snorted. "What could be a bigger problem than a call from the Oval Office and me with no answers?"

The senator moved uneasily. "Not here. Three o'clock—my office."

As he spoke, the double doors jolted open.

A surgeon in rumpled scrubs strode into the hall. His eyes were lined with fatigue as he tugged off his surgical mask. "Gentlemen, I believe you were waiting for some news?"

Chapter Three

"ANNIE, WAKE UP."

Someone was shaking her. She blinked and saw Taylor holding out a portable phone.

"My friend the admiral just phoned, asking a lot of questions. He wanted your number, so I got down here pronto." Taylor gestured with the phone, keeping the receiver covered. "I think this is someone from the Navy, but she won't tell me anything. She'll only speak to you."

Annie glanced at the clock.

It was 5:30 A.M.

She shoved a tangle of hair out of her eyes and took the phone. "This is Annie O'Toole."

Papers rustled, and a woman answered. "One moment, Ms. O'Toole."

Annie was put on hold. She looked at Taylor and shrugged. "Wake me up at five-thirty, then put me on hold."

"Ms. O'Toole?" The male voice held the faintly flattened vowels of the Midwest, heavy with authority.

"Yes, that's right."

"I see that you've left a number of messages requesting information about the officer wounded on the schoolbus in Washington. May I ask how you know this man?"

"I met him last month while he was here on his boat."

Taylor's eyebrow rose, but Annie paid no attention. She gripped the phone, her heart pounding as the silence stretched out. She could almost sense the man's wariness.

"Ms. O'Toole, are you interested in his welfare?"

"I'm very interested."

"In that case, you won't mind answering a few questions. When did you last see him?"

Annie had the sharp sense that her answers were being recorded. Possibly there were other people in the room listening to the call. The thought left her chilled, even though she had nothing to hide.

A chair squeaked. "Ms. O'Toole?"

She glanced out the window, down to the windswept beach where she had first seen Sam cruising into the cove. Her heart did a little flip-flop at the memory. "About six weeks ago. When he left, he told me he was headed for the Baja coast."

"How did you two spend your time together?"

Alarm bells began to clang. "Sam helped me with some repairs here at the resort, we enjoyed some local wine and we did some stargazing."

"Did he discuss his work with you?"

"No."

"He told you why he was headed south?"

"For a vacation." Annie frowned. "Why are you asking me all these questions."

"Let's be frank, Ms. O'Toole. Were you and Sam intimate?"

Annie slammed down the phone without thinking. "That's *your* answer, pal. Who do you think you *are*?"

"You need to disconnect," Taylor pointed out gently, taking the phone and breaking the connection. "But that was very nicely done just the same."

"He was asking about us—personal things. Why should I tell a stranger about my private life?"

"No reason at all." Taylor frowned at Annie. "What are you worrying about now?"

"That I destroyed any chance of getting news about Sam." Annie rose to pace in front of the window. "Good work, Annie. Bite the hand that was about to feed you."

Taylor smiled as the phone rang again. "Apparently not."

Annie forced herself to wait for the third ring. This time she heard a different voice.

"Ms. O'Toole, this is Admiral Ulysses Howe. I apologize if my aide was abrupt to you a moment ago."

"Is this call being recorded?"

There was a pause. "Why do you ask?"

He hadn't answered her question, which meant the answer was probably yes.

"You need to understand our situation, Ms. O'Toole." The admiral spoke slowly and carefully. "We have a media frenzy here at the moment."

"But I'm not a reporter."

"Just the same, everyone is demanding answers, and giving answers to the wrong people can be dangerous."

"I'm not dangerous. I just want to know Sam's condition."

There was another pause. "Sam is alive. I can't say the outlook is rosy, but he's tough and he's a fighter."

Annie's eyes blurred with tears and she struggled for composure. Sam wasn't dead, thank God.

But something didn't make sense. "I don't understand all the secrecy, Admiral."

"One slip and we'll have tabloids, career reporters, and cranks beating down the doors of every naval hospital in the country. They'll demand medical information and one-on-one interviews. Hell, they'll steal hospital uniforms and sneak into treatment rooms, trying to get an exclusive on America's latest hero."

Annie froze, seeing every detail exactly as he had described. "What can you do to stop it?"

"Keep this quiet. That officer will not be harassed on my watch. Can I count on your help, Ms. O'Toole?"

"Me?" Annie frowned. "Of course. You mean that I should stop leaving messages and bothering your people?"

"No, I'm not asking you to stop your calls. I'm asking for

your support under conditions of absolute secrecy. Are you prepared to give that?"

Annie didn't hesitate. "I am."

"You're decisive. That's good. This puts the ball back in my court. I'll contact you shortly, Ms. O'Toole. Meanwhile, I appreciate your commitment."

"*What* commitment?"

"When Sam leaves the hospital, he's going to need a secure and isolated location for his rehab. I happen to know that your record of recovery with top athletes is formidable. I spoke with one of them just this morning." The admiral named a high-profile quarterback who had come to Annie off-season for ankle-strength training and spine flexibility. Now he was playing better than he had in years.

"I merely redirected some limiting behaviors. He's a hard worker and an amazingly well-conditioned athlete."

"So is Sam. I'm sure he'll perform just as well for you."

"Admiral, you're not being very clear."

"You'll have all the details shortly, Ms. O'Toole. Your contact's name is Mr. Teague. Meanwhile, this must remain absolutely secret."

"Of course, but—"

"A final warning. If you reveal any detail of what we've discussed, the government will deal with you harshly, make no mistake."

Before Annie could blurt out an answer, the line went dead.

"What's going on? How is Sam?" Taylor demanded.

"I'm not sure." Annie stared at the phone. She knew Sam was alive, but very little else. And the admiral's warnings infuriated her. It didn't take threats to ensure that Sam's secret was safe with her.

"Well?" Taylor said impatiently.

"No details. I promised."

Taylor looked annoyed. "Is he alive?"

Annie nodded.

"What else can you tell me?"

"Not much." She'd worked with sports stars, movie stars, and models, but never with the military. Annie stared out at the ocean and wondered exactly what she was getting herself into.

❖ ❖ ❖

AT FIRST THERE WAS ONLY PAIN.

Like thunder, it battled up and down his chest. He tried to talk, but some kind of mask covered his mouth, so he forced himself to relax and assess the situation, the way he'd been trained.

A night dive?

Had he surfaced too fast and blacked out?

Sam McKade raised one hand, grimacing at the immediate kick of pain. Tendons, muscles, bones, skin—everything was on fire at once.

Then his vision blurred, and he knew he was going under again.

But he had to stay awake. There was something important he knew, something he had to pass on.

By sheer force of will he kept his eyes open, fighting to stay conscious though every breath was a torment.

Panting, he stared at the blurred shapes around him.

A room? Chairs? There were clicking noises and something pressing on his face, his chest. A bed beneath him?

None of that mattered. All that mattered was getting where he needed to go and reporting.

Reporting *what?*

His fists clenched. He struggled to focus, but there was nothing beyond the pain, no urgent knowledge to hold him awake, tense and shaking, gripped by dread.

Something moved at the corner of his vision. A shadow slid out of the darkness. Grunting, Sam forced his body away from the blow he sensed was coming.

The shadow was right above him now, its outlines blooming into hollow eyes and a black mask. Something tugged at Sam's wrist, and he saw the flash of metal.

A syringe.

The same instincts that had saved his life a dozen times made Sam twist sideways and roll across the bed. He struck out blindly, heard a curse, then the sound of a falling chair. Something slapped his arm.

The shadow blurred again. As it faded, Sam heard a low cry. It took him a long time to realize the voice was his.

The blurring was everywhere now. He was panting, fighting to breathe, when light flooded the room.

"Commander, stop!" Footsteps raced toward him. Sam was blinded by light, his eyes still adapted to the dark. "You've knocked off your oxygen mask and your IV is out." Soft hands pressed at his face. "Stop fighting me or you'll hurt yourself."

The darkness was growing, taking him down. "Someone here." He struggled to speak. "Can't—stay here."

"Now you just relax. Let's get your oxygen back on. You'll feel better then."

Another voice, another set of hands. Sam felt the prick of a needle, then the slow numbness dripping into him, blurring pain and memories.

Not yet.

He had to explain.

Had to report that the danger was here. Somehow it had followed him.

Then the pain fell away, and there was nothing at all left for him to remember.

Chapter Four

FORTY-EIGHT HOURS LATER, ANNIE WAS STILL WAITING FOR NEWS.

She had scanned every news channel, hoping for an update, but no one was talking about Sam's condition, unofficially or otherwise. The silence was driving her crazy.

With a sigh she forced her mind back to work. July was her busiest season, and with Summerwind fully booked, she had her hands full hosting special events, local wine tastings, and gourmet dinners. Usually she enjoyed these unique promotions, but Annie couldn't pull her thoughts away from Sam.

Wherever he was.

Despite Taylor's pointed questions, Annie kept her silence, and her sister had stalked off in no good humor. But Annie knew that Taylor's anger would pass and then she would be back to help.

The hard truth was that Annie needed Taylor's help more than she ever had before.

She was finishing a memo for a gourmet cookoff hosted by three famous California chefs when her computer screen filled with fuzzy red lines. Annie sighed. One day she would have to track down the annoying glitch.

Right now it was at the bottom of her list.

She looked up as her head housekeeper huffed into the room. "*No mas, señorita.* He cuts the towels again."

Annie rubbed her neck. "You mean the Olympic fencer in the Monterey Suite?"

"*Sí, sí.*" Her housekeeper smoothed her pristine white apron. "He cuts holes in all my towels. A riposte, he calls it. Now I have two dozen new towels and all are slashed."

"Give him replacements from last year's supply and keep a

record. We'll charge him for the new ones. Any other problems?"

"The test pilot in room twenty-two. He pays to lose weight, then hides a television set, two bottles of gin, and a box of Twinkies in the closet." She sniffed. "He promises me three hundred dollars if I do not tell you."

Annie had to smile at the man's ingenuity. "Tell Major Prescott that the television and alcohol go or he goes. We'll negotiate about the Twinkies."

The housekeeper bustled out happily and was immediately replaced by Annie's head chef.

"A problem, Zoe?"

"I'm going to kill them all. I've got the knife ready."

Annie sat back, looking interested. "Your old boyfriends?"

"The rabbits. This time they hit the bok choi and white strawberries. It's a war out there, Annie."

Aware that a chuckle might lose her one of California's finest chefs, Annie kept her face sober. After a last, disgusted look at her computer, she stood up. "Let's go have a look. Maybe we could throw my monitor at them. It doesn't seem to be good for anything else but crushing small animals."

❖ ❖ ❖

WHEN ANNIE RETURNED FROM HER JAUNT, SHE WAS TIRED, HUNgry, and more than a little irritated. The rabbits had done more damage than she realized. The orchard and gardens would have to be carefully fenced. Otherwise, her chef was history.

She glanced at the new faxes, snagged a cup of coffee, and headed down the corridor to her office. She was absently scratching a mosquito bite when she saw the glow of light above her desk.

Annie froze, certain she'd turned off the desk lamp before she'd left.

She put down her coffee on an end table and inched closer. A man was sitting at her computer. He appeared to be inputting a stream of programming code, humming happily, completely at home.

Furious, Annie shouldered open the door. "You have exactly sixty seconds to tell me who you are and what you're doing at my computer."

Chapter Five

HER VISITOR CLOSED DOWN THE COMPUTER WITHOUT EVEN looking, his dark features unruffled. "You must be Annie O'Toole."

"You've got thirty seconds left. I have a direct line to my head of security and any calls automatically ring through to the local sheriff."

"Good protocol. I like it."

The man was tall and broad shouldered, like the football players Annie often worked with, but he met her eyes squarely, with a focused intelligence and lazy good humor Annie didn't expect in a professional athlete who crashed his body for a living.

He steepled his fingers. "You shouldn't reveal your security details to a stranger, though. What's the point of an alarm system if everyone knows how it works?"

"Time's up." Annie reached for the intercom to her head of maintenance, who doubled as her "head of security." "Reynaldo, I need you in my office. Make it pronto."

The stranger raised one eyebrow. "Message received, ma'am. Here's mine. The name's Ishmael Teague. I believe you're expecting me."

Annie recalled her strange conversation with the admiral, who had promised someone named Teague would answer all her questions. She crossed her arms uncertainly. "Who sent you?"

"Admiral Howe."

"Why didn't you call?"

"Orders, ma'am. I was told to get here on the double. I would have been here two hours ago if I hadn't missed the turnoff from the coast road. This place really is the back of beyond."

"That's the point. People need to escape from the noise and the rat race sometimes." Annie continued to watch him warily. "You haven't told me why you're here. I doubt it's for our seaweed wraps."

"Consider me your support team. I'll be helping you with Sam and keeping an eye on things."

Annie drummed her fingers on the windowsill. "What kind of things?"

"I've got training as a medic. I'll also help with press, security, and whatever else you need."

"Why would the press be involved, Mr. Teague? I thought Sam's stay here was a secret."

"Mistakes happen. That's when I do my best work." He smiled calmly, looking remarkably like Denzel Washington. "And call me Izzy, please."

Annie had the sense there was a lot that Ishmael Teague wasn't telling her, but her concern for Sam outweighed any other worries. "What's Sam's condition? I'll need a complete medical report before I can start planning his rehab regimen."

Izzy pulled a thick folder from the leather briefcase on her desk. "Everything you need is in here: X-rays, progress notes, surgical evaluations. The man's lucky to be alive, considering the fall he took. He's going to need a lot of work."

Annie reached for the folder. "I'll see that he gets it." She skimmed through Sam's medical chart. A chill set in as she looked through the X-rays.

Dislocated shoulder.

Possible nerve damage in the left arm.

Reconstructive work on the left knee.

Most of the cartilage, tendons, and muscles in his shoulder had been stretched and separated from connecting tissue. In addition, he had localized trauma to head, chest, and torso. Fortunately, no spinal damage was indicated, but he'd been rushed into surgery twice in the last ten days. The X-rays were invaluable, showing Annie the exact areas they would need to strengthen. His shoulder was going to take special attention, as was his knee, which would require a stabilizing brace for at least four weeks.

Her job wasn't going to be easy, but it wouldn't be hopeless either. He'd been incredibly lucky to escape serious internal injuries.

When Annie came to the neurological evaluation, she stiffened. She scanned the page, stopped, then reread the report.

She looked at Izzy. "You've seen this?"

He nodded.

"But this says—" She struggled with shock. "This says that Sam can't remember."

Chapter Six

"IS THAT TRUE?"

"It's true." Her visitor wasn't smiling now. "Amnesia induced by trauma." He leaned back in her chair, his eyes hard. "Do you want to back out, Ms. O'Toole? The physical work alone will be demanding. If you factor in Sam's mental state and disorientation, your job's going to be damned ticklish."

"Why didn't Admiral Howe tell me about this when he called?"

"He wasn't certain then. Sam hasn't stayed conscious very long. When he was conscious, the pain was overwhelming, so tests were impossible."

Annie closed the file, gripping it tightly. "Is there any evidence of brain damage?" she whispered.

"None so far."

"I want the truth, Mr. Teague."

"Call me Izzy, please."

"Fine. I need all the cards on the table, Izzy. What's Sam's exact mental condition?"

"First answer a question. Are you still in?"

Annie squared her shoulders. "Of course I'm in. Why would Sam's loss of memory change anything?"

"Some people might consider it too big a burden. I'm glad you're not one of them." He gently slid the file from her fingers and returned it to his briefcase. "You can finish reading this later. Here's the bottom line. Sam's mental condition is guarded but optimistic. There should be a gradual recovery of his memory, but the time frame is uncertain. He's been on numerous medications since the surgery, and those could be a factor, too."

Annie took a deep breath, digesting the news.

"Now I'd like to go over some mission objectives with you."

"Mission what?"

"Sorry." Izzy scratched his jaw. "What I mean is, we need to work out Sam's schedule, your responsibilities, and what you're going to say to your staff."

Things were moving too fast. Annie had a sudden sense that her life was about to change in ways she couldn't imagine. "Why should I tell them anything?"

"Sam's presence here has to stay secret. That means his quarters will be off limits to anyone but you and me. You'll need a good reason for that."

"Lots of high-profile guests come here to recover from cosmetic surgery. My staff won't question a private visitor if I explain we're doing special rehab."

"Good. That makes one less hole to plug." Izzy swung back to her computer, rebooting the system. The new screen image was crisp, without any sign of jagged red lines. "I changed your BIOS and operating system while I was waiting for you."

"How? That bug has been driving me nuts for a month."

"It was a simple reroute. Then I added a few subroutines."

"You're not going to start speaking Computer, I hope."

Izzy grinned. "I'll try to restrain myself. The point is, your system needs to interface with my equipment. When Sam gets here, we'll use yours for basic communication and logistics, so I've added a little encryption program, along with some speed modifications. You'll love it."

Encryption program?

Speed modifications?

Yet again Annie had the premonition that she was getting in over her head. "I can handle a computer, but you just got way out of my league."

Izzy's smile was reassuring. "No problem. It's designed to be user friendly." He glanced down at his watch. "I'd better get us both a cup of coffee, because we have a lot of ground to cover. You're going to need an updated security system for your personal quarters and courtyard. I presume that Sam will stay in your house?"

Annie nodded. "That's the best way to monitor his progress."

"The security installation shouldn't take more than a few hours. I'll need you to carry a pager at all times, along with a secure cell phone." He handed her a slim gray unit wired to a low-profile earplug.

Annie grimaced. "I have to carry this all the time?"

"After a while you won't even know it's there. I'm also installing a private intercom, so Sam is never out of touch."

Though her head was spinning, Annie managed a laugh. "Why do I feel as if this is a Bond film and you're Q?"

Izzy's grin was a cocky slash. "I'm way beyond Q, ma'am."

Outside the door, Annie's fax machine beeped twice and Izzy pushed to his feet. "I expect that's for me." With an easy stride he covered the distance to the machine and scanned the newest sheet.

Only because she was watching closely did Annie see his jaw tighten. "What is it?"

Worry flared in his eyes, just for a second. "It's nothing. Sam's holding firm, and everything's on schedule."

"What was in the fax, Izzy?"

"Just transport options. We'd better get to work."

Annie noticed that he folded the fax carefully and slid it into his pocket. What she didn't know was that the words, written in code, would have made no sense to her anyway.

❖　❖　❖

"I WANT ANSWERS NOW."

Admiral Ulysses S. Howe glared at the frightened surgical nurse. "How did an intruder get past my guards?"

"I didn't see anyone. None of us did, sir. Just an orderly and someone from maintenance, but neither went into any patients' rooms."

"I'll have that checked."

The nurse shifted uncomfortably. "When the patient woke, he was confused and upset. He'd already torn off his oxygen mask, and his IV was out."

"Don't you people have equipment to monitor things like that?" Howe shot back. "This is intensive care, damn it. What the hell went on in here?"

"The monitor was working, but the attendant had a priority call from the security desk downstairs. That's why it took a few extra seconds for him to notice the problem in Commander McKade's room."

And those few seconds could have cost the SEAL his life.

He'd damn well check out that "priority call," Howe thought grimly. He was sure he'd find that the call couldn't be traced. "I want to know who was in his room."

"I doubt that anyone was." A graying man with a faint southern accent finished checking Sam's pulse, then stood staring down at his sleeping patient.

"Are you telling me McKade was hallucinating? We're talking about a man with fifteen years of field experience and a chestful of medals."

The surgeon shrugged. "We see it all the time in postsurgical patients. Anesthesia and pain leave them disoriented. They wake up and see . . . things." He nodded to his worried nurse. "You can go now, Eileen. You did the right thing, calming him down, then paging me."

"What about the cut on his arm?" Howe said after the door had closed. "Did my officer imagine *that,* too?"

"As the nurse said, he'd been struggling. He could have caught the needle when he tore out his IV."

"I don't want guesses, Doctor. You've got one hour to tell me exactly what caused that slash on his arm."

"Of course, sir."

Admiral Howe looked up at the sound of angry voices echoing down the hallway. He raised a brow at the surgeon.

"The senator from Montana has been camping out near the nursing station, hoping for news. He's becoming very persistent."

Howe chewed angrily on his unlit cigar. "Doesn't the man have legislation to shape, interviews to give? More votes to buy?" he added under his breath.

"I've put him off, Admiral, but he's getting nasty. He keeps trying to sneak onto the floor."

"Trust me, the man has been sneaking around from his first day as assistant to the attorney general of Montana." The admiral listened to the echo of angry questions. They were soon drowned out by another voice, one that Howe recognized well. So the president's aide had tracked McKade here, too.

FUBAR was the expression that came to mind.

There was going to be hell to pay. Unless someone pulled a truckload of strings, Sam McKade was going to become a political football.

Not on *his* watch, the grizzled officer swore. After flying a desk on the Pentagon's E-wing for the last thirteen years, Admiral Howe knew whose strings to pull.

The door opened. A Navy guard looked in, his face carefully expressionless. "Sorry to intrude, sir, but Senator Jeffries is making a fuss out here. Also, your son is downstairs in the lobby waiting to take you to your physical."

"To hell with my physical."

The guard cleared his throat. "Lt. Howe said to remind you that you've postponed twice this month, sir. If you don't come down, he said he's coming up."

"Later," the admiral snapped.

What he meant was *never*.

He glared at Sam's surgeon, including him in the orders that followed. "This patient is to be kept completely isolated. I want one of my guards in the room with him at all times."

The surgeon said nothing, and the guard waited impassively. Only Admiral Howe knew the reason for all the secrecy.

During three months of deep cover work in California and

Mexico, Sam McKade had targeted serious problems in the Navy's weapons research program at China Lake. He was on his way to report in person to Admiral Howe and his staff when he'd jumped aboard that school bus. Now three months of highly sensitive information was locked inside his head.

Admiral Howe had to keep his asset alive—and awake—long enough to convey the results of his investigation.

Howe left the surgeon to his work and strode off the ward with the senator close behind. "Admiral, I must protest this high-handed—"

"Later," he barked, barreling into the elevator.

He found his son pacing restlessly at the first-floor nursing station.

"How's he doing?" his son asked.

"You know better than to ask for that kind of information."

Lt. Peter Howe glared suspiciously at his father. "Don't tell me you're planning to cancel *another* physical."

The admiral ignored the question, frowning at his son's cast. "How's the arm?"

"It was a simple fracture. They say I'll be back to work in about two weeks. Stop changing the subject. Your doctor's been holding all his patients for the last hour so he could fit you in, and you're not missing another physical."

The admiral sighed. Physicals were worse than piloting a rowboat in a force-ten gale. After the annoying questions, they got out the gloves and the *real* torment began.

Suddenly the admiral smiled. Maybe a physical was a good idea after all. Even the president's top aide couldn't follow him into an examining room while he was getting gowned and prepped for a rectal exam.

"Miss my physical? I wouldn't dream of it." Howe hid a smile at the surprise on his son's face. "Now, enough about my health. Tell me about this new task force you've been assigned to. Better yet, come home for dinner tonight and give me the full story."

Chapter Seven

ANNIE'S FAX MACHINE CHATTERED NONSTOP FOR THE NEXT FOUR days. In between making final arrangements for Sam's arrival, Izzy scanned the incoming flood of reports and schedules. A Navy doctor was to accompany Sam on the flight, and Annie had already faxed him a list of questions.

Next had come the question of security. Turning over her guest list had pained Annie keenly, but Izzy had explained it was necessary. Since Annie suspected he could assemble the information from other sources, she'd finally given in.

Not that she thought the honeymooners in suite 36 posed a threat to world freedom. On the other hand, maybe the rabbits did.

It was almost two in the morning when Annie finally walked Izzy to her guesthouse, which was separated from the main house by a courtyard and a small garden. Hiding a yawn, she checked that he had fresh towels, then added a down comforter.

"Anything new I should know about?"

"Nothing crucial. Sam's itinerary is set, barring any last-minute medical complications. They're still watching that metal plate in his knee." He frowned. "I know you haven't had a lot of time to deal with this. Why don't you catch some extra sleep in the morning while I familiarize myself with the resort and your staff?"

"Can't." Annie fought off another yawn. "I'm a basket case without my morning run. After that I have two honeymooning couples arriving, and I want to be on hand to greet them."

"Your call." Izzy took the stack of towels and tossed the comforter on the couch. "Just remember, as far as your staff knows, I'm here to handle the upgrades on your computer system and check out resort security, but I'm fully prepared to handle whatever else you want to throw at me." He took a sleek laptop computer from his flight bag and set it carefully on the dresser. "Sam's going to need *you* a heck of a lot more than he needs me, so consider me at your disposal. I can handle follow-ups, guest bookings, and inventory checks. I can even calculate your payroll."

"Something tells me doing payroll's not in your usual job description," Annie mused.

"I put in some time on a cruise ship last year. It was an interesting experience."

"Why am I thinking murder, mayhem, and national security threats?"

His lips curved. "Beats me. Let's just say, I know the drill."

"I'm sure it would make an interesting story. Then again, you're probably not allowed to discuss any of it."

Izzy smiled and said nothing, pointing to Annie's cell phone. "Remember to keep that with you. It's programmed so all you have to do is punch the star key if you need me."

"I seriously doubt that I'll have any emergencies involving inventory or staff payroll." She examined the high-tech phone as if it might bite her. "On the other hand, if my test pilot doesn't agree to ditch his stash of gin, I may need you to escort him from the premises."

"Not a problem." Izzy finished checking the room, then headed back to the door. "After you."

"Are you going somewhere?"

"I'll see you to your house."

"That's not necessary. It's just across the courtyard and we haven't had a robbery here in ten years."

"I'm glad to hear it, but from now on it's SOP."

"Silly old plan?"

Izzy's eyes glinted. "Standard operating procedure."

Annie went very still. "Is Sam in some kind of danger?"

"There's no reason to think so."

"In that case, am I?"

Izzy continued to stand in the doorway. "None that we're aware of."

"Then why all these precautions?"

Izzy motioned her outside, all the time scanning the darkness. Annie realized he had memorized the layout of the resort and its outlying buildings. Beneath his engaging facade, the man had a razor-sharp intelligence and years of solid experience. Annie was also sure that most of his work was classified.

Why had the Navy sent a smart, experienced operative to protect a wounded man from possible media exploitation?

It didn't add up.

Surf rumbled in the distance as they cut through the dark courtyard. "Well?"

"Twenty million viewers saw Sam save that bus. The Navy can use that kind of good publicity."

"It's better than sexual harassment suits," Annie murmured. "So they're going to get as much mileage as possible out of their newest hero."

Izzy moved a branch out of Annie's way. "Every journalist in America wants a piece of this story. If his location is leaked, Summerwind is going to be knee-deep in Mike Wallace wannabes."

Annie frowned. If Izzy was right, Sam could lose the peace and quiet he needed for recovery, and she would lose all her high-profile clients, who guarded their privacy obsessively. "What's the problem? The Navy has taken precautions so that no one will know Sam is here." She stopped in the darkness, struck by a sudden, uneasy thought. "Unless there's a slip at your end."

Izzy said nothing.

"That's the real reason you're here, isn't it? Somehow the news has gotten out."

They were outside the garden around her house now. Moonlight had turned the hollyhocks into a row of dancing silver petals. After scanning the darkness, Izzy climbed the steps, tried Annie's door, and frowned.

"I told you to keep this locked." Before she could protest, he stepped inside, switched on the inner light, and vanished.

Another security check, Annie realized.

Some powerful people were taking Sam's safety very seriously. But she wanted the whole story, not a carefully edited civilian version. When Izzy reappeared, she was waiting, arms crossed. "I agreed to help Sam, but I didn't agree to take on a bodyguard, no matter how helpful. I also don't like having the Navy's mess dumped in my lap."

"I've told you everything I know."

Oddly, Annie believed him. "What about the leak?"

"Let the experts handle that."

She fingered the sleek cell phone. "All this cloak-and-dagger stuff feels ridiculous."

"When you accepted Sam's care, you accepted the whole package," Izzy said gently. "As far as the Navy's concerned, that's nonnegotiable."

"In other words, tough." Annie's voice was tight. "If I had any sense, I'd back out now."

"I don't think so. You care too much."

She took a slow breath, trying to gauge his expression in the half-light. "Why is he so important?"

"He's the Navy's biggest hero," Izzy said softly. "He's also the man you're going to put back together."

"What *else* is Sam Mitchell?"

"His real name is McKade." Izzy walked her to the door. "Sleep well, Annie. Be sure to lock up after me."

❖   ❖   ❖

SECOND BY SECOND.

He drifts, slipping down into dreams.

Instead of a hospital bed, Sam McKade finds a place where torn ligaments, battered knee, and burning shoulder are forgotten, a place with golden sun and waves slapping on a fiberglass hull. Here are calm seas and wind out of the west as he drifts with sails slack.

It is good to be in that place, wherever it is, with the smell of the sea in his face.

His mind clicks, a new image rising. He recognizes her scent even before he sees her face, challenge in her eyes and laughter floating on the steady wind. The teak deck rocks gently as she walks toward him, barefoot, wearing his old 49ers jersey, a copy of the one Montana wore on his run to glory.

He is on the verge of gruff questions and reckless promises in that moment. He hovers on the brink of emotions too dangerous to explore.

But she gives him no time, tossing a wet fish at his chest. "There's dinner. Better get going, ace."

He catches the fish in one hand, flings it high over his head, back into the blue water, never taking his eyes from her face. "I have a better idea."

Stripping off his T-shirt, shucking his sneakers, he comes for her, scooping her up and leaning dangerously over the rail.

Her eyes are huge. "You wouldn't!"

"Afraid I would."

His mind clicks again, fast forwarding to Annie's body locked against him as he drops over the rail, savoring the cool slap of the sea when they hit.

Like a precious cargo he carries her back to the surface, already peeling away the red jersey and tonguing the cool skin beneath until she shivers against him, presses hard, wanting what he wants.

Click-click.

Images race. Her legs long and bare as she licks warm marshmallows from his fingers, laughing at their mess.

Click-click.

Her body bent above him, first tentative, then strong with need that leaves her panting, searching, straining.

Click-click.

Their fingers locked in the bright flare of blood and muscle and his sudden knowledge that she is crying. But she never explains and he is too careful to ask questions as they lie spent beneath a world of stars.

Click-click.

Again the memories, this time in broken conversation.

"I have to go back too many guests four meetings tomorrow a new receptionist—

—stay—

—interviewing a chef meeting my sister for lunch ordering a dozen chairs for the—

—stay, Annie—

I can't no I can't I really can't—"

Collapsing on the deck, their clothes in a tangle, the sky black silk shot through with hot white stars as he pulls her down, down to meet his body, hard with desire.

Click-click.

Click-click.

The images race by as Sam McKade tosses in his hospital bed far away from Summerwind's quiet cove. The memories burn hot and sharp as stars—Canopus, Vega, and Orion with his belt of fire.

But like stars at dawn, the images fade and break and he wakes, knowing somehow that in waking he will forget not only her name but everything else that truly matters.

❖ ❖ ❖

HE OPENS HIS EYES IN A COLD HOSPITAL ROOM. HE LIES BATHED in sweat, feeling something move close.

When he reaches up, the thing with no name flows through his fingers, elusive as sea wind, the what or who or why of it lost beyond reclaiming. He is left with a sadness beyond words.

Chapter Eight

FIVE.

Six.

Seven.

Annie's brain slowly began to clear as she finished her first set of predawn stretches. Mist curled around her, ghosting through the twisted cypress trees above the beach.

She had to forget the cloak-and-dagger stuff. Her sleep had been fitful, broken by unsettling dreams. Being around Izzy was making her paranoid.

As she jogged in place, two otters played a game of touch football in the kelp beds, and she felt her tension lift. Everywhere she looked was sand and sea. She'd loved this beach since she was old enough to paddle through the surf and watch a pod of dolphins click out indecipherable questions. Summerwind commanded a view of twenty miles of coast and Annie savored that beauty, turning slowly, letting the wind play over her. There was no place more beautiful.

She turned to find Izzy rounding the path from the resort, his nylon jacket snapping in the wind.

Who else? Annie thought. Her staff knew that her morning runs were sacrosanct, disturbed for nothing less than fire, bankruptcy, or earthquakes.

She waited with her hands on her hips. "I run alone, Mr. Teague."

"Not anymore you don't, Ms. O'Toole."

Polite but relentless, Annie thought. "That's ridiculous."

Izzy raised his hands, palms up. "Rules."

Fuming, Annie set off at a hard clip. When she glanced

back, Izzy was maintaining a three-yard distance. Curious, she speeded up.

He did the same.

So he'd done this sort of thing before. Probably he'd been assigned to accompany diplomats, military officers, or government officials.

The least she could do was give him a workout.

She followed the narrow path over the dune to the beach. Wind tugged at her clothes as she lengthened her stride along the damp, packed sand at the water's edge. There Annie lost herself in the cry of seabirds and the beauty of the dawn streaking red in the east.

Jogging in place, she stared back at Izzy. "Forget about maintaining a polite distance. If you're going to run, come up here and give me some competition." She jumped agilely across a narrow arm of the creek that ran down to meet the sea just beyond the resort's boundary.

Annie knew every curve and rise of the coast. She'd run this way a thousand times, first as a girl, then as a woman. Thanks to the magic of the changing light and windswept water, no two runs were ever the same.

"I love this place." Somehow the words spilled out, part of an emotion she couldn't contain.

"I can see why." Izzy trotted beside her, matching her stride.

Annie was irritated to see that he hadn't even broken a sweat. "Do you do this often?"

"Run?"

"Run as part of security backup," Annie clarified.

"Now and then." He scanned the slope as he spoke. "Seldom in such beautiful terrain—or such pleasant company. The last man I ran with barked orders into a tape recorder for forty minutes straight." He shook his head. "Kind of spoils the point of getting away and recharging, if you ask me. Of course, he wasn't asking me."

Annie watched him survey the beach, then study the upper orchard. He was very good at his job, she realized. Sam would be in excellent hands.

Izzy turned. "Do you always come this way?"

"Most of the time. If there's a storm heading in from sea, I stay close to the woods." She frowned at his silence. "What aren't you saying?"

He matched her pace without any sign of exertion. "In the future, I suggest you vary your route."

"For security reasons?"

He nodded. "SOP."

Standard operating procedure.

"I'll consider it," she muttered.

His gaze moved back along the cliffs. "So you and Sam got pretty close while he was here."

Annie tensed. "Is that a simple question or the start of a fishing expedition?"

"Just a man making pleasant conversation."

Like hell it was. Annie wondered, not for the first time, how much information the Navy had collected on her in the last week.

She brushed the hair off her face, hating the thought of being watched and followed and discussed. "If you want details, you'll have to ask Sam."

"Right now that's not possible. That's why I'm asking you."

Annie rolled her shoulders, fighting a wave of tension. "Sam helped me with some repairs, and I invited him up to the resort for dinner. We ate several times on his boat, watched the stars come out, traded tall tales. End of story." She climbed the path over the dunes, drinking in the panorama of brooding clouds and rugged coastline. "It's your turn. How long have you known Sam?"

"I'd heard his name mentioned a few times, but I didn't get to know him until about six years ago. We were assigned to a . . . project . . . together overseas."

There was something in his eyes, Annie thought. Something hollow. "From your expression, I'd say it was unpleasant."

His brow rose. "Most people say I have a top-notch poker face."

"I'm not most people. Reading faces is part of my job."

"I'll remember that," he muttered, matching his pace to hers along the trail that looped across the top of the dunes. "We did what we set out to do. That's all that matters."

"I'm sorry," she said quietly.

"For what?"

"For whatever left that look in your eyes."

He shook his head. "Let's switch topics, shall we? You're starting to spook me."

"In that case, why don't you tell me what's in that file the Navy has on me?"

"What makes you think there's a file?"

"Your people have gone to immense trouble to protect Sam. I'd say they've culled a deskful of information, including reports on my staff, my sister, and the resort. Am I close?"

"Inquiring minds want to know," Izzy murmured. "I'm not at liberty to give details, but I'll tell you this. There's zero tolerance for slipups in this case. Careers will crash and burn if anything goes wrong, so the Navy is being exceptionally thorough."

Annie drew a sharp breath. "That means my file must be *really* big. No, don't bother to deny it. I knew what I was getting into—I just didn't like it."

Izzy focused on a line of fog brushing the far cliffs. "Sam's worth it, Annie. He's a good man. Those kids aren't the only people he's rescued from tight situations."

"So tell me what you two did overseas that was so important—"

There was a flash of movement from the orchard. Annie gasped as Izzy drove her backward, out of sight behind the dunes.

Sand blew in her face, and she heard Izzy curse as he

shoved aside his windbreaker, pulling a gun from a shoulder holster. Annie pushed to one elbow, looking across the sand.

"Stay down." Izzy's voice was curt. "Don't move unless I tell you."

Sand rustled as he crawled up the slope, hidden in the lee of the dunes.

Annie discovered the hardest thing was waiting, wondering if they were a target. Anyone could be hidden in the shadows at the edge of the orchard, friend or foe.

She lay stiffly, listening to the wind hiss over the sand. A lifetime later Izzy's shadow fell over her face.

"All clear. How do you feel?"

Confused. Angry. "Like I'm entitled to some answers." Annie brushed sand from her legs. "What was that flash?"

"One of your guests practicing with a foil."

"The fencer who's been shredding my towels. I'm glad he's found a better practice area."

Izzy glanced down, frowning. "You've cut your knee."

"It's nothing."

He held out a hand, helping her to her feet. "I'll still take a look when we get back."

"All I really need is answers." As they crossed a meadow beneath the resort's main building, Izzy seemed in no mood for conversation. The silence gave Annie time to sort through the facts, and they didn't add up.

She turned at her door. Her knee ached, but she barely noticed.

Izzy followed her to the kitchen. "Caffeine would be wonderful about now."

"You talk, and I'll cook."

She broke eggs in an iron pan and pulled out handmade stoneware plates, piling Izzy's high with homemade bread, fresh melon, and a Southwestern omelette. "What's going on?"

Izzy ate by the kitchen window overlooking the hillside.

The beach was deserted, but his eyes kept flicking down to check. "There was no sign of anyone else when I got there."

"But you suspect there may have been someone else. Not just the fencer?"

"It's not about what I suspect, Annie. It's about being prepared for any threat." Izzy blew at his steaming mug of coffee, took a careful sip, then sat back. "Zero tolerance for slipups, remember?"

"I remember. And if any reporters show up, I'll have Reynaldo or his men escort them off the premises. It's happened before and we've never needed a gun or any fancy security equipment."

"This is different." Izzy cradled the coffee mug between his hands.

"Why? What are you really worried about?"

Izzy rolled the cup slowly. "Sam's made enemies over the years. With the kind of work he does, making enemies is inevitable." He looked up, watching Annie's face. "Some are overseas, but some are the homegrown hate-group variety."

The words left her cold.

Shadow warriors, wasn't that what Izzy was saying? Men who carried out covert operations and high-risk missions in places where normal rules didn't apply.

Annie kept her voice light. "So you're telling me Sam's more than a cute face in a nice white uniform?"

Izzy laughed grimly. "You could say that. He's one of the Navy's best and brightest. Unfortunately, now that his face has been splashed across twenty million TV screens, he's not anonymous anymore."

Annie tugged off her sweatshirt and slid into the chair across from him. "So Sam's in danger?"

Izzy pushed away his coffee, frowning. "With a little persistence someone could track down a policeman on duty that day, ask a few questions about traffic, and find out which hospital Sam was taken to. You get the picture."

Annie did indeed, and it frightened her silly. "How can the Navy prevent that?"

"Right now every detail about his life and whereabouts has been locked up like Fort Knox. They're taking all the usual precautions, plus some new ones made up just for the occasion."

"But because the Navy is a big, cumbersome bureaucracy, mistakes can happen. Information can be leaked." She sat back tensely. "That's why you're here. In case someone gets through."

Izzy studied her for a long time, then nodded.

"Exactly how dangerous is this going to be?"

"You want the official answer—or the truth?"

Annie stared down at the coastline where sunlight touched the waves. "That answers my question. It also tells me why you wear a gun."

A muffled sound came from Izzy's jacket. He pulled out his pager and studied it in silence.

"Well?" Annie demanded.

He pushed away his plate and stood up. "Sam's move may be delayed." His expression told Annie nothing.

"Why?"

Izzy stacked his dishes in the sink. "I can't tell you because I don't know."

"Can't you find out?" Annie's hands were trembling.

"This is the Navy we're talking about. Right now the rule is *need to know*."

"Well, *I* need to know if Sam's okay. I also need to know when he's arriving."

Izzy stared down at the beach. "When I find out, you'll find out. Right now, that's the best I can do."

❖ ❖ ❖

"WHAT ARE YOU DOING OUT OF BED?"

"Walking." The man in the hospital gown grimaced. "Trying to."

Admiral Howe shoved his unlit cigar in his pocket and took Sam McKade's arm. "You're barely off the IV, you young fool."

"Six hours." Sam hid a wince as he tried to lift his left leg, encased hip to ankle in a removable brace. "Almost."

"It's too soon," the admiral snapped. Secretly, he was elated at the sight of the SEAL's fierce determination to recover. "Get well before you start trying to line dance."

"Never was much of a dancer." Sam took four more halting steps. "Sir."

The man had to be in massive pain, yet Howe knew from his nurse that McKade was pocketing his pain meds and flushing them down the toilet.

Real grit, the admiral thought, well pleased. Maybe he could leave the hospital sooner than his doctors predicted.

"When did you have your last pain pill, Commander?"

The media's unknown hero, looking tense and dangerous in several days of stubble and pain lines that bordered his mouth, simply shrugged. "A while, sir."

The admiral hid another smile. Stubborn bastard. Not that he'd have it any other way. "When your nurse comes back, you're to take whatever pills she gives you. Is that understood?"

Sam grimaced. "Take them—as in swallow them, sir?"

"That's an order, sailor."

Sam glared down at his leg brace. "Aye, aye, sir."

"Good. How's that leg feel?"

They started another slow circuit around the room. "Like shi—" Sam cleared his throat. "Like a garbage scow plowed through it, sir."

"I expect so." Holding his officer's arm, the admiral guided him through another two steps. "At least you're learning how to use a crutch. What about your shoulder?"

"It's not as bad, sir."

Not as bad as *what*?

But Howe was wise enough not to ask. A man had to keep his pride when his body had come close to being shattered.

"We'll get you started on therapy tomorrow, if your doctors clear you."

"I'd like that, sir." Sam struggled through another circuit. "The sooner the better. I want to get back to the team."

"Of course you do." Howe patted his pocket, pressing his battered cigar and trying to decide how to ask his next question.

Straight out was always the best.

"Any pain from that head wound?"

"Only when I breathe." The SEAL smiled crookedly. "Sir."

The admiral coughed, hiding a chuckle. "All to be expected. How about your recollection of the accident?"

Right now that's all they were calling it. *The accident.*

"Still pretty hazy, sir."

"How about prior to the accident?" The combat veteran kept his voice carefully neutral. "Any recall before the hospital? Over the last month, say?"

McKade frowned. "Nothing, sir. I keep trying to dig. It feels—important somehow." His jaw tightened. "I get back to when I woke up, and the pain started."

"And before that?"

The SEAL's voice was hard. "Nothing, sir."

Hell and hell again, the admiral thought. He needed the information Sam McKade had buried in his head. He needed it fast, before the problems at the Navy's weapons program got any worse.

One attempt had already been made on the commander's life inside a secure Navy hospital ward, and Howe had to assume that someone with excellent sources was prepared to kill to keep that information hidden.

Howe took out his cigar. "Give it some time, son. You were torn up pretty bad. Concentrate on building your strength and charming that young nurse who keeps flirting with you."

Sam scratched his jaw. "The blonde, sir? She's married with three kids and a husband who flies a Pave Low chopper out of Little Creek."

Howe shook his head. The nurse didn't look old enough to date his son, much less have three kids and a hotshot pilot for a husband.

"How'd you learn all that?"

The young officer shrugged. "People talk to me. I must have that kind of face."

Harrison Ford on a good day, the admiral noted. Yes, women would talk to this man. So would men. It was something about the way he met your eyes, afraid of nothing, but prepared to treat you as an equal, no questions asked.

Howe saw that McKade's eyes were narrowed with fatigue and his movements were slowing. He glanced down at his watch. "I'd better get the lead out. I've got another finance meeting on the Hill." He helped Sam maneuver to a chair. "Get some rest, Commander, and call me if you need anything. Even if you just want to talk."

Or if you remember.

But Howe didn't say the words. The SEAL had enough to weigh him down right now. His neurologist had reported that there was no sign of brain damage, and Sam was expected to recover the lost chunk of memory eventually.

But would it be soon enough?

Others had proposed hush-hush experimental stimulants and deep hypnosis. Some crank had even pushed for electroshock therapy. For now, the admiral had tabled all such discussions.

But he couldn't hold out forever. He would give his man another week to remember. After that, like it or not, he'd have to get tough.

But first McKade was going to take a trip out West.

Week
Two

Chapter Nine

ANNIE O'TOOLE STOOD IN THE DARKNESS, DISORIENTED AND restless.

At 2:00 A.M., the night air was cool. She shivered a little as lights cut through the distant sky.

A helicopter churned closer. The knowledge that Sam was on board left her nerves jumping. She had read his medical file a dozen times since his transport was finally cleared, and the details were carved into her memory. But how would he look and what would he say? Most of all, would he remember her at all?

The file said nothing about that.

"Ready for your new patient?" Izzy stood beside her on the deserted inland road, connected to his cell phone via a small earphone. Annie was coming to see that the man made staying in touch a high art form.

"Absolutely." *If you discount my breathing difficulties.* Annie stared at the approaching lights. "I just wish I could be sure that no one else knows about this."

"The Navy is doing everything they can to take the heat off. They sent out two other choppers tonight from different bases, each bound for a different destination."

"Decoys?"

Izzy nodded. "It's unlikely that anyone will track Sam's flight here."

"But it's not impossible."

Izzy stared into the darkness. "Nothing's impossible."

The hum of motors grew louder. Annie picked out a darker shape against the racing clouds. "I want to do everything I can for him," she said. "But I need to know his outlook. His commitment. How much he'll remember . . ."

"The medical team at the hospital has filled in a few details about the accident, but they don't want him to be overloaded right now." Izzy turned, studying Annie in the darkness. "They've decided not to tell him about what happened before the crash. The neurologist felt it would be best for him to piece things together as part of his recovery."

"So he doesn't know that he's been here before? He won't know me or that we've met?"

"That's about the size of it. The less he's told, the better. His medical team plans to use his rate of recall to assess the recovery."

Annie laughed tightly. "Sam is going to be furious when he finds out that his doctors want him purposely kept in the dark."

"Probably," Izzy agreed. "But it's not our call. His medical team thinks it's the right approach, and that means you two relate strictly as patient and therapist. They don't want him to be sidetracked by personal issues from his past. Right now he has to focus on regaining his fighting performance."

"I don't like lying," Annie said tightly.

"We don't have to like it."

Izzy looked up into the darkness. The air churned. Suddenly lights cut across the slope, trees shaking in the sudden turbulence.

There were no markings or military identification on the helicopter that hovered the meadow. The high-tech black body looked sinister, like something out of a movie. The Navy was taking no chances with Sam's safety.

Thanks to some juggling, most of Annie's guests were gone, and all but her essential staff had been given time off. The remaining workers had been briefed to avoid Annie's house and to hold all their questions. As far as they knew, Izzy was her only visitor. Now the rest depended on Sam and his determination.

And how much pain he could endure.

Annie had studied his files and spoken to his doctors. She knew he would be facing an enormous amount of pain, especially at first. For his therapy to work, pain would be his constant companion.

She raised her chin, reminding herself to stay calm, to make her concern purely professional. But she kept seeing Sam's face as he'd waved good-bye from the cove.

And then his bloody, broken body captured by a hovering news team.

The lights grew brighter. Against the drone of motors, night turned to blinding day. Sand and pebbles snapped against Annie's face as she was blown back by turbulence from the blades. Izzy grabbed her arm as the chopper landed and a man in a black jumpsuit leaped to the ground.

Dry mouthed, Annie watched him confer with Izzy, then lean inside the helicopter.

She hadn't smoked a cigarette in eight years, but she had a sudden urge for one now, watching a gurney being lowered to the ground.

Izzy pointed down the hill toward his van, and two men in flight suits hefted the gurney over the ground. Annie followed, picking up bits of conversation as they walked.

"So *this* is the Shangri-la you promised me, Teague? Can't see much in the dark, but the sea must be close, judging by that wind."

Sam, Annie thought. Her throat tightened painfully.

"Just over the hills," Izzy said. "How are you doing, ace?"

"Great, as soon as you get me out of this torture device. Tell me about the therapist you found for me. A real dragon lady, right?"

"She has to be a dragon to put up with a hard case like you."

"Guess you're right." Sam gave a low bark of laughter. "Hard on the eyes, is she?"

"See for yourself."

Annie walked ahead, opening the door to the car. With light filtering around her, she took a breath and turned, facing Sam.

His face was pale.

His eyes held no hint of recognition.

It doesn't matter, she told herself. They'd told her to expect this.

She cleared her throat. "I believe I'm the dragon lady in question."

"Things must be looking up." Sam's hand rose, curled around her wrist. "Where have you been all my life, beautiful?"

Annie couldn't speak, assaulted by memories.

"She was doing better things. Why waste her time with a saltwater cowboy like you?" Izzy said.

"Better than being a digital desk jockey like you," Sam countered. He didn't look away from Annie's face as he spoke.

"Says you. Now let the woman do her work."

Sam released her hand reluctantly. "Fine. Just get me out of this damned gurney. I can walk with a little effort."

Izzy glanced at the man in the black jumpsuit, who pursed his lips and shook his head.

Annie gripped the car door, fighting to keep her hands steady. She couldn't let any of them see how shaken she was. So what if Sam didn't remember her? This wasn't *personal*, after all. Her memories would have to be buried deep, where they couldn't interfere with the difficult job before her. "Into the car, tough guy. We'll negotiate the details of your therapy when we get to the house. Then you'll find out exactly what a dragon lady I can be."

❖   ❖   ❖

THE VAN HELD THE GURNEY AND THE NEW ARRIVALS WITH INCHES to spare. Annie couldn't see much of Sam until they pulled into the driveway that led up to her house.

Take this one step at a time, she thought. At least he was strong and his outlook was positive.

Then she looked down and saw that his hand was wrapped around the edge of the gurney's metal frame, clenched tight.

Pain.

And he would never show it.

"I'd say you could use some medication, Mr. McKade." That was how she'd been instructed to address him. Mister. No military titles. Annie wondered if it was his real name. He'd called himself Sam Mitchell before.

His eyes hardened. "I had a shot two hours ago."

Behind Izzy the doctor frowned and shook his head slightly, raising six fingers.

"Fine, fine. We'll work out the details later." Right now her patient needed rest, not arguments, Annie decided. She opened the door and jumped down. "Tomorrow I'll give you the grand tour, including the exercise area and whirlpool. I hope you like exercise, Mr. McKade."

"Call me Sam." *As if they were strangers.*

"Sam it is."

"And I like exercise just fine. Always have." For a moment his eyes were troubled. "At least I think I do. My memory's a little whipped right now."

"No problem." Annie forced her voice to stay light as she guided the group inside. "You're right down this hall." She pointed to a room dominated by a wall of windows framing the dark coast. Only a few lights rocked, far out at sea.

"The king-size bed is yours. You've got a remote control for lights, television, and curtains."

"All the comforts of home."

"That's the idea. This handset will page me, wherever I am."

"Seems like a lot of bother for one man." Sam sat up awkwardly on the gurney. "When do we start the therapy?"

"Tomorrow."

Sam nodded, fighting to keep his eyes open. Only tension and pain were keeping him awake now, Annie realized.

Moving behind him, she beckoned to the doctor, holding

up thumb and two fingers as if for an injection. When he
nodded, she placed her hands on Sam's face. "Why don't you
close your eyes while we help you onto the bed? No sense getting dizzy." As she spoke, she massaged his forehead, placing
her hands along his face.

"Nice hands," he murmured.

Annie could feel him fighting the tension, fighting sleep.
Teaching him to relax would be one of her biggest challenges,
since he would fight any hint of weakness.

"Let's get you into bed, shall we?"

His eyes didn't leave her face. "Best offer I've had in weeks."

Annie helped him maneuver to the bed using crutches. After
he was settled, she stood behind him and covered his eyes, massaging his face. Then she nodded at the doctor, who held a prepared syringe. "My hands are going to be important, Sam. Focus
on them so you can learn to direct the healing process."

"You've got my complete focus, ma'am."

"Good. Stay with me." Annie skimmed the muscles at his
jaw, feeling his tension. "Still with me?"

"Oh, yeah." His eyes were closed now.

Deception was rotten, but sometimes it couldn't be helped.
Annie nodded at the medic. The syringe slanted down,
touched Sam's arm, slid home.

He tried to sit up. "What the—"

Annie held him still. "Don't tell me a big tough guy like you
is afraid of a teeny widdle needle?"

His lips curved in the hint of a smile. "Yeah, I'm shaking in
my boots, Doc. Whatever you do, just don't stop doing that
thing with your fingers."

One hurdle crossed, Annie thought. The pain medication
would soon help him sleep. "What I'm doing is cranio-sacral
massage and counterpoint balancing, with a little acupressure
thrown in for good luck."

"Lost me there." He sighed, turning his head toward her
hands.

"No need to move. I'll do all the work."

"This must be illegal. Probably breaks some AMA protocol. Or maybe that's FDA." His words were beginning to slur.

"We're in California. The only thing that's illegal here is not recycling."

"Never felt anything so good." His mouth tightened suddenly. "I don't think I have. Can't remember. Tried damned hard, but I can't."

"There's no rush," Annie said soothingly. She moved down to massage his neck and shoulders. "Give it time."

"Funny." His eyes opened, narrowed against the pain. "Your voice. It almost seems . . . familiar."

Annie kept her smile impersonal. "I bet you use that line on all the ladies, Mr. McKade."

"Sam." He shook his head, his face so pale that Annie hurt inside. "Wouldn't use a line, ma'am. Not with someone special like you," he said gravely.

Emotions fluttered, but Annie shoved them away. "I'm delighted to hear it, Sam. Now close your eyes and relax. You've got all the time in the world."

He studied her face, frowning. "No. I have to remember."

"Cool down, Sam." Izzy touched his arm. "What do you have to remember?"

Sam's hand closed to a fist. He stared down at his locked fingers, breathing heavily. "It's right there. That close." He looked up at Izzy. "They didn't tell me where the accident happened. All I see are buildings. There are sirens everywhere and I'm trying to hang on, to hold it all together. For them, but I don't remember who."

"You saved over forty people, ace. That makes you America's reigning hero." Izzy spoke with just the right edge of challenge. "If you weren't so dog ugly, I'd have to be jealous."

"A hero," Sam repeated. His eyes closed slowly. "Can't remember."

The pain medication finally kicked in, pulling him under.

He wouldn't have to fight anymore, Annie thought, or pretend he wasn't hurting.

She nodded at the medics, who pushed the gurney outside. On the bed Sam muttered, but didn't wake. She started to move her hands away, but he made a low sound of disapproval.

"Don't stop now, Doc. Just . . . getting good."

Izzy studied Sam gravely. "We're going to have our work cut out for us." His voice was low. "The big fool will be fighting his pain every step of the way."

"Fighting can be good." Annie slid one hand gently over Sam's hair. "And we'll be here to help him fight."

"You okay?" Izzy asked softly.

How can I be okay? I touched this man. That night under the stars, I gave him a piece of my heart. He went away without a real good-bye, and now he's come back a stranger.

Though her eyes burned with unshed tears, Annie straightened her shoulders and smiled. "I'll survive."

◇ ◇ ◇

SOMETHING WAS WRONG.

The pain was back, but Sam was already used to feeling pain. This was different.

He lay staring into the darkness, his whole body tensed. More of his imagination? First the surgeries. Then they'd pumped him full of medications in spite of all his protests.

He tried to block out the crushing pain, but he couldn't focus, couldn't see, couldn't—

Remember.

Not one damned thing prior to waking up in the hospital.

His name?

Okay, he knew that much. *My name is Sam McKade.*

His lips twisted. He only knew *that* courtesy of a frowning doctor from the naval hospital. Even that might have been a lie.

He went through his usual inventory, testing legs, arms,

hands, fingers. Every muscle was weak, but they functioned, even if any movement made his left shoulder ache like hell.

He needed to get going, to start building himself up. He didn't have much time before . . .

Before what?

He tried to sit up. Instantly pain shot up his chest and clawed down his arm.

His fingers gripped the bed, tightened. Damn it, before *what*?

The darkness offered no answers as he fought for clarity, caught on the razor's edge somewhere between pain and sleep. Something whispered that he couldn't trust anyone, that things weren't what they seemed. Gritting his teeth, he blocked the dark slide to oblivion because he had to. Because he needed to remember.

Before it was too late.

Chapter Ten

ANNIE AWOKE TO THE CRACK OF SHATTERING GLASS. DISORI-ented, she stared into the darkness, remembering she wasn't alone.

Sam.

She lurched from her bed, running down the dimly lit hall to the guestroom. "Sam?" she called breathlessly.

Through the faint moonlight she saw him, stretched across the bed, one arm caught in the sheets. His hands opened and closed as if trying to hold something that kept slipping away.

There was blood on the sheet. More blood at his shoulder. His body was rigid, every muscle of his chest defined.

Something stabbed her foot as she crossed the floor, but Annie ignored the discomfort. Sam's doctors had warned her to approach him slowly, never taking him by surprise. By training and experience, his instinct was to attack first and ask questions later. That instinct would only be sharpened by his disorientation and pain.

"Sam, can you hear me?"

"That you, Doc?" His voice was hoarse.

"Right here. What have you been doing, reenacting World War II in here?"

"Yeah. Feels like Normandy, except my side lost," he muttered. "Gotta get up. No time to waste."

"You're going nowhere, big guy."

"Have to go. Have to tell them—"

When Annie touched his face, he was burning up, his eyes delirious. "Everyone's asleep, but you can call whoever you want in the morning. Since you've made a mess of that wound on your shoulder, we'd better fix it."

He stiffened when she touched his arm. His mouth flattened to a hard line.

"No arguments. You're taking some pain medicine."

"Like hell," he said. "Don't need it. Do that thing with your hands and I'll be fine."

"You take half your meds, and I'll give you half the massage. Then we'll clean up that wound, because it's got to be hurting like hell." Annie waited impatiently. If he didn't agree, she'd have to call Izzy for firepower.

"Don't want the medicine." The words were slurred. "Can't—think. Need to remember."

"You can remember tomorrow," she said softly. "If you don't sleep, you won't be good for much anyway."

"Not good for anything now." His hands opened, and one callused palm locked over hers. "Do it," he rasped. "But only half."

The stubborn, proud fool.

Annie found the bottle Izzy had given her and tapped out one pill. "Take this. Here's a glass of water."

She watched him grimace as he swallowed. When he sank back, his eyes narrowed on her. "Your turn, Doc."

"You think I break my promises?"

"I don't know you well enough to say."

One brow raised, Annie sat carefully beside him, feeling the heat of his body through her thin nightdress. Ignoring the instant skim of heat where her body touched his, she reached down to his neck.

"Close your eyes. Focus on my hands." Slowly, she worked her way along locked muscles and tender nerves until she felt his breath hiss free.

"Those hands of yours ought to be insured, Doc."

"I'm not a doctor."

"Who the hell cares?"

The compliment made Annie smile. "Don't tell that to the AMA unless you want me behind bars." She traced the top of his right shoulder, kneading smoothly. Suddenly his arms tightened.

"Let it go, Sam."

"Can't."

"Who are you fighting, the world or yourself?"

She heard him curse. "Both. Whenever I close my eyes I see a road with someone right behind me. I don't turn back but I can hear the engine. Louder, louder. And if I don't hurry—" He blew out a hard breath. "Sometimes it's so close I can touch it. Then later, I think I'm dreaming. Maybe I'm ready for a padded cell."

"Stress can play nasty tricks. Let it go," Annie repeated softly. "There'll be plenty of time to remember."

He moved his arm restlessly. "I can't. Too important."

"Trust me, fighting isn't going to help."

"Fighting's . . . what I do best." There was a grim edge to his voice. "Too late to change that now, Doc, even if I wanted to."

Annie frowned in exasperation at the nickname. "Put it away, Sam."

"Can't. Call it a—a guy thing."

"So here's a girl thing: no rest, no therapy. *Capice?*" She moved away, glaring down at him.

He opened one eye. "Hell, don't stop now. I was just starting to feel human again."

Annie's foot was throbbing. She must have cut it on something during her rush down the hall. She hid a grimace as she moved around him, smoothing his blankets. "Too bad, ace. It's my game here, with my rules and my scorecard. If you don't accept that, we might as well stop now because I can't help you."

"Izzy was right. You *are* a dragon."

"Absolutely. I breathe fire and consume chivalrous knights on a regular basis. Do you accept my terms or not?"

"For now."

Annie sensed it was all she would get. Sighing, she bent closer, massaging his back. "Always fighting," she muttered.

"Like I said, it's what I do best." His hand rose, cupping her hip through her cotton nightgown. "*Almost* the best." There was a faint curve to his lips.

Annie stiffened. Did he expect personal services along with the therapy?

She looked down, ready to set him straight. "There's another rule you should know about." She caught his hand and set it on the bed, but the second she let go, he moved it back. "Sorry, but this one's nonnegotiable."

No answer.

"Sam?"

His hand opened, and his breath came low and regular. He was already asleep.

❖　❖　❖

IZZY FOUND HER AT THE KITCHEN TABLE TWENTY MINUTES LATER, picking glass splinters out of her feet.

"I saw the light," he explained when she waved him inside. "What happened?"

"Sam woke up. I finally got him settled and changed the dressing at his shoulder."

Izzy frowned at her feet. "Looks as if you had a tussle in the process."

Wincing, Annie drew out a particularly nasty sliver of glass. "I heard a noise and I raced to his room. By the time I realized he'd knocked over and broken a glass, it was too late to put on slippers." She dropped another sliver into the saucer beside her. "Do you think this qualifies me for hazardous-duty pay?"

"I wouldn't hold out hope. Your resort fees aren't exactly cut-rate." Izzy pointed to her heel. "Need some help with that?"

"I'm almost done."

"In that case I'll take a look at our hero before I shove off."

When Izzy returned, he looked at Annie curiously. "The man's dead to the world. Pain pills?"

"He agreed to take half."

"Whatever your secret is, keep it up." He watched Annie position a bandage over her right heel. "How was he when he woke up?"

"Definitely disoriented. Very determined to push himself."

"That figures. Did he say anything else?"

Annie pressed a bandage on her other foot, then sat down. "He mentioned having a recurrent dream, something about being on a road and hearing a noise behind him, but not being able to see what it was. He was lucid enough to describe the dream, but he's afraid he's missing something." Annie frowned. "Whatever it is, it feels darned important to him."

Izzy drummed lightly on the table.

Annie waited, trying to read his face. "Was there a project he was working on, something that he left hanging?"

"If there was, the Navy didn't give me any details."

"Maybe you need to find out. Something's gnawing at him, and eventually he's going to need answers." She glanced at the clock and stood up. "I didn't realize it was so late." She suppressed a yawn.

"You want me to take a shift here? I can bunk on the couch in Sam's bedroom."

"No, I'll finish out the night." Annie felt intensely protective about Sam, though she didn't want to explore the reasons why.

"In that case, I'll come by at seven. Anything big happening tomorrow?"

"Things should be fairly quiet since most of our regular guests are gone. My major headache is the new cedar whirlpools, which don't heat properly. The company is sending a troubleshooter to check out the problem."

"You want me to handle that for you?"

Annie nodded, only too glad to leave the problem to Izzy. If he fixed her computer, he could probably fix a whirlpool, and she was getting tired of fighting a battle to make the manufacturer take responsibility. "Next on my list is trying out some new mud wraps. Care to volunteer?" She had to laugh at his instant expression of distaste. "What, not interested?"

"I'll definitely pass on *that* assignment."

"Your pores will never forgive you." She grimaced as she walked him to the door. "I guess I won't be running for a few days."

"Just as well. I can't watch Sam and tag along with you at the same time."

"Are you saying I can't run alone while Sam is here?"

"Only the beach is out. If you stay inside the resort, you should be safe. For the moment."

"That's ridiculous."

"No, that's standard operating procedure," Izzy said calmly. "Remember to lock up after me. I'll be listening."

Chapter Eleven

SAM WAS HALF-DRESSED AND STRUGGLING TO STAND UP WHEN Annie checked on him at dawn.

"What do you think you're doing?"

"Getting dressed."

Irritated, Annie moved in front of him. "Why didn't you call me?"

"After shaking you out in the middle of the night, I figured you were entitled to your sleep."

"If there's a problem, call me. That's what I'm here for." Annie studied his face. "How's the pain?"

He was pale but determined. "Better than it was. I want to start my therapy today."

"Fine. We'll begin with some stretches, then see what comes next."

"Don't pull your punches," he said flatly. "I'm here to work." He looked down, frowning. "What happened to your feet?"

"Just some blisters from running. Let's get started on knee extensions with your right leg." Annie watched him carefully as she adjusted the position of his knee.

His face was strained, but he gave no sign of complaint.

"Good. Now let's run through some triceps work on your right arm." She handed him a ten-pound dumbbell. He gripped the weight easily, moving it up and down in a smooth motion that showed he was no stranger to free weights. Of course the left arm would be the real challenge. "Now another set."

His eyes narrowed as she gave him a heavier weight. He curled his fingers awkwardly, breathing in little puffs. After half a set, his muscles rebelled.

"Take it slow." Annie resisted the temptation to help him complete the move, knowing he had to find his own limits, even if they were painfully less than he hoped. When she finally called a halt ten minutes later after another set of exercises with his good arm, Sam was sweating.

She followed up with a slow massage to cool him down and relax him.

"How about some breakfast after this?"

"Great," he murmured, eyes closed. "I'll have steak rare, with an extra helping of steak rare. Oh, yeah, steak rare on the side."

"Very funny." She headed for the kitchen and returned with a tray. "You've got two poached eggs, one grapefruit, and oatmeal on the side."

"Oatmeal? You must be kidding."

"Complex carbohydrate with tons of fiber. Great food value for the calories."

Sam examined the bowl as if it were pond scum. "Who cares about food value? There's a steak somewhere with my name on it."

"It will still be there tomorrow. Try your eggs."

As she held out Sam's plate, the phone rang.

"Annie," her assistant said, "we've got a problem down here. Someone stole the new shipment."

"Not the organic Hungarian facial gel?"

"Gone. All twelve boxes."

"Try the linen room. There's a new woman in housekeeping and she may have moved them by mistake."

"Will do."

When she put down the phone, Sam's eggs were gone and he was grinning. "Hungarian facial gel?"

"Don't knock it. Those bottles cost two hundred dollars an ounce."

"Good thing I don't need my pores cleaned."

Annie gave him a measured stare. "I don't know about that."

He glared. "No way. Don't even think about it. Things could get nasty fast."

Annie took his plate. "Funny, Izzy said the same thing."

The phone rang again, and this time it was Annie's chef. "I told you this would happen. Last night they got all my baby carrots. Damned rabbits—I swear I'm going to shoot them all."

"I'll talk to Reynaldo, and we'll get the carrots fenced off this afternoon."

"It's me or those rabbits, Annie. You can consider that an ultimatum."

Sam's brow rose as Annie put down the phone. "More trouble?"

"Rabbits got the baby carrots."

"That's serious?"

"Trust me, it's the worst. It's the rabbits or my head chef and I'll never find anyone half as creative as Zoe." She sighed. "I'd better go find my groundskeeper and devise a plan of attack."

Sam put out his hand, holding her still. "You're dead on your feet. Izzy's here to troubleshoot, so let him earn his pay. Come to think of it, he could probably set up some kind of electronic barrier to keep your four-legged intruders at bay."

"I'd kiss his feet if he could." Annie shifted uncomfortably, aware that his hand still covered hers. When she tried to pull free, his fingers tightened.

"Stay for a few minutes." He studied her face. "You look exhausted, and I'm pretty sure that's my fault."

"I'll catch a nap after my afternoon staff meeting." She stiffened under his continued scrutiny. "What?"

"Are you sure we haven't met before? Something about your voice is damned familiar."

Annie swallowed. Every instinct clamored for her tell him the truth. Now, not later.

But she bit back the words. The experts had spoken: for the moment, ignorance was best. "If we'd met, I'm certain I'd remember."

"Yeah. I felt that way, too. With that hair of yours and that sexy voice, you'd be a hard woman to forget."

"Another line?"

Sam's eyes glinted. "No way." He looked down and saw his hand wrapped around hers. "Sorry. That was out of line."

"No offense taken. Just don't try it again," she said coolly, "or I'll have to break your good arm."

Annie looked up as her doorbell rang. "That must be Izzy, right on time."

He looked crisp and well rested, even bigger than she remembered in a black turtleneck, black nylon pants, and high-tech running shoes. "How's our hero?"

"Come see for yourself."

Izzy followed her down the hall and stood in the doorway, studying Sam's tray. "Oatmeal?"

"It's all her idea. I had my heart set on a steak so rare it was still mooing."

"Glad to see you're keeping him in line. I'll take over now." Izzy snagged Sam's unused mug and poured himself some coffee from the pot. "By the way, your assistant said you should call her right away. Your sister dropped by looking for you. I also gather there's a guest crisis." Izzy seemed to be fighting a smile as he blew on his coffee. "Seems that one of your new arrivals called the front desk in hysterics." Izzy crossed his arms. "She swears all her underwear was stolen last night."

"Welcome to the glamour and excitement of resort living," Annie muttered.

◇　◇　◇

"When did you realize your underwear was missing?" Annie steepled her fingers, smiling at her panicky guest, a well-known self-help author on the talk-show circuit.

The writer tugged at the black hair that spiked around her face. "Last night. But who would steal my suitcase? All it had was my *underwear*." There was a note of hysteria in her voice. "I know I had it when I checked in."

"We'll find it, don't worry." Annie made a mental note to call her friend at the trendy boutique in nearby Carmel and arrange for the purchase of new lingerie to soothe her guest. "We'll make arrangements for you to pick out some replacement pieces in Carmel. And of course we'll extend a complimentary day to your visit to make up for any inconvenience you've been caused."

The woman drummed her fingers on the cover of the book she carried, which happened to be her newest release, already a national best-seller.

Thirty Days to a Stress-Free Sex Life.

Now, there was a hot topic, Annie thought. "I hear your book is number four on *The New York Times* list this week. Congratulations."

Her fingers tightened on the book. "I wish I could enjoy it but I've got Larry King at the end of the month, and my people are in touch with Oprah's people." She held up crossed fingers. "My agent tells me it could be huge." She stood, tucking the book carefully beneath her arm. "I'll accept your offer and try to stop worrying, even though the idea of a stranger having my intimate things gives me goose bumps."

"I'm sure there's a perfectly good explanation," Annie said calmly. "Until we find out, why don't you just relax and enjoy your shopping spree in Carmel? Consider it research. After all, new lingerie could help destress anyone's sex life."

"Exactly. In fact, that's chapter four. What woman feels sexy in threadbare flannel pajamas?"

Annie smiled as she steered her guest toward the door. "In that case, enjoy your research."

With one crisis narrowly averted, Annie sank into the chair behind her desk. First predatory rabbits, now missing underwear.

Maybe the *rabbits* had the underwear. Maybe they were

planning an all-night orgy to celebrate the purloined frisée and baby carrots. The surreal image helped to dissipate the headache building at Annie's right temple.

She eyed the couch longingly, wondering if she had time for a nap. Izzy had phoned to say Sam was sleeping, so she was free there. *Go for it.*

She was all set to stretch out on the couch when her intercom beeped.

"Annie, I think you'd better come down to guest registration."

"Can't it wait?"

"I'm afraid not." Her assistant sounded upset. "Remember Tucker Marsh?"

"I remember." A cutthroat lawyer, Marsh headed one of Silicon Valley's most predatory bankruptcy firms—and he had the attitude to match the job. "He stayed here last month, didn't he?"

"One and the same. He's been arguing with anyone who will listen, swearing he has a reservation. I told him that was impossible, because we're accepting only a few visitors right now, but he refuses to leave until he's spoken with you."

Annie gave a last, longing glance at the couch. "I'll be right down."

❖   ❖   ❖

AN HOUR LATER, PUNCHY WITH EXHAUSTION, ANNIE OPENED THE heavy oak door to her courtyard. Marsh had proved every bit as irritating as she remembered, and she had the headache to prove it.

The boxes Izzy had left in her courtyard were gone, replaced by partly assembled exercise equipment. With a dozen wheels and pulleys, the structure looked like nothing Annie had ever seen before.

"Nice," she said. "What kind of mileage do you get on that thing?"

Izzy adjusted the padded seat, then set down his wrench. "It's a prototype I'm testing for a company in Seattle. I figure we'll let Sam beta test it since this puppy has infinite resistance settings and full range of motion at all stations."

Annie ran a finger along the leather seat. "I'm impressed."

Izzy frowned. "You look more tired than impressed. Did you find the missing underwear?"

Annie sighed. "Don't ask. How's Sam?"

"Rested and ready to work. Your chef sent up some truly amazing seafood tacos about an hour ago, and Sam only complained once that they weren't steak." He crossed his arms. "How about you?"

"I don't eat much red meat these days. It's hell on the system."

"I wasn't asking about your food choices, Annie. You look beat," Izzy said patiently. "What can I do to help?"

Annie stared up the hill toward Zoe's organic garden. "How good are you at trapping rabbits?"

"Call me Davy Crockett."

"My chef will be thrilled because they've decimated her organic vegetables. You won't shoot them, will you?"

"Negotiating generally doesn't work too well with rabbits," he said dryly.

"But the thought of all those fluffy little bodies and big soft ears—"

"Don't worry, I'll trap them and put them in cages. Your man Reynaldo already suggested taking them up to the national forest and letting them loose."

Annie and Izzy turned as Sam tottered into the courtyard, balanced on a pair of new aluminum crutches.

"Letting *what* loose?"

"Rabbits. You should have called me before you tried them," Izzy said sharply.

Sam's mouth was set in a tight line. "It's time I started managing for myself."

Annie wanted to argue but didn't. She had to let him go at

his own pace, within reason. Of course, knowing Sam, it wouldn't be within reason.

"You'll move better if you hold the left crutch higher." She studied his posture critically. "Shift your leg forward, too." She leaned closer, adjusting the position of his body. "See?"

Annie watched him slowly negotiate the length of the terrace. He frowned, concentrating on every step. She interrupted to adjust his posture again, then watched him make another circuit.

Izzy shot her a questioning look, but she shook her head slightly. She meant to work Sam hard, right to the edge. Tiring him would help take his mind off the rest of his problems. The trick, she decided, would be to go just far enough.

She stopped him in the middle of his fifth trip. "Now you're holding that left crutch too high. Turn your wrist the way I showed you, but lean slightly to the right." She gripped his waist, adjusting his hand as she spoke. "Like this."

Sam gave no sign of noticing when her breast brushed his arm and their thighs touched.

Annie *definitely* noticed.

Every nerve tightened and her heart punched in her chest, leaving her awash in memories.

Sam stripped down to a pair of cutoff shorts, leaping from the deck into the churning sea.

Sam feeding her roasted marshmallows that ran between his fingers and stuck to her face.

Sam standing on the beach and brushing her hair gently from her forehead, just before he kissed her.

Why did her life seem to start the day they'd met?

She looked away, overwhelmed by thoughts of those lost pleasures. Twilight had fallen, leaving the ocean heavy and sullen. Far away near the horizon a gray whale breached, then fell back in a spray of churning foam. "I—have to go, Sam. Paperwork. I've got lots of paperwork," Annie blurted out. "You can work with Izzy. I'll check in after dinner."

"Annie." The word was a rough question. "What's got you so jumpy?"

The strain was tying her in knots. Even now she felt the brush of his thigh and the rough strength of his hand. The rest of her memories were even more intimate. How could she go on pretending that they were strangers? "I'm just thinking about work."

"You weren't like this a minute ago." Sam maneuvered closer, his crutch tapping. "Tell me what happened."

She couldn't face his probing eyes. Her emotions were too raw. "Let's talk about you instead. In a few weeks you'll be jumping hurdles. That's the kind of man you are. Tall, dark, and stubborn."

His eyes hard, Sam looked from her to Izzy. "What is it you both aren't telling me?"

"What does it feel like?" Izzy countered.

"Forget the Socratic method. I want answers, damn it."

Izzy stared back impassively. "If you want answers, then think harder. It's something you're supposed to be good at."

Sam's hand clenched on his crutches. "What's she hiding? Why did she go pale a minute ago?"

"Because you stepped on my foot," Annie snapped. "Now, if you're finished with the interrogation, I'm going back to work. I still have a resort to run."

"Annie, I—"

She strode past, her body stiff. The slamming door echoed through the quiet courtyard.

"Hell." Izzy rubbed his jaw and sighed. "Nice work, McKade."

Chapter Twelve

ANNIE SAT IN BED, HER KNEES PULLED UP AGAINST HER CHEST. Working with Sam was going to be far worse than she'd thought. Why had she imagined she could conceal their past?

She stared into the darkness, feeling trapped. She hadn't lied to her sister. What had happened with Sam had been brief and reckless and unexpected. They had never mentioned love and Annie had no illusions about them sharing any kind of future.

None of that made any difference.

The fact was, she hadn't had a lot of experience with men. Her work at the resort kept her too busy for much of a private life.

She had had a few pleasant encounters, nice while they lasted, but nothing that had outlived the eighteen-hour days and seven-day weeks that were her routine.

She lay back with a sigh, punching her pillow. Above the sea the moon was torn silver caught between racing clouds. Storm coming.

Winds from the west.

Probably rain.

Storms, she could manage. Men were something else. Particularly the tall, dark, and stubborn variety like Sam.

Annie gave her pillow one last punch, then closed her eyes, determined to put the past behind her. Tomorrow she was going to show Sam that he was just another patient.

She'd show *herself*, too.

◆ ◆ ◆

Alexandria, Virginia

Rain hit the glistening street. All around him, the cars were expensive and the yards were perfectly manicured.

Quiet little street.

Quiet little world.

The man crouched between a vintage Triumph and a silver Mazda. Unmoving, he watched the darkness, checking for any signs of surveillance. By nature he was patient, and his training had honed that patience tenfold.

Seeing nothing, he allowed his body to relax as he stared up at the dark apartment on the third floor.

His lips twisted.

Sam McKade, the perfect hero in his perfect little world. But not for much longer.

McKade wasn't going to be recuperating, not this time. He'd already traced the Navy's reigning hero to two possible locations. When he realized one was an upscale resort and spa on the California coast, he'd almost laughed. But his sources had never been wrong yet, so he was headed west as soon as he finished a few last details.

Starting here.

"You're damned good, McKade. Fortunately, I'm a lot better. Proving that is going to be a pleasure." He checked his watch, made another inventory of the tools he'd need for his mission: glass cutter, lock pick, crowbar, surgical gloves. Everything the well-dressed burglar needed for a night out on the town.

The thought amused him, and he smiled as he moved away from the Mazda. Still crouched, he turned toward the small side yard.

Something glinted down the street, inside a parked Explorer. Instantly he flattened, rolled hard, crawled two cars forward, then hunkered down to reconnoiter.

He caught another glint, light on glass.

Field glasses, he decided. Maybe even a night scope, although the streetlights would make night vision hell to use.

He waited, certain the street was being watched, but no car doors opened and no motors kicked in. Staying low, he crawled beneath a food truck and two SUVs, then bellied his way up a drainpipe that let him out on the perfectly mowed lawn of the public library.

As he surveyed the street, the hair rose along his neck. He knew he hadn't imagined the glint of distant glasses.

Now the night's B and E would have to wait.

He took one last look at Sam McKade's silent apartment, stripped off his surgical gloves, and tossed them into the drainpipe. He smiled, just a little, at the thought of their faces when they finally understood. But they wouldn't understand for months, of course.

He cut through an alley, circled two streets over, and swung into his own transport. He actually caught the surveillance team leaving the Explorer as his own battered District of Columbia utility truck lumbered down the alley where he'd parked it several hours earlier. The truck was authentic, right down to the employee ID taped on the dash. Only the plates were lifted, and there was no way the theft would show up on any computers yet.

Humming softly, he passed the two arguing men and vanished into the night.

❖ ❖ ❖

"There was no one there, I tell you."

"Bullshit." The man called Fanelli stared down the street, watching a utility truck turn around the corner. "He was there. I made him through the glasses, right next to that silver Mazda."

"You had too much Thai food for dinner, man."

Fanelli rubbed his neck. After twelve years on the force, he knew when surveillance had been blown. "We better call it in anyway." There was a lot of pressure from the chief on this one.

The two cops moved uneasily, staring up at the dark apartment, wondering who lived there and why they'd been assigned to watch both entrances, night after night.

Had to be someone damned important, but neither of them said it.

"Hell with this." Fanelli stared at the drizzle captured beneath the streetlights. "Let's check out the premises, just to be sure no one got inside. Then I'm getting my sorry butt somewhere warm. Five minutes for some decent coffee won't make any difference. You ask me, this whole assignment is chicken-shit anyway. Let the G-men do their own work."

He turned up his collar and strode down the sidewalk, unaware that the utility truck had cut its lights and eased into a spot less than six cars behind him, where its driver had a perfect view of the whole street.

Chapter Thirteen

THE SUN HAD BARELY TOUCHED THE TREES WHEN ANNIE HEARD the scrape of metal, followed by the thunk of a falling body. Her heart raced as she sprinted toward Sam's room.

He was balanced with one shoulder against a bookshelf while he tried to reclaim his fallen crutches.

"Is there a medical name for your particular form of insanity?" Annie demanded.

"Sure." Sam caught the edge of the crutch and pulled it up slowly. "It's called work."

Annie guided him into the nearby chair and took his crutches. "Breaking news. Any work you do gets supervised by me. That's what the Navy is paying me for." When he tried to stand up, she blocked him, hands against his shoulders. "Is anyone home?"

"There was no need to bother you."

"Wrong. You're *supposed* to bother me."

"Go back to sleep." His eyes were hard and focused. "You need your rest. You don't sleep very well."

She stared at him, hands on her hips, entirely oblivious to the way her worn Lakers' T-shirt flirted with the soft curve of her thighs. "Do you want to repeat that?"

Sam's gaze flickered to her legs, then quickly away. "Hard not to notice. The bed creaks, then you turn over and hit the wall. Pretty noisy." He ran his tongue over his teeth. "You talk a hell of a lot, too."

"I talk in my sleep? No way."

Sam shrugged lightly. "Only two of us in here, unless you had company last night."

Annie glared back in silence.

"Okay. Wasn't me, so it had to be you." He raised a brow. "No one ever told you that? Not anyone you slept with?"

Aware that her T-shirt was riding up, Annie yanked it down angrily. "None of your business."

"I'll take that as a no," he said coolly. "Could annoy someone trying to sleep next to you. Especially if he was bone tired from—" He cleared his throat and chose his next words carefully. "From a strenuous night of world-class sex."

"What makes you think sex with me would be world class?" Annie knew it was the wrong thing to say as soon as the words left her mouth.

He angled a lingering glance from her flushed cheeks to her bare feet. "Oh, yeah, Doc. Gotta be world class with a body like that. You're in prime physical shape, good muscle tone from all those massages." His eyes glinted. "Makes me feel a little distracted just thinking about it."

It was making Annie a lot more than distracted, but she refused to dwell on their last sizzling encounter, when they'd torn off each other's clothes beneath a starlit sky on the deck of his yacht.

She felt her cheeks flush again.

"Something wrong, Doc?"

"Stop calling me that. I'm your physiotherapist, not your doctor."

"Whatever you say."

"And my sex life is *none* of your business."

"Too bad." He started to say something else, but stopped himself. "Message received." His eyes slanted toward her legs again, and he looked away. "Any other rules I should know about?"

"One, you wake me if you have a problem."

"Aye, aye, sir."

Annie ignored the challenge in his voice. "Two, any exercise you do gets done with my—or Izzy's—supervision."

He took longer to answer this time. "How do you define exercise?"

"Anything, mister. If it's more strenuous than yawning, I want to know."

"Bossy, aren't you?"

"You haven't seen anything yet. I've eaten two-hundred-eighty-pound linebackers for breakfast." If there was a double meaning there, Annie didn't want to think about it.

Sam met her angry gaze with a faint smile, which only flustered her more. "Is that story they tell true?"

She crossed her arms, then dropped them when she realized it hitched up her T-shirt a good three inches. "What story?"

"The one about you and the NFL quarterback. I hear he tried to sneak in a football before you thought he was ready to start throwing again."

"The next morning he found a dozen pieces of boiled pigskin mixed in his jalapeño omelette," Annie finished coldly. "Yes, it's true. Now do you agree to rule number two or not?"

"Noticed that, did you?" Sam rubbed his jaw slowly. "Don't suppose you'd accept a *maybe*."

"Don't suppose."

"Hell." He studied the brace on his leg, then shrugged. "Agreed. Anything else?"

"Five minutes for me to make coffee, five minutes for me to dress."

"No need to bother dressing on my account. That T-shirt is the best fashion statement I've seen in quite a while."

"Very funny." Annie gave the Lakers' shirt a last tug, relinquishing the idea of another hour's sleep. "See you in ten minutes. Do not *think* about moving until I get back."

"Sure thing, Doc. I won't think about anything." He watched her huff outside, then permitted himself a wide grin. "Except maybe that gorgeous pair of legs you've got," he muttered.

❖ ❖ ❖

WHEN ANNIE RETURNED, SHE WAS DRESSED IN LYCRA CAPRIS
and a matching Lycra exercise top that bared most of her
midriff.

"Looking good, Doc," Sam murmured.

"Save your flattery." She put a bottle down beside him.
"Here's your water. Drink frequently, whether you're thirsty or
not. Dehydration can be a real problem during exercise."

Sam didn't appear to hear. He was staring at her feet. "What
happened?"

"Nothing happened."

"You've been walking funny ever since yesterday."

"I always walk funny when I get four hours of sleep." The
world wasn't fair, Annie thought. How could he look so
rugged, so calm?

So gorgeous.

He was supposed to be the sick one. Instead he looked relaxed and focused, his unruly hair and two-day stubble dangerously sexy. A black turtleneck only added to his dangerous
good looks.

Going without sleep made men look tough and adventurous. It made *women* look scary.

Annie tried not to think about the dark circles and puffy
eyes that marked her own restless night. "Can we stop dissect-
ing my walk and get to work?" She cut off his answer, pacing
briskly to the terrace outside his room.

"What's the rush?"

"I've got an early meeting with my accountant."

"Sounds like loads of fun."

"Yeah, Arnold's a real laugh fest." She opened a wooden
storage chest and pulled out a big blue ball. Made of soft rubber, it bounced smoothly when she dropped it. "This is your
new best friend. You two are going to spend lots of time together. You can start by sitting down on it."

Sam stared at the ball with disdain. "I don't have time for children's games. I need to get back in shape. That means hard work to get me strong and mobile. Maybe then I'll—"

Annie sat down on the ball and stared up at him. "Maybe then you'll *what*?"

He looked over her shoulder. "Remember."

She nodded slowly, understanding what drove him so relentlessly. "Being strong will help, Sam, but it may not bring all the answers."

"I'll have to risk that. My options are a little limited right now. Can we get down to some real work?"

Annie stood up and rolled the ball toward him. "Be my guest. It's harder than it looks, trust me."

"It's just a big ball. How hard can it be?"

"Try it."

"The only hard thing will be maneuvering with this damned brace." More irritated than ever, Sam propped one crutch against the wall and sank downward.

Annie forced herself not to help him as he tottered slightly, then settled on the ball.

"I don't see what's the big deal. Anyone can sit on a—"

Without warning he slid backward. Muttering, he pushed back up, opening his legs for balance. Even then he shifted slightly, rolling from side to side, his abs working to keep him upright. "I can feel this all through my back."

"That's the idea. This ball uses the stabilizing muscles in your back as well as your abs and thighs. It also develops upper-body strength and helps your balance." She smiled innocently. "Especially with the ten-pound dumbbell I'm going to give you."

"Ten pounds is nothing." He took the weight, working hard to stay upright. "What do you want to me to do now, balance plates?"

"We're going to work your right shoulder, tricep, and delt. At the same time, you'll be strengthening your back and abs on the ball. Hold the weight at your side, without moving your arms. Exhale as you raise your shoulder, inhale as you lower."

He worked through the movements stiffly, as if it were a fight to make his body listen, but the movements gradually became smoother.

For thirty minutes they focused on his good arm, running through front and side arm lifts, hammer curls and biceps curls, all seated, which demanded torso strength and concentration.

At the end of his workout, Sam was flushed and sweating slightly. Annie noticed his mouth twitch whenever he bent his left elbow.

"Let's take a break."

"I want to keep going."

Annie blew out an irritated breath. "Your elbow's bothering you, Sam."

"Nothing big. I didn't even use that side yet."

Frowning, Annie lifted away his weight. "Pushing through warning signs is a dumb idea."

"Are you calling me dumb?"

She shook her head. "I'm calling you dumb and stubborn."

He said nothing, massaging his elbow.

"Let me do that." She checked the joint, feeling for resistance. "How long have you had this knot on the back of your arm?"

"Don't remember. Maybe I hit it when I fell last night."

"You *fell* and you didn't call me?"

"There was no need. I handled it myself."

"I'm supposed to be helping you, Sam. H-e-l-p. That means you *call* me if you have a problem."

"I was clumsy and I slipped. There was no blood and the pain was minimal, so I decided to let you sleep." His eyes narrowed. "It was the least I could do after ripping into you yesterday."

An apology?

Annie opened her mouth for a scathing answer, then closed it. *No emotions,* she told herself. *Nothing personal.* "Next time wake me up. Meanwhile, I want that swelling on the back of your arm checked out."

"Fine." Sam pulled a towel from the nearby table and wiped his face. Annie saw his jaw harden at the movement. "Right after we finish the workout."

"You're insatiable, do you know that?"

"Am I?" Something flickered in his eyes. "I don't know what I am. I can't *remember* enough to know." He wadded the towel tightly between his fingers. "Not one damn thing that matters."

Annie touched his arm gently. "You're too stubborn to let anything get past you for long."

"Was that a compliment, Doc?"

"Probably not."

"Good. I don't think I like compliments. Criticism is more useful. Now tell me what's really wrong with your feet."

"I told you, I—"

"That was the lie," he said patiently. "Now try the truth."

Annie winced as her heel brushed against one of the dumbbells on the floor. "If you must know, you knocked over a glass the night you arrived. I wasn't wearing slippers." She omitted the part about the glass slivers she'd dug out for an hour afterward.

"Why didn't you say something?"

"At the time I was a little distracted trying to keep you in bed."

"Hell." His gaze rose slowly, following the trim line of her body. He took her hand and brushed it with his lips. "Sorry for that."

Annie shivered, trying not to feel.

Trying not to remember.

"Sorry for what?"

He gently kissed her open palm. "For causing you pain."

"Forget it."

Sam traced the inside of her wrist. "I don't think I can."

It took all Annie's strength not to lean closer and pull his mouth up to meet hers.

She stepped back, clearing her throat. "Let's get to work. But first you take your pain pill."

"Already had it."

Fine. If the stubborn fool wanted to play this game the hard way, so be it.

"Let's work on your leg. Lateral lifts."

Annie was rolling out a padded exercise mat in the living room when she heard him stop. He was staring at her, one shoulder against the door. "Are you involved with anyone?"

Annie finished straightening the mat. "Why?"

"Just wondering."

And you can keep right on wondering, she thought as she sat on the mat and motioned him down beside her. "Lie on your side."

"Aren't you going to give me an answer?"

"No. We'll start lateral stretches with your good leg. Extend your top leg slowly, keeping your foot straight. Inhale while you lift, exhale while you lower. Take your time, and don't force it."

Sam stretched out awkwardly beside her, grimacing as he raised his foot. "Tell me about him."

"No more questions."

He raised a hand in acquiescence. "The last thing I want to do is pry into your private life."

"I'm delighted to hear it. No, don't move that bottom leg." She watched critically to be sure he didn't put pressure on the brace, then adjusted the position of his knee, supporting it with one hand. "That's good."

He gave her a crooked grin. "It would be even better if you'd raise your hands a few more inches."

Annie felt heat touch her face. "Keep your overheated fantasies to yourself."

"I try, but you keep distracting me."

"Next are forward extensions."

Sam's eyes narrowed. "So it's strictly business, that's what you're saying?"

"With the rehabilitation program I have planned, neither of us will have time for anything else."

Annie was painfully aware of the brush of his body as they worked through two sets of forward extensions. He was panting now, his face pale, but he still hadn't asked for a break.

"Now for the kickback. This one looks easy, but I warn you it isn't. You'll be working all the muscles in your back, so stop immediately if anything hurts."

Despite his casual nod, Annie knew he had no intention of stopping for anything short of a complete joint dislocation.

"Lie down on the exercise ball and put your hands on the floor."

"Sounds like this could be interesting."

"Focus, McKade. I want to see your stomach in, back straight, chin tucked. Look straight down at the floor and hug the ball."

"If you say so, Doc."

Annie watched him work his way into the position. "Now lift your right leg as far as you can. Knee straight, remember. Keep the motion slow and controlled with the ball beneath you, so you really feel the muscles work." His movements were jerky and Annie could see that he was surprised at how much coordination and concentration were required.

"Not as easy as it looks," he muttered.

"Don't pull anything. All your muscles get a workout with this one, but you have to start out slow. Remember, you're healing muscles now, stretching them gently, not bulking them up."

He finished another lift and Annie saw his mouth flatten to a line. His focus was almost palpable.

"Are you sure you took your pain medicine today?"

"Sure I'm sure." He drew a hard breath. "I think I'll stop at ten."

"I was going to suggest five."

"What kind of a wimp do you take me for?"

The kind who would risk his life to save a bus filled with children. The kind who would tear a muscle before he'd show any weakness, Annie thought.

She watched Sam force himself through another lift, breathing hard. His eyes were tense, his body stiff. "Damn it, Sam, stop pushing."

His face was lined with strain as he rolled over onto his back.

Annie ran her hand along his shoulder, raging at herself for not halting him sooner. Not that the big gorilla would have stopped without a tranquilizer gun. She traced his elbow. "How does this feel?"

He shrugged. "A little tender."

She touched the lump on the back of his arm. "This?"

He grunted. "The same."

Annie massaged the area with long, slow strokes. It took longer than before to relax him. "Macho heroics will land you back in the hospital. You should have told me about the pain."

He closed his eyes. "I could handle it."

"And when you're back in a hospital bed, it will be a huge waste of the taxpayers' money." He stiffened as she touched the inside of his elbow. "In the future, if it hurts, tell me. If I say stop, you stop, no questions asked." She raised his arm, guiding it in a slow circle. "Better?"

He nodded, his breathing level. "I'll try to watch the macho heroics, I promise."

"This isn't a joke, Sam. One more stunt like that and I'll have you flown out of here."

"I need to work." He looked tired, infuriated at a body that wouldn't do exactly what he told it to do.

"All in due time."

Keys rattled at the side door. Sam tried to sit up, but Annie held him still.

"Anybody home?" Izzy opened the door from the patio,

looking from Annie to Sam. "Am I interrupting something? This feels like the last episode of *Survivor*."

Neither Annie nor Sam laughed.

Izzy crossed his arms. "Let's have it. Why all the tension?"

"Because Sam's being an idiot."

"A macho hero idiot," Sam offered dryly.

"He could have hurt himself badly."

"But I didn't."

"How do you know?" Annie shot back. "That elbow is probably a mess inside."

"My body, my choice."

"Whoa." Izzy stood carefully between them. "Take it easy, you two. I'll check Sam out. As it happens, the team from Bethesda just sent me some more equipment, and I have to run tests on him anyway. Looks like my medic training's going to be helpful."

Sam muttered a few pithy phrases, which Izzy ignored as he reached into his jacket.

"By the way, here's that refill for painkillers."

Annie stared at the bottle. "When did he run out of pills?"

"Last night. I ordered more as soon as the pharmacy opened."

"You lied to me." Annie glared at Sam. "Why am I surprised? Mr. Macho all the way, aren't you?"

"I work better when I can feel my body." Sam grimaced, as if looking for a comfortable position. "You're making a big deal out of nothing."

"Am I? Maybe we should just quit right now. Otherwise, I might murder you myself."

"Hell of a way to go, Doc," he murmured. "I could die of pleasure from one of your massages."

Annie picked up the blue exercise ball and tossed it to Izzy. "Call me when the Boy Wonder here grows up. Until then, this is a complete waste of everyone's time."

Chapter Fourteen

"WANT TO TELL ME WHAT THAT WAS ALL ABOUT?" IZZY WATCHED Annie stalk out of the room, then turned to study Sam.

"I got her steamed."

"No kidding."

"I didn't tell her about the pain pills," Sam said tightly. "Then I asked if she was involved with anyone."

"Not your business, is it?" Izzy stared at the bar of sunlight cutting across the exercise mat. "I suggest you spend your time getting well, not asking Annie personal questions. How's your shoulder?"

Sam rotated his arm slowly. "It hurts."

"How much?"

"Like a fragmentation grenade."

"I take it you didn't tell Annie that."

Sam merely snorted.

"She's got a point, macho man. She's supposed to be clued in so she can monitor your progress."

"You want me to snivel about every little ache and pain?"

"We're not talking about little aches and pain. Annie's your on-site caregiver, and she needs to know if you've taken your meds or not."

Sam's mouth flattened. "You, too?"

"Face it, friend. You're an important asset to the U.S. Navy, and I'm under orders to get you back on your feet pronto. Don't make my job any harder than it is."

"The woman makes me nervous. I don't know why, but she does." Sam stretched out on the mat and glared up at the ceiling. "And to hell with dredging up an hourly list of physical complaints. I don't want anyone tallying my vital signs and medications. I just want to be left alone to recover."

"No can do, sailor. You need Annie's help to recover. Do you think the major league football teams send their golden boys to just anyone?"

Sam sighed. "She definitely knows her stuff. I can feel every muscle after that workout she designed. The moves were just hard enough."

"Damned right she's good, so start paying attention. You two have to communicate or she'll pull the plug. She's serious about this."

Sam eyed him suspiciously. "How do you know her so well? Are you two involved?"

Izzy's expression didn't change. "What if we were?"

"I'd wish you well." Sam sat up awkwardly, glad to take Izzy's hand when it was offered. "And then I'd try like hell to take her away from you."

"Save your effort. We're not involved. I doubt that Annie's been involved very often. From what I can see, her work comes first."

"Been reading her file?"

"No need. Spend two hours watching her juggle demanding guests and complicated staff assignments and you'll see for yourself." Izzy crossed his arms. "How interested are you?"

Sam reached for his crutches and heaved himself to his feet. "Enough to wonder what makes Annie O'Toole tick." He studied his fingers, which were wrapped around the handle of the crutch. "You could help by finding out if there's anyone special in her life."

"Answer the question. How personal is this becoming, McKade?"

"I'm not sure. After all, everything's personal." Sam smiled tightly. "And everything's professional. I think Khrushchev said that."

"Or Bill Gates."

"Let's say I was *very* interested in her." Sam glared at the exercise ball. "What would I do about it? My memory's a little rusty and I keep coming up blank as far as recent social encounters." He frowned. "If you know what I mean."

Izzy cleared his throat. "Are you asking me for dating tips?"

"Hell, no. I just have a few general questions. You could steer me straight. Like that."

"Shoot."

Sam toyed with his towel. "If this was a normal situation, I'd ask her out for dinner. Maybe take her to a noisy country place for some dancing. But this isn't a normal situation," he said grimly. "What would a woman like Annie want? Hell, I'm in a brace and I'm sleeping in her guest bedroom."

"Maybe you should decide what *you* want first. Your life isn't exactly your own right now, McKade."

"I keep telling myself that. But there's something about her, some kind of electric hum whenever I'm around her. It just keeps pulling me in." He tossed down his towel. "This makes absolutely no sense," he said in disgust. "We're strangers and this is business. Why should I be thinking about her as if—as if it's personal?"

"You tell me."

"Maybe it's the way she smiles when I get something right. Or maybe it's that don't-mess-with-me look she flashes when she thinks I'm pushing too hard."

"Which is just about always," Izzy said dryly.

"Look, are you going to give me advice or not?"

"I thought you said you didn't want—"

"Never mind. She's not the only woman in the world. It's just this crazy situation, with the two of us cooped up together. That's all it is."

"Whatever you say."

"Damned right." Sam rubbed his neck. "Forget I ever brought it up."

He looked at the bottle of pills on the nearby table. "Let's get these tests done, Einstein. I don't want to throw off my results by taking any meds beforehand."

"You're a real hard case, you know that?"

"I try my damnedest." Sam moved awkwardly to the door and stopped when he saw the elaborate equipment lining the terrace. "What's that, retrofitting for the Mir space station?"

"Close. This baby does everything but give next year's stock quotes. Once I get you hooked up, the boys at Bethesda will be pulling in EKGs, blood pressure, and muscle diagnostics while you go through prearranged workouts."

"Whoopee. I always wanted to be a human guinea pig," Sam said darkly.

"A very high-profile human guinea pig," Izzy murmured as he watched Sam sit down and go to work.

◇ ◇ ◇

PAIN CRAWLED ALONG HER SHOULDERS AND HER STOMACH growled.

Annie ignored both.

Her morning meeting with her accountant had quickly gone from bad to worse. As always, he railed at her for keeping too many personnel on her payroll and for giving them too many benefits. Annie explained for the hundredth time that a resort was nothing without excellent, experienced staff in a high ratio to the guests.

The accountant had yawned, the way he always did.

Ignoring her irritation, Annie grabbed a cup of coffee and a handful of trail mix, then headed into her office to scroll through the morning's E-mails and sign off on a dozen faxes. After that she had to check an order for aromatherapy oils and finish planning next month's wine tasting.

She was halfway through when her desk phone rang.

"You've got to get down here, boss."

Annie recognized the note of hysteria in her assistant's voice.

"More rabbits, Megan? If the new cedar whirlpool has over-flowed I'm going to shoot someone." *Maybe myself*, she thought.

"No, it's Mr. Congeniality and he's on the warpath."

"Tucker Marsh? What has he found to complain about?"

"Where should I start? Not enough Cybex equipment. Not enough trainers. Not enough towels. There was something else, but I couldn't make it out. And I swear to heaven, he's wearing a cashmere warm-up suit. Genuine cashmere. He's headed your way, so brace for impact."

As Annie put down her phone, she heard footsteps in the corridor. Thanks to Megan's call, she was waiting for Marsh with a confident smile.

And he really *was* wearing cashmere, she saw.

She steepled her fingers calmly. "Is there a problem, Mr. Marsh?"

He took the power spot, bracing one hip on her desk and smiling down at her. "Not if you can explain why I can't get a massage and no trainers are available."

"We have two trainers on duty today."

"Both of them are busy," the lawyer said tightly. "I couldn't even speak to them directly."

"I'm sorry for the wait, but you were notified that some of our services would be scaled back this week. You insisted on staying anyway."

"No trainers. No massages available until late tonight." His brow rose. "I can't even arrange a decent meal."

"The menu has been reduced only slightly," Annie countered. "Any reasonable requests will be cheerfully honored. I'll be happy to talk to the chef personally."

The lawyer shook his head coolly. "Forget the menu. I'd rather have you fit me in for a massage. I'm told you're dynamite."

If reptiles could smile, they would look like this, Annie thought. "I'm afraid that won't be possible."

"Why, Annie?" He leaned in closer. "You don't mind if I call you Annie, I hope." He reached out, brushing her arm with a gesture that looked carefully casual.

Annie stared down at his hand. "Actually, I do mind. And I would prefer that you remove your hand."

He looked down and laughed. "Can't say I noticed."

Like hell you didn't, she thought.

She waited for him to move his hand before speaking. "Perhaps you should reschedule your visit, Mr. Marsh. I'm sure you'd be more comfortable when our full staff is present."

He smiled, his teeth very white and perfectly capped. "I don't believe I will."

Annie said nothing as she moved around the desk, out of reach of his carefully orchestrated touches. "I'm sorry to hear that. Since you choose to remain, you'll need to understand that some services may be restricted."

"All I really want is a deep-tissue massage. My partner's wife is still raving about your magic touch." He smiled thinly. "Apparently you made time stand still for her."

Suppressing a shudder, Annie crossed to the door. "The circumstances were different last year when Ms. Winston visited."

Marsh ignored her pointed position at the door. "Everyone has been asking about Summerwind. I would hate to give a negative report."

"Any travel agent will confirm that what agrees with one guest may not work for another. That is one reason we do no advertising and rely on referrals from satisfied guests."

Marsh followed her with sharp eyes. "I'd hate to break your winning streak." He moved closer, resting his hand on her shoulder. "On the other hand, I'm sure we can find a satisfactory resolution. Perhaps over a quiet dinner?"

Annie felt the first stab of uneasiness. "I'm afraid that won't be possible. I have other plans for the evening."

For the merest moment, his hand tightened. Annie stepped away, holding the door open pointedly.

Marsh's face suffused with color. "I like a good challenge, Ms. O'Toole. Any of my clients will tell you I thrive on it."

"I'll be sure to remember that. Was there anything else?"

His eyes turned icy. "Just one. Tell your security man to stay out of my way. I don't like being followed."

Annie blinked. "You mean Reynaldo?"

"Not him. A big, muscular fellow in a blue nylon wind-breaker."

Izzy.

"I'm sure that was a simple misunderstanding."

"No, I was hiking past the gardening shed and he warned me off."

"That path leads up to my private quarters. It's always closed to guests."

Marsh's eyes narrowed. "Funny, I didn't notice any signs."

"There are two of them, clearly posted." Annie fought to keep her voice calm.

"Maybe I wasn't paying attention." Marsh shrugged. "All I wanted to do was to enjoy the grounds. Heaven knows, the last thing I wanted to do was disturb your privacy."

That's exactly what he wanted. And he was enjoying this, she realized. Every nasty second from opening argument and counterattack, to the final confrontation.

He started to move closer, but Annie raised her palm, blocking his approach.

"You're wasting your time, counselor. We have a business relationship, not a personal one. As a lawyer, you should understand the difference—and why it's dangerous to confuse the two."

"Perfectly." His smile was cold. "And as a man, I can regret the fact. But don't worry, I never take no for an answer, Annie."

"You'd be a fool not to."

"I am many things, my dear. A fool is not one of them." Marsh moved toward the door, in the process managing to brush against a delicate Murano vase holding a single white rose.

The vase toppled before Annie could react, shattered into a thousand bright fragments on the pink Saltillo tiles.

Marsh prodded the glass with the toe of his polished loafer. "So lovely, yet so fragile." There was nothing warm in his eyes. "Be sure to send me a bill for the damage."

Annie managed to keep a cool smile in place as Marsh strolled outside. She noticed he was careful to walk over her rose, grinding it down into the shattered glass.

◆ ◆ ◆

ANNIE WAS SHAKING WHEN SHE REACHED THE GATE TO HER courtyard.

Wind whipped at her face as she opened the back door and let herself into her favorite room, a study warmed by yellow walls and a red tile floor. After slipping off her shoes, she took a bottle of spring water from her refrigerator and crossed to the window overlooking the beach. She took a deep breath and stood for a long time, watching otters rock in the kelp beds. Usually this view of sea and sand filled her soul and brought her peace.

Not today.

She couldn't erase the memory of her ugly encounter with Tucker Marsh. An experienced lawyer, he obviously enjoyed throwing his weight around. Annie knew if she tossed him out, she would face a nasty lawsuit.

A viselike pain settled around her forehead and the bottle in her hand shook slightly.

Outside the wind tossed the ocean into whitecaps. A rising bank of clouds signaled a storm.

She had to keep her head. Her lawyer could tell her how to handle Tucker Marsh. Even if he decided to play hardball, she'd hold her ground. There would be no private dinner—or any other personal contact.

What if he went after the resort?

Annie shivered. Wasn't it worth a few casual touches if it meant Marsh would leave Summerwind alone? And if Marsh wanted *more* than a few casual touches?

Something gripped her shoulder.

She spun around, and the bottle flew from her hand.

Chapter Fifteen

"Rough afternoon?"

Annie stood stiffly, surrounded by puddled water, feeling her heart pound.

"Don't move. You'll slip." Sam leaned a crutch against the wall and tilted her face up to his. "You look beat. If I were a real macho hero, I'd pick you up and carry you to that couch, but so much for fantasies." After some fumbling, he managed to pick up the fallen plastic bottle and toss a towel down over the water. "Watch your step."

Annie didn't move.

"Go sit down, Doc. That's an order."

"I don't want to sit down." Annie was barely aware of him guiding her to the couch.

"Want something to eat?"

"No."

"Want to yell at me?"

"*No.*"

"How about a drink?"

Annie shook her head.

"I suggest a single-malt scotch, nicely aged and smooth as silk."

"I don't want a drink and I don't want to talk."

"In that case we could just sit here and glower at the sea. Or maybe not."

His crutches tapped away over the tiles and a few moments later she heard him return. Something cold met her fingers.

Annie looked at the inch of amber liquid in her glass. "I don't want it."

"Tough."

Maybe she *did* want it. Maybe the whiskey would chase away the memory of Marsh's smug face. Annie took a gulp and promptly broke into raw coughing.

"Serves you right. Good scotch isn't meant to be guzzled."

"I don't need the whiskey. I'm fine."

The ice cubes in her glass began to rattle, and Sam curled his fingers around hers, holding the glass steady. "Tell me what happened."

"No." She took another careful gulp of scotch, grimacing as it burned over her tongue. "Why does this taste like diesel fuel?"

"Call it an acquired taste."

Annie stared at her glass. "The rotten, sniveling weasel."

"You bet."

"I'll cut him into tiny pieces if he goes after me, my staff, or this resort."

"Damned right." Sam frowned. "Who exactly are we cutting into pieces?"

Annie paid no attention. "He's going to be sorry he came here, sorrier still that he broke my favorite Murano vase."

"Who, Annie?"

She took another angry gulp of whiskey. "Tucker Marsh, of course. The man who would be king."

"What's he got against you?"

"I wouldn't go to dinner with him—among other things."

Sam's voice tightened. "*What* other things?"

"He seems to want me as his latest wall trophy. Or maybe I should say bed trophy."

Sam gripped his crutches, his face hard. "Which suite is his?"

"He's in one of the guesthouses near the lap pool." She took another gulp of whiskey, trying not to wince. "He'll be the one in the cashmere warm-up suit."

"Did he touch you?"

"Once or twice." Even now Annie flinched at the memory. "But he was careful to make it seem like an accident."

Sam didn't answer. He was already halfway to the door.

"What are you doing?"

"Nothing. Stay here and rest."

Annie took a good look at his face, and what she saw frightened her. "You can't deck him, Sam."

"Trust me, decking the man is only the start of what I have planned."

Crutches or not, Sam would be deadly, Annie realized. She shot to her feet. "He's a guest here, and this is business. I fight my own battles."

"Oh, he'll be all yours, just as long as I have a few minutes with him first."

Annie caught his arm. "If you touch him, he'll ruin you. He'll make up a story about cold-blooded assault and he'll find ten upstanding citizens to back him up. After he's done, your reputation will be in shreds. You'll be lucky to get a job cleaning boats in Ukiah."

"I'll chance it."

"But I won't." Annie moved, blocking his path. "You're not going, Sam, I mean it. Even if I have to take your crutches and hold you down."

"Go ahead and try."

Annie went still, shocked by the fury in his voice. He seemed a stranger, his eyes glacial and his face strained. She had the strange sense he didn't hear her. "Let it go, Sam. I'll handle this snake through legal means."

"In the end it's always lawyers protecting lawyers and the hell with everyone else. I've seen it too damned often. The dirty ones go free and the innocent ones pay." The words seemed to churn up from some deep, bitter space inside him. "They're so clever you never trap them, never see what they are until it's too late. This time one of them is going down hard."

Annie was certain he wasn't listening to her.

Memories? Was his past finally coming back?

"This time I've got proof." He was muttering, completely oblivious to her.

Annie took his hand. "Can you hear me, Sam?"

"Hear what?" He looked down, his eyes narrowed. "What's wrong?"

"You. You said they weren't getting away, not this time. You said you had some kind of proof."

Thunder rumbled in the distance. Sam stared out the window for a long time, then shook his head. "For a moment it was real, Annie. Somehow I know it was deadly important. Now it's gone again."

"You'll remember."

"Will I? Maybe I'm a burnout. Maybe I'll always have this hole where my memories should be."

"Do you want to give in? Say the word and we'll stop." It was a calculated challenge, and Annie prayed she hadn't pushed too hard. He had already driven himself harder in two days than most men did in two weeks.

"No." He braced his good shoulder carefully against the wall. "I'm not throwing in the towel. But what I really want to do is *this*."

His fingers framed her cheeks, and the brush of his mouth came without warning. Annie barely heard her own sigh of pleasure. She was already leaning closer, her arms sliding around his neck, her body warm and restless.

After so many days of worry, she couldn't focus on the reasons this was wrong. All she knew was how good it felt to touch him.

Her fingers slid to his shirt. Blindly, she tugged at the buttons, burrowing to find the heat of his skin while he took her mouth again, harder now, his hand opening at her hips and urging her against his thighs, his own need blatant.

Annie closed her eyes as he fisted her skirt and shoved it

upward to explore the curve of her hips. She tilted her head, opening her mouth against his, giving a tentative brush with her tongue. Sam's rough hands tightened, anchoring her as their bodies met.

"More," she whispered.

Sam pulled away, breathing hard. "I want you. God help me, right here and now."

"So why are we still talking?"

His hand rose, cupping her breast. He frowned as he felt the signs of her arousal. "Because we both need to know what we're getting into, Annie."

Reality and logic were returning and she didn't like the feeling one bit. "I won't read anything into this if you won't. Or are you telling me you've changed your mind?"

"Does it feel as if I have?" His face was strained. "I'm just trying to keep things straight."

"I'm not. I'm tired of keeping things straight. For once I want to be completely bent, absolutely reckless."

Her heart pounding, she stared up at him, feeling the tension in his body. "You're supposed to grab me hard and jump me, McKade."

"I'm considering it," he said thickly.

"Consider it faster." She wanted to be witty, sophisticated, confident.

Grace Kelly in *To Catch a Thief*.

Audrey Hepburn in *Breakfast at Tiffany's*.

"My palms are sweating," she muttered. "I think I'm going to faint." Was there lightning outside or had she only imagined it?

Sam tucked a strand of hair behind her ear. "Take a deep breath. That should calm you down."

But Annie didn't want to be calm. She didn't want to think too much either. Right now *not* thinking felt wonderful.

She closed her eyes, hyperaware of his leg moving between hers. "Breathing doesn't help."

"It's like that sometimes."

She leaned into him, remembering every detail of his body. He had been a slow, powerful lover, and their nights together had left Annie shaken by her sensual response.

Then one morning he had sailed away with no promises and no explanations.

Could you ever go back? she wondered.

Sam's eyes darkened as she found the button at the top of his jeans. His stomach was hard and muscled, and touching him felt so good it left her dizzy. "Done considering yet?"

"I was done two days ago," he muttered as he freed her skirt.

❖ ❖ ❖

OUTSIDE IN THE COURTYARD, IZZY FROZE, ONE HAND ON THE doorknob.

He heard the low rustle of clothes, saw the two shadows framed by the window. The silhouette told him all he needed to know.

That was one hell of a kiss.

And it looked like a kiss was only the start of what they had in mind.

He took a step back, wondering what the people in D.C. would say about this development. Izzy decided they weren't going to find out. Annie and Sam were two good people who deserved all the happiness they could find. Regulations or not, he wouldn't interfere, nor would he report this.

His pager began to vibrate. Wind snapped up from the beach as he scanned the terse message.

Code Red.

He suppressed a curse. Sam's level of security had just been upgraded.

He didn't waste time pondering the cause. After a final glance at the pair in the window, he headed for a quiet spot to contact Washington and find out what the hell had gone wrong now.

◊ ◊ ◊

"ARE YOU SURE ABOUT THIS, ANNIE?"

"You don't see me running away, do you?"

Sam's fingers covered hers, then tightened. "I can't carry you to bed. Hell, there's a lot I can't manage to do right now. Maybe this is a bad idea."

Annie smiled. "I can walk just fine." Her smile faded as Sam continued to stare at her. "What's wrong?"

"Sorry." He tilted his head, frowning. "Touching you like this feels strange."

Annie felt a sudden jolt of nerves. "Strange how?"

"Familiar." He studied her intently. "Did we meet somewhere before the accident?"

There was that shaky sense of lightning somewhere close again. *Calm, Annie. Remember this lie is for Sam's good, no matter how much it hurts.*

She kept her voice steady even though she was jelly inside. "If we'd met, I like to think you'd have more than a vague impression."

"You're right." He shook his head. "I've gone back and forth, questioning every thought and searching for the memories so often that everything's tangled up together. I guess that's what happens when you get thrown from a bus."

Annie didn't move. "How do you know that?"

His brow rose. "Because . . ." He frowned. "I just do."

"You *remembered*, Sam. No one told you the details of your accident."

"Someone must have. Probably a nurse in the hospital."

Annie shook her head, gripped by excitement. "No details, doctor's orders. You were supposed to remember by yourself. And you just did."

He rubbed his neck slowly. "Okay, maybe. Just a little. I'm almost afraid to believe it."

"It's just the start. Congratulations."

He didn't smile back. "I've got a long way to go, Annie."

"Is that supposed to frighten me off?"

"I think it's supposed to frighten *me* off," he muttered.

One part of Annie's mind warned that touching him like this was folly. He had an amazing body, one that had already begun to heal. When he was whole he would walk out of her life again, without a backward glance.

But the sane, reasonable part of her mind paid no attention. The drum of her pulse drowned out all logic and thought of tomorrow. Her skirt rustled, slipping to her feet, and she heard Sam's breath catch.

He slid her white camisole upward. Her nipples rose tight and hard against his palms. "We should probably stop right here."

"Do you want to stop?"

"Hell, no. Then I wouldn't get to see the rest of you. I've never wanted anything so much."

Annie shivered at the urgency in his voice, at the friction of his callused hands. She stepped out of her skirt. "Then don't stop."

Before she could finish, a sharp crack echoed through the courtyard. Cursing, Sam grabbed her waist and pushed her forward. "Down, down. *Now!*"

Chapter Sixteen

SAM HELD ANNIE BENEATH HIM, IGNORING HER MUFFLED PROtest. Warnings screamed in his head, sounds mixed with jagged images. Memories, he realized.

The humid darkness of a South American jungle.

A rocky bay somewhere off the coast of Thailand.

No details. Just the pounding adrenaline burst that signaled danger.

Sam was trying to see outside when he felt Annie tug at his wrist. "Stay low," he snapped. "They could be targeting the window."

She finally managed to work her head out from beneath his shoulder. "*Who?* What are you talking about?"

"Save the questions."

"Sam, I don't think—"

His hand clamped down over her mouth as a shadow moved along the wooded slope beyond the window. "Don't move. Is that understood?"

Feeling her tense nod, he pushed away and crawled awkwardly toward the door, cursing his clumsiness. Every nerve was on alert and his heart was pounding.

Head low. Limbs tucked. Present the smallest possible profile while moving fast and silently.

Patterns were returning. He realized he was used to quick response against hostile fire. Most of all he was familiar with being a target under the worst kind of odds.

Through the swaying foliage, Sam saw the shadow flicker, weaving closer. By instinct, he reached for the knife strapped inside his boot. Except the knife wasn't there.

He cursed softly, feeling the deep prick of habit and training.

Stay low.

Never offer a target.

Always have an escape route.

"Sam? Annie?" A familiar voice drifted from beyond the window. "You two okay in there?"

"Hell." Grimacing, Sam pushed to his feet to find Izzy silhouetted against the gathering twilight. Izzy had a pistol flat against his thigh, muzzle facing the ground.

"Yeah, don't shoot. We're here. Give us a minute."

Sam grabbed his crutch and maneuvered to his feet, shirt in hand. He was all too aware that Annie was watching him, her face pale and anxious.

Irritated too, he realized when his sweater was flung against his chest.

"Don't forget *this*."

"You're angry."

"As amazing as it may seem, I don't enjoy being tossed to the floor, caveman style. If it was necessary, I want to know why." Her hands trembled as she glared up at him. "What's going on, Sam?"

He extended a hand to help her up.

Annie stared as if it were toxic waste.

"Look, Annie, it was pure instinct."

"I thought I knew what I was getting into, but I don't." Her voice was tight. "How much danger are you in?"

He jammed a hand through his hair. "I don't know," he said with absolute honestly.

"Then find out," Annie said. "That didn't feel like a practice drill, Sam. On some level you were *expecting* to be attacked."

His eyes darkened. "If you want me to leave, I'll arrange it. Just say the word."

She started to speak, then looked back toward the window, where twilight was slipping into true night. "They told me there would be some precautions. I knew about the need for secrecy, of course, but nothing like this. Not jumping at shadows and expecting armed attacks."

In the dim light from the window, Sam saw the fear in her eyes, and now it was mixed with anger—probably at what she considered her weakness. As a civilian, she wouldn't understand that fear was a valuable and natural survival mechanism, not a sign of weakness.

There was a light tap at the door.

"Coming." He was relieved to see that she had pulled on her blouse and was stepping into her skirt. He moved to help her fasten the last button, but even that small contact made her stiffen and push away his hand.

"Annie, we need to talk."

"About what?"

He caught her wrist gently. "About us."

"*What* us?" She moved out of reach, her body stiff. "I have to go."

"Damn it, we need to talk."

"Would that change anything?" She looked pale and drained. "You're a stranger, Sam. In more ways than I realized." She bent and swept up her shoes. "We both need time to think before things go any further. *If* things go any further."

She was right, of course. Only that made him cut off a curt answer.

"I'll be back later. Don't bother to wait up."

❖ ❖ ❖

SAM PROWLED RESTLESSLY ON HIS CRUTCHES, WATCHING IZZY make a fresh pot of coffee. "What happened out there?"

"Lightning hit a tree up in the orchard."

Lightning.

Not gunfire, Sam thought.

Not hostile pursuit.

"Any sign of intruders?"

Izzy shook his head. "Only old Mr. Harkowitz sprinting past. Seems he enjoys wearing a flesh-colored suit for the shock value, but the lightning was too close for comfort. He looked a little shaken. So did Annie," Izzy added.

"I noticed." Motionless before the big window, Sam studied the distant gray swell of the Pacific. "Is she in danger?"

"Hard to say. Your presence has been buried in as many false leads as possible. The Navy even—"

"Is Annie in danger?" Sam repeated stonily.

"Possibly." Izzy took a hard breath. "Probably."

"Why, damn it? Her only crime is helping me." Sam's eyes narrowed. "She's not part of this, is she? Don't tell me she's done government work."

"Hell, no. The woman can't lie to save her life."

Sam watched the sea pass from gray into formless black. "I guess I knew that," he said grimly. "It's easy to forget there are honest people left."

◇ ◇ ◇

Alexandria, Virginia

The tidy Alexandria street was crowded. School out, kids playing, pedigree dogs barking.

Perfect little street.

Perfect little world.

The deliveryman in the brown uniform hiked two heavy boxes onto his hand truck and wheeled them deftly up the sidewalk and around to the side door, where he pulled out a clipboard.

Clipboards were the best kind of camouflage. Give a man a clipboard and he immediately assumed authority and blue-collar authenticity. No one looked at him twice.

As usual, his contacts had told him exactly what to expect.

The deliveryman made a big production of ringing the side

bell, except that his finger was two inches away. Several people glanced over casually, then dismissed the sight of the man with a clipboard. He opened the door, palmed his lock pick, and maneuvered his boxes into the building's quiet foyer. From there, no one saw him take the elevator to the third floor and jimmy the lock in nine seconds. It helped that the two D.C. cops outside had just been summoned to a violent domestic argument two blocks away.

Nothing left to chance.

He listened, heard no alarm or sounds inside, then opened the door. After slipping on surgical gloves, he started taking the room apart, quiet and thorough. In eight minutes he had checked the drawers, explored beneath the beds, examined the books.

Absolutely nothing.

But there had to be something useful here. He reviewed his instructions, then checked his watch again. Eleven minutes since he'd entered the apartment. *Think, damn it.*

He studied the neat bookcases, the comfortable sofa, then checked the walls for hollow sections.

Nothing.

He was sweating when he went back into the kitchen, knowing the search was taking too long and cursing his failure. There had to be something in here. There was no other room left. When he lifted the range top, his lips pulled back into a tight smile.

A key was taped out of sight near the back of the metal cover. He pulled it free and read the number cut into the plastic body.

A safe deposit box?

He shoved the key into his pocket and closed the range, checking that everything was the way he'd found it. Then he opened the door and maneuvered his hand truck back out into the hall and carefully removed the plastic gloves.

No one had seen him. He checked as he returned to his truck, but no one was paying any attention to the man with the hand truck and the brown uniform.

He'd done it.

Buoyed by a rush of triumph, he packed up the truck, checked his mirror, and pulled slowly into the afternoon traffic, thinking about how he'd spend the next hundred thousand dollars.

❖ ❖ ❖

"HE JUST LEFT." THE UNSMILING FEDERAL AGENT STUDIED THE street from the apartment across from Sam McKade's building. "Our person on the third floor heard him enter the apartment." He spoke quietly into the phone, eyes to the street below. "He was inside for fourteen minutes."

He listened and nodded. "It should have been enough time."

Down below a truck motor growled to life.

"Virginia plates." The agent read a string of numbers into the phone. "Run them down while I check to see if he found our surprise in the kitchen." His eyes were hard. "Then let's find out if our little fish will lead us to a nice, big fish."

❖ ❖ ❖

STONES CLATTERED IN THE COURTYARD.

Opening the curtain, Sam saw Annie stretching against the wall, sleek in navy spandex. "She's going out."

"Good thing, too. She looked pretty upset. Running might calm her down."

Sam didn't turn from the window. "Go with her."

"No can do. My orders are to stay with you. The storm's moved inland, so there's no problem."

"Orders be damned. Go with Annie. I'll be fine here."

"Damn it, Sam, you know I can't."

"Stow it, Izzy. She could be a target. I can take care of myself for a few minutes."

"How? By hitting an intruder with a crutch?"

Sam made his way to the couch. He sank down, dropped his crutches, and pulled open the bottom drawer of the nearby chest. "Me and my friend Glock here will play host while you're gone."

"It's against procedure."

"Maybe I don't care." Sam laid the gun across his lap and smiled. "You have ten seconds. Get out of here or I'll shoot you myself."

Izzy shook his head. "Since you put it so graciously."

❖ ❖ ❖

REALIZING SHE HAD COMPANY, ANNIE STOPPED JOGGING IN place. "Where are *you* going?"

"With you."

"Sam's the one who needs guarding."

"Sam can take care of himself for a little while." Izzy glanced over the beach and up to the orchard. "What's your route?"

As before, his gaze ranged over the path through the dunes, across the beach, and up to the meadow.

The man wouldn't miss a single blade of grass, Annie thought. "Through the meadow and down to the beach," she said, taking the lead.

Izzy nodded. Without a word he moved to Annie's right.

To keep his firing arm clear, she realized.

In case someone might be lurking in the trees.

She suppressed a shiver, knowing better than to argue. Izzy was as bad as Sam when it came to stubbornness and duty. "What was that noise?"

"Lightning. Scared Mr. Harkowitz pretty bad. He ran by in his swimsuit faster than usual."

"He's a nice man. He lost his wife last year, so we let him be outrageous. It doesn't hurt anyone." Annie wound through the meadow. "How were Sam's test results?"

"Just short of amazing." He skirted a fallen log, his breath coming easy. "I've seen a few surprises in my days as a medic, but nothing close to this. His right leg appears stable, with excellent mobility. The X-rays also show solid improvement in that left knee. The partial joint replacement they did worked like a charm."

"What about his shoulder?"

Izzy's eyes narrowed. "There are some signs of inflammation. The medical team in D.C. will decide if he needs treatment."

"He's doing too much." Frowning, Annie jumped the narrow creek at the meadow's edge. "He's pushing himself too hard."

"The nature of the beast, I'm afraid. If you can figure a way to hold him back, be sure to let me know."

"Oh, there's a way. I can throw in the towel unless he agrees to drop back to a semi-reasonable pace."

"You'd quit on him?"

"I won't stand by and watch him damage a joint." Annie's voice was flat. "I've seen it before with dancers and major-league quarterbacks. The body can only be pushed so far, and like it or not, the body always has the last word."

"I guess that's why you're so good."

Annie's head tilted. "I don't follow you."

"You know just how far to push, right up to the edge but no further."

"I'm not a mind reader." Annie panted, running as she spoke. "There are all kinds of signs if you know what to look for. Pain is a pretty good gauge, too. If he were a different man, I'd say Sam had reached his limit, then passed it." She stopped on the path over the dunes, staring down at the waves churning toward the beach.

She took a deep breath. The beauty of the ocean rocked her and left her awed, as it always did, distancing her problems and offering clarity. *One more reason I can never leave Summerwind,* she thought. *No place else will ever fit me this well.* "He's in pain, Izzy. All the time, I imagine. But he doesn't complain, not ever."

"It's his way."

"It's a stupid way." Annie dragged in another breath of air. "He could damage his tendons or ruin that knee stabilization. There's no reason for heroics. It's just Sam and the exercise mat. No one's watching him now."

"He's watching," Izzy said quietly. "For a man like Sam, that's all that matters."

"Big stubborn idiot."

"You want him to leave?"

"Absolutely." Annie bent forward, working out a knot in her calf. "Unfortunately, another part of me would never forgive myself for tossing him out now," she said tightly.

"So what happens next?"

"Heck if I know." Annie rubbed her shoulder absently. "I need time to think. As a therapist, I can't support unreasonable behavior."

"Perfectly logical."

Annie glared at the flat blue line of the horizon. "If Sam wants to kill himself, he can do it without me."

"True."

"Stop agreeing with me."

"Whatever you say," Izzy said equably. "Just answer one question."

"Maybe."

"I don't suppose your irritation has anything to do with why Sam was so late answering my knock."

Heat bloomed over Annie's cheeks. "Of course not."

Izzy shrugged. "Just asking."

"We were talking." She dragged her toe in a wavy line over the sand. "At least we started out talking. Then things went south."

"Things often do."

"Before I knew it we . . ." Annie kicked away the line of sand she'd traced with her shoe. "Everything got crazy. Absolutely unexpected."

"The talking, you mean?"

"No, not the talking." She drew a long breath. "He's an amazing man, and his willpower is remarkable." *So is his body*, she thought. "Maybe I'm losing my focus. The medical books warn you about patients who develop an emotional attachment to their caregivers."

Izzy frowned. "Transference, you mean."

"Something like that. It can go the other direction, too."

"Is that what's happening here?" Izzy asked quietly.

"I don't know." The words were angry, jangled. "I don't think so. I don't want to think so. We have a past, Izzy, even if Sam doesn't remember it." *My body can't forget either*, she thought.

"That could be a problem." Izzy scanned the beach, then glanced casually along the tree line. "You're both under a lot of pressure. Why don't you take a day off and relax with one of those spa treatments Summerwind is so famous for?"

Annie shook her head, watching clouds blanket the cliffs to the west. "Time off won't help. I don't think anything will help. He can't remember and I can't forget." She hugged her chest, shivering slightly. The wind was sharper now, gusting in off the sea. "We'd better get moving."

"You're cold? Sorry, I should have noticed."

"Not cold." Annie looked up the slope. "Call me paranoid, but I just can't shake the feeling that someone's been up there watching us. And I *don't* mean Mr. Harkowitz."

Chapter Seventeen

SAM WAS WAITING WHEN IZZY PUSHED OPEN THE DOOR FROM THE courtyard. "Where's Annie?"

"She said she'd shower and change at her office."

Sam slid the Glock out from beneath a pillow and holstered it silently. "You escorted her down?"

"Every inch of the way. Especially now."

Sam frowned. "Run that by me again."

"She said someone was up in the woods watching us. At least that's how she felt." Izzy glanced around the room. "I figured I'd check in here, then circle back for a closer look."

"All quiet here. Go check. After that, stay with Annie." Sam rubbed his shoulder slowly. "I still don't see why she didn't come back here first."

"I think she's feeling a little hemmed in."

"What's *that* supposed to mean?"

"Relax, McKade. She needs a little space, considering the way you two have been on top of each either." Izzy cleared his throat. "In a manner of speaking."

"Did she tell you that?"

"Not exactly."

"What *did* she tell you?"

"Taking these security precautions has hit her pretty hard. She's not used to this kind of life."

"Most people aren't."

"Then give her a little space. And you can stop pushing yourself, too. Annie's afraid you're going to do some serious damage."

"I don't have time for pampering." Sam stared down at the beach. "I need to get strong again."

"Remember anything more?" Izzy asked casually.

Screaming. The sick sense of falling. "Nothing helpful," Sam said. "Tell Annie not to worry, I know my limits."

"Tell her yourself." Izzy pocketed a small pair of high-tech binoculars and a digital camera. At the door, he turned. "Better yet, *show* her."

◇   ◇   ◇

"WHERE IS HE?" TAYLOR O'TOOLE WAS DRESSED IN SKINTIGHT black pants and a white shantung blouse. Her windblown hair fell around her face as she charged into her sister's office.

"Hello to you, too, Taylor."

"Stop stalling. Where *is* he?"

"Where is who?"

"Mr. Atlas with all the gorgeous muscles. The Denzel Washington look-alike." Taylor frowned. "The man you're having mind-numbing sex with."

Annie turned, hairbrush in hand. "Mind-numbing sex? Now there's a charming phrase."

"Don't argue word use with me." Taylor lifted the spandex unitard from a nearby chair and shook her head. "How do you wear these things without looking like a blimp?"

"Must be my years of clean living." Annie snagged the workout suit and tossed it back onto the chair. "What's got you in such a lather?"

"*You,* of course." Taylor straightened a vase of flowers, aligned a framed photo of Annie's staff, then sank onto the elegant rattan sofa. "I want the truth."

"I don't know what you're talking about."

"Don't push it, Annie. You don't return my calls and you're never here when I drop by for a talk. What gives?"

"Nothing gives. I've just been busy."

Taylor's eyes narrowed. "What's going on between you and that Denzel Washington fellow?"

Annie put down her hairbrush. "Nothing. He's a consultant doing some work here."

"That's not what I hear. It's personal. Wilma, over at the bank, told her brother, who told his wife, who happens to be married to my plumber."

"Did they happen to say *how* personal? Maybe they gave you some dirty details," Annie said dryly.

"No details. Your Denzel's a mystery. They say he's big and gorgeous and follows you everywhere." Taylor picked up a tube of mango-chamomile lotion and rubbed some on her hands. "Nice stuff."

"Thank you. My Denzel, as you call him, is merely doing some security work for me and checking out my wiring."

Taylor's lips curved. "I'll bet he's checking out your wires. Listen, Annie—"

"No, you listen. I'm having the guesthouse and main house security upgraded and I want it done fast. I also need changes in the security system at Summerwind. There's no mystery about any of it." Annie rattled off the prearranged story set up by the Navy in case of local questions. "Check the San Francisco directory. He's right there under Arcane Electronics."

Taylor's eyes narrowed. "Arcane?"

"He likes to keep a low profile. Most of his clients are Fortune 500 companies, and their privacy is crucial."

Taylor's lips pursed. "So he's *really* just working on your security?"

"Afraid so."

Taylor sighed. "I was hoping you were caught up in a hot, reckless affair. Speaking of affairs, have you had any news about your wounded hero?"

Annie turned away, walking into the private bathroom next to her office. "He's under medical care. They wouldn't tell me where. Military rules and all that."

"Are you going to see him?"

Annie toyed with her hairbrush. "I hope to. That depends on what I hear from the Navy." Uncomfortable at the lie, Annie turned to the mirror and ran her brush through her damp hair. "No more questions. Your problem is you imagine too much."

"My problem is a sister who tells me *nothing* that matters." Taylor crossed her legs and studied her lizard sandals. "Such as about your Denzel." She watched Annie reach for the white cotton camisole draped over a chair. "You're not wearing *that*, are you?"

"You have something against pima cotton?"

"If you're going to have a torrid affair with world-class sex, you need to dress for the part."

"I'm not having a torrid affair," Annie said firmly.

"You will someday, so you need to be prepared."

Annie shrugged out of her robe and pulled on the camisole. "I don't think I'd look good in black lace and breast spikes."

"That's hardly your only choice. Just ask the author of *Thirty Days to a Stress-Free Sex Life*."

"Since when did you start reading Nikki Jerome's sexual self-help book?"

Taylor pursed her lips. "My editor sent it to me. I keep telling her that in a flat economy death sells, but she insists sex sells better. She might be right, since the book just jumped to number three on *The New York Times* best-seller list." She frowned. "Maybe I should give my hostage negotiator a sudden, steamy encounter with his dead partner's wife. Or maybe with one of his suspects. What if he—"

"No book plotting, Taylor." Annie pulled on a plain white half slip. "You got all of the creative flare in the family. I got the boring managerial skills."

"You have flare. It's just your lingerie that's boring. Remember, men want excitement, danger, mystery."

"Then they'll have to read your books." Annie tried not to remember the moment of sheer insanity when Sam had pulled off her blouse, and she had ripped off two of his buttons while attacking his belt. She looked away to hide a flush. "The Queen of Sex is pretty stressed out, by the way. I just spoke to her an hour ago."

Taylor sat up straighter. "Nikki Jerome?"

Annie nodded. "Ms. Stress-Free Sex herself. Between Larry King, Oprah, and a national media blitz, she's seriously wound up."

"Larry King? Please, I should have it so hard."

"Your books are wonderful," Annie said, instantly loyal. "You have fabulous reviews."

Taylor sniffed. "I've never been invited to Larry King. Not even for a call-in."

"Blackmail a politician or start a new religion. You'll be one hot ticket."

"Very funny." Taylor tossed Annie her white terry cloth spa robe. "Follow me."

"Why?"

"No questions." Taylor grabbed her Louis Vuitton bag and opened the door to Annie's private patio overlooking the two outdoor pools. She motioned to the teak chaise. "Sit down. We've got some serious business to take care of."

"Taylor, I can't—"

Her sister waved down the hill and one of Zoe's staff waved back.

"What's going on?" Annie asked warily, belting her robe.

"R and R. Yours." Taylor smiled at the man in the white kitchen uniform who appeared at the patio's edge. "Just put the tray down over there, please."

"Put what down?" Annie started back inside, but Taylor blocked her way.

"*Sit.* I still have part ownership in Summerwind, remember? I could make life very messy for you." She waited until Annie was sitting down, then dug into her big leather bag, removing a dozen plastic bottles and a lacquer box. "Close your eyes and prepare for a little vacation. Zoe's made a spectacular seafood salad with blue-corn muffins. While you eat, I'm going to do your toenails. Then maybe I'll do a hot stone massage."

"I don't have time for this."

"Listen to yourself. You're supposed to be a model of stress-free living and glowing health. It's time for you to practice what you preach."

Annie studied the plates. The corn muffins smelled delicious. Down the hill the swimming pools sparkled invitingly, framed by the ocean in the distance.

"You win. Who could resist?" Annie sank onto the chaise and slid off her shoes. "Just don't try anything outrageous."

"Who, me?" Taylor slid a towel under Annie's feet and went to work. First came a fragrant salt rub rich with lemon and rose oil. After Taylor was done buffing, she cleaned Annie's skin with a damp towel and smoothed on orchid-scented almond oil.

"Now for stage two."

Annie could barely keep her eyes open. "There's more?"

"We'll moisturize those cuticles, buff up your nails, then put on a nice polish. I'm thinking iridescent crimson." She chose a bottle from the dozen or so inside the lacquer box. "Here it is, direct from Paris. Hot Affair."

"I'm not contemplating an affair," Annie said firmly.

"No one ever does. Usually they just happen." Taylor slathered a second gel onto Annie's feet, then slid on thick cotton slippers.

"Rabbit slippers?" Annie smiled at the big ears. "Very sixth grade."

"Don't laugh. That cotton holds the moisturizer like nothing else. When I'm done your feet will be front-cover special."

Annie closed her eyes and inhaled the fresh sea air, feeling totally relaxed and just a little reckless. She wondered what Sam thought of iridescent red toenails.

"Supposing someone was thinking about having an affair,"

she said quietly. "Not me, just someone. Why bother?" Annie squinted up at the big clouds sailing through the sky. "I mean, the risks are terrible, the timing is crucial. And all for what, a few scattered minutes of forgettable groping?"

"If the groping is forgettable," Taylor said, "you're with the wrong man."

With Sam it had been unforgettable.

Don't think about Sam. This is strictly hypothetical.

"Okay, even if the sex is passable, then what? You have to schedule times to meet, then shave your legs, put on all kinds of makeup, and go talk about things you're not even half-interested in. Like quarterback slumps and season playoffs. What's the point?"

Taylor took off the rabbit slippers and put cotton balls between Annie's toes, then went to work with the iridescent nail polish.

It *did* look good, Annie decided. Very sexy with the metallic sheen. Not that *she* cared whether Sam liked it or not.

"The point," Taylor said, "is that you're connecting. You're letting yourself find out about what you like and don't like. That's hugely important."

"Why?" Annie persisted. "One day it's over and he's gone and all you've got is a dull razor and blurred memories. What's the good of that? Where does it take you?"

Taylor sat back, surveying Annie's cotton-studded feet. "Very nice. Very *French*. But I can see you're got some seriously warped ideas about sex, which we'll have to work on."

"There's nothing wrong with my ideas about sex," Annie said defensively.

"Not if you live in 1950. Listen, sex doesn't have to *take* you anywhere." Taylor rummaged inside the lacquer box. "You can't pencil it into your date book or write it up in one of those boring business reports you do twice a year. But it will put the glow back into your life—assuming you choose the right man." Something flashed in Taylor's hand.

"What's that?" Annie leaned forward, frowning.

"A toe ring."

"Why would I want a toe ring?"

"Because they're silly and fun and have no earthly use. Because they're not *boring*," Taylor finished.

Annie studied the little silver band Taylor slipped onto her toe. "What next, an ankle bracelet?"

"Heaven forbid. Those are *so* last Tuesday."

Leave it to Taylor to be up on every trend.

Annie frowned. When had she stopped being adventurous and spontaneous and trendy?

When Mom and Dad died. When you had to take over Summerwind and Taylor was off in the Greek Isles somewhere with an Australian actor.

Not that Annie was bitter. Okay, maybe a little.

Taylor pulled out the cotton balls and nodded. "Excellent. You'll have him eating out of your hand."

"*Who?*"

"Anyone you want. Now finish your salad. Next is stage three."

Annie was afraid to ask. "I've already taken an hour off. This was wonderful, I'll admit, but I have to go."

"Not yet." Taylor pulled a spray can and a piece of spandex out of her leather bag. "First I'm doing your hair." She shook the can. "Just a few sun streaks here and there. Very natural."

"Streaks?" Annie croaked.

"Stop complaining. I'm an expert at this. When Noel ran off and left me stranded in Greece, I actually made money this way."

"You never told me about being stranded."

"Too depressing. The man was scum, pure scum." Taylor shook the can some more. "But amazing in bed. Such a waste." She tossed the spandex to Annie. "Go put this on."

Annie held the red fabric strip by one finger. "A tube top? I haven't worn one of these since second grade."

Taylor sighed. "What *have* you been doing with your life?

Go, go." She waved her hands. "You need serious work, my dear. Luckily, you're in the right place. I'll add a few streaks today and cut in a few layers. You're going to look like a million."

"A cut, too?"

"Live dangerously." Taylor was completely serious as she touched Annie's shoulder. "You always took responsibilities too hard. It's why you're so good with Summerwind. But sometimes you need to kick back and relax. Just for once let me help."

Annie nodded slowly, feeling a sudden jolt of love for the sister she'd always admired but had never understood. "Okay. I'm ready to live dangerously."

"Excellent." Taylor studied Annie's slip beneath the terry cloth robe. "Unfortunately you're still a case for Lingerie 911. It's definitely time to ditch the white cotton. I'll meet you tomorrow at three."

"I can't. I've got two massages scheduled and—"

Taylor leveled a polished fingernail. "Forget the excuses, pal. Consider yourself shanghaied."

"Taylor, I can't go anywhere tomorrow."

"No? Then maybe I'll have to track down your Denzel and find out what's really going on. You never could lie worth a damn, even though this time you did better than I expected."

"This is blackmail."

"Possibly, but you work too much. That's why I have a full day of R and R planned for you tomorrow. Spa products and all." Taylor smiled wisely. "Consider it consumer research."

Annie had to admit that Taylor's pampering had left her feeling mellower than she'd been for days. Maybe she *should* delegate more and take a little time off. She glanced at her feet. Even that silly toe ring was starting to grow on her.

"I'll try, Taylor. Really, I will."

There was a tap at Annie's door, and her assistant looked in. "Zoe says she's bringing up a dessert tray. All chocolate, all sinful."

Taylor's brow rose. "I can't miss this." She held up a lock of Annie's hair. "Now for some streaks."

◇　◇　◇

"I LOOK LIKE A SURFER." ANNIE SQUINTED IN THE MIRROR, checking her hair from every angle. "It's got all kinds of colors. And what about these little spiky pieces around my face?"

"They're perfect. You've always had wonderful cheekbones, but now they're a real knockout."

First toe rings, now the bleached blond surfer look.

Annie studied the red tube top Taylor had insisted she wear with a skinny white linen skirt and a clingy red sweater.

In an odd kind of way, it all worked. Just like Taylor to suggest things that seemed crazy but pulled together with a bang.

"You like it." Taylor gave Annie's hair a final snip. "Go on, admit it."

"Yeah, I do. Give up writing and you'll make a mint down in the salon." Annie studied her hair again and smiled. "It's got sort of a Meg Ryan thing about it now. Thanks for all this, Taylor. I feel like I could tackle the Mongol horde after that pampering."

"Let's hope you don't have to. Don't ditch the toe ring, either. It's adorable."

"I won't. It goes with the reckless blond look. Except I was never reckless."

Only once.

With a man who couldn't remember a single detail.

Taylor swung her big bag over her shoulder and smiled. "Stick with me, kid. I'll give you lessons in reckless. I've been practicing all my life." She looked away, her eyes unreadable. "Sometimes I think that's all I've done."

"No way." Because the air was charged with unspoken regrets, Annie took her sister's arm. "I can't image a better older sister."

"When I was there. Which wasn't often."

"You had your dreams, I had mine. Now you've got a wonderful career and I've got Summerwind. Things worked out just right."

"I suppose they did," Taylor said slowly. "You really love this place. It's amazing how everything shines. Even your staff seems to be having fun. That's quite a gift you have."

"Almost as good as giving killer highlights." Annie ruffled her hair, delighted by the wild sheen. It was her all right, the secret, hidden her that no one but Taylor had ever glimpsed beneath Annie's tidy, careful veneer. "I owe you," she said.

"Don't worry, I'll collect tomorrow. Prepare for a serious makeover."

"Makeover?" Annie said warily. "But you already did my hair. What more is there for you to change?"

Before Taylor could answer, she was drowned out by the shrill blast of the fire alarm.

Chapter Eighteen

THE SOUND CAME FROM THE KITCHEN. ANNIE YANKED ON HER shoes and raced down the hall, with Taylor right behind her.

Zoe's staff was clustered outside the big kitchen's double doors, and there was no sign of smoke, Annie noted. Not that she would take any chances.

"Everyone outside." Annie had to shout to be heard above the wail of the alarm. "You, too, Taylor."

"No way," her sister shouted back.

"What about you?" Reynaldo, her head groundskeeper, hovered anxiously at the doors to the kitchen. "If *you* stay, I stay. The fire trucks should arrive any minute." He frowned. "Your hair is very nice."

"Thanks. But we'll be lucky to see a fire truck inside of twenty minutes. The coast highway is down to one lane again, remember?" Annie reached for a fire extinguisher. "Outside, all of you."

Her assistant pushed through the half circle, standing beside Reynaldo and looking at Annie. "Cool haircut. And I'm staying, too."

"No way." Annie looked up in relief as Izzy appeared at the side door. "Mr. Teague will take you outside, then he'll come back to help me. I assure you, we'll be fine."

Taylor gave Izzy a thorough scrutiny, then reluctantly followed the uneasy group outside. After he secured the door, Izzy turned to scan the corridor. "No smoke in here."

Annie was only a step behind him as he pushed open the big silver doors to the kitchen, where her chef was poised on a ladder above the ventilation hood.

"Zoe, what's going on?" Annie shouted.

"You tell me. This damned thing's been screaming ever since those two pool repairmen came through here to check the fuse box. I think maybe they crossed some wires." She climbed another rung, peering up at the commercial smoke detector. "This unit looks okay. The green power light is on and the wires are intact. Only problem is there's no fire."

"Let me take a look." Izzy helped Zoe down, then climbed up. He traced the exterior wires, checked the contacts, and probed the alarm box gently.

Nothing happened.

He opened the metal lid, then gently closed it again.

The noise stopped.

Annie breathed a sigh of relief. "Now what?"

"I'm taking this puppy down to examine. I'd also like the name of the company who installed it."

"I've got the information back in my office somewhere." Annie stared at the gray metal unit. "We've never had problems with the alarms before."

"It was probably your pool men at work, just like your chef said. Don't worry, I'll check the fuses and power lines while I'm here."

"You can check power lines?"

Izzy chuckled at Annie's look of surprise. "It's not exactly Fermat's last theorem, you know. By the way, nice toe ring."

Annie was saved from embarrassment when her assistant opened the outer door. "Is it safe to come back in?"

She was moved aside by Taylor, followed closely by Nikki Jerome.

"Have you found my suitcase yet?"

"I'm sorry, Ms. Jerome. We're still looking."

"But those are my private things. My *underwear*. It's sick."

"I understand perfectly, but—"

"How can you understand? It didn't *happen* to you." The author opened and closed her hands. "I need to rest and relax, but I can't focus while my clothes are missing."

Probably another complimentary night's stay would loosen her tension, Annie thought cynically. "I'll talk to my staff as soon as I'm done here."

"What if he's doing something perverted with them?"

Perverted?

Behind her, Taylor rolled her eyes as Nikki Jerome shifted her book under her arm. "Just let me know if you hear anything." She looked down at Annie's feet. "Nice toe ring. I see you like Hot Affair polish."

Taylor beamed. "She *loves* Hot Affair polish." She glanced at Izzy, who was leaning against the stove. "I don't believe we've met. I'm Taylor, Annie's sister. I understand you're checking Annie's wires."

Annie heard the subtle innuendo, even if no one else did.

Izzy's lazy smile didn't waver. "Upgrading the security system. It's nice to meet you, Ms. O'Toole."

"Call me Taylor, please."

Annie was saved from more of her sister's questions when a white police cruiser pulled into the parking lot. "What does the sheriff want?"

"Beats me." Her chef cleared her throat. "Maybe he wants to see your toe ring, like everybody else."

Chapter Nineteen

ANNIE MET THE SHERIFF AT HER DOOR, SMILING WARILY. "Did you come to tell me you'd caught the ax murderer?"

The officer slid his cap back and scratched his head. "No one phoned in a murder."

"Sorry, Buzz, that was a stupid joke. It's been a really long day."

Buzz Kozinski was only a few inches taller than Annie, but his rugged frame made him seem much larger. "Nothing serious, I hope."

"Clients, mostly. And according to my chef, rabbits are taking over the world."

Buzz's eyes narrowed. "Rabbits?"

"Don't ask. The real problem is the fire alarm, which just went crazy for no apparent reason."

"You want me to look at it?"

"Thanks, but someone's already checked. It appears that one of the workmen bumped the fuse box. On top of everything else, we're in the middle of installing new cedar whirlpools on the upper terrace."

"So I noticed." The sheriff leaned against the side of his cruiser. "By the way, nice haircut. Changed the color too, didn't you?"

"It was an impulse thing."

Buzz rubbed his neck, looking faintly uncomfortable. "I hear you've got someone redoing your security."

"Word travels fast." Annie wondered if he had heard the rest of the gossip, linking her with the gorgeous mystery man who looked like Denzel Washington.

"Everything okay here?"

"Sure, Buzz. It's just usual maintenance. The fire alarm is a minor nuisance that we'll get sorted out."

Annie motioned him inside, considering how to deflect his curiosity. "How about a double hot chocolate?"

"Only if you have one, too."

She steered him to the dining room. "That stuff is loaded with chocolate, whipped cream, spices, all sorts of sinful calories." She motioned to one of the kitchen staff. "Hot chocolate for two."

As soon as the steaming cups were delivered, Buzz leaned back and studied her. "Nice toe ring."

Annie studied her foot. "It was all Taylor's idea. Did you know she's staying this time, Buzz? She bought that house she was renting."

"Well, it's about time she settled down. Maybe she can help you out here at Summerwind. You look tired."

"Oh, shucks, you always know how to make a girl feel beautiful."

"I mean it." He toyed with his cuff. "I worry about you. I haven't forgotten how much I owe you for all the help you gave me when Emmalou—" His fingers tightened.

"Buzz, you don't need to go into this."

"The hell I don't. You know how bad she was feeling at the end, how much pain there was. Without those massages and the water therapy you arranged, she would have been in a lot more pain. I know you didn't charge even half your usual rate."

"But I—"

"Let me finish." His voice was surprisingly hard. "I never did say thank you for that. After Emmalou passed on, I guess I went to pieces. Nothing much seemed to matter. It wasn't that we hadn't expected it, since she'd been fading for over a year." He traced a line in the whipped cream with a spoon, his brow set in hard furrows. "Then the time came and she was gone, really gone, with no chance that I'd ever hear her call my name or walk in the front door, trying to hide another stray cat under her coat." He drew a rough breath. "Yeah, I went to pieces all right."

Annie covered his hand. "You were entitled. You'd been together for fifteen years, hadn't you?"

"Sixteen in November. Married right before I left for my last hitch in Asia. Best thing I ever did." He shook his head slowly. "Where did that come from? Don't mean to bore you with my stories."

"She was a lovely woman, Buzz. I felt as if I'd lost my closest friend."

"A lot of people felt that way about Emmalou. I didn't realize how many good friends she had until . . ." He pushed away the hot chocolate. "The point I'm trying to make is that I owe you. If you need any help, you call me, okay? Day or night."

"How good are you with aromatherapy products?"

Buzz didn't laugh. "I'm dead serious about this, Annie. Why the hell are you running this big place alone anyway? You could sell for major bucks, then settle down and raise about ten kids of your own."

"Summerwind's not for sale." The snap in Annie's voice surprised them both. "Grandpa left this resort to Mom and Dad, and I promised them I'd keep things going. We've almost paid off our last mortgage and in four years I plan to buy a few more acres up the hill. We'll establish separate casitas for families who want privacy while still having access to all our resort and spa facilities. After that I—" She stopped. "My turn to run on."

"You always did have a carload of ideas, Annie. I just don't like you throwing your life away on a never-ending flow of rich strangers."

"It beats digging ditches. Sometimes." She cradled her chin in her hands. "So what brought you up here?" She raised her hands in mock fear. "Hey, if it's about those parking tickets—"

Buzz's mouth twitched. "Yeah, you're a real hardened criminal. Remind me to put out an APB on you." He turned his cocoa mug slowly. "Actually, the reason I came was—"

He was interrupted by the wail of his beeper. He consulted the screen and shook his head. "Another accident on that damned coast road. The state ought to do us all a favor and shut the blasted thing down."

"I saw a car almost go over once. It scared me senseless," Annie said.

"You should be scared. Emmalou hated that stretch, too. She told me that . . ." His voice trailed away. "There I go again."

Another pager went off. This time it was Annie's. Buzz watched her intently. "More problems?"

Annie scanned her pager and stiffened. "That's it, I'm going to kill someone. Better hang around and save yourself a trip for apprehension. Two months, seven service calls, twenty thousand dollars, and one of the new cedar whirlpools just flooded. Could you please lend me your gun?"

Buzz tried to hide a grin as he stood up. "I'd say any jury in the state would acquit you for just cause."

Halfway to the door Annie stopped. "What *did* you come up here for?"

Buzz motioned to the sidewalk. "Have a look."

A brown suitcase stood beside a bank of hollyhocks.

"It's not one of mine. Where did you find it?"

"Edna called me from the café. A woman left it after lunch, and Edna remembered that she mentioned coming here to rest. Edna said she was a nervous type with spiky black hair, just wrote some kind of book."

"Nikki Jerome! You've got her underwear!" Annie swept a kiss against Buzz's wind-burned cheek. "Blessed, blessed man."

The sheriff rubbed his face, trying to hide a flush. "I had to open it to check for a name and there sure seemed like a lot of underwear for one person. Of course I haven't been out on a date since the first Reagan administration, so what do I know?"

"You should go out again, Buzz." Annie touched his arm lightly. "Emmalou would be the first to agree."

"Hell." Shoulders stiff, he fiddled with his hat. "I wouldn't know where to begin."

"Just think about it. In return, I'll remember to call you if I need any help."

"You got yourself a deal. Now go find your pool repairman and teach him a hard lesson about customer satisfaction."

"Good advice." Annie turned to find Izzy cradling her defective smoke detector. "If this is bad news, I don't want to hear it."

"All in all, it's fairly positive."

"Good. First let me introduce our sheriff. Ishmael Teague, meet Buzz Kozinski."

The two men shook hands politely, but Annie sensed that behind their smiles they were sizing each other up.

"I'd better let you get on with your work," Buzz said after a thoughtful silence. "Remember to call me if you need anything."

Izzy watched the officer amble to his cruiser. "Seems like a nice fellow."

"The best. Some people think he's too provincial to conduct a real criminal investigation, but he's patient and he's ruthlessly thorough. In fact, he just solved the case of the missing underwear."

"Sounds like you've known him a while."

"Fifteen years." Annie waved as the patrol car drove past. "He lost his wife, and things have been pretty rocky for him but I think he's finally coming back." She glanced at the smoke detector and sighed. "What did you find?"

"Some of the circuits were twisted in the fuse box. I checked with the manufacturer. According to them the circuits might have rattled loose if you've had a lot of earthquake activity."

"Nothing major for three years."

Izzy turned the unit between his fingers. "Probably not caused by a quake, in that case. I'll keep digging. In the meantime, I installed a new detector and I'll check your primary fuse box next."

"It's near my office. I'll come along and show you." Annie headed down the corridor at a brisk walk.

"Everything else okay?" Izzy asked casually.

"I'm really backed up from spending so much time with Sam. Not that I regret it," she said hastily.

"What's to regret? You have no peace, no privacy, and no free time. But I'll take over tonight. I was thinking he could try the whirlpool up at your place, just as a change of pace."

Annie suppressed a sharp image of Sam rocking against her in the hot, swirling water. "Good idea. Anything to keep him from the free weights." She cleared her throat at the thought of Sam clad in nothing but foam. *No way.* "Just be sure that leg stays out of the water."

"Roger. Anything else I can do before I head back?"

"Want to try out some chamomile toning gel?" Annie asked, then chuckled at the look of sheer disgust on his face.

◇ ◇ ◇

AS HE CRUISED THROUGH THE PARKING LOT, BUZZ WATCHED ANnie talking with her visitor. The man held himself with quiet confidence and looked as if he worked hard at staying in shape.

Buzz grimaced, suddenly conscious of his own expanding midriff. The fact was, he'd let himself run down since Emmalou had . . .

Left him.

That's the way he usually thought of it. But gone was still gone.

The pain receded slowly. Emmalou would have wanted him to keep an eye on Annie.

He glanced in the mirror, frowning. Her friend in the windbreaker seemed like a decent type, but he decided to do his own checking. He pulled out a notebook, trying to remember the man's name.

Teague. What about his first name?

Israel? No, Ishmael. At least a name like that should be easy to track. Assuming it was real.

As a police officer, Buzz had access to a wide array of resources, and he decided to call in some favors. He couldn't allow a stranger to cause Annie any trouble.

Emmalou would expect it of him.

❖ ❖ ❖

"A TOE RING?" SAM PUT DOWN THE DUMBBELL HE'D BEEN CURL-ing. "Annie?"

"It looked kind of cute, especially with the red polish on her toenails. And she did something to her hair. It's all shades of blond now with different lengths. Taylor says it's the newest thing."

"Who's Taylor?"

"Her sister. Lived in Europe awhile, then moved to San Francisco. Now she bought a house nearby."

Sam ran a towel over his face. "Did she swallow your story about doing security work?"

"No reason for her not to. Although for a minute I thought—"

"What?"

Izzy shrugged. "Maybe she thought Annie and I were up here—well, you get the picture."

Sam ignored a little stab of jealousy. "I suppose Annie gets that reaction a lot. Being a single woman doing hands-on therapy with athletes and movie stars, I mean."

Izzy nodded. "That little tube top was probably her sister's idea, too."

Sam looked down the hill toward Annie's office. "One of those skimpy knit things? No sleeves?"

"That's the kind."

"What color?"

"Red."

A muscle moved at Sam's jaw. "You'd better go back down and check out that fire alarm. See if any wiring is damaged. And keep an eye on Annie. I don't want a bunch of rich guys hitting on her." He glanced around the room, frowning. "But first help me find the binoculars."

Chapter Twenty

WHEN ANNIE FINALLY TRACKED DOWN NIKKI JEROME, THE AU-
thor was covered with sweat, pumping away on a stationary bi-
cycle.

"Good news, Ms. Jerome. Your suitcase has been found. It
appears you left it in the café in town the day you arrived."

"Impossible," the author panted. "I had it when I checked in."

"Apparently not. The manager at the café remembered you
mentioning Summerwind and asked the sheriff to check it out.
I've sent the case up to your room."

"Thank heaven. The thought of a stranger with my private
things made me *nuts*." She stopped pedaling and ran a hand
across her neck. "I guess I owe you an apology."

"Don't worry, stress busting is our specialty."

"So it seems." The author combed her fingers absently
through her damp hair.

"Is something else bothering you?"

Nikki Jerome slid off the bike and walked to the terrace, the
curtains drifting around her. "How well do you know Tucker
Marsh?"

More than I want to, Annie thought. "Not very well. Has
something happened?"

"You could say that." The author toyed with the belt of her
robe. "I met him in the exercise room and he noticed my book.
He's worked with a few authors in plagiarism cases, so we began talking. He asked about my representation and said he
could do better for me. When he asked me for lunch to discuss
it, the idea seemed perfectly reasonable." Her brow furrowed.
"We talked for a while, but all he wanted to discuss was the
cases he's won. And then he . . ."

"Go on," Annie said.

"Then he got touchy—a pat on the shoulder, a touch on the waist. After his third glass of wine, things changed." She took a hard breath. "He touched me under the table, and I told him to stop."

"Did he?"

"He told me to drop dead." The writer laughed cynically. "He also said I was a big girl and if I didn't want to play ball I shouldn't get out on the court." She stared out toward the garden. "I was vulnerable, and he knew it."

"Did he threaten you? Harm you in any way?"

The author shook her head. "He came right to the edge a few times, but never went over." She was silent for a long time, staring down at the beach. "I think he's done this kind of thing before, Ms. O'Toole."

It was possible. Tucker Marsh's ego was colossal. No doubt he considered female intimidation and sexual harassment to be his God-given right.

Annie realized she'd have to take immediate precautions. "If he tries anything else—if he even whispers in your direction—I want to know. Bring me times and locations. Meanwhile, steer clear of him and I'll alert the staff. Unfortunately, unless he does something overt, I can't have him thrown off the premises."

Nikki Jerome nodded slowly. "Not without one hell of a lawsuit."

"Let me worry about that. I want you to forget Tucker Marsh and enjoy yourself. If he tries to bother you again, I'll take legal action against him." Annie glanced at her watch. "Aren't you due down in hydrotherapy for a watsu session with Sumner? I guarantee when he's done, you're going to be melted butter."

But Annie's smile faded the second the author strode out. She refused to let Tucker Marsh sink his fangs into one of her guests.

She drummed one hand on the counter.

Legal advice first. Time to contact her lawyer in Santa Cruz.

Alex took her call immediately. "Annie, it's wonderful to speak to you. Are you still holding that wine-tasting dinner next month? If so, put me down for four tickets."

"Consider it done." Annie hesitated. "The fact is, I need some advice."

His chair creaked. "Professional advice?"

"I'm not asking for new massage techniques, if that's what you're asking."

"I might surprise you. I lived in an ashram in India for a year before I passed the bar."

Annie was astounded. She had never guessed her fast-track, button-down lawyer had a fuzzy New Age side. "Did India help you get in touch with your inner Buddha? Or was your inner child interested in torts?"

"Actually, it was both." He chuckled. "Things were certainly simpler then. But you didn't call to discuss metaphysics. What's the trouble?"

Annie took a deep breath. "One of my guests had an unpleasant encounter with another guest."

Alex's voice turned hard. "There's a lot of that going around. Was rape involved?"

"Nothing so overt. He put his hands on her, got a little pushy and crude. He told her he could help her career, then got huffy when she tried to leave." Annie chewed her lip. "I'm starting to think he makes a practice of this."

The lawyer's chair squeaked again.

"Well?" she demanded. "Talk to me, Alex. What are my options?"

"It's not a lot to go on, Annie. If you want to pursue legal action, you'd need a sworn statement from your guest detailing exactly what took place at the resort."

"It didn't happen on the grounds. They'd gone into town for lunch."

"If this didn't happen on your property, I'm not sure you have a solid reason to be involved."

Annie stiffened. "But it's *wrong*."

"Of course it is. Proving that is something else entirely."

"Have I ever told you how much I hate cynical people?"

"It's called realism, not cynicism. Unless I'm mistaken, that's what you're paying me for. Is there anything else I should know?"

"One thing." Annie took a breath. "The man involved is Tucker Marsh."

"*Capo di tutti capi* of litigators? Damn, Annie, you know how to find the hot water, don't you? The man's only lost three cases in seventeen years. In a courtroom he's like a great white shark on steroids."

"He also skirted the edge with me," Annie said tightly.

"The bastard. Was he physically intimidating?"

"Verbal, but using more force in grabbing my arm than he should have."

"Did he leave marks? Do you have pictures?" Her lawyer's voice snapped like bullets.

Annie glanced down at her wrist. "No."

"Look, Annie, as angry as this makes me, I'm going to give you this straight. I've heard some unpleasant rumors about Marsh, but not one has ever stuck. One of his paralegals sued him for sexual harassment about three years back."

"What happened?"

"He tore her to pieces. He prolonged the case, smeared her personally and professionally, then summoned a who's who of California notables as character witnesses. She ended up losing—and paying all the legal fees." He cleared his throat. "The last I heard, she was selling shoes somewhere north of Fargo."

Annie stared at the phone. "Are you telling me to forget this ever happened?"

"I'm telling you to think long and hard about what you want to do next. I'll back you fully. Just call me when you decide and we'll hammer out a strategy. I've always wanted to go shark hunting."

Annie had to chuckle. "Now I know why I pay you those huge retainers."

"One last thing. Who's the mystery man who looks like Denzel Washington?"

"You, too?"

"My cousin works at the bank, and we got to talking."

"Am I the town's only topic of conversation?"

"At least your news is good news. I'm glad you're involved with someone, Annie. It's about time."

"Save the congratulations. He's just here to do some upgrades on my security system."

"Sure, Annie. No need to shout."

"I *wasn't* shouting. I was . . ." She took a breath, glaring at the little silver toe ring. "Talking very loudly. And I'm going to say good-bye before I do it again."

Annie heard him chuckling as she hung up.

Chapter Twenty-one

"WHAT DO YOU MEAN, SHE'S EATING DINNER AT HER DESK?" SAM glared at Izzy. "Whose mush-for-brains idea was that?"

"Hers. I believe it's called multi-tasking," Izzy said dryly. "You SEALs have even been known to do it on occasion."

"Annie needs to rest."

"I doubt that she can. You've been taking up a big chunk of her work time, if you recall."

"If that's supposed to make me shut up, think again." Sam grabbed his crutch. "I'm going down there."

"It's supposed to make you feel guilty," Izzy said. "And you're going nowhere."

"To hell with procedure." Sam lurched to his feet. "And just for the record, I don't need your help to feel guilty. I know Annie didn't bargain for what she's gotten into. Where's my damned shirt?" Irritated, Sam searched through the exercise equipment at his feet.

A towel struck his face.

He caught it with one hand.

"Try that instead. Annie said you're ready to do some water therapy in her outdoor whirlpool, so let's go."

"I don't want to do therapy. Not unless she's there to snap at me when I do something wrong." Sam turned the towel in his hands. "Is it my imagination or am I losing my mind?" he asked quietly.

"Could be that thing."

"That's helpful, Teague."

Izzy scratched his jaw. "That transference thing."

"Between me and Annie? Like hell." Sam flung the towel over his shoulder and stretched his sore muscles. "We're too smart for that." He sniffed. "Too experienced." He slid his fingers around his crutch, then looked thoughtfully at Izzy. "You think?"

"It happens. Annie said it was fairly common."

Sam's eyes narrowed. "You talked about it with her?"

"Just checking for feedback."

"I don't want to hear this. Not one damned word. I'm changing into my swimsuit." Sam lumbered into the bedroom, his crutches tapping. Clothing rustled, then he emerged. "You can tell me what she said when we get to the hot tub."

Izzy gave an innocent smile. "I thought you didn't want to—"

"Stow it, Teague."

◇ ◇ ◇

ANNIE MADE A FINAL SKETCH, THEN PASSED THE PAPER TO HER assistant. "What do you think?"

"The blue glass bottle will be beautiful with the picture of Summerwind's cove on the label. We can sell a million of those rose and sage salt glow scrubs. There's a glass supplier in Oregon who's willing to ship small quantities. I've also found a printer for the labels. He'll do gold foil letters, the way you requested, and he's sending some samples early next week."

"Great work, Megan. I want this line to be special." Annie stared at the framed picture of her mother. "Mom and Grandma swore by natural ingredients. They always regretted that they couldn't find a big company to produce their natural products."

"So you're doing it for them."

"Maybe I'm nuts. It's going to be a huge amount of work, more than you or I can handle."

"Reynaldo's niece just finished college. She doesn't want to move back to San Francisco, so maybe you could find something for her here."

Annie felt the crushing weight of responsibility. With sixty people on her staff, she did not bear the burden lightly. "The line could fall flat. Where would she be then?"

"Packing to move to San Francisco, just the way she is now. At least she'd have some solid work experience under her belt. That's gold on anyone's résumé."

"What was her major?"

"Journalism."

Annie shook her head. "She'd be wasting her time here."

"Journalism was her *mother's* idea. She wants to own her own chain of beauty supermarkets one day, showcasing natural products collected from around the world."

"No kidding." Annie stared at her half-eaten sandwich. "But what if—"

"Forget what-if, boss. Give her the facts and let her decide. You don't have to play God. Even *He* took one day off to rest."

"There's blasphemy in there somewhere, but I'm too tired to find it." Annie stood up wearily. "I'll talk to her tomorrow. After she hears the raw, unvarnished facts, if she's still interested—"

"She will be. She thinks you're a cross between Mother Teresa and Martha Stewart."

Chuckling, Annie glanced at her watch. "Take an hour off for a massage tomorrow, Megan. Indulge—and put it on my account."

Her assistant smiled impishly. "That makes my fifth massage this month, but who's complaining? Thanks, boss. You're the greatest."

The impulsive compliment left Annie strangely touched. With dedicated people like this, Summerwind had a solid future, and that thought pleased her very much.

❖ ❖ ❖

AT ELEVEN O'CLOCK ANNIE WAS DRAINING HER FOURTH CUP OF coffee, but her paperwork was nearly finished. She'd finished the press release for next month's wine tasting, revised the resort's Web site, and gone over chemical reports on the salt-water hydrotherapy pools.

To top off a long day, Tucker Marsh had dropped by a little after ten. Cocky and grinning, he had perched on the edge of her desk while he tried to look down her blouse. For ten minutes he'd listed all his criticisms of the resort staff and why Annie should handle him personally.

Annie pretended to remember a late appointment with her groundskeeper, but Marsh had insisted he would accompany her to the building at the far side of the complex.

When Marsh finally left, she'd been thoroughly shaken, and she was certain that he knew it.

Afterward, she'd called Reynaldo, her head of security, and ordered all the staff to keep a close eye on the lawyer. At the slightest hint of impropriety to any guest or staff, Annie swore to kick him out on his cashmere-clad backside. Lawsuits be damned.

Annie stretched, glad the day was finally over. Standing alone in the silent wing of offices, she was struck by the personal legacy of the resort and its three generations of visitors. It had been her grandparents' dream, then her parents' pride, and Annie had caught the bug. Summerwind was a magical place, perched above the beach, and Annie liked to think her guests took a little bit of that magic with them when they went home. Now she was tackling her parents' final wish, bringing a line of natural face and body-care products to the world beyond Summerwind.

Crazy, she thought. But designing the spa products was exhilarating and Annie sensed they could be a huge success. Maybe she needed to go crazy more often.

She picked up a framed postcard from Venice, a memento of her parents' honeymoon years before. Beside it stood a huge stuffed gorilla with red sneakers, a gift from Taylor on Annie's twenty-first birthday.

Everything here was business, but it was also intensely personal. Her parents had planned for Summerwind to feel like a home away from home and Annie worked hard to retain that mood. After all, didn't everyone want a place at the beach?

As she was turning out the light, Annie glanced at her telephone log. It was facedown, resting on the left corner of her desk, though she always kept it beside her phone.

She stood uneasily, trying to remember if Megan had moved the log during their last meeting. Or had someone else been in her office tonight?

No, it had to be Megan. They had gone through a stack of files together and probably moved the phone log in the process. That had to be the explanation.

She snapped out the light, plunging her office and the corridor beyond into darkness. As her footsteps echoed in the silence, she was suddenly aware of how alone she was now that the office staff had gone home. Even the security office was two buildings away.

Too far to hear her scream.

"Idiot." She gripped her handbag tightly and straightened her shoulders. She was imagining things. No one was going to break in, pin her to the wall, and hold a knife to her throat.

The crunching came from the shadows to her left. Annie's pulse spiked and she sank back against the cold stucco wall with her heart slamming in her chest.

"Annie, are you there?"

A flashlight beam cut through the darkness, glancing off her face.

Izzy.

She gasped in relief.

"Hey, what is it? You're shivering."

"Nothing's wrong." *Only a major heart attack.* "I was just . . . fixing my shoe. The strap was—it was loose."

Izzy flipped on the light, looking down at her face.

Annie didn't need a mirror to know that she was probably the color of snow on snow. She felt almost as cold, too.

"Annie?" Izzy touched her arm gently. "Talk to me."

"It's nothing, okay? I didn't expect anyone to be around this late."

His frown told her he wasn't buying it. "Come on."

Annie didn't budge. "Why are you down here?"

"Sam sent me to get you. He was worried."

"I had a press release to finish, a new skin-care line to re-search and—" She sighed. "Why am I explaining? This is my work, and that's that. If Sam doesn't like it, he can just go—"

Rubber soles squished behind them. "He can just what?"

He was almost the color of snow, too, Annie saw. In an at-tempt to conceal his face, he wore a baseball cap pulled low and the collar of his jacket turned up. Annie guessed that his windbreaker concealed a holstered weapon.

"What are *you* doing?"

"Getting you. What kind of crazy plan was that, working until midnight?"

"The only crazy one here is you." Annie glanced around, checking that they were still alone. "Why aren't you up at the house asleep?"

"Why aren't you?"

"Forget about me. Tomorrow's going to be a big day for you. Trust me, what you've done up to this will feel like ballroom dancing compared to tomorrow's workout."

"I'm quaking all right." Sam moved closer, studying her face. "Nice haircut."

"Thanks," she said stiffly.

"You look worried. What's wrong?"

Annie switched off the light and started toward the door. "You'd look worried too if strangers kept looming toward you out of the shadows."

"What strangers?" Suddenly tense, Sam pulled her around to face him. "Who was here?"

"You." Annie cleared her throat. "And Izzy, of course."

"You said strangers."

Annie shrugged dramatically. "What do I know? Standing here in the dark everyone looks like a stranger."

Sam's eyes were cold. "No one else?"

She shook her head. No way would she wring her hands and whine about Tucker Marsh. The man was her problem to handle, and Sam wasn't involved.

"Why do I think you're lying?"

"Beats me."

"Nice toe ring," Sam said gruffly. He leaned in closer and sniffed. "What's that smell?"

Probably her circuits burning, Annie thought. "The lingering bouquet of four cups of coffee?"

Sam shook his head. "No, it's sweet like fruit and fresh grass. It smells nice."

He had good taste in fragrance, Annie conceded. "It's my grandmother's recipe for apple-lavender body cream. An old family secret, I might add."

"You'll make a lot of money with it. Not that I'm an expert in things like that."

The compliment softened Annie's irritation. "How was the whirlpool?"

"Izzy isn't tough enough."

"No?" Behind him, Annie saw Izzy frown, then point to his left shoulder.

So Sam's shoulder had acted up. He had probably tried to push right through until the pain stopped him.

Annie immediately revised the program she'd been planning for the following day. "I'll have to see that Izzy gets tougher," she lied. "Any other problems?"

"Izzy told me about the fire alarm. I want to look into that."

"It was a simple circuit problem."

"Maybe." Sam stared up the hill as they followed the narrow

path through landscaped banks of trees. "Have you known your sheriff long?"

"Buzz? Fifteen years." Annie raised a brow. "Why?"

"Just wondering. He seemed . . . taken with you."

Annie stiffened. "You were watching?"

"German lenses don't miss much. The casita has a good view of most of the resort and all the beach. Good tactical advantage. I like that red tube top you're wearing, too," he muttered.

"You *watched* me?" Annie repeated.

"I was worried about you." Sam's jaw tensed. "Are you two seeing each other?"

Annie just kept walking.

"Well, *are* you?"

"That's none of your business."

"Isn't it?" Sam's voice fell. "Not too long ago we were ripping off each other's clothes. Now you look right through me. If you're seeing someone else, I want to know."

Annie felt heat flood into her face. "Maybe you should define seeing. Do you mean are we dating? Good friends? Reckless, passionate lovers?"

"Any of the above," Sam said grimly.

Annie heard the crunch of gravel and realized Izzy had fallen back, giving them some privacy. "Who gave you the right to monitor my private life?"

"I guess I have this whole thing wrong. When you yanked off my shirt and went for my belt, I was stupid enough to think it meant something."

So had Annie, but she didn't like the possessive tone Sam was taking. She didn't need him controlling her private life—not that she *had* one.

"I guess you thought wrong." Relieved to see the casita before them, she shoved open the door, stormed into the pantry, and pulled down the first bottle she found.

"Where are you going?"

"Out to get drunk, and you're not invited. Don't wait up."

"Annie, don't do this."

"Watch me." She sailed past him, not stopping for Izzy, who was leaning against the big oak at the front of the drive.

She stalked along the lighted path at the back of her property. At the top, she turned and called down to Izzy. "I know you're there, so you can stop hiding."

A branch moved.

Silent as a shadow, Izzy appeared on the flagstone path. "I don't think he meant what he said."

"I think he meant every word." Annie cradled her bottle stiffly. "You can go back now. My sister's house is right up the hill through the trees."

"I'll just tag along. I'd appreciate it if you didn't come back alone," he added.

Annie sighed. "Stop worrying, will you? I probably won't be back until morning anyway."

She turned before he could raise any other objections, but when she reached her sister's door, she could still feel him behind her, a silent guardian.

On the fourth ring, Annie heard the scrape of slippers.

The peephole slid open.

"Annie?" The door opened with a creak. "What are you doing with that bottle?"

Annie strode inside. "You and I are about to get seriously drunk."

Chapter Twenty-two

TAYLOR STARED ANXIOUSLY AT HER SISTER. "GET DRUNK? THIS isn't like you."

"Maybe I'm tired of the old me. Maybe I want a *new* me." Seated on Taylor's overstuffed leather sofa, Annie swirled her glass of scotch, which was considerably emptier than it had been fifteen minutes ago.

She finished the rest in one gulp, coughing slightly. "This isn't working. Let's try some of that vintage port you're always hoarding."

Taylor looked at Annie's empty glass. "I don't think you should. You've already had two beers, remember?"

Annie swept to her feet, only swaying a little. "In that case, I'm leaving. You're no f-fun." She blinked at Taylor's Tiffany light, which was moving oddly. "*You* always get to break the rules and live dangerously, but I have to do the normal things." She frowned. "The boring things that no one else wants to do."

"That's not true."

"Name one time I broke the rules." Annie crossed her arms, watching Taylor sip her scotch.

"Third grade. You threw up on Tommy Clanahan's spelling book, then buried it in the science fair compost pile."

"Doesn't count," Annie said stiffly. "I was sick that day."

"So?"

"So he'd also put a frog in your locker. I was paying him back."

"Tommy Clanahan did that?" Taylor shook her head. "You never told me."

"No need. I handled it just fine my own way." Annie swayed

slightly and decided sitting down would be a good idea. "Name another time."

Taylor drummed her fingers on the carved oak coffee table. "High school, freshman year. You sneaked out during second period study hall. You made a rope out of panty hose, as I recall. I never could figure out where you got them."

Annie smiled faintly. "Stole them. Raided the locker rooms while the seniors were at basketball practice. Best fun I ever had." Her smile faded. "Did you *hear* that?"

"You mean the part about the senior basketball practice?"

"No, the part about the best fun I've ever had, which is seriously pathetic. What have I been doing for twenty-seven years if stealing panty hose is my highest idea of fun?"

"I'll tell you what." Taylor gripped her hand. "You helped Mom and Dad build something special here. You were their rock, Annie. Both of them said that."

"Yeah." Annie rolled her shoulders. "A rock. Big deal."

"Hey, take that back, pal. It *is* a big deal. Summerwind is one special place," Taylor said hotly. "People love it here. They have fun, they learn things, and they go away feeling better. That's the best part of all."

Annie glared at her empty glass. "So what?"

Taylor studied Annie carefully. "Is this some kind of hormone thing?"

"What's that supposed to mean? You're the one who turns into Bride of Frankenstein for three days every month."

"I know. That's why you're starting to frighten me. You're supposed to be the steady, calm O'Toole sister. Floods, earthquakes, tax audits—nothing shakes you. There must be a law that says Annie O'Toole can't agonize over the wasted opportunities of life."

"Why?"

"Hell, I don't know. Because that's the way it's always been."

Annie set down her glass with a snap. "That's about to change."

"You're serious, aren't you?"

"Should I start quoting *Richard III*?"

"Well, now, *this* calls for serious ammunition." Taylor pulled out a new bottle. "Single malt, eight years in lovely oak caskets. Here's to the death of the noble-minded and long-suffering Annie O'Toole."

"Didn't you tell me not to mix port and scotch?"

Taylor shrugged. "You only live once. Of course, you might curse me in the morning." She frowned as she opened the bottle. "So no-good Tommy Clanahan put that frog in my locker. Who knew?" She filled Annie's glass, then her own. "Any idea where little old Tommy is now?"

"Not a clue."

"Little old Tommy weighs about four hundred and fifty pounds and runs a car dealership in San Jose. Word is, if you renege on a loan, Tommy will come lean on you." Taylor grinned. "Literally."

"What about his high school sweetheart?"

"Lou's an exotic dancer in Seattle. Something to do with snakes. I actually interviewed her for my last book."

"Maybe Tommy's frog turned her on." Annie took another drink and studied her toe ring, which she had come to like hugely.

"Lou is one sharp customer. In her line of work, you have to be part psychiatrist, part psychic. If she doesn't tune in to her customers' fantasies inside three minutes, she doesn't make the big bucks."

Annie frowned. She, on the other hand, knew next to nothing about tuning in to fantasies—her own or anyone else's.

Take Sam's, for example.

Her stomach went quivery at the memory of their last out-of-control encounter in her living room. He still had amazing hands.

And they'd been mere seconds away from . . .

Definitely don't go there.

"So what's big in the fantasy department these days, according to an exotic dancer in Seattle?"

"Male or female fantasies?"

"Male."

"Anyone particular in mind?"

Annie glared at her sister over the rim of her glass. "None of your business."

"Fine. Just fine," Taylor said soothingly. A smile flirted around her mouth. "Don't suppose it's the man you're shacked up with? Denzel, who's checking your wires."

"I told you—"

"Okay, okay." Taylor sat back, crossed her legs thoughtfully. "Fishnet stockings are big this year."

"With what?" Annie looked confused.

"With nothing."

Annie stared down at her legs, one eyebrow raised. "How do you hold them up?"

"Garters are selling like hotcakes."

Annie sat some more, considering. "That's all?"

"That's the word in Seattle."

Annie shook her head. "They must be drinking too much Starbucks out there. That's . . . well, nobody in their right mind would dress like that."

"It isn't exactly a ballet recital," Taylor said carefully. "It's just you and him."

Annie stiffened. "Who said anything about *me*? This is a general discussion of social trends."

"Sure." Taylor stuck her tongue in her cheek. "A general discussion. Speaking generally, I hear bondage is pretty big too."

"Bondage? That's disgusting. Depraved. What woman wants to be tied up?"

"Not the woman," Taylor said patiently. "The guy."

Annie stared at the fire. Now it was her turn to drum her fingers on the coffee table. "You mean that she gets to tie *him* up? To do whatever she wants to him until he . . ."

"That's the general idea."

Annie took a substantial drink of scotch, choking back a cough. "How do you lead into something like that? You don't just pull out a rope and say, 'Lie down, honey, time for some nice bondage.'"

"With the right guy, you might not have to say anything."

Annie sank back against the couch. "No, it would never work. I'd get nervous and throw up." She cleared her throat. "I mean, a *person* would get nervous and probably throw up. Not me. Not anyone I know."

"Annie."

"This is just general supposition."

"Annie." This time Taylor said the word firmly, reaching for her sister's arm. "Being in love and wanting to turn up the heat is nothing to be ashamed about."

"Love," Annie squawked, "who said anything about *love*? One minute we're discussing recreational trends and the next minute you're talking about *amore* with a full orchestral background." She stood jerkily. "If a person wants to know about current fantasies, why can't you leave it at that? What's wrong with a few simple, sordid fantasies?"

"Nothing."

"In my book, love is a four-letter word. Love is unpredictable and messy."

Taylor sighed loudly.

"You don't believe me?"

"You've always been transparent, Annie. You were the one who cried at weddings and went nuts at the World Series playoffs. It's just the way you're made."

"Maybe I've changed," Annie snapped. "Maybe I'm turning over a new leaf. Why can't I have some fun?"

"No reason at all."

Annie glared at her empty glass. "And for the record, my life's great, absolutely great. I finally meet the man of my dreams, but he proceeds to vanish without a word. After that, he nearly dies before a viewing audience of millions, only to reappear in the dead of night, strapped to a gurney." Annie swallowed hard. "He also has no memory that we've ever met. What's not to like about that?"

Taylor sat up straight. "What man of your dreams?"

"Forget it. I didn't breathe a word, understand? Not a word."

"But you just said—"

Annie focused hard, realizing her slip. "I said nothing."

"You did! Tell me every detail."

"There *are* no details."

"Why, is he in the mob?"

"He's *not* in the mob. No one's in the mob. In fact there *is* no one."

Taylor stalked to the phone.

"What are you doing?"

"I'm calling Buzz. Only a policeman could get you out of this mess."

"I don't need any help, Taylor. I'll be just fine."

"There you go again," Taylor said angrily. "The great Annie O'Toole wouldn't dream of accepting help from anyone, not even her sister. Make that *especially* from her sister."

Annie turned slowly. "I'm picking up hostility here. Lots of hostility."

"There's more where that came from." Taylor slammed down the phone. "Did you ever stop to think that maybe I might want to change, too? Maybe I'm tired of being the flighty one, the one who skips out at the first hint of responsibility."

Annie opened her mouth, then closed it again. "I'm not stopping you."

"Of course you are. One saint in the family is fine, *two* is overkill. It's all been arranged: you get to be Mother Teresa and I get to be Goldie Hawn in *Protocol*." Taylor pulled her knees up, hugging her chest. "I'm the one who was caught smoking cigarettes behind the library in third grade. I'm the one who dyed my hair green for senior prom, then made a miniskirt out of duct tape."

Annie was stunned to see that Taylor was crying, gulping as she stammered out the words.

"But I thought you liked being outrageous," Annie said, totally confused now.

"I had to do something for attention. You were always there, Miss Picture-Perfect Straight A. Let's face it, you were the blue-chip standard as far as this town goes. While you were busy being the Rock, I was frantically playing the Rebel. Being outrageous was my only escape from total invisibility."

Annie felt her irritation zing away like a punctured balloon. "Why didn't you say something?"

"It wasn't your fault that you were perfect." Taylor gave a shaky laugh. "Besides, I soon discovered that having wild, abandoned sex in the backseat of a souped-up red Camaro had a way of taking the edge off the pain."

"I'm sure it did." Annie knew a moment of pure jealousy. Why hadn't *she* had wild, abandoned sex in the back of a red Camaro—or any other car? She sat without moving for a long time, then sank down beside her sister on the couch. "So what do we do now?"

"I don't know about you, but I'm going to finish this glass of scotch, get really drunk, and throw up painfully in the morning."

"Sounds good to me. What about after that?"

"I'm open for suggestions."

"What about this hostility we've been nursing for years?"

Taylor shrugged. "I'll let you scream at me if I can scream at you."

Annie refilled her glass and raised it high. "You go first."

Taylor cleared her throat and summoned a low growl that climbed into full gear as Annie joined in. The noise grew to a shrill crescendo, then broke into raucous laughter.

In the silence that followed, the two sat side-by-side, warmed by the golden dance of the fire. The scotch wasn't hurting their mood either.

Taylor shook her head. "Don't blame *me* if you have the mother of all hangovers tomorrow."

"I won't."

"That's what they all say."

"Care to elaborate on the wild, abandoned sex?"

Taylor sniffed. "Only after I've had a few more drinks."

"You know, all these years I've envied you. You had flair and imagination and you weren't afraid of anything."

"I was a misfit," Taylor said softly. "I was afraid of *everything*."

Annie stared at the dancing embers. "Not to me. To me, you were the perfect big sister." She blinked hard. "I think you still are. To me you were never a screwup."

"Oh, hell, Annie. There you go again, being Mother Teresa."

They were both crying, both a little unsteady, when they sank into an awkward hug.

Chapter Twenty-three

DAMP AIR BRUSHED ANNIE'S FACE, SLICING IN OFF THE SEA. GASP-ing, she wobbled off Taylor's porch, then stopped. "I'm not supposed to do this."

"Get drunk?" Taylor asked, equally wobbly.

"Go back to the resort alone." Staring into the darkness, she replayed Izzy's warning.

Taylor clutched her arm. "This is too cool. Is he on some kind of covert operation?"

"Hardly."

"So who is he?"

"I can't tell you that."

"Why?"

"I can't tell you that either."

"What *can* you tell me?" Taylor asked irritably.

Annie thought it over. "He has one cute butt."

"Maybe I'd better check out this guy myself. Come on, I'll drive you back in the golf cart." Decidedly unsteady, the two made their way along the porch to Taylor's small stucco garage.

"Are you sure?" Annie wondered if driving was a good idea. Speaking for herself, she was seeing double.

She frowned at the garage light.

Make that triple.

Of course Taylor had a lot more experience with this alcohol stuff.

Annie stared at the gleaming vehicle. "I don't know about this."

"What?" Taylor slid behind the wheel. "This will be a cinch." She waved one hand. "Head 'em up, move 'em out. Don't worry, the golfmobile only does seven mph."

Annie had barely fastened the flimsy seat belt when Taylor shot across the driveway, front-ended the lawn mower, and jumped the curb, burying the front wheels in a jade plant.

So much for head 'em up, move 'em out.

Taylor grabbed her arm. "You okay?"

"Other than the whiplash?" Annie stood unsteadily, eyeing the fresh furrow in the lawn. "Martha Stewart wouldn't like this."

"I never cared for the woman. C'mon, let's walk."

Why not? Anyone within half a mile had already heard the crash of the golf cart. Secrecy and stealth weren't exactly an option.

Taylor took her arm as they lurched down the path, which seemed considerably darker and steeper than it had four hours ago. "Tell me more about your mystery man."

"Can't."

"C'mon. I'm drunk, but I'm not that drunk. He has to be the man in the yacht." Taylor smiled darkly. "I also know he has a fabulous butt."

"Who told you that?"

"You did, about five minutes ago."

"Oh. Right."

Annie was having a hard time getting that particular image out of her head, but she plodded on in silence. Taylor leaned closer, her voice falling. "Don't look now, but we're being watched."

"Where?" Annie whispered.

"By the avocado tree."

When Annie saw the outline of broad shoulders in a nylon windbreaker, her tension lifted. "It's okay. I know him."

"Your mystery man?"

"Not exactly."

"I *want* some answers."

"Don't ask." Annie wasn't feeling so good. The cold air was

making her dizzy, and her knees were showing an unaccountable tendency to lean to the right.

"Here he comes," Taylor whispered as Izzy loomed out of the foliage. Annie wasn't sure, but he seemed to be fighting a smile.

"Evening, ladies. Nice night for a walk."

"Grand." Annie focused hard on walking in a straight line.

Beside her, Taylor was busy studying Izzy. "We met this afternoon. You're here to redo Annie's security."

"That's right."

"Have you ever written a book?"

"Can't say as I have."

Taylor stared some more. "Didn't I see you at the Edgar Awards last year?"

"I'm afraid not."

Annie sighed. "Give it up, Taylor. You don't know him, and he's not a writer. He does security." Among *other* things, Annie thought.

Taylor frowned. "But what else is he?"

Annie stopped walking and looked at Izzy. "What else are you?"

Izzy gave a slow smile. "Tonight I'm whatever you want me to be, ladies."

The answer was so outrageous that Annie began to laugh, and when she laughed, she lost focus on her knees and plowed into Taylor, who fell against an oleander brush. After hard concentration, the two managed to pull themselves upright.

"Feeling no pain, are you?" Izzy drifted closer. Annie was pretty sure it was to render aid if needed.

She was having none of it.

She drew herself up to her full height. "We can manish—manage perfectly on our own, thank you."

"No problem. I'll just hang back here in case you need me."

"Won't," Annie said.

"Might," Taylor muttered, hooking her arm through Annie's and squinting down the hill.

"Want to tell me about that crash I heard?" Izzy followed them down the gravel path.

"Golf cart." Taylor sniffed. "Never did like the game. Hit a stupid little ball in a stupid little hole. Curse a lot while you do it."

Izzy coughed. Annie thought he might be muffling a laugh.

"I know we've met before." Taylor studied Izzy again. "Were you in San Diego last March?"

"No."

"What about New Orleans at the library conference?"

"I'm afraid I missed that one."

"I know your voice." Taylor smacked her forehead. "Why can't I place it?"

"You don't know him," Annie said wearily, tugging her sister down the path. "Give it up. He's from one of those three-letter agencies." Annie frowned. "I think."

"No kidding."

Izzy said nothing, his face carefully expressionless.

"If you were, you couldn't talk about it. I know because I wrote a book about that once."

"You wrote a book about *everything* once," Annie muttered.

They were at the front of Annie's casita when Taylor stopped and snapped her fingers—after a little struggle. "*The Farewell Code.*"

Izzy's brow rose. "I beg your pardon."

"*That's* where I heard your voice, researching my last book."

"You must be confusing me with someone else." Izzy produced a key and slipped inside, then return to hold the door open.

"I never forget a research source." Taylor was indignant. "You were the one who helped me with the encryption techniques. We did most of the communication via E-mail, but we talked on the phone twice. *That's* where I heard your voice."

Annie wasn't sure if it was the alcohol or the light, but Izzy seemed to stiffen, looking uncomfortable.

"Must be someone else."

"Are you a hit man?"

Izzy crossed his arms. "Not that I recall."

Taylor squinted, checking him out thoroughly. "Are you the one with the cute butt?"

"Taylor!" Annie swayed. To her dismay, her knees were wobbling again.

Damned scotch anyway.

"I'm not feeling so good. I think it's time for the painful throwing up."

"No, that's tomorrow," her sister said wisely. Her voice fell away she saw a movement behind Izzy. "Well, well," she murmured as a man loomed out of the shadows.

Taylor took in the naked chest with ridged muscles and the worn jeans that hugged his thighs. "So this is what you've been hiding up here." Her eyes widened as she got a closer look at Sam. "Wait a minute. He's the man from Washington. The one on the bus."

"No, he's not. And you never saw him," Annie said sharply. She straightened her shoulders. "I'm going to sleep. Things are getting very fuzzy." Especially her brain.

She lumbered past Izzy, carefully avoiding Sam though he turned to watch her pass. By a miracle she managed to clear the top step without plunging onto her face.

Taylor smiled broadly at the two men. "Don't mind her. It's the scotch. Or maybe it's the port and the beer. Annie never could drink." She sized up Sam, then sighed. "She's definitely right about one thing. You do have a fine butt."

◇　◇　◇

"DON'T SAY IT. NOT ONE WORD." SAM GLARED AT IZZY AS HE paced the living room.

"Who, me?"

"And stop looking so damned innocent. Her sister recognized your voice. How did *that* little fact slip past you and all our crack operatives in D.C.?"

"She writes under a pseudonym, M. M. Taylor. No one connected that with Annie." Izzy stared down the dark hallway, looking a little ill. "What do we do now?"

"Gut it out. Maintain complete denial." Sam gave an irritated sigh. "They're both seriously looped so they probably won't remember anyway. What about that crash we heard?"

"Annie's sister front-ending a lawn mower in the golf cart. That's when they decided to walk."

"Mixing booze and a concussion isn't a good idea. I know, because I tried it once in Puerto Rico." Sam paced to the hall and listened intently. "Why are they so quiet? Maybe something's wrong."

"Stop worrying, McKade. They're drunk; it's not life threatening."

Sam glared down the hall. "Who's worried? If they want to get blotto, that's their problem. The idiots." He turned his head, listening. "It's too quiet. I'm going down to check on them."

He moved down the hall, stopping just outside Annie's room.

When he looked inside, his lips twitched. "The wages of sin," he murmured.

Annie was stretched out cold on the bed, both shoes off and one arm dangling. On the far side of the room, Taylor lay prone on the couch, a pillow over her head, snoring faintly.

"Complete and absolute idiots."

Sam was fighting a grin as he covered them both with blankets. When he finished, he found Izzy waiting outside. "Dead to the world, both of them."

"Taylor thinks I'm a hit man," Izzy said calmly. "Or she did until she saw *your* face. Your cover's blown to hell, McKade."

"We'll deal with that tomorrow." Sam frowned at the light already touching the bay. "Except it already *is* tomorrow." He rubbed his shoulder, which was aching again. He thought about his painkillers, but fought the temptation. "I still don't like those false alarms at the main building. Are you checking out Annie's smoke alarm units?"

Izzy suppressed a yawn. "Already in the works."

"Then hit the sack. I'll listen for the Bobbsey Twins."

Sam thought he heard Izzy mutter something about "a fine butt" as he headed outside to the guesthouse.

Chapter Twenty-four

ANNIE AWOKE TO PUCCINI AND KETTLEDRUMS. SHE OPENED her eyes and immediately winced as light drilled into her cortex.

Hungover, all right.

She breathed very carefully, trying to make the nausea go away before she attempted to sit up. Somewhere in the distance she heard the sound of the shower going off and a door opening. Even that distant noise left her head ringing.

"How are we doing?"

She recognized Taylor's voice, disgustingly cheerful.

"*We?*"

"Figure of speech, of course."

"Other than the occasional twitching and an uncontrollable need to purge my entire stomach, I'm feeling fine."

"It will pass." Taylor, the voice of experience.

The drums and the Puccini went on hammering inside Annie's head.

"How about something to drink? Maybe a cold Coke?" Taylor asked.

"Only if it's got a good stiff jolt of Demerol. Or maybe I'll go straight for the curare."

Taylor rolled her eyes. Even that much movement made Annie's stomach pitch.

"Drink this."

Annie sniffed the mixture Taylor was holding out. "What's in it?"

"Trust me, you don't want to know. Just hold your nose and get it down."

Annie closed her eyes and swallowed, gagging as she caught

the taste of raw egg mixed with garlic, honey, tomato juice and assorted herbs. White-faced, she sank back against the pillow. "Well, that was way beyond unpleasant."

"If it didn't taste so bad, it wouldn't work. What you need now is a cold shower."

Annie shuddered at the thought of moving. Add in frigid waves of water drilling on her cranium?

No way.

She cradled a pillow over her throbbing head. "I'll just stay here and expire quietly."

The pillow slid from her head. The covers were yanked free. "Rise and shine. Trust me, a shower will do wonders. It has to be really frigid, of course."

In Annie's book, the only thing worse than a cold shower was a frigid shower. Or maybe a root canal with no anesthetic.

"Definitely count me out."

Taylor gripped her arm and pulled her upright.

"Sadist," Annie muttered.

"Wimp," Taylor shot back.

"Anything else I need to know before I expire?"

Taylor turned the shower on cold. "Just one."

Strange things were happening to Annie's stomach in the wake of the drink Taylor had given her. She didn't like the loud rumbling or the general distress. "Let's have it."

Taylor looked apologetic. "You asked about the painful throwing up part? Now is the time."

The door closed quietly behind her.

Almost immediately Annie felt her stomach declare a full-scale mutiny.

◆ ◆ ◆

WHEN ANNIE EMERGED FROM HER BEDROOM, HER SKIN WAS BLUE and her body frozen, but the cold shower had made her feel partially human again. In the process she had also won a precarious cease-fire with her rioting stomach.

She shuffled down the hall, targeting the scent of fresh coffee coming from her kitchen.

As she came to the door, Sam turned, cup in hand, looking disgustingly rested. "So you're alive."

"Maybe we should define 'alive'."

"Breathing unassisted."

"That I can manage. Probably."

"Taylor put another drink here for you before she left. If it doesn't kill you, you should feel better soon." With a towel over one shoulder, he looked good enough to eat. His hair was tousled from a recent shower and his chest was damp. He smelled wonderful, like citrus and leather.

"Other than the unbearable nausea and excruciating headache, how do you feel?"

Annie covered her ears. "Could you please not shout? At least until the glass slivers stop drilling into my forehead."

His eyebrow rose. "That bad?"

With a sigh, Annie slid into the booth before her kitchen window. Clouds dotted the horizon, and a dozen sea otters raced through the kelp beds.

Very perky. They were smart enough not to drink anything but seawater, Annie thought grimly.

A wonderful fragrance filled the air as Sam slid a cup into her hands. "Coffee, very weak. Cream and sugar?"

At one time he had known exactly how she liked her coffee. Annie remembered how he'd made a big deal out of adding skim milk, then one spoonful of honey.

Now he didn't have a clue.

She closed her eyes. *Don't go there. At least not until your head seems less likely to explode.*

"Skim milk in the door of the fridge. One tablespoon of honey." She drew another careful breath. "If you don't mind."

"Honey?"

Her lips tightened. "So sue me."

"It's just a little . . . exotic."

Eccentric. That's what he'd called it the first time he'd watched her mix the ingredients.

Forget about that. Remembering makes it hurt more.

"You had a few calls," Sam said, settling across from her.

"Someone from the resort?"

"A lawyer named Alex. He said he needed to talk to you."

Annie gasped, staring at the clock. "Why didn't someone wake me?"

"Taylor tried about five times. The lawyer said no problem, that he'd call you tonight after his meetings."

Annie rubbed her forehead. "I needed to talk to him."

"Anything urgent?"

"Financial stuff." Annie looked away. "You know."

"If you need to talk, I'm available. I've become something of an expert on dealing with unplanned stress."

His voice had a husky quality that made the hair rise on Annie's neck. "No need, but thanks for the offer."

"In that case, how about a massage?"

Annie was trying to come up with a polite way to refuse when Sam's strong fingers circled her neck and shoulders, then fanned out over her back.

Heaven.

"No, thanks," she mumbled. But her head tilted, giving him better access to her aching shoulders.

Laughing, Sam moved closer, framing her spine and working back up again.

"You're pretty good," Annie said grudgingly.

"It pays to learn from the best. Lift your arm."

She complied without thought, feeling him slide in behind her and turn her gently. Her body melted under his careful kneading, muscle by muscle turning hot and loose beneath his hands.

Those same hands were doing hot, fluttery things to her stomach. If she hadn't been so nauseated she might have jumped him.

"Feeling better?" he whispered.

"Ummm."

"How's the nausea?"

"Down to seriously unpleasant. Nice job."

"Always glad to be of service." Annie felt his lips brush her forehead. "Great hair." His fingers moved around her waist, working small, intoxicating circles of absolute pleasure.

Suddenly she stiffened as she felt his palms skim across her breasts.

In a second, her insides were mush. Desire skittered wildly, leaving her dry mouthed and edgy. She turned her head, staring up at Sam.

His smile was wicked. "Anything else you'd like? I'm feeling like a whole new man, thanks to you."

Annie swallowed back the gut answer. Dragging him down onto the kitchen table for blind, abandoned sex was probably not her best life choice right now.

Even if it *was* incredibly tempting.

"Anything you want, just name it," he murmured, feathering the exquisitely tender skin behind her ear. "I'm open to suggestions."

She resisted the urge to tear off his sweat pants and pin him to the floor. That qualified as another unwise life choice.

She cleared her throat. "M-more coffee," she rasped.

His eyes darkened. "Chicken."

Damned right, she thought. Besides, she probably had repulsive hangover breath.

She closed her eyes as he did something with his fingers that had her pulse spiking. Pleasure zones were surging to life all over her body, her hangover nearly forgotten. "Hey, I'm still in a subhuman condition here."

"You don't look subhuman. You've got the sexiest shoulders." Her robe inched downward. "Nice definition in your upper arms. Not much, but just right. Amazingly sexy."

"It's from the m-massage work I do." The floor was looking better every moment.

"It's a major turn-on." He kissed one shoulder, then the other, nipping lightly with his teeth. "Makes me want to see a whole lot more."

Annie swallowed hard. Maybe she should forget about aiming for wise life choices. The kitchen floor was looking irresistible, especially when Sam kissed the hollow at her shoulder, stroking gently with his tongue. Who knew a shoulder could be so sensitive?

She yelped when she heard Izzy call out from the living room. "Whenever you two are done in there, I could use some help."

"Go away," Sam called thickly. "We're busy."

Annie opened her eyes and discovered that he was studying a major expanse of cleavage exposed beneath her robe. Her face flaming, she jerked her robe back in place and lurched to her feet. "What are you, some kind of undocumented Third World virus? I'm around you five minutes and I lose all semblance of sanity."

Sam grinned, looking immensely pleased at the compliment. Except that it was supposed to be an insult.

"It's your call," he said in that same sexy whisper that turned her insides hot and slick.

"Not interested." One of her bigger lies, Annie thought.

"Maybe you could find some of that lavender body lotion. I'd rub it in very carefully. Anywhere you wanted."

Her heart took a sharp left turn into the insanity zone. "N-no thanks."

"You sure about that?"

"Absolutely."

His grin widened. Annie followed his glance downward. It was centered on the front of her robe where her nipples stood outlined, dark and tight and clearly aroused.

"Make one comment and you're toast."

His mouth twitched.

"Not one, understand? I'm getting dressed." Annie lurched toward the door.

"Aren't you forgetting one thing?"

Her mind, Annie thought. But she wasn't about to admit that. She didn't turn around. "Like what?"

He was behind her before she knew it, tall, dark, and absolutely dangerous. "I was thinking we could start right about here."

Chapter Twenty-five

ANNIE COULDN'T MOVE, COULDN'T BREATHE. "START WITH what?"

His mouth settled on hers, pulling out a sigh. Biting gently, he drew her closer, and as he did, his hands slipped inside her robe.

The Puccini and kettledrums faded, replaced by Eric Clapton and a throbbing guitar solo.

Oh, boy.

Annie's brain fogged, and she sank against his hard body, giving her mouth over to the smooth glide of the kiss, the practiced slip of his hands.

When she came up for air, she was horrified to find her robe making its way toward her waist. "We can't do this."

He nuzzled her ear. "Why?"

"Izzy's out there, for one thing."

"To hell with Izzy. To hell with the whole U.S. government." He pulled away far enough to look into her eyes, his face grave. "I've thought about this since I heard your voice in the darkness the first night I came here."

Not the first night, Annie thought.

A lie.

What happened when he realized it was a lie?

He stroked her shoulder, his lips tracing the little hollow near her collarbone. She shivered at the warmth of his mouth, the exquisite tenderness of his touch.

Suddenly her sensible, practical life choices were fading fast.

"Sam, I—"

"God, you're beautiful. When your voice goes husky like that, I can't see straight." His fingers eased over her hips, drawing her against his locked thighs. "I want to be inside you, Annie. I want it slow and long."

The words had her head spinning. So did his callused fingers as they slid over her aroused breasts.

When she didn't answer, he drew her hair from her cheek and studied her gravely. "Any thoughts about that?"

She took a hard breath. "I want a lot of things, Sam. A red Ferrari. A week in Paris. A private tour of the White House. That doesn't mean I get to have them."

His mouth curved. "I'm better than a red Ferrari. Better than Paris. Believe me."

She did believe him, and that made matters worse. Right now everything about him made her think of sex. She closed her eyes as he nuzzled her jaw. How did the man reduce her to mush this way?

"There are rules, Sam. This probably breaks them all."

His eyes were dark, hungry. "We're adults, we're both free. Anything else is irrelevant."

"But you—"

On the desk beside them the phone rang. Their eyes locked, and neither one moved.

"You're going to have to face this thing that's happening between us sometime," Sam said hoarsely. "We both are."

The phone continued to ring.

Annie sighed and pulled away.

"Let it ring."

"I can't. It could be a problem at the resort." She swept up the phone. "Yes?"

There was a slight pause. "Oops. Hope I'm not interrupting anything."

Taylor.

Annie gripped the phone, trying to focus as Sam kissed the sensitive curve of her ear. "N-nothing major."

"You sound out of breath. Still hungover?"

Annie cleared her throat, hiking up the sleeve of her robe. "More or less. What was in that drink you gave me—besides hemlock?"

"I'll give you the recipe when you're not feeling nauseous. Is your friend still there?"

Annie closed her eyes as Sam drew her back in his arms. "My friend?"

"The one with the eyes that don't miss anything. And the cute butt," Taylor added helpfully.

Annie swallowed. "He's here." And he was nibbling on her earlobe in a way that would soon have her begging for mercy. "But you've never heard of him, understand?"

"Sure, whatever. I just wanted to be sure you weren't suffering from whiplash or something."

She was suffering all right. Any minute she might tear off her robe and slide right down onto the floor, throwing her heart away on a man she barely knew.

For a second time.

Annie took a shaky breath. "I'll survive the whiplash. The hangover's a little uncertain."

"I told you to go easy on the scotch."

His expression unreadable, Sam skimmed his knuckles over her chin. Without a word, he turned and brushed lightly across the tips of her breasts.

Her breath caught hard.

"You okay, Annie?"

"Fine." *Terrible.* "G-great." *Crazy.* "But I have to go. I need to get dressed. I need—"

Sam. Naked and inside her.

It *had* to be the hangover, Annie told herself as his lips replaced his hands, sliding over her breasts with a slow, patient intensity that missed nothing.

Annie bit back a gasp. Her robe slid lower. She almost dropped the phone, but Sam caught it and held it to her ear.

"Talk," he whispered. "Don't stop on my account."

Annie covered the receiver. "Stop," she whispered. "I can't think straight when you—"

"I don't want you thinking straight," he said hoarsely. "I want you out of your mind, just as hot as I am." His eyes were glinting as he kissed his way down the center of her robe, opening it slowly.

"Annie, are you all right?"

"What? Oh, I'm fine, Taylor. Maybe a little hot. From the hangover. Like that," she said breathlessly.

"You don't sound okay. I'll see you later for a massage."

"Taylor, I don't have time for—"

"You *never* have time. That's why I booked us for three o'clock."

Desire was blurring Annie's vision. "But I—"

"In the meantime, don't do anything I wouldn't do. Fortunately, that leaves you a whole lot of ground to cover." Taylor laughed softly. "And you can tell *that* to your friend with the cute butt when he's finished kissing you."

"Who said—"

"*Such* an innocent." Taylor was laughing as the line went dead.

"Well?"

Annie gripped the phone irritably. "Well what?"

"The call. Your sister, I take it?" Sam set the phone back in its cradle. "Sounds like she doesn't miss much. She won't talk, will she?"

"You can trust her. She knows this is important." Annie frowned. "That doesn't mean she won't waylay me and demand details."

Sam nudged the belt of her robe. "Maybe we should work on that. Who knows, we might even make it into one of her books."

"Forget it." Annie was thinking again, and she wasn't liking what she saw. She couldn't afford to succumb to his charm again while the situation was so complicated—and her own emotions so raw. "I have to go."

"You can't keep running, Annie."

"Who's running?"

"You are. We both know it. But when you stop, I'm going to be here waiting. Just remember that."

Irritated, she tugged her belt from his fingers. "Very smooth. I bet that line gets all your women flustered, panting to fall into your bed."

"You're the only one I want."

"Probably because I'm the only one who ever said no."

"You're wrong." His finger traced her check. "But I won't push you. For now. And you'd better hurry, because your assistant called. You're supposed to introduce the spa cuisine demonstration, and it begins in . . ." He glanced down at his watch. "In eight and a half minutes."

Annie stifled an oath. How could she have forgotten? "I'll never make it now." She jammed a hand through her wayward hair, then caught the dress Sam tossed to her.

"I found this in your closet. Your shoes are over by the couch. Get going, Doc."

"But my—"

Two pieces of lingerie came hurtling her way.

I can do this, Annie thought grimly. "Turn around," she ordered.

With a shrug, Sam turned. Annie dropped the robe and yanked on panties, camisole, and dress, then jammed the buttons closed, her eyes on the red wall clock.

Six minutes.

She straightened her collar. "I need my—"

Her brush landed beside her on the couch.

"Thanks."

"My pleasure."

Annie smoothed her hair, swept up her purse from the desk. Five minutes.

"All done. I'm out of here." She rolled her shoulders. "Minutes to spare."

Sam was smiling broadly when he turned around to study the finished effect.

"What's wrong?"

"Your shoes."

Annie looked down. She was wearing one red sandal and one leopard-print pump. "It's a fashion statement," she snapped.

Sam continued to smile.

"So who's stressed?"

"Not you. No, ma'am."

"Then what's so funny?"

"Not a blessed thing." Sam tossed her the other sandal, then opened the door. "You've got four minutes left, Doc. Go knock 'em dead."

❖ ❖ ❖

THE COOKING DEMONSTRATION WAS A HUGE HIT.

Annie sat back with a sigh, watching Zoe orchestrate a four-course gourmet meal for twelve executive men and women who were one step closer to living a healthy, stress-free life, thanks to exercise instructions, gourmet recipes, and a sample of her lavender-glow kelp-and-marine-salt scrub for face and body.

But the only body Annie had in mind was lean, six foot four and drop-dead fabulous.

Right now that body was adding dangerously to her own stress level.

Smiling, she shook the last hand, and passed out the last sample of Summerwind Sea and Sand Body Glow. As she did, she tried not to think about the man in her casita who made her own body glow outrageously.

"I have one question, Ms. O'Toole." The guest was trim and

stylish in purple capris, pink sandals, and a leopard-print turban. Her white hair was impeccable, and she didn't look a day over sixty, though Annie knew she was closing in on eighty. "Yes, Ms. Sanderson."

"Coco, please. I liked what you said about finding the moment and staying with it. But it's not always easy, is it?"

"If it were easy, there wouldn't be monasteries in Asia filled with people trying to get it right."

"I suppose not." The woman nodded slowly. "Well, my question concerns sex. Are you for or against?"

Annie crossed her arms, watching the guests crowd around Zoe and her amazing grilled salmon with corn relish and organic basil vinaigrette. The dishes smelled heavenly, but Annie wished the dry taste in her mouth would go away. After four hours, it was all that remained of her hangover. Or maybe it was the remains of Taylor's hangover remedy. "Are we being theoretical here, Coco?"

The tiny woman in purple stared out at the sea lions in the bay. "Sex is never theoretical. My first husband told me that the night we met, and he was right. I was in the chorus in a revival of *Mame* on Broadway. Frank was escorting a dozen shipping millionaires from Osaka. I still remember that flutter when he looked at me." She turned back from the window. "Five husbands, six children, twenty-one grandchildren, and I still remember Frank and that first amazing flutter."

Annie waited, trying to figure out the question. "A flutter is good."

"It's good when you're twenty. It's not so good when you're sixty-three. Well, actually I'm seventy-nine, but that's no one's business."

Annie heard the polite warning and smiled. "Damned straight. My lips are sealed."

Coco tilted her head. "I like you, Ms. O'Toole."

"Call me Annie, please."

Coco nodded. "With pleasure. I won't take up much of your time, since I can see you're a busy professional woman dealing with her own points of stress."

Was she ever, Annie thought. But the guest always came first. "Take your time."

The slender woman looked out the window some more. "I've had five husbands. You'd think that would be enough." She fingered her bracelet, a hammered slide of gold and platinum that probably cost about a mouth's stay at the resort. "But someone came into my life. My family thinks I'm crazy, and my friends are aghast, but he makes me feel it all again. The flutter, you know?"

Annie knew *all* about the flutter. She was starting to wish she didn't. "That sounds wonderful."

Coco nodded, her eyes still on the seagulls. "That's what I thought at first, but why should I have all that again? My life is calm, well ordered. I've got friends, family, responsibilities. He makes me feel like I'm twenty, and I'm not even talking about the sex, which is absolutely amazing." She fingered the bracelet, frowning. "He's fifty-four, Annie. Not much older than my son." Her eyes clouded. "He says we could have ten good years, maybe more. I love him, but at my age, why should I jump off that cliff again?"

Annie tried to come up with an answer. "Because you're alive. Because you've got things to learn and share. And because it's a pretty amazing cliff when you find it." Annie's lips twitched. "And because the sex is stupendous."

Coco laughed, a smooth ripple of sound. "Indeed, it is." She stood some more, her brow wrinkled. "Relationships 101. I wonder if we ever learn all the lessons."

Annie searched through her bag and pulled out a book. "This might help."

The woman scanned the foiled title. "*Thirty Days to a Stress-Free Sex Life*. It better not take any longer or I might not be around for the last chapter."

"I have a feeling you're going to outlive all of us."

Coco patted her turban and smiled. "I'm definitely going to try. And I appreciate the book. The next thirty days should be most invigorating. I had a feeling you could help, because you know how it is."

"I do?"

"The flutter. The zing." The tiny woman nodded. "I saw it when you rushed in this morning. The way you carried yourself, trying not to look distracted. Smiling when you thought we weren't watching."

Am I that transparent? Annie wondered.

"Yes, this is the tricky time, isn't it?" Coco cradled the book. "The tricky time when sex turns to something more. Watch yourself, Annie. Remember, that first step is amazing, but it's a long way down to earth."

Chapter Twenty-six

WHAT WAS IT ABOUT SEX?

Annie drummed her fingers on her cluttered desk. Good sex was unpredictable, time-consuming, and often messy, and it grabbed you by the jugular when you least expected.

Not sex, a voice whispered.

Love.

Annie stiffened.

No way. Not a chance.

Zippo.

Love was *not* involved here, not in a thousand years. All she and Sam had was a volatile chemistry, an arresting physical awareness.

And the sex *had been* amazing, Annie thought, feeling that familiar zing.

But it wasn't love or anything close. She had her resort, her career, her friends, and Sam had his own demanding career. This chemistry between them was going nowhere beyond a few pleasant hours in bed.

But a quiet voice intruded. *What if there could be more? Plenty of people manage to mix careers with full private lives.*

Suddenly Annie wanted all that. She wanted to be like Coco Sanderson, with memories of a rich, full life. With a house full of photographs instead of a full Rolodex and calendar full of business meetings with people she barely knew and hardly liked.

Annie closed her eyes. She had a thousand things to do. She didn't have time to be indecisive and moody while she obsessed over the merits of recreational sex. Fantasies were lovely, but this was daylight. She had decisions, responsibilities, and a resort to manage.

And no matter what she decided, Sam would be gone in a matter of weeks.

She simply *wasn't* going to tumble into an affair. She wouldn't put her heart up for target practice a second time.

There was a tap on her door. "Buzz called," Annie's assistant said. "So did your sister. I left a phone slip there on your desk."

"Sorry, they're lost beneath the last batch of supplier files. Who knew that finding a source for rosemary and lavender essential oils could be so difficult?"

Her assistant frowned. "Well, you'd better call Taylor back. She sounded edgy."

"Taylor always sounds edgy. It's that writer thing."

"No, she was worried about you. She wanted to be sure you don't sneak out and miss your three o'clock appointment."

"I'm not sneaking anywhere, don't worry."

"You also had a call from a reporter for the *San Francisco Chronicle*. She wants to do a lifestyle piece on the resort. New answers to old problems, that kind of thing. She sounded smart."

Annie shook her head. "You know the rule, Megan. No publicity. People pay to come here to get away from all that. Tell her the usual. We appreciate the interest from such a fine publication, etc., etc."

"I think you're making a mistake." Megan's voice grew firmer. "The right kind of publicity would be priceless, especially with this new line of body products."

Annie considered it. "If she calls again, get her name and number and tell her we'll be in touch."

"But—"

"Thanks, Megan. I know you'll handle it gracefully. Then why don't you break for lunch?"

No publicity was her parents' policy, and Annie meant to

maintain it. She'd launch her new spa products strictly by private mailings and word of mouth, then see what happened.

Annie rubbed her eyes. She'd hit a few more files before she took a break for lunch herself.

She was elbow deep in lavender sachets when the phone rang. With Megan at lunch, Annie took the call, muttering when it turned out to be someone trying to sell a time share in Aruba.

After pouring a fresh cup of oolong tea, she pulled out a new batch of lavender samples, some from as far away as England and France. Pricey, but quality counted. Given the competition in high-end beauty products, Annie knew her line had to be smarter, fresher, and more effective to have a chance at success.

She jumped as the phone rang again.

"No, I'm *not* interested in a time share in Aruba."

There was a moment of silence. "Why not?" It was Buzz Kozinski.

Annie drew a slow breath. "Sorry, Buzz. Just some back and forth with a pushy salesman."

"You want to borrow my gun for a few hours?"

Annie could almost see the grin on his calm, ruddy face. "I smell a trick question here."

"No trick. I've had my fill of pushy phone solicitors, too. Only thing worse are their pushy lawyers."

Annie thought of Tucker Marsh and suppressed a shudder. "No argument there. But I'll pass on the gun rental, Buzz, kind as it is. What can I do for you?"

A chair creaked. "I've been thinking about that fire alarm. Did you have the units checked out?"

"It was a short in the fuse box. One of the repairmen must have mangled the wiring."

"No other problems?"

"Just an obnoxious lawyer and a bad-tempered whirlpool."

"Is the lawyer a guest?"

"Afraid so."

"Anything you need my help for?"

Annie was sorely tempted to lay out the problem for a sympathetic listener, but she resisted the urge. *The buck stops here*, her grandma had said, long before Truman hit the White House. "It's nothing, Buzz. I appreciate your support, but I'll handle it."

"You sure? You want to make a complaint, I'll be there in ten minutes."

"Thanks, but I was just letting off steam. It's been one of those days." And the hangover hadn't helped.

"I know all about those days. Matter of fact, I just picked up a shoplifter over at the Stop 'n Buy. He stole some lighter fluid and set fire to the mayor's car. Claimed she was in league with the Russian mafia, and they've been abducting people and selling their organs to wealthy Arab oil sheiks."

"Interesting theory." Annie frowned. "The mayor's okay, I hope?"

"Just fine. Unfortunately, her black BMW is toast."

"And I thought *my* day was bad."

Out of the corner of her eye, Annie saw her door open. Suddenly her day got a whole lot worse. Tucker Marsh strode toward her, his eyes small and mean. "I want to talk to you."

"I'm on the phone, but I'll—"

He crossed his arms. *"Now."*

"I believe you'll have to make an appointment, Mr. Marsh."

"Forget an appointment." He watched her with predatory intensity as he moved around the desk. "It was bad enough when I couldn't get a decent meal. Now I can't book a massage or get private exercise training. Everyone claims to be busy."

Because she had warned them to provide no private services to Marsh until further notice.

Annie pushed to her feet, her heart pounding.

"I'll be with you in a second, Buzz." She put down the phone, studying Marsh coolly. "You were told when you registered that services would be scaled back this week. You do remember, don't you?"

"I remember every word." Marsh leaned over the desk. "Your services are inadequate. I expect a complete refund."

Annie had the sudden sense he had done this before. He probably considered it a pleasant game to bluster his way out of paying for his vacations.

She picked up an onyx letter opener and tapped it against her wrist, letting him wait for an answer.

"Well?" he snapped.

"Your money will not be refunded. If you choose to leave early, we will cancel the bill for any remaining days."

"You must be nuts. I'm going take you apart in court. When I'm finished you won't be able to *pay* people to come to Summerwind."

"Is that a threat?" Annie asked, her voice like silk.

Marsh leaned over the table and caught her arm. "What the hell do you think?"

"I think that you've had your way too often. If you pursue this course of action, I'll release the sworn complaints of women whom you have harassed and intimidated. I will add my own complaint to those."

His fingers tightened. "Big talk. But that's all it is."

Annie pointed up to the security camera, which was directed at her desk. "I wonder how your outburst will look on video in the courtroom." She pushed away his hand. "I expect I'll have bruises here in the morning. Those should look interesting on film, too."

Unnerved, Marsh glanced up at the camera. "You can't videotape without a posted notice."

"It's right beside the outer door. I suppose you were too intent on threatening me to see it."

He moved away, smoothing down his windbreaker, already playing to the camera. "Naturally I'm upset. I'm seriously dissatisfied with your services. I intend to register a complaint with the state tourism board as soon as I get back."

Annie studied him coldly. "Harassment in any form is not only unethical but illegal. I think I'll discover you have a pattern of such behavior."

Marsh moved from foot to foot, and Annie could see his jaw twitch. "What are you suggesting?"

"That you've done this kind of thing before, Mr. Marsh."

"That's bulls—" He glanced up at the camera. "Baloney," he snapped. The arrogance surged back. "You should be worrying about your defense in court."

Annie clicked her tongue. "Should I? Lawsuits are unpleasant and expensive." Her voice fell, confiding. "I think I'll make a few calls and check out how many other times you've done this. It should look nice in my file."

Marsh's hands opened and closed as he stared at her. "You won't find a thing."

"Let's see." Annie reached for the phone. "And now I'm going to finish my call."

She was trembling when he stormed out, trembling so much that it took several seconds to hear Buzz's voice.

"Stay put. I'm coming right over. No one can talk to you that way."

Annie sank into her chair, shaken. "I can handle this, Buzz."

"I heard enough to know he threatened you. I can bring him in and question him. I figure I can hold him for at least a few hours."

"He's a pro at this and I need more ammunition before I take him on. But I hope you'll be a witness, if this comes to trial."

"You've got it." There was a long silence. "I hear Taylor's golf cart got pretty banged up last night."

"You heard about that?"

"People love to talk. Any particular reason Taylor's golf cart got banged up?"

"We were a little drunk." Way more than a little, Annie thought.

"You sure you're okay?"

"Just fine. It was one of those sister things." Make that twenty-seven years of buried sibling rivalry, Annie thought. A hangover was a small price to pay for purging years of painful misunderstanding.

"Well, if you decide to run Attila the Hun in for an afternoon behind bars, it would be my pleasure to oblige. Consider *that* a sheriff thing." He was silent for a few moments. "Did you really get him on camera?"

Annie smiled faintly. "No. That camera hasn't worked in three months. But Marsh doesn't know that—and he never will."

Chapter Twenty-seven

ANNIE HAD JUST GONE BACK TO MAKING FILES OF HERB SAMPLES when she heard the sharp click of stiletto heels.

Today Taylor was wearing black leather pants, a leopard-print sweater, and black alligator ankle boots with four-inch heels. "Amazing. I actually found you."

"The MTV awards are on the other side of the hall," Annie said.

"Very funny. Let's go."

"Look, Taylor, I'm buried here. I can't possibly—"

"*Now,* ace. Otherwise I'll call in the marines."

Annie's eyes narrowed. "What marines?"

"The one with the cute butt. With that body, if he's not a marine, he's something close, so don't bother lying."

Annie sat back with a sigh. "You're impossible."

"Only when it's necessary."

"I have to be back in an hour."

"Two."

Annie tapped two fingers on her desk. "One and a half."

Taylor smiled. "Three. You work too damned hard."

Annie reviewed her day. Hangover. Temporary insanity with Sam. Another confrontation with Tucker Marsh. Hardly a stellar success so far. Probably an hour break couldn't make matters any worse.

And she definitely needed to relax. If she could relax, she might be able to forget about Sam.

About his incredible body, his amazing hands.

About that skillful mouth and how it drove her crazy.

Earth to Mars! No more thinking about the man in her casita. She closed her files with a snap. "Let's go."

❖ ❖ ❖

HE SAT IN THE DARKNESS, CRADLING A COLD FOSTER'S, DEAFENED
by the energetic wail of a singer in a red cowboy hat with
rhinestones the size of golf balls.

He hated country music, but his contacts always set the
meet location via pager with no callback number. Each time, a
different place.

Never a place like this though.

All he could do was sit and sweat, watching dancers shuffle
past and wishing he could cover his ears.

Another drink of beer.

Another glance at his watch.

Someone ambled past on his right, a little too close and too
fast. He relaxed when a waitress in pink cowboy boots bent
down beside him. "A call for you, sir."

He nodded. He had been contacted by different people over
the last year, some men and some women, but never in person.
Their voices were always digitally altered, but over time he
could recognize differences. Today's caller was one he'd heard
several times recently. A powerful person, you could tell that
from the way he spoke.

Someone used to giving orders, not taking them.

"Did you get a fix on that item we discussed?" His contact's
voice was sharper than usual.

The man at the table frowned. "It's some kind of locker key,
just like you thought. I tried National and Dulles, but no
match."

"What about Union Station?"

"No good. They changed to all-plastic keys two years ago.
Most other places have phased out their public lockers for security reasons."

His waitress came back with a new drink, and he paid with
a smile, which faded as soon as he was alone again.

His contact went on curtly. "It has to be somewhere in the

downtown area. We had McKade under constant surveillance before he jumped on that school bus."

He remembered that day all too well. Every plan shot to bits in minutes.

He sat back, frowning at the country singer who was wailing on the narrow stage. "Except for the time he was in the men's room at the Federal Triangle Metro station. What if he slipped out a window?"

There was a long silence. "You mean that he could have dropped something off nearby, then hustled back."

The man at the table fiddled with his drink. "That's what I came up with. It's a long shot, but I made some calls and found out they still have employee lockers at the Old Post Office. It's a short walk from there to the Federal Triangle station."

"Check it out." The order was curt.

First things first, the man at the table thought. "What about my money?"

"Same place. The deposit will be made in the usual amount. If you find that locker in two days, the payment will be tripled."

The line went dead.

Tripled.

He put down the phone and stood up, tossing an extra bill on the table for the waitress. The money had been good before, but now it was incredible. If he had to take some risks, so what?

He smiled at the singer with the red cowboy hat on his way out.

❖ ❖ ❖

SAM WAS SWEATING HARD, CURLING A THIRTY-POUND WEIGHT with his good arm and trying not to think about Annie. He especially didn't want to imagine the soft curves hidden beneath her silk robe. About the heat of her skin and the husky rasp she'd made when he'd leaned into her and nuzzled her breasts.

He nearly dropped the weight.

Damn it all anyway.

Cursing, he pulled the weight onto his chest and began doing sit-ups, ignoring the dull ache at his left shoulder.

"Better slow down, McKade. That makes forty."

"It doesn't count until you hit two hundred," Sam said irritably.

"That was then, this is now." Izzy tossed him a bottle of water. "You're in rehab, not BUD/S, remember? Take five."

Sam sank onto his side, frowning. Annie had left over an hour ago, but he couldn't think of anything else. Hell, he could almost smell that soft perfume she wore, mixed with the apple scent of her shampoo.

She didn't go for makeup or daring clothes. Not much in the way of jewelry either. She dressed for comfort and ease, since she was always on the move.

He liked that.

He could imagine her leading a tai chi class or demonstrating water aerobics in the outdoor pool. He mused on that for a while, certain she wouldn't go for a thong or some ridiculously miniscule bikini.

Too bad.

He suspected that Annie was nothing like his usual choice of companion. He had a sense that he preferred women who showed their assets in tight spandex and probably laughed more than they should. Then again, having deep conversations in bed didn't seem like something that was high on his agenda.

Until Annie.

He enjoyed talking with her as much as he enjoyed touching her, and that was saying a lot, considering that he wanted to touch her every second he was awake.

But he also liked the way her eyes carried a challenge and her laugh rippled softly in her throat, building until it poured out in a husky rush.

Even her laugh left him rock hard.

With a grimace, he headed for the big Swiss exercise ball. If he was lucky, a few dozen leg lifts might clear this haze of painful lust.

But probably not.

Chapter Twenty-eight

ANNIE SIGHED. "FINE, TAYLOR. BUT TWO HOURS, TOPS. I'VE STILL got the payroll to finish."

"Forget about the payroll." Taylor pointed her to the door. "You have more important things to worry about than money."

"Like what?"

"Sex, power, and lingerie." She gave Annie a despairing look. "Your underwear has the sexual punch of a peanut butter sandwich."

"We can't *all* dress like Madonna." Grumbling, Annie followed Taylor down the hall. "Where are we going?"

"You'll see."

They passed Megan and the chef, who were both smiling broadly. Clearly they were in on Taylor's plan, whatever it was.

"What's this all about?" Annie hissed.

Taylor pushed open the door to the therapy rooms. "If you're going to have an affair, you have to do it right."

"Who said anything about an affair?"

Taylor shook her head. "So naive. As if you could fool your sister. Now be quiet and pay attention." She turned the sign on the door so it read Closed, and bustled inside. "To have an affair, you've got to learn to relax."

Annie crossed her arms. "Who said I—"

"Don't insult my intelligence by denying that it's on your mind." Taylor opened the glass door to the outdoor pool, where steam rose gently over heated salt water. "Lesson number one: build a mood." She swept her Louis Vuitton bag down onto a deck chair. Annie knew the bag dated back ten years to Taylor's first trip to Paris. It was her most prized possession, after her computer and an amazing black leather jacket she'd picked up for a song in Florence.

Taylor took out a plastic bag and scattered rose petals over the water. "Color and fragrance spur the imagination, and imagination is all.

"Lesson number two." She reached back into the bag and held up a pair of cotton mitts. "Exfoliating gloves. Trust me, he's going to loooove the feel of your skin after these. Now for lesson three."

"Heavy animal tranquilizers?"

"Very funny." Taylor pulled out a shallow glass bowl, set it on the tile near the pool and filled it carefully with water. After that she lit six small candles and floated them in the water, scattering a final handful of rose petals between the drifting candles. "You're good to everyone else. Now it's time to be good to yourself."

Annie stared, on the verge of tears. "You planned this all for me?"

"You have a problem with that?"

Annie shook her head. "I don't know what to say."

"Just say thank you and smile. I'm allowed to take care of my best sister." Taylor frowned. "Especially when she's being an idiot and working herself to death, oblivious to the hunk standing in her kitchen."

"He's a client, Taylor." Annie had been trying hard to remember that.

"Like *that* makes a difference. When the man looked at you, I could feel the recoil all the way across the porch." Taylor took a deep breath. "If you're worried about making time, I'll even fill in for a couple of days."

"*You?*"

"Don't act so shocked. I worked the resort from the ground up, remember? Mom and Dad saw to it that I put in my three summers as a fitness coordinator. I used to be damned good at motivating the guests."

Annie couldn't speak. For Taylor, this was the supreme sacrifice. "You'd do that for me?"

"An offer is an offer. Just don't take too long deciding, or I might change my mind. I'm starting to feel faint at my generosity already." She dug to the bottom of her bag. "And don't go all giddy on me, because there's one more item of business. Your lingerie has *got* to go."

Annie tugged at her white camisole, outlined beneath the top of her knit dress. "What's wrong with my underwear?"

"You want a list?"

"Sorry, Taylor. I appreciate the offer, but I'm just not a black lace kind of woman. I don't own any push-up bras or fishnet stockings."

"About time we changed that." Taylor had a wicked gleam in her eyes. "Especially since you're one of the few people I know with the body to wear that kind of stuff." She tossed a bag at Annie. "Go change."

Annie pulled out a scrap of black lace, hardly big enough to cover the essential areas dictated by civil code. "No way."

"Try something else."

Annie reached in the bag again, pulling out a feathered and beaded bra in gleaming satin. "This?"

"Trust me, he'll go nuts when he sees you."

Annie shook her head and delved in once more, hoping for something more sedate. Instead she found a scrap of snakeskin spandex. Confused, she turned it right and left, up and then down. "I don't understand. How does it go? There are too many openings."

Taylor sighed. "You are *such* an innocent." She held up the spandex underwear. "They go like this."

Annie flushed slightly. "You mean—"

"Yeah. They're great with the fishnet stockings. He'll be begging for mercy."

"I really don't think—"

Taylor pointed toward the dressing room. "Go try them on. The red thong might be a little much, but give it a go."

Red thong?

Annie looked into the bag, feeling slightly faint. "What's wrong with white cotton?"

"Nothing—if you're having a slumber party with five of your twelve-year-old girlfriends. For crying out loud, you're twenty-seven, Annie. It's time to let things rip a little. Every item in that bag is guaranteed to be Big O material. Trust me, he'll go berserk, and what woman doesn't want to make a man crazy sometimes?"

Put that way, there was some tortured logic to what Taylor was saying. Annie felt a little flutter in her chest at the mere thought of Sam's hot gaze running over her.

Then his hands.

Then that hot, clever mouth.

"Fine, I'll try them. But this stays strictly between us. It doesn't go into any book."

"Of course not. My lips are sealed. Not a word."

After Annie disappeared into the changing room, Taylor frowned. "On the other hand," she mused, "this could make a fabulous opening for chapter six." She pursed her lips. "With the right details changed, of course."

As clothes fell to the floor behind the door, Taylor considered the idea. "Don't forget to try the red lace," she called out thoughtfully.

❖ ❖ ❖

SAM PUT DOWN HIS DUMBBELL, WINCING. HIS SHOULDER WAS ON fire and his leg felt like a truck had run over it. Day after day he was pushing hard, fighting to get back up to speed, but he still hadn't remembered anything significant. The specialists said he would remember with time.

But how *much* time?

When Izzy signaled Sam to take a secure call a few minutes later, Admiral Howe didn't seem to be too pleased with the situation, either.

"Slow down the rehab schedule," the admiral ordered. "I don't want to see you back in a hospital bed."

Sam grunted.

"I'm not hearing you, McKade."

"Yes, sir. I won't push too much." Like hell he wouldn't.

"What have you found about those fire alarms?"

"Izzy's still checking, but it appears to be defective wiring."

"The problem is recent?"

"Yes, sir."

"Keep an eye on that. I never have believed in coincidences." The admiral cleared his throat. "How are you getting along with Ms. O'Toole?"

Sam rubbed his shoulder irritably. "She's doing her job, and I'm doing mine."

Sam could almost see the admiral's raised brow. "No problems of any sort?"

"No problems." *In a pig's eye.*

"Izzy says she's good, and he's damned particular about who he praises."

"She knows all the moves. Except for my knee, my lower-body recovery is about 90 percent. Of course this blasted shoulder is a different matter entirely."

"Stay with it. That was one hell of a tumble you took." A little silence fell. "Remembered anything yet?"

"A flash here and there," Sam said tensely. "Nothing that holds still long enough to make sense."

"The trauma, coupled with your post-op medications, can make recovery unpredictable. Don't let it get you down."

"I feel like a piece of cardboard, sir. There's nothing I can connect with." Sam stared out at the gray surf. "Nothing that feels like *me*."

"There's another problem." Admiral Howe's voice hardened. "Someone broke into your apartment in Virginia."

Sam frowned. "Don't you have a surveillance team there?"

"Night and day. But he was allowed to pass."

Sam ran through the possibilities. "Because you wanted to see where he might lead you."

"That's the plan. Do you have any other clues that might help us in the meantime?"

Sam desperately wanted to say yes. He put one hand against the window, fighting to dredge up some detail out of his memory. As he stared at the gray water, he saw a flash of blurred images.

People. Noise and laughter. The glint of sunlight against silver. And through it all a sick stabbing in his stomach and a sense of betrayal.

He didn't have a clue what any of it meant.

"I can't remember anything else, sir. Sorry."

"The memories will come. Until then we wait." The admiral cleared his throat. "But we go by the book on this, understood? I'm the quarterback here and the play's in motion. You're to go by the book or we'll lose a whole lot more than yardage," he added grimly.

"Aye, aye, sir."

"Good. Now get back to work, Commander. No pain, no gain. Just stop short of putting yourself back into the hospital."

◆ ◆ ◆

ADMIRAL HOWE HUNG UP THE PHONE, THEN STOOD BY THE WINDOW, staring out at the Washington Monument in the distance.

He imagined Lincoln, grave and brooding in the twilight, with eyes that had seen the full pain of political betrayal and a country split in two. The image moved him, as it always did.

He turned away, studying the half dozen framed photos that were the only decoration on his oversize desk. He looked at them often while he worked, for they were his lifeline in a world where trust was nonexistent and lying was an art form. Sometimes it bothered him to see how well he'd come to fit into that world.

But it never bothered him for long. Duty was duty, after all. And business was business. He hadn't gotten to the top by being weak or indecisive.

He frowned as he picked up the photos, one by one. His wife with their youngest daughter, skiing in Vermont. His two Great Danes rolling in the snow. His son with his friends at their raucous graduation from prep school.

Finally he came to the edge of the desk and a shot of him and his two sons playing down-and-dirty football with Sam McKade at the family's sprawling estate in McLean. As he studied the photos one by one, memories slipped through his fingers like sand.

A hell of a thing not to be able to remember your own past. It was almost inconceivable to him. No wonder Sam McKade was edgy.

The admiral watched the flow of evening traffic, an angry beast scrambling along the Beltway. He didn't want to think how big a problem he was facing, but he was paid to think so he pulled out the surveillance photos taken in Alexandria. The federal agents on site had verified that the apartment had been entered and the key they had planted had been taken. The trap was laid.

Now they were assembling a full file on the man in the delivery van. Ex-army, he had a list of aliases and questionable skills that he occasionally sold to the highest bidder.

But they still hadn't reeled in the big fish.

Howe knew that the key was supposed to accomplish that.

He didn't like playing in the dark, but they seemed to have no choice as long as Sam's memory was blocked. He wondered again what information the SEAL had unearthed in Mexico while he was undercover. His reports had been uncharacteristically terse, deferring full details until their appointment in Washington.

An appointment that Sam had never kept, thanks to a runaway bus and a near-fatal act of heroism.

They had come so close to knowing everything about the network of greed and betrayal eating its way through the heart of the government and its armed services. But not close enough.

Not without Sam.

Howe picked up the phone and told his aide to call his driver. Staying here in this silent office to brood was pointless. He needed to relax, and he'd do that best at home in McLean. Being with his family always made him feel better, though he could never discuss the problems he carried home with him.

Later he'd contact Izzy and find out how things were *really* progressing out at the resort.

Chapter Twenty-nine

"HOW DO YOU LIKE THE CLOTHES?"

Annie tugged at the belt of her big terry robe. "Let's just say I can't believe people really wear this stuff. *Normal* people, that is."

Taylor waved a hand in front of Annie's face. "Hello? Welcome to the twenty-first century. Donna Reed doesn't live here anymore."

"Easy for you to say. You're not the one strapped in under here."

"The thong?"

"No way. That was giving me rug burn in very uncomfortable places."

"A minor drawback." Taylor shrugged. "But men love the stupid things."

"Then let the men wear them." Annie yanked her robe open. "This is the best of the lot, and I *still* feel ridiculous."

She held her robe stiffly, offering a glimpse of a red lace demibra with ultrasheer cups. The matching panties were held together by tiny strings at each hip.

"Not bad," Taylor mused.

Annie shot her an angry look. "I'm more out than in with this bra. I can't figure what's keeping it up."

"That's why they call it a miracle." Taylor crossed her arms smugly. "And because of the miracle it can work in your sex life."

"*What* sex life?"

"My point exactly."

"Maybe I don't want a sex life," Annie said glumly. "My life is already too complicated."

"Honey, *no* one's life is that complicated. You're going to knock him out. Now go put on the leopard bodysuit."

Annie returned to the dressing room, reluctance in every step. "If I catch pneumonia, you're footing my medical bill."

"You never get sick. It's disgusting how healthy you are." Taylor paced outside the door. "Did you know that some of the guests have a pool going on the identity of your visitor?"

"Maybe they should get a life," Annie called grumpily.

"For your information, the bets are currently running neck and neck. Half say you've smuggled Harrison Ford inside. The other half are putting their money on Brad Pitt."

A feather went flying over the dressing room door. "Aaaargh."

"Actually, your mystery man has a cuter butt than either of them. Hard eyes, but a cute butt," Taylor mused. "How's the leopardskin doing?"

The door opened, and Annie emerged in skintight spandex. One strap was twisted over her shoulder, the other was locked around her neck.

"Help."

"Stop wiggling." Taylor tugged the straps—which were actually formfitting sleeves—into place low on Annie's shoulders, then stood back to survey the effect. "Impressive. Or it would be if you'd stop twitching."

Annie peered at her image in the mirror. "I don't know, Taylor. It's incredibly revealing." She turned to one side and then the other, frowning.

"It doesn't show much skin."

"It doesn't need to. You can see everything else, because of the way it clings. I can't even wear any underwear."

"Better and better. Just sit back and watch him drool."

"He won't drool."

Taylor lowered the sleeves again and smiled lazily. "Wanna bet?"

Annie took another look at herself in the mirror. "I feel like a complete fool."

"You don't look like one. That's what matters." Taylor pushed her back toward the dressing room. "Go change. Next stop, a massage with those lovely hot stones. Then it's straight into the saltwater pool."

❖ ❖ ❖

SAM WAS HALFWAY TO THE SHOWER WHEN IT HIT HIM.

Easy, pal. It's here, right in front of you.

He didn't move, afraid any distraction would scatter the gossamer web of memory drifting at the edge of his mind.

A number?

A number that felt damned important to him?

The patterns started to unravel, and Sam cursed, afraid he couldn't hold them together. Looking up, he saw the sports jersey tossed over a chair in Annie's bedroom. He could make out the folded hem and the edge of the number.

He felt sweat brush his brow as he searched for a memory. He had a sudden flash of a man racing down the gridiron, arms outstretched.

Red and white. It had to be Joe Montana, Sam thought. No one else came close. After four Super Bowls, the man was a legend.

Then he saw a number, white on red, so clear he could touch it.

16.

Montana's winning number for the 49ers. What was it supposed to mean?

Sam's hands were unsteady and his mouth was dry, but he didn't let go of that precious thread. Maybe the number would mean something to the people back in D.C. Or maybe it was the colors that were important.

He pulled out the secure phone Izzy had given him and dialed grimly, cursing all the things he still couldn't remember.

❖ ❖ ❖

Mmmmm."

"You say something?"

"Not me."

Steam billowed over the granite tiles. Annie's head rested against a towel as hot salt water swirled over her while the ocean shimmered beneath her in a forty-mile expanse of blue glory.

They were outside steaming away their toxins in 102 degree water. According to Taylor, every ten minutes made their bodies one year younger. Annie figured she was just about to start elementary school. Her face was swathed in a chamomile-yogurt mask, cucumbers covered her eyes, and her muscular system was the consistency of hot tapioca.

Taylor gave a long sigh. "This is the life. Tell me again why we don't do this every day."

"Because we can't afford it."

"Says who? You can afford it because you're the owner. I can afford it because I'm a major shareholder and you'll give me deep discounts to stifle any shareholder dissent." Taylor pushed away a slice of cucumber and opened one eye hopefully. "Right?"

"Not if you keep pushing that trashy lingerie at me."

"It's for your own good. Wear it just once, and you'll see what I mean." Taylor's lips curved. "I'll expect a complete report afterward, of course."

"You're impossible."

"Thank you." Taylor raised one arm and stretched languorously, watching steam spiral around her. "If my life came with a sound track, I'd be humming along to Yanni right now."

"Better than listening to William Shatner sing 'Rocketman.'"

"'I'm not the man I used to be-e-e-e.'" Taylor rolled her eyes and made a gagging sound, which made them both laugh wildly. "What would your sound track be?" Taylor demanded abruptly.

"I'm too tired to think." Annie brushed at the water. "Maybe Enya. No, Eric Clapton. 'If I could change the world.'"

Taylor gave another sigh, studying the water with regret. "It's almost four. Too bad I have to go."

"Same here," Annie murmured. "Too bad."

The steam shimmered.

Neither of them moved.

"Do you ever wish you could start over?" Taylor asked gravely.

"As in wear diapers again?"

"Not that far back. Just a decade or so, when life started to get interesting." Taylor turned her hand and watched water slide down her fingers. "Back to, say, high school. Fall 1980s. Early Metallica."

"Not me. I hated high school. You were the one with all the dates and the boys who watched your every move."

"They were watching yours, too. You just didn't notice."

Annie sniffed. "No way." She shifted one of the cucumber slices.

"You always had your head in a book so you never saw." Taylor's eyes narrowed. "I, on the other hand, was the first one to stay out all night, the first one to sneak into the drive-in. I was always looking for the next big experience, even if it was a bad one."

"You really wish you could go back?"

Taylor shrugged. "I wish I'd slowed down and enjoyed things. If you charge headlong at the stream of life, you end up with windburn. Or shin splints. Or something." She shook her head. "On that obscure note, I'm leaving. I've got to go kill someone."

Smiling, Annie tossed her a towel. "Who gets it today?"

"A lawyer who's been two-timing his wife and his mistress.

He's also been skimming from his oh-so-proper Boston law firm."

"I like it." Annie thought about Tucker Marsh and his threats. "Just don't make it quick. Draw it out. Make him suffer."

"Is there something you need to tell me?"

Annie pulled on her terry robe. "Nothing that I can't handle."

"Remember, I'm here if you need me. Any and all details welcomed. Moral support dispensed as required." Taylor slid the towel over her shoulder. "There's always a chance I can work you into a book somewhere."

"Quote me and you're a dead woman."

"Hmmm."

Annie shook her head, well aware that warnings made no impression on Taylor, who was busy digging in her Vuitton bag. "Catch."

Something flew toward Annie. She caught it, frowning at a small foil square.

"Keep it. Use it," Taylor said.

"I don't—"

"You might. New century, new rules, love. A woman doesn't leave it to the man."

Annie blew out an irritated breath, then pocketed the foil square in her robe. She had an uncomfortable suspicion that Taylor had the mature approach, but Annie wasn't about to carry around a condom.

On the other hand, she wasn't going to leave it here for a guest to discover.

She watched Taylor toss beauty items into her designer bag. "Do you really need a pair of fake leather capri pants and three tubes of mascara with you at all times?"

"Faux, not fake. And the answer is yes. Absolutely. A woman's got to be prepared for all eventualities." She turned to give Annie a searching look. "Wear the red lace. He'll be crawling in five seconds."

◇   ◇   ◇

CLEANSED, GLISTENING, AND EXFOLIATED, ANNIE CROSSED the courtyard toward the kitchen, feeling like a new woman. The wind was picking up and her hair flew into her eyes. To the north she saw the sharp outline of lightning.

There was a sense of unreality about the unnatural darkness. Or maybe it was just her body, weightless and sleek from two incredible hours of pampering.

Only one unpleasant sight spoiled her rosy mood.

A workman was crouched near the new whirlpool, checking chemical readings in a test kit. Annie scowled at the familiar logo on his khaki uniform.

This was the fifth workman this week. If he told her there was *another* problem, she was going to rip the whirlpool out of the ground and send it back in little pieces. Nothing was worth *this* much aggravation.

Squinting into the wind, she stalked toward her unsuspecting target.

"Don't tell me it's overflowing again," she snapped.

The man jumped, nearly dropping his test kit. "Jeez, I didn't hear you back there."

"Sorry." Annie held out a hand. "I'm Ms. O'Toole, the manager. I hope you haven't found any more problems."

"Not so far." He squinted up at her behind his dark glasses. "Your chemistry looks fine. PH is normal and chlorine reads just in zone." He pulled a wrench from a big aluminum toolbox. "Your intake filters look cloudy, though. I thought I'd clean them out before I finished. Dirty pipes can be a bitch." He cleared his throat. "Begging your pardon."

Annie noticed a line of foam at the top of the pipe. "Could that be what's causing these maintenance problems?"

He scratched his neck slowly. "Might be. You get a fair

amount of leaves and debris up here, and that can be a killer. Your staff needs to skim everything at least twice a day, and be sure to cover the tub at night as a precaution, as well as before any major storm." He glanced up at the sky and shook his head. "Starting right now. Those clouds could rip any second."

Sand and dry leaves danced along the path as he spoke and he clutched at his cap to keep it from blowing away.

"I'll get one of the maintenance people right away."

"Sooner the better." He tightened his wrench, then went to work on the filter. "I'd better get moving, too. No sense staying around water when the lightning starts. I got hit once and it's not something you forget." He rubbed his wrist unconsciously as he spoke, and Annie wondered if that was where he'd been struck.

"Thanks for all your help."

"Don't worry." He patted the top of the filter. "When I'm done, this baby's gonna purr."

Halfway up the path, Annie had another thought. "Do you have a card?" she called. "If I have another problem with the filters, I'd like to call you directly."

"Can do, ma'am." Squinting, he fumbled in his toolbox, producing a folded and soggy set of business cards. "Doused them at my last service call." He pulled one out for Annie, tapping the number at the bottom of the card. "The name's Dooley. I'm usually in the field, but you can always reach my pager. You got a problem with the pumps or the filters, give me a shout, 24/7."

He gave Annie a little two-finger wave, checked the sky again, then went back to work on the filter, muttering about the dangers of silt impaction.

A drop of rain hit Annie's shoulder. She knew she had to find Reynaldo and make certain he understood the new maintenance requirements. The quickest way would be to use the phone in her office.

Rain splattered over the flagstones as she reached the main

courtyard. One of the maintenance staff was walking toward her office, and Annie ran to cut him off.

"Reynaldo?"

He didn't turn. Annie couldn't see his face with his hat pulled low against the wind.

Frowning, she crossed around in front of him. "Enrique?"

"*Sí.*" He turned as she did, keeping his side to her.

"I need some help up at the new whirlpool. The cover needs to be put down before the storm hits."

"Big winds, *sí*." He turned up his collar, pointing toward the covered walkway. "We go this way."

"Yes, but—"

He moved ahead of her, his voice muffled by the whine of the wind while Annie followed in growing irritation.

She stopped near the therapy rooms, just outside a walled terrace. "Can you turn around, please? I need to talk with you."

"No talk."

"Why in the world not?"

He shrugged, moving toward the wall, which was covered with jasmine. Annie's breath caught as he pulled her back against a trailing bank of white petals. "Because of this," he said roughly.

Chapter Thirty

"WHAT IN THE WORLD—"

His mouth moved over hers, unexpected and hot with demand. Heat slammed through her chest and streaked down to her toes, making her tremble.

Desire or not, fury clamped down hard. She shoved at his hat and sent it flying. "You big idiot. You're not supposed to be down here."

Sam's face was lined with strain. "I was worried about you. You should have called in."

"I was fine."

He leaned back against the stucco wall and nuzzled at her neck. "What's that perfume you're wearing? Something with strawberries and roses."

Annie closed her eyes as his fingers fanned out over her hips. "Rejuvenating facial complex."

"Good name," he said. "I'm feeling very rejuvenated."

"Stop, Sam. You shouldn't be here. Your orders—"

"To hell with my orders. I kept seeing you cornered with a pushy guest. He was running his hands over your shoulders, biting your ear. Looking at your breasts. The thought is still driving me crazy."

Annie softened slightly. Jealousy she could understand. She had spent a lot of time thinking about Sam with other women, and the experience hadn't been pleasant. "No one has been running his hands over me except some wretch in a wrinkled gardening uniform." She fingered Sam's collar and winced as rain hit her face. "Can we carry on this argument somewhere dry?"

"It's not an argument." Sam nudged her along the wall

toward a big glass door leading to the yoga room. "It's a discussion." He opened the door and pulled her inside.

Into the cool silence.

Into the darkness.

Into his hard arms.

He was working on the buckles at her shoulder straps and Annie felt one slide free. She knew she had to tell him to back off, to wait, to be reasonable.

She was trying to tell herself those things, too. But all she could think of was how he'd feel naked against her, how his body would pin her against the cool floor, how he'd find her heat, make her laugh, make her moan and gasp his name, the way he'd done before.

"Annie." It was a harsh rush of sound, his face all dark planes and shadowed need. "If you're worried about—"

"I'm not worried." Her hands were at his shirt, digging and pulling.

"It has to be here," he muttered. "I can't wait."

She closed her eyes, turning in his arms. "Here? But what if someone—"

The other buckle slide free, and her dress coasted over her shoulders, down to her waist, across her hips.

To the floor.

She heard Sam curse, his fingers tensing on her wrists.

The red lace. She'd finally agreed to wear it after Taylor's badgering.

Annie's face flamed in the darkness. The lingerie was sheer, high cut, and outrageous, absolutely unlike her.

Silence fell like a hot weight, broken only by Sam's hard breathing.

"Damn."

Annie swallowed.

"That's . . . lace. What there is of it." He took a deep breath. "Red. Very red."

"So?" Annie tried to feel beautiful, confident, like a woman who wore red lace all the time. "Is there a problem?"

"Yeah, there's a problem." His jaw clenched. "You're beautiful. And I'm so hard I can't move."

Her lips curved and she made a silent note to thank Taylor. "How hard?" Her hands skimmed his chest, then opened to pull him against her until she felt the awesome reality of the answer. "Strike that question."

Rain struck the big glass door at her back. Sam's eyes narrowed as laughter carried over the nearby courtyard, followed by the race of feet.

He moved in a blur, silently locking the door, his eyes on Annie's face. "Now."

Not a question. More like an act of nature, Annie thought, pulled closer, swallowed by the darkness in his eyes.

Her only answer was a nod, since she didn't seem to have air to speak.

Someone clattered up the outside stairs and tapped at the door. "Anyone in there?"

Sam covered her mouth with one finger, pulling her back into the shadows. Annie's gaze didn't leave his face as the knocking continued.

"It's locked." The door shook again. "Let's try the other side." The sounds drifted away, muffled by the rain.

"Can they get in?" Sam's voice was harsh. "Is there another door?"

Annie tried to focus. "One. It—it's closed unless a class is in session."

"Class is definitely in session, but it's going to be a private one, just you and me."

He caught her waist and lifted her up onto the seat lined with cushions, surrounded by yoga and nutrition magazines.

"Is this is going to be extreme yoga?" she asked breathlessly as Sam swept the magazines away with one hand, then pulled her long silk scarf over her head.

"You have no idea *how* extreme."

As Annie stared back at him, the rain and the shadows were forgotten. The cushion was soft beneath her hips and the scent of incense lingered from the morning's yoga classes.

She shouldn't be here, she thought dimly.

She shouldn't be anywhere else.

He terrified her.

She was terrified he would stop.

"Annie." He slid one hand into her damp hair.

Her bra opened, lace straps sliding off her shoulders and down over her arms.

"I couldn't stop thinking of you," Sam whispered. "Night and day, you wouldn't let go of me." His hand rose, brushing her breasts, making her forget to breathe. "How about you?"

"Me, too."

"Every time I heard your voice, I wanted this. I thought you'd see."

"How? You never give away anything."

The red straps fell, pinning her arms as Sam leaned down to find her with his mouth.

Annie closed her eyes at the sharp, jolting pleasure of his tongue. This was Sam, she thought. She'd wanted him, touched him, then watched him walk away, watched him almost die. Now fate had tossed him back to her and she wasn't going to waste any more time worrying about what she couldn't control or foresee.

She shoved his shirt free, raking her nails gently over his chest. New scars gleamed, pink outlines against tanned skin, and Annie touched them one by one with her lips.

There were tears in her eyes when he cradled her face.

"I'm not worth a single one of your tears," he said grimly.

"Say that again and I'll have to get nasty."

Behind them rain hammered at the window. His hands

tightened in her hair. Annie saw the question in his eyes and touched his cheek, nodding blindly.

"What about your shoulder?" she said.

"Hurts like hell." He smiled faintly. "You'd better go easy on me."

"Take off your clothes and come here," she whispered. "I want to touch you."

Sam shoved down his zipper and stepped awkwardly from his khaki work pants, leaving white cotton against hard, tanned skin. He took her mouth, whispering her name hoarsely, and Annie realized his hands weren't steady.

Intrigued, she reached for the taut skin clearly outlined by white cotton, shocked when he caught her hand and pinned it hard against his chest.

"Why?"

His jaw moved. "I couldn't take it. I'm right at the edge already, Annie."

Her smile was uncertain. "So what are you . . ."

His eyes were on her face as he moved between her legs, stroking beyond her final barrier of lace. "One thing at a time."

His eyes dark slits, he explored her, finding silken folds and wet heat. Annie stiffened beneath waves of hot sensation as he stroked, searched. Deep, deeper, until she couldn't seem to take in air.

It was better than before. Now Annie knew how close she'd come to losing him forever, and the knowledge left her ashamed of the lie she had to maintain.

"Sam, I have to—"

"Shhhh."

"No." She swallowed, fighting her way through waves of pleasure. "About us. You and me."

His movements grew slower and more intimate. "What about us, Annie?"

There was an edge to his voice that hadn't been there before, telling her his control could shred at any second.

"This." She closed her eyes, feeling the stroking heat of his hands. Every sense ached, fully sensitized as she shivered in the cold air, surrounded by the hammering of the rain, the scream of the wind.

His hand twisted. Her last piece of clothing dropped to the floor. Sam's eyes narrowed as he nudged apart her knees and stroked slowly.

She tried to speak and failed. "What, Annie?" He pulled back, then filled her again, finding a rhythm in his taking that made her mind go blank.

She shook her head, gripping his waist, unable to speak. Something was tearing inside her, clawing free and breaking loose. She felt his hands, the heat of his locked body against her hips, all part of an unbearable weight of intimacy.

With a stranger.

Yet not a stranger.

Then the thing she couldn't name surged free and she moaned as pleasure exploded and her body went liquid, contracting against his hand.

Her eyes flashed opened and she felt the burn of his eyes, but his fingers didn't stop. "Sam, I can't—"

"Again, honey. Trust me."

Trust me.

Annie caught a harsh breath, feeling the lie locked in her throat. "Sam, we need—need to talk."

"I don't want to talk. I want to watch you go crazy again."

Annie gasped as he traced the exquisitely aroused bud of nerves. She throbbed at the slightest touch, pleasure cresting all over again.

Then Sam's mouth took hers and she gripped his shoulders, sliding to meet the thrust of his tongue, lost to everything but his touch, pushing blindly against his hand as he stroked her. She unraveled, lost against him, lost in what he was doing to her.

Pleasure.

Once.

Again.

Long, dizzying waves of sensation gathered heavily, surging through her. Now she was hot, liquid with wanting him.

Liquid with the memories of how he'd taken her before, rocking her until pleasure snarled and screamed through her veins. She shuddered, feeling him sheathe a second finger in her heat.

In that instant, Annie recognized the simple, damning truth. This was far more than wanting. This hammering at her chest, like a primal breath trying to claw free, was a thousand times more dangerous than idle desire.

She'd loved this man since the day he rounded her cove, fearless at his sails, fighting to hold course in a snapping wind.

She'd loved him when he'd offered his life for forty-seven children on a bus headed straight for hell.

She wouldn't let him go again, not without this.

"You're dangerous," she said huskily.

"Not half as dangerous as you are."

Dangerous? Annie let herself think about being the kind of woman who always wore red lace underwear and carried a foil packet in her wallet.

The kind of woman who saw what she wanted and let herself have it, the way she was going to let herself have him now.

Maybe she *was* a little dangerous.

She slid her legs high, circling his waist, and the movement pressed him against her in a wet slide of friction.

"Damn," he said raggedly.

She smiled, suddenly fearless. Or maybe brazen was the word. Amazing that it had taken her twenty-seven years and one pair of red lace underwear to see the light. "Something wrong?"

His hands opened, gripping her hips as she moved against him. "Not that I've noticed."

"Then what are you waiting for?"

His body was still. "For the top of my head to bounce back off the ceiling."

"Forget about your head." Annie reached up to him and their mouths fused hungrily. He felt wonderful against her, and he felt even better when she took his weight in her palm.

His jaw worked hard. "I need something."

"So do I," she said, stroking down his length.

"My pants." His voice was unsteady. "I need my wallet."

Annie fished the pants from the window seat with one toe while Sam simply stared at her, looking as if he might beg fairly soon.

Taylor was right. Sex, lingerie, and power could be a lot more fun than she'd expected.

Sam frowned as he searched his wallet. "I thought I had one in here."

Annie realized he was looking for protection. "Try the pocket of my dress," she blurted. "Taylor gave it to me. She said I needed . . ."

"I may have to kiss your sister when I see her next." Sam fumbled with Annie's dress. "Which pocket?"

"Right top."

Fabric rustled. "Found it. I only hope she got my size."

"I didn't know that there were sizes. Taylor didn't say—"

"There aren't." He leaned down, fighting a smile, then kissing her, rough now, not gentle, nipping her mouth and driving his tongue across hers until her nails dug into his shoulders.

Then he pulled away, ripping at the foil and sheathing himself.

Annie watched in fascination.

This was Sam. Sam wanting her, Sam staring at her with his face tense and his beautiful, scarred body hard with need for her.

Her heart took a jerky little sidestep in her chest and she raised her foot, trailing her toe across his rigid stomach.

He caught her ankle, turned it slowly, and planted a kiss on her tender sole. If Annie's heart hadn't already been oatmeal, it would have melted then.

"You smell amazing."

"Eucalyptus steam bath. Strawberry-mango face gel."

"How did you get to be so damned smooth?"

"Taylor's exfoliating gloves."

He skimmed a hand along her thigh. "Here, too?"

"Yep."

"I'll have to buy us a few dozen." His hands moved down her back, opening over her hips. "Later."

"Much later." Annie was mesmerized by the desire she saw in Sam's face. "I'm not letting you go for hours."

"Hell." Sam's body went still. "I didn't think I could want you more. Then you say something like that, looking at me as if I'm important, as if I'm special and you couldn't want any man more—"

"I couldn't." She traced his shadowed face. "And you are."

Neither moved, their bodies touching, the bond between them fierce.

He breathed her name and Annie sighed as he leaned down, gripping her hips, moving against her, inside her, filling her in one driving thrust that had her wanting until she couldn't breathe with it.

Her body felt strange, hot and out of control, like the body of a woman who always wore red lace underwear and always carried protection, just in case. Annie wondered if she'd been that kind of woman all along, only she hadn't known it.

Then she couldn't focus on anything because their fit was too slick, too tight, and something was pulling her up, rocking her into him, sucking her into the pounding rhythm of her heat to his.

She gasped his name, caught in the magic of touching him this way, holding him as he moved inside her. Annie wanted to tell him how special it was, that she'd never been so lost before, never known it could be so deep or blinding or perfect.

No more wishing he was here, she thought. *He's real and he's alive and he's inside me, not a dream or a dim memory.*

She closed her eyes, wanting to hold this gift, to hoard the sweetness of the night around them, the rain on the windows, the smooth stucco tiles beneath her hand with Sam warm and deep and relentless inside her.

She could feel him in perfect, minute detail, his biceps straining at her back, his naked body slick with their sweat as he rocked, rocked, rocked against her.

Suddenly it wasn't a fantasy anymore, not remotely a game. It was her and Sam, together again, only now they were hot and wet, panting and straining and holding and taking, and the taking had never been so deep or amazing or so filled with risk.

She opened her eyes to find his gaze on her, fierce and black, as if he were thinking the same thoughts.

"How?" His voice was low and strained. "How can it be so much better than I imagined? How can you make it so damned good to touch you?"

Annie only shook her head as he opened his hand, sliding between her legs, finding the perfect way to make her mind do that blank thing again.

Something tore away and left her shuddering. The world blurred and the shuddering went on for maybe a few hours and then Annie felt tears slip down her cheeks while the ringing lifted from her head and the feelings started to loosen so she could finally breathe again.

This is incredible, she thought.

This is Sam filling me and it's worth every risk.

He traced her damp cheek, his jaw outlined by shadows as he said something she couldn't hear. Then he kissed her hard, sliding his tongue deep and flicking his fingers over her and she came again, this time clutching his locked shoulders, feeling the hammer of his heart, the bunch of his straining muscles.

Hers. This. All hers.

She must have said the words aloud because Sam said yes, he was and it was, and he never stopped moving as he spoke, never stopped driving into her until Annie realized the other two times had been only rehearsal and now, now the real show was starting.

Too sudden for words, she was *there*, mindless and hot, coming in high speed and full Technicolor. Sam said her name, coming with her, stretching her, opening her, taking her so hard that she shuddered and bit his taut shoulder and said *harder* just like a woman who owned red lace would do.

"Jesus," Sam rasped, moving just the way she'd asked, his hands on her hips as he watched her. "I wanted you," he said. "Wanted this. Every time you were around me I thought about this."

"So did I," Annie said, fearless, shuddering from the inside, holding him deep and taking him with her until he stiffened. Gripping her hips, he drove against her in a way that made Annie come all over again, in sheer shock at the pleasure of him losing himself inside her.

They were both gasping then, their bodies hot in the cool, rainy night.

Oh, boy, was Annie's final thought.

❖ ❖ ❖

THIS TIME THE SHUDDERING WENT ON FOR MAYBE A DECADE BEfore Annie opened one eye. She was slick with sweat, bone tired, shaking.

Entirely sated.

Sam looked to be in about the same state.

She slid back against the wall, as limp as the rain pooling over the flagstones and flowing down the windows.

Women who wore red lace probably felt that way a lot, she decided. She was going to have to invest in a whole wardrobe of red lace.

She drew a long breath. "Is there a word for what just happened?"

"Insanity. Even by California standards." He moved stiffly, taking his weight off her and pulling her against him on the cushioned seat. "Having sex that good is dangerous. I think it makes you go blind. Or bald."

Annie ruffled the hair at his forehead. "Still here."

"Glad to hear it." She heard the smile in his voice.

Rain hammered at the windows in heavy sheets. Neither spoke for a long time. When Annie looked up, she realized Sam was watching her.

"What?"

"Just replaying the last twenty minutes." He seemed to be waiting for her to say something. After a while he pushed up onto one elbow. "I don't think I've ever lost control that way. You hit me like nerve gas."

"Gee, thanks."

"That was supposed to be a compliment. You were overwhelming. And that red lace." He shook his head. "I'd ask you to frame it, except then you couldn't wear it." He tried to stand up and winced. "My leg's paralyzed."

Annie shot forward. "Sam!"

"Only temporary. You grabbed me with your hand when you—"

"Why didn't you say anything?"

"At that particular moment I wasn't feeling any pain," he said dryly.

Frowning, Annie reached for his leg. "Let me take a look. You might have done some real damage."

Sam hauled her back down beside him. "Relax, Doc."

"But—"

"I'm okay." He brushed his fingers through her hair. "Actually, I'm damned fine."

"In that case, I'd better get dressed." She looked around for her clothes. "Someone might come in."

"The door's locked," he pointed out.

Words backed up in her throat. She wanted to tell him how perfect it had been to touch him and how she wanted to do it again, right now. But there was something guarded in his face that hadn't been there before and suddenly she was very conscious of her nakedness and his hand on her hip.

"You're shivering," he said.

"Am I? It must be the cold."

Gently, he turned her face toward his. "Talk to me, Annie."

She couldn't. All the bravado had fled, and now she felt like an awkward teenager. "Talk about—what?"

"About us, for a start."

His focused stare was beginning to irritate her. "You want a performance critique, McKade? If so, you're out of luck. I was a little distracted just now."

"Who needs a critique? We both know what happened."

Annie crossed her arms. "You mean in addition to reasonably good sex?"

"It went way beyond good," Sam said harshly. "I'd say we burned away the whole top of the chart."

Annie figured he'd know more about that than she would. Her experience prior to Sam had been singularly underwhelming. She wondered where the conversation was headed and why he was so distant.

"Okay, it was excellent sex. I'd say we got to fifteen on a scale of ten. Not that I was counting." Shivering, she clutched at her nearest item of clothing. Unfortunately, that happened to be the red lace panties.

"I'm getting dressed," she said firmly, refusing to dwindle into postcoital dithering.

He watched her wriggle into the lace, his eyes dark and intent. "Why are you rushing?"

"Being found naked in the yoga room with one of my clients isn't at the top of my wish list." She dispensed with her bra and tugged on her dress, stuffing the bra in her pocket.

"Ever done that before?" Sam asked quietly.

Annie spun around. "Is that what *this* is about? Are you asking for a report on my sexual history? If so, you can go jump off the Big Sur Bridge."

"All I want is one little part of your history," Sam said.

"And that's supposed to make me feel better? I've got news for you—"

"Annie, I know."

"Know *what*? That I kissed Walter Hendrickson behind the soccer field when I was seven and he was nine. That I had my first date when I was fifteen and three-quarters. He took me to the Artichoke Festival and my father drove us home. As you can guess, not much happened with my father in the front seat. Then about a year later I—"

Muttering, Sam caught her hand and pulled her down onto his lap. He winced slightly as he settled her onto his good leg. "Not that. Not about Walter Hendrickson or the artichokes. About *us*. I know what happened between us this summer, Annie. *I remember.*"

Chapter Thirty-one

ANNIE FELT THE BLOOD LEAVE HER FACE. SHE STARED AT HIM helplessly. "*Us?* You and me?"

Sam nodded, his eyes unreadable.

"How?" she whispered.

"The last two nights I've had flashes. I put them down as incredibly explicit fantasies, something I've had a lot of since I came here. Then yesterday, when you kissed me, I started to think they were more than a product of my fevered imagination." His hand tightened on her arm. "When we made love—"

"Had sex," Annie corrected tensely.

For several moments he didn't speak. "Whatever you want to call it. When it happened, when I felt you take me inside you, it triggered a whole flood of memories."

"I see." Annie was sweating. "So you remember . . . everything?"

"Close enough." His jaw tightened. "Why, Annie? Why didn't you tell me we'd been lovers?"

Bad, Annie thought.

Worse than bad.

He was right to be angry, of course. Not telling him about their past was a form of betrayal, even if it hadn't been her choice.

"Exactly how much do you remember?"

"Enough. Or are you the one who wants a performance critique?" His tone was harsh.

With good reason. If the roles were switched, she'd be pummeling him right now, not talking. "I wanted to tell you, Sam."

"All it took was three words. 'We were lovers.'"

Annie stared down at the dark tangle of their clothes. "They told me not to."

"They?"

"The people in Washington who set this up. Izzy and I weren't supposed to give you any details. They wanted you to focus on your recovery, not the emotional entanglements of your past."

He was silent for long moments. "What about you? What did *you* want, Annie?"

"I wanted the best for you. I still do," she said quietly. "No matter how it hurt you—or me."

He turned away with a muffled curse. "I want to believe you. I hate being handled. I hate being lied to." He glared out the window. "Most of all, I hate knowing what was new and special to me was old hat to you."

"Not old hat. When you were here, it was like a dream. Then you left and I—" She stopped, crossing her arms and shivering.

"You said you hated good-byes. You made it sound like a game that day. Just wave at me from the beach, that's all you wanted."

Not a game.

Simply a way of salvaging her torn pride, Annie thought.

"But it wasn't a game, was it?" His eyes narrowed. "I hurt you. I can see it now." He drew her fingers through his. "You've hidden it all this time, haven't you?"

Annie stared at their locked hands. She'd thought her life was rudderless and without meaning. Every morning she wondered how she'd face the pain of his leaving.

She'd told no one about that, not even Taylor. They had made no promises, no plans, no vows of love eternal. They'd both been realistic and practical, or so it had seemed at the time. Yet Annie had never forgotten his face, his hands. His laugh.

"How bad was it, Annie?"

"No big deal. I managed."

"You just picked up and went on."

"That's right."

His thumb brushed her face. "Then why this?" His voice was rough with emotion as he traced a tear down her damp cheek. "You're crying, Annie."

"Don't think it means anything. Good sex always leaves me weepy."

"Great sex," he corrected. "And I was the first man you'd been with in four years. I remember *that* conversation perfectly."

Heat flashed into her face. "I never said—"

"Yeah, you did." He cradled her face gently. "You were sitting on the deck, dressed in my T-shirt and not a lot else, as I recall."

Annie shut her eyes. She didn't want to remember the brush of the wind and the feel of his hands. She wasn't going to cry about the past. "What if I did say it? I could have been lying."

He traced her lower lip with his thumb, making Annie shiver. "First I walk out and leave you flat. Then the Navy in its infinite wisdom sends me right back here to you for fixing up, and you do it. Beautifully. Without a word of protest." He drew a harsh breath. "You're something else, Annie O'Toole."

"You weren't complaining ten minutes ago."

"I'm not complaining now." He raised her hand to his mouth and kissed the curve of her palm. "I'm trying to think of some way I can repay you for what I put you through."

"There's no need."

"Maybe I'll decide about that."

Annie's heart took a jerky little sidestep as he found the hem of her skirt.

"Did I ever tell you my favorite fantasy? It involves women who wear red lace."

There was a sensual scrape to his voice that made Annie way too warm. They couldn't do this again. She wasn't cut out to be reckless and outrageous. She had to say no right now, before he

fogged her brain again. As the professional here, it was her job
to take charge, to set boundaries and—

She leaned against him. His fingers drifted up her thigh and
Annie swallowed hard as her brain started to fog.

Someone tapped on the shuttered window behind them.
With a yelp, she shot out of Sam's arms and saw a shadowed
figure standing outside the glass door.

Sam stayed low, just out of view. "It looks like one of your
staff."

"Reynaldo," Annie said after a moment. "You shouldn't be
here." She looked down. "You *definitely* shouldn't be here
naked."

"I'm working on that part." Clothing rustled frantically.
"Give me a second."

He dragged on his pants while she fumbled with her dress.
"Go out through the changing rooms." Annie pointed. "Use the
door at the end of the hall. It will lock automatically behind
you."

Sam's eyes narrowed. "What about you? I don't want you
wandering around here alone. Izzy told me that lunatic lawyer
came to harass you again."

"Tucker Marsh left five hours ago. Two maintenance men escorted him to his car and watched him drive away."

"Too bad," Sam grumbled. "I'd still like to kick his ugly—"

"I smell testosterone," Annie muttered. "I think I can manage to talk to Reynaldo without risking life or limb."

Sam kissed her shoulder. "Call Izzy as soon as you finish,"
he said tightly. "He'll walk back with you."

"Sam, I don't need—" Annie saw the flare of worry in his
eyes and gave up arguing. "Okay, I will. Promise. Now I have
to go."

He squeezed her hand, then released her, staying out of
sight behind a stucco pillar as she opened the door.

Her maintenance foreman was pacing outside. "Are you

safe? One of the guests called about banging noises by the whirlpool. Then I looked through the window and saw something moving in here." He peered into the darkness behind Annie. "Why didn't you turn on the lights?"

"Why?" Annie cleared her throat. *Think, think.* "Because I . . . I knew I wouldn't be long and I wanted to save electricity." *Feeble, Annie, incredibly feeble.*

Reynaldo peered some more. "There was no one else here?"

"Not a soul." As she closed the door, Annie moved in front of Reynaldo, blocking his view of the room. She saw Sam vanish down the back corridor. "Everyone must be inside because of the storm."

"Not everyone." Reynaldo sounded upset.

"Is it Tucker Marsh?"

The old man rubbed his neck. "It would be better if I show you."

Annie fought a premonition of doom. "Tell me."

Looking uncomfortable, he gestured down the hill. "A window was broken in your office. Everything was thrown to the floor. Papers, files, shelves. *Dio mio.*"

Annie froze. "Was anyone hurt? Megan?"

"No one. Just these things of yours."

She drew a sharp breath, all too aware of the likely culprit. "Things can be replaced." She searched in her pocket for her keys and turned to lock the door.

As she did, Annie saw the dark shape in the middle of the floor.

Sam's wallet.

He must have kicked it there when they—

She took a breath, focusing her tangled thoughts. She had to get the wallet. Sam's safety was at stake. "I'll be along in a second, Reynaldo. I remember something I left inside."

"Then I will wait for you," he said firmly, flashing a light through the door as she opened it.

Annie definitely didn't want him to wait and see her picking up a man's wallet. "You can start ahead. I'll be done in a moment."

His eyes narrowed. "If you are longer than that, I will come back for you."

Annie watched him stride toward the main offices. When he reached the sidewalk, she opened the door and raced for the fallen wallet, gripping it with a sigh of relief.

Behind her, wind gusted through the room, heavy with rain. Annie heard a click, and then the wind stopped.

"Reynaldo?" Frowning, she turned. "I said—"

But it was Tucker Marsh standing behind her, carefully locking the door.

Chapter Thirty-two

ANNIE STOOD UP SLOWLY. "THIS ISN'T A JOKE."

There was an ugly smile on Marsh's face. "It isn't?" He reached out, drawing the curtain.

Annie's heart began to pound. "Unlock the door now."

His smile grew uglier. "There's no need to go yet."

"Have you heard *anything* I said?" As she spoke, Annie slid Sam's wallet down into her pocket.

"Every word." Still smiling, Marsh swept her scarf off the window seat. She realized it must have fallen when she and Sam—

Don't think about that.

"Now I know who trashed my office."

"That would be breaking and entering. Maybe even a felony." He tried to sound shocked. "I could be disbarred."

Annie's heart was pounding. "Get out of my way, Marsh."

"Not just yet." He studied her thoughtfully. "I've got plans for tonight." He pulled her scarf gently through his fingers. "First we're going to have a little talk." *Snap.* "Then we're going to find a nice, private spot." Another *snap.* "We'll get comfortable." *Snap-snap.*

"No." Annie's heart was trying to claw its way out of her chest.

"I'm afraid so. Then you're going be very nice to me." *Snap-snap-snap.*

Annie swallowed hard. "Why would I do that?" She kept her voice cool.

"Because I want you to." *Snap.*

"You disgust me," Annie hissed. She darted to the side, then cut toward the door, but Marsh caught her with one foot, sending her face first against the glass. She hit hard and fell sideways, lights exploding inside her head. Through a curtain of pain she felt a movement behind her.

"You'll do everything I tell you tonight. Those are the rules. Just our little game."

Her hands jerked, caught behind her, knotted tight by her scarf.

Marsh pushed her against the glass. "I tell you and you do it." His voice was calm, almost without emotion. "That's all you have to know tonight, Annie."

He shoved her again, holding her against the heavy pane until Annie heard ringing in her head.

She had to distract him, free the lock and kick open the door.

He gripped her hands, shaking his head. "I'm afraid no one will be coming to check on you. They're all busy at your ruined office. And I believe there's going to be a fire in the kitchen any second."

"Damn you, Marsh."

He pushed her against the glass, his eyes without emotion. Annie kicked out, slashing at his knee. When the pressure left her hands, she staggered back, running to the end of the room.

She hit the next door with her shoulder, banging it open with a crack, then jumped back into the shadows with Marsh right behind her, cursing in the darkness.

Twenty feet to go.

She slid out of sight behind a pillar, trying to rein in her labored breath. Marsh careened past, and she stayed hidden, struggling to free her hands. As his curses grew dimmer, she bolted for the door on her left, which opened into the women's dressing room. From there she could circle around to the back door and vanish before Marsh realized it.

Suddenly the scarf bit into her hands, pulling her backward. "You're still not doing what you're told, Annie."

"I never will."

Marsh jerked the scarf, drawing her toward him, and Annie stumbled, then managed a wild kick that struck his shin.

"First your sister, now you."

Annie felt a jab of fear. "What about Taylor?"

His palm cracked against her cheek, sending her back against the wall.

Through a blaze of pain she saw the silk scarf fall at his feet. Blood trickled from her mouth and the wind screamed, but she focused on the big clay bowl beside the door.

Marsh didn't notice her inching toward the door. "You're not playing by the rules, Annie. Neither of you. I don't like that."

"What rules?" She inched cautiously toward the bowl. "The ones that say you always win?"

"Stop moving," Marsh hissed.

Almost there.

Annie lunged, digging her fingers into the bowl. She threw a candle and two Yanni CDs at Marsh, then kicked over the bowl and hurled an aromatherapy pillow at his head.

Not the best artillery.

Marsh ducked the first three and caught the pillow, his eyes small and mean. "You want to go to sleep, Annie? You want that with me?" He dropped the pillow and went for her, and as he did Annie screamed, rolling the bowl at his feet and running wildly for the front door.

Glass shattered.

The front door flew open in a fury of rain and icy wind. Annie realized she was pounding at Reynaldo's chest, with Izzy right behind him.

It took her a moment, even then, to stop fighting and take a long, shaky breath. She looked down at Marsh, who was twisting and cursing on the floor, surrounded by clay fragments.

"I worried when you didn't return. Your friend also was worried." Reynaldo gestured to Izzy, who was busy tying Marsh's hands with Annie's scarf.

Both men stiffened when Annie turned into the light.

"You are hurt. I will phone the doctor."

"Later," Annie said shakily. "Reynaldo, I want you to take pictures of my office, then make another set here. After that I want you to take Mr. Marsh to the county hospital and stay while he is examined," she added tightly. "The sheriff will need all this information when I file my complaint for assault."

Her hands were trembling now, knocking together so hard they hurt, so she locked them at her waist. "I need someone to check on my sister, too."

Reynoldo nodded to one of his uniformed staff waiting outside.

The two men pulled Marsh to his feet. He rolled his shoulders, trying to be in control.

"Too bad about the misunderstanding." He tried to smile, casual and confident. "When you asked me to meet you out here, I assumed you were playing straight. I would never have lifted a finger to touch you otherwise."

"Great piece of fiction," Izzy said coldly. "Better remember it for the sheriff."

Reynaldo gestured to his staff. "Take him to the Blazer. Hold him if he tries to leave."

As Annie watched them vanish into the fury of the storm, every nerve in her body screamed. It took her a moment to realize that Izzy was slipping his windbreaker around her shoulders.

"Ready to go?" he asked quietly.

"I have to c-call Buzz. I need to file a report."

"Up at the house."

After a moment, Annie nodded. "I'm not feeling so great."

"Most people wouldn't," Izzy said calmly. "By the way, I liked how you used the Yanni CDs as artillery. Also the body brush. But the clay bowl did the real damage."

Annie laughed. Actually, it was closer to a gasp, but Izzy didn't point that out. "Who says the New Age is dead?"

"Tucker Marsh probably wishes it was." Izzy closed the door and locked it with a key Annie didn't know he had, then took her arm. "I'll get you up to the house, then come back and board up this broken glass."

"I'm not really upset." Annie swallowed, staring at the scattered glass. "The main thing is that I stopped him. I plan to see that he never does this again."

"You've got a solid case."

"It was some kind of game to him." She shivered. "He kept talking about rules."

"There will be a lot of rules where he's going," Izzy said grimly. "Right now, let's get you warm."

"I'm not cold," Annie insisted between teeth that wouldn't stop chattering. "I'm just f-fine." Things were getting a little blurry so she leaned into Izzy, squinting against the rain and watching the lights dance up the hill at her casita.

Thinking about Sam.

Wanting his arms around her.

"What about Taylor?"

"Reynaldo's man has a walkie-talkie. He should be checking in any minute."

"Marsh mentioned Taylor, Izzy. I need to know she's safe."

"I'll handle it as soon as we get you home."

"I'm fine," Annie kept repeating, realizing it wasn't true, shaking hard now and feeling pain dig into her right temple. There was an ache at her mouth that made talking hard, but she talked anyway.

Maybe to distract herself from how much she was shaking.

"I made him stop. I did it, didn't I?"

"Two Yanni CDs would scare the hell out of me," Izzy said, guiding her uphill through the rain. "You were smart and brave, Annie. You did a fine job. Damned fine."

"I did," she told herself.

Then the door was flung open and Sam lurched toward her, saying, "Where is he?" and "I'll kill him this time."

Annie shuddered and ran toward him in the rain, as fast as she could, which wasn't fast at all.

Chapter Thirty-three

IT WAS ALMOST NINE BY THE TIME ANNIE HAD PHONED BUZZ TO report the attack. Before that she had called the security staff to check on Taylor again and also make certain there had been no more accidents at any of the resort facilities. Then, fighting exhaustion, Annie had insisted Izzy take photographs of her face and the angry bruises on her neck and arms.

All the while Sam watched, his face like granite. "The bastard can't walk away from this."

"He won't. Buzz is taking Marsh into custody as soon as the ER team checks him out."

Sam stabbed at the air. "Not good enough."

"It has to be good enough. You're *not* getting involved."

Behind her, Izzy put away the camera and pocketed the film for safekeeping. "She's right, McKade. Let it go. The rest is up to the police."

"To hell with the police," Sam snarled. "If he rots in jail for a hundred years, it's still not enough."

Annie sagged against the wall, completely drained. "I'm going outside."

"Why?" Sam demanded. "You should be in bed."

"I'm too wound up to sleep. Maybe I'll use the hot tub. The rain's nearly stopped."

"It's got to be fifty degrees out there," Sam said worriedly.

"I'm going out." Annie felt boxed in and didn't know why. Maybe she was afraid of her dreams if she fell asleep.

"I'll go with you." Sam took her shaking hands between his. "I don't want you alone."

She raised her chin. "I'm just fine."

"Who said you weren't?" Sam turned carefully. Behind

Annie's back, he gestured to Izzy, making the movement of swallowing pills. Izzy nodded, holding up one finger.

Sam shook his head and held up two. When Izzy had gone, he pulled Annie against his chest. "It's okay, ace. You slew your dragon tonight. Now you need to kick back and rest."

"No good," Annie said tightly. "If I fall asleep I'll see his face. F-feel his hands."

"Come to bed," Sam said gently.

She stiffened. "Sam, I can't."

"To sleep, nothing else, Doc." He brushed her cheek. "Don't make me carry you or I'll blow my shoulder all to hell and ruin your work." Sam slid an arm around her waist, feeling her shake and hating the man who had done this to her.

He smoothed back her hair. "You're going to have one amazing black eye tomorrow. Feel free to blame me if you want. Tell everyone that Han Solo did it."

Annie tried to smile, but ended up wincing as Sam changed the cold cloth on her forehead. "It doesn't really hurt." She rubbed her wrists restlessly. "I'm just a little edgy."

"Sure you are." Sam gently washed her face, glad that she couldn't see the bruises. Then he held out a glass of water.

Annie blinked. "What's that for?"

"These two pills. Your doctor had one of Reynaldo's people pick them up in town. Izzy just brought them from the office."

Annie shook her head. "I don't need medicine."

"Two against one. Izzy's on my side in this, so stop talking and open up."

"But—"

Sam caught her midsentence, dropping one pill in her mouth. He moved the glass up against her lips, waiting for her to swallow.

"Now another."

Annie downed the second pill, frowning at Sam all the while. "Satisfied?"

"Not until you're in bed under the covers, sleeping like a baby."

With a sigh, Annie bent for her shoes.

Sam pushed her hands away, stripping her with careful efficiency, then drawing the covers around her. Her face was colorless and strained as he turned out the light.

"Check the pocket of my dress."

"Only if you promise it's not a Yanni CD."

Annie shook her head. "Your wallet. I found it on the floor. It must have dropped when we . . ."

Sam frowned. *When we had hot, grinding sex.*

But he didn't trust himself to think about the earlier part of the evening. What Annie needed was rest, not another bout of incendiary sex.

Wonderful as it would be.

Especially when she moved beneath him, drawing her legs around him and making those husky little moans that left him so hard that he couldn't see straight.

Enough of the flashback, McKade.

He stood holding his wallet, furious. He should never have forgotten it. That single piece of carelessness had brought Annie into danger.

You're losing it here, pal. Really losing it. You're thinking like a fifteen-year-old, and that's dangerous for both of you.

But all he could think of was that red underwear she'd worn, and how beautiful she'd been, the way she'd shuddered beneath him, whispering his name and knocking him silly.

"Sam?" she said sleepily.

He pulled up a chair beside the bed and sat down. "Yeah, beautiful."

"I'm not beautiful."

"The hell you aren't. Hasn't anyone ever told you that you look like Meg Ryan?"

Annie smiled softly. "You did. The first time we met."

Sam frowned. He hadn't remembered that. What *else* had he said?

"Don't worry." She put her hand on his arm, almost as if reading his thoughts. "It will come back."

"It better," he said savagely. "I'm getting tired of waiting for all the details."

"Are you still angry that I didn't tell you before? I wanted to, you know."

"I'm mad as hell," he said huskily. "But not at you. You did what you were told would be best for me. It's other people that I'd like to strangle."

"They did what they thought was right, too."

He didn't say anything, saving up his anger for the medical geniuses who had decided to play God with his memories.

"Reynaldo told Izzy you went back inside for some reason. Was it because you saw my wallet?"

"I wasn't trying to be heroic, Sam. I just reacted."

"And then Marsh found you." He touched her bruised mouth very gently. "I'd say you're the bravest woman I know."

"Probably not."

"So I can't thank you for saving my cover?"

"Afraid not."

"For protecting me from a horde of predatory journalists?"

"Nope."

"Not even a few tabloid hacks?"

Annie shook her head. Sam saw that she was fighting a yawn. He repositioned her ice pack, which was slipping down her forehead. "Feel better?"

"The pills are making me sleepy."

"That's the general idea, Doc."

"Who put you in charge here, McKade? You're *supposed* to be the patient."

"Yeah, but I'm good at being in charge."

"We'll see about that." She yawned. "Tomorrow's another day."

Sam nodded, staring at her with almost painful tenderness. He wasn't going to leave her side while she slept.

He turned as he heard a light tap at the door.

Izzy was holding out a cell phone. "The admiral," he said quietly.

There was only one admiral as far as Sam was concerned, and that was his superior officer. Bad news traveled fast.

He took the phone, planning how to put the best spin on what had just happened.

"McKade, is that you?"

Sam moved outside so he wouldn't wake Annie. "Right here, sir."

"What the hell's going on there?" the older man barked. "First I hear about problems with fire alarms and overflowing hot tubs, and now there's an attack on Ms. O'Toole. Has there been an infiltration at the resort?"

"No, sir. The attack was unrelated to my presence here. The man in question appears to have a personal grudge against Ms. O'Toole."

"She's not hurt, is she?"

"Some bruises and a nasty cut. But she's tough."

"The bastard should be keelhauled." The admiral cleared his throat. "No one has discovered your presence there, I hope."

Only because Annie had been smart and resourceful. He'd been a witless fool to leave his wallet.

And Annie had paid for his mistake.

Sam took a sharp breath. "No one, sir. I understand the staff are taking bets as to whether I'm Harrison Ford or Brad Pitt, in physical training for a new movie."

"She handles them, does she?"

"She's not saying."

"Closemouthed. That's good. McKade, I'm taking a lot of heat for keeping a lid on this thing, and you might have to move at short notice. I've done everything possible to plug the usual sources here, so if anyone talks, it's at your end."

Sam hoped it was true, but he also knew that the military's bureaucracy could be a big, unfriendly place. "I'll keep that in mind, sir."

A chair creaked. Sam had a sudden image of Admiral Howe in a cozy study, surrounded by pictures of his family and all the presidents he'd served under. Sam realized that he'd been a guest in that study on a number of occasions. He stiffened at another memory.

A quiet afternoon. A muddy free-for-all on a huge lawn that stretched down to a sleepy river. He remembered cheering, the smell of burning leaves and cigar smoke. Sam's eyes narrowed as he pictured the admiral hunched over an antique desk, puffing on his third cigar of the night, leaving the room veiled in smoke.

Then suddenly there was more.

"McKade, you still there?"

Sam gripped the phone, willing the blurred images to slide into focus.

He heard shouting and laughter. The sound of crunching leaves. Then wild cheering.

"McKade? What's going on?"

Sam was sweating now, his pulse fast and hammering. "I'm remembering something. Mud, sir. Cheering. It feels like fall. Maybe." Sam dug for answers. He prayed and sweated and searched through the shattered debris that was his memory.

Nothing. Another wall.

"I can't see. It might have to do with the number sixteen, sir, but I don't know why." Sam laughed grimly. "And this makes me sound like a kook."

"I want to hear about anything you remember, no matter how small." The admiral cleared his throat. "I'll run it past the people here and see if anything clicks. What about the accident?"

"Noise. Screaming." Sam looked out the big window at the blackness of the sea. "Pain."

The admiral's chair creaked. "McKade, I'm going to give this to you straight. There's a lot riding on this and some key people here are pushing for medical intervention."

"I'm not following you, sir."

"*Drugs*, damn it. Pentothal or worse. I've been fighting this, but I can only hold out so long. I thought you should know," he said gruffly.

So now they wanted to reach inside his head and pick through the shattered fragments of his memory. Sam bit down a wave of fury. "I appreciate the notice, sir. I'll let you know as soon as anything else surfaces."

"I know you will. If all else fails, I'll simply take off for my annual Alaskan hunting trip a little early. Let them try to catch me in the middle of Kodiak bear country."

Sam smiled. It was good to have a power player watching his six o'clock.

"I'd better go before my wife catches me with another cigar. She swears she's going to banish me to the guesthouse if I don't cut down and my son's almost as difficult. Amanda's been asking after you, by the way. She pesters me for news every day since that damned television extravaganza. I told her you were in Bethesda, recuperating. We sent you flowers, and you answered with a cordial note, by the way."

Sam grinned. "I did, did I?"

"Short but to the point. Peter says hello, too."

"Peter?"

"My older son. He got a promotion last week."

"Congratulations, sir. You must be very proud." Sam frowned. As hard as he tried, he couldn't summon up a memory of any of the Howe family, but he remembered their big house and the cool grass near the river.

He heard a car horn at the other end of the wire.

"I'd better go. Peter is determined to chauffeur me to another doctor. Something about my eyes. Why can't they let a man grow old in peace?"

Sam heard another blast of the car horn. "Give 'em hell, sir."

"Count on it."

Izzy was standing at the door when Sam put down the phone. "Good news or bad?" he asked.

"I remembered something." Sam frowned. "*Almost* remembered, at least. It had something to do with the number sixteen. The admiral's people are checking it out."

"Anything else I can do to help?"

Sam rubbed his neck. "A week in Tahiti would be pleasant."

"Not in the budget, ace."

"Then I guess I'll just sit here and watch Annie sleep."

Izzy grinned. "Almost as relaxing as Tahiti. She's damned brave, you know."

"I know," Sam said tightly.

"Good." Izzy nodded and headed to the door. "If you need me, I'll be out in the courtyard keeping an eye on anything that moves."

Chapter Thirty-four

Rush hour on a Thursday afternoon.

Washington's Old Post Office complex, now converted to 35 upscale shops and an impressive food court, was packed. Two medical conventions were in town and their ranks were well represented in the airy Romanesque building on the corner of Eleventh Street and Pennsylvania Avenue. A class of fourth graders from a local District of Columbia school was holding an art exhibition on the plaza level and a trio of young jazz musicians entertained shoppers at the entrance to the food court.

Good targets, he thought.

He clicked off the shots and imagined the immediate chaos. The scenarios were satisfying. He'd have his escape routes if he needed them.

He already knew where the employee lockers were, of course. He'd committed every detail of the building's structure to memory, down to fire alarms, help desk and restrooms.

His contacts had insisted on that. Everything had to be checked out completely before he tried the key.

Now he sat at the edge of the food court, holding a paper he only pretended to read and a glass of wine he only pretended to sip. He'd circulated through the building for three hours, waiting for the warning sense of faces seen once too often, but there had been none.

He sat holding his wine, reviewing his careful instructions and forcing himself to wait. When the afternoon crowds were at their peak, he folded his paper neatly, tossed his plastic glass into the nearby trash bin, and strolled toward the jazz trio near the stairs.

When he slipped past, brushing them slightly, none of the musicians noticed anything unusual.

By the time they did, it would be too late.

❖ ❖ ❖

"RAY, YOU HAVE A CLEAR LINE OF SIGHT?"

"All clear, Bishop. No one near the lockers. No one near the outside corridor, either." Crouched inside two specially connected lockers, the federal agent wiped sweat off his neck. "Good thing, too, because this place is as packed as Times Square on New Year's Eve. You know you can rent this place? It'll only set you back twelve large."

"More than an honest civil servant like me can afford."

"You sure that intel was solid, sir?" Ray sounded edgy.

"It was solid." Bishop, the operation head, stood at a French pastry shop. Dressed in a crisp white jacket, he watched every movement on the floor in front of him. He didn't know why their target was so damned important, only that there were others involved, and the others were higher up the food chain. "He'll be here. No more chatter," he added curtly.

The jazz musicians were swaying, straining to reach that perfect chord while bystanders tossed dollar bills into an open guitar case. There was no need, of course. They had been hired for a substantial fee and tipping was unnecessary.

But some habits die hard.

Bishop saw movement the same second his lapel microphone began to squawk.

Shit.

"Ray, are you clear?"

"All clear, Bishop. What's the—"

"Stand by," he interrupted curtly. What the hell was a SWAT team doing at the back entrance, loaded for bear? And why the hell hadn't he been notified of a situation in progress under his damned nose?

Interdepartmental rivalry, of course. Sheer bureaucratic incompetence, too. But now he needed *answers*, not incompetence.

"Kelly, report," he snapped.

"Movement in the loading area. Damned if that's not a SWAT van." The agent on the roof breathed sharply as if trying to find a better vantage point.

"Stay low, Kelly. Repeat, stay low. I don't want you made for a hostile target." Bishop was sweating now, aware of the consequences of failure and furious at the thought of hours of careful planning going up in smoke. He fingered the comm unit inside his white jacket and spoke quietly. "Dade, this is Bishop. Patch me through to whoever is running that damned SWAT op."

"Roger, sir."

But the connection was interrupted. "Ray, here. We have motion at the stairs. Appears to be one man." The agent sounded edgier than ever.

"Kelly, notify SWAT team that we are mobile. All officers engage, locker corridor."

The music suddenly stopped. The bystanders fell into a hush. A dozen black-clad SWAT officers in tactical body armor swarmed through the room, wrestling the musicians to the ground and kicking their instruments aside.

Bishop was on the run.

Why the SWAT team *now*?

"Report contact at lockers." Ray's voice was tight. "Going out."

Bishop heard the metal door bang open and Ray yelling, "Freeze!"

A *boom* roared through the line. Bishop, already at the mouth of the corridor, grabbed reflexively at his earpiece. "Ray, do you read?"

No answer.

Downstairs the tourists began to scream as they realized a
SWAT team had deployed around them with weapons drawn.

*Nice move, you bastard. There will be a stampede in here
shortly, and you'll blend in, just another face in the crowd.*

The screams from the plaza level rang in John Bishop's ears
as he caught up with the other team members. Ray was
sprawled next to the open locker. The floor was red where he'd
fallen. "Suspect is on the run. *I want him alive.*"

Bishop's hands wrapped around his service pistol as he sank
down beside Carlos Ray's motionless body in its darkening red
pool, fighting his grief at the sight of a good man down.

"Report," he snapped.

His earpiece squawked. "Kelly, sir. I apprehended the target
at the service elevators."

"On the move," Bishop said curtly. It took him less than
thirty seconds to reach the elevators.

Kelly was cuffing a man facedown against the floor.

Bishop nodded to his agent, who pulled the suspect to his
feet. He had to fight an urge to take blood for blood.

"I want a lawyer."

Bishop recognized the man from the delivery van instantly,
but gave no sign of it. He motioned to another agent, who read
the suspect his rights with harsh, barely controlled anger.

Bishop turned away while the murderer demanded a lawyer
again. Bishop was putting it all together now. The SWAT call
had been a diversionary tactic, a carefully timed anonymous
tip—apparently having to do with the musicians in the food
court. Just the sort of thing to set up panic among D.C. law en-
forcement.

He looked down at Carlos Ray, at the blood soaking his shirt
from his head wound, then put away the emotions until he had
the luxury of mourning a man he'd considered one of his closest friends. Right now he had a job to do.

This was one interrogation Bishop wanted in on. He wanted

to lean hard, then lean again, and he swore he wouldn't stop until he'd squeezed out every useful piece of information.

Not that it would bring back his friend.

The suspect was still shouting for a lawyer when Bishop motioned to one of his agents. "Take him out the front way."

"Sir?"

"The front, I said. And don't rush. They'll have someone in place, watching the building."

Too bad they hadn't gotten any higher up the food chain with this op. Letting the suspect leave the apartment in Virginia had been a calculated plan, but despite all their surveillance, the man had been damned careful never to make contact with his handlers.

The one phone call in the nightclub had come out of the blue. The surveillance team hadn't been able to make a trace in time.

Bishop wanted those handlers bad. Someone was going to pay for Carlos Ray's death.

His voice hardened. "Be sure that the suspect's visible when you take him outside, understand? I want them to know that their little fish just got hooked. Let *them* sweat for a while."

Week
Three

Chapter Thirty-five

SAM AWOKE IN A COLD SWEAT, THE COVERS TWISTED AROUND HIS legs. He heard the roar of a bus and children screaming and it took him a minute to realize it was a dream.

Another damned dream.

He shook his head, angry that the dreams were getting sharper, wondering when he'd stop dreaming about the accident and start remembering something useful.

For an instant images flashed before his eyes. He caught the sound of water slapping and trucks backfiring. Or was it another kind of motor?

Suddenly the noise began again, and this time it was one voice, high and thready.

Not a dream. It was Annie.

He was down the hall in two seconds, Glock level while he scanned the room at a crouch.

Annie was alone, sheets at her chin, looking pale and frightened and trying not to. "You can put away the gun. I had a bad dream."

"I know how that feels." Sam put down the Glock and sat beside her. "Marsh?"

She nodded mutely, reaching out for his hand.

"Yeah, you'll probably have a few of them."

Annie didn't say anything, but her grip grew tighter.

"Want to talk about it?"

She shook her head, her face too pale, her eyes too dark. "No. You're sure Taylor is okay?"

"Izzy checked right after Reynaldo did."

"Does she know about me?"

Sam shook his head. "You can tell her yourself tomorrow when you feel better."

Annie nodded. "That would be best. I don't want to worry her." She took a hard breath. "About the dream—it was raining and he was there, laughing. He had the scarf again, and I couldn't get away from him. I was so cold."

So frightened.

Sam guessed she wasn't giving him all the details, but he got the picture. "Scoot over."

She was shivering when he lay down beside her and pulled her against his chest. "Cold," she said.

"It's the storm."

Both of them knew it wasn't.

She turned into his heat, putting her arms around his waist, shivering hard. "Would you stay for a while?"

"My pleasure."

"Sorry to whine like this."

"Yeah, you're a real whiner." Somehow Sam kept his voice light. "No question about it."

"Do you get dreams?" she asked softly.

He frowned over the top of her head, his fingers tightening. "Sure I do."

"What do you do about them?"

Gut it out.

Throw up.

Tell yourself it's normal to see dead people all around you and be scared spitless.

"Just remember it's a dream. The dreams go away, Annie."

"Will they?"

Sam sure as hell hoped so. "Sure they will. Scout's honor."

She pressed closer. Sam felt his body react instantly, hard with need for her.

But he only touched her hair, drawing her head down against his shoulder. There were a lot of things he wanted to do in bed with Annie O'Toole.

Right then, holding her gently while she slept was good enough.

◊   ◊   ◊

"Sam."

The whisper brought him awake in a blur, grabbing for the gun tucked under his pillow.

"Only me. Izzy."

Annie murmured and turned away, asleep again in seconds as Sam eased away from her. He glanced at the alarm in the darkness and shook his head.

"I held her off as long as I could," Izzy said apologetically.

"Held who off?"

"Taylor. She's out in the courtyard and she swears she'll call Buzz if I don't let her in to see how Annie's doing."

"Hell," Sam muttered.

The horizon was hidden by a gray wall of clouds. His brain felt equally fogged as he dragged his fingers through his hair and sat up. "Let me throw some clothes on. Then you can send her in."

He stood up carefully, trying not to wake Annie. He was reaching for his jeans when Taylor burst through the door.

"How is she?"

Sam jerked the jeans in front of him. "She's asleep," he said gruffly.

Taylor's face was white and she seemed oblivious to his near nakedness.

"Let's go outside for this," Sam muttered. As soon as Taylor turned around, he pulled on his jeans and followed her down the hall. "The doctor sent something to help her sleep."

"Why didn't she call me herself?"

"I don't think she wanted to worry you. She looked pretty shaky."

"I'm her sister," Taylor hissed. "She's supposed to worry me." She stalked into the living room, her expression stony. "She always does this, so damned determined to handle every little thing by herself. I could strangle her."

"She doesn't like to bother people."

"Of course she doesn't. Saint Annie never wants to upset anyone. That's why I have to hear everything secondhand!"

She made a watery sound and Sam realized she was crying.

Oh, hell, not that. He could handle grenades, artillery, and heat-seeking missiles.

Anything but tears.

"I'm going to kill that maggot."

Sam assumed she was referring to Tucker Marsh. "Get in line," he said grimly.

"You get what's left of him, pal. I've already talked to a doctor friend who told me about a nice little injection that will leave him impotent for life. Then there's a nasty alkaloid from Guatemala that will give him blinding headaches, followed by gradual vision loss and muscle wasting."

Sam winced.

"After that, I'm going for the big stuff. I'm going to tie him down and cut off his—"

"Whoa." Sam cleared his throat uneasily. "I don't think the publicity would help Annie or the spa very much. Legal eagle neutered after spa weekend from hell?"

Taylor rolled her shoulders as if they hurt. "He deserves it. He should have his miserable skin flayed, inch by inch."

Sam couldn't have agreed more, but he wouldn't let Annie's sister get involved. "Your sheriff will handle him."

"Marsh is already in custody in town. I just checked. But Buzz has gotten calls from three judges who are aghast at what they call an unfortunate misunderstanding. What if Marsh gets out on bail?"

"Don't worry, he won't get near Annie," Sam said grimly. "From now on she won't be going anywhere alone."

"Nice thought, but she won't listen." Taylor sighed. "She'll nod and she'll take normal precautions, but with Annie Summerwind comes first."

"Not this time."

Taylor measured him slowly. "You might be the one to convince her." Her brow furrowed. "You look pretty dangerous yourself."

"I can be," Sam said quietly.

Taylor studied him some more. "I gather that nobody's supposed to know you're here."

He nodded.

"But I know."

"If you talk, I guess I'll have to kill you."

Taylor smiled faintly. "Can I steal that line for a book?"

Sam crossed his arms. "It's all yours."

"I suppose you know there's a pool going." Taylor paced to the big window. "As of last night, the bets were running in favor of Han Solo." Taylor's eyes narrowed. "Myself, I think she'd be better off with the Wookie."

"Hard to find a massage table big enough for a Wookie," Sam said dryly.

Taylor rubbed her arms. "So what happens now?"

"Annie rests, whether she likes it or not. She also cuts back on her work, like it or not. Izzy and I will handle her protection."

After a long time, Taylor nodded. "Okay, that works. I just wish I could do something, too. I hate being the spacey, scattered one."

"Anyone who thinks that has to be blind."

"Thanks." Taylor sniffed once, then picked up her big leather bag from the sofa. "I'm going to sit with her. But don't plan on going anywhere." She leveled a finger at Sam. "I have a lot more questions for you."

❖　❖　❖

ANNIE AWOKE DISORIENTED, HER FINGERS CLUTCHING AT THE sheets. Her temples throbbed and her mouth hurt. She took a shaky breath, remembering the night before.

"Sam?" she whispered.

"Hey." Fabric rustled. "Glad you finally woke up."

"Taylor?" Annie reached out for her sister's hand. "What are you doing here?"

"You think you could keep me away?" Taylor turned the bedside lamp to a dim setting, stiffening when she saw Annie's face. "Marsh did that?"

Annie gave a little shrug.

"I'm going to eviscerate him," Taylor hissed. "I'm using manicure scissors, and they're going to be very dull when I do it."

Annie's hand tightened. "Don't. And don't encourage Sam, either."

"That man doesn't need any encouragement, thank heaven. He likes Marsh even less than I do." Taylor studied Annie in silence, her eyes anxious. "Want to talk about it?"

"Not yet." Annie sat up carefully. "Marsh mentioned you being a problem. Did he try something?"

Taylor pursed her lips. "I ran into him after I left the spa yesterday. He got too touchy-feely when I dropped a towel. He also implied that you and he were enjoying hot sex."

"*What?*"

"Don't worry, I knew it was a lie." Taylor smiled thinly. "That's why I gave him a karate chop in the family jewels. He didn't look too happy when I left." Something came and went in her eyes. "Forget about Marsh. What do we do now? Getting drunk is out," Taylor said. "Having an orgy is no good either, since your hunk looks like the possessive type, at least where you're concerned. Since the orgy's canceled, I thought we could watch QVC and shop for fake leather, but my Visa card is maxed out, so scratch that. That leaves the fallback plan." She rummaged in her purse and brought out two videotapes. "We've got *Multiplicity* and we've got *Godzilla*." Taylor's eyes narrowed. "You sure you don't want to talk about anything first?"

Annie shook her head, plumping up her pillow. She tossed Taylor the remote. "Crank up the terror of the sea."

❖ ❖ ❖

TWO HOURS LATER THEY WERE SIDE-BY-SIDE ON THE BED, FINISH-ing their third bowl of popcorn. Taylor had had to go home for more popcorn, but after that they'd settled in for some serious film criticism.

They had trashed the acting, the special effects, and the scene in the Park Avenue tunnel when the phone rang.

"Annie, this is Buzz. How're you doing?"

"Pretty good."

"What's that banging noise?"

"Godzilla just dive-bombed a New York taxi cab. Taylor came down and we're watching movies."

"It's good she's there."

Annie glanced at the bedside clock. "Buzz, you didn't call me at five-forty-five to make small talk."

"No, I didn't. You feel up to taking a little walk down to the main building?"

Annie sat up stiffly. "What's wrong? Has someone been hurt?"

"Not exactly. I think you'd better have a look. Bring Taylor and that big fellow named Izzy."

"I don't understand, Buzz."

"You will."

❖ ❖ ❖

THE ENTRANCE TO THE MAIN COURTYARD WAS FILLED WITH light, most of it focused on one of the second-floor guestrooms.

"I don't like the look of this." Annie tried to walk faster.

"No need to rush. Whatever is up there doesn't seem to be going anywhere."

Annie squinted through the shadows. "Why would Buzz call me if it wasn't important?"

"Beats me," Taylor said calmly.

Annie saw two police cruisers in the front parking lot. Buzz was talking on a cellular phone and a uniformed officer was striding toward the outside stairs.

Quiet as always, Izzy moved ahead of Annie and Taylor. In protective mode, Annie realized, his jacket open so he could reach his weapon.

Goose bumps rose over her neck. "What's going on?"

"I'll find out," Izzy said.

Not without her, he wouldn't. Annie pushed on doggedly, ignoring a throb in her ribs where Marsh had flung her against the door.

Several guests were gathered on the lawn, dressed in bathrobes or sweat suits. They were pointing up at the balcony, too.

Suddenly Izzy went still.

"What is it?" Annie demanded. "What's wrong? Has there been a crime?"

"I'd say it's a crime all right." Izzy stepped out of the way. "Have a look."

Annie stared up at the brightly lit balcony. She took a breath and then looked again. "Dear Lord," she whispered.

"I doubt He's involved in this," Taylor murmured.

Annie rubbed her eyes. "Is that what I think it is?"

Taylor nodded slowly. "A naked man. Singularly unattractive, too." She crossed her arms and rocked back on her heels. "I could just swear the naked butt in question belongs to Tucker Marsh."

"Why is he standing up *there*?"

"I do believe our boy's handcuffed to the balcony railing," Taylor murmured. "Looks like he's blindfolded and gagged, too."

Annie suddenly felt faint. "Oh, no." She looked around wildly. "If Sam did this, I'll—"

"Sam was asleep when we left. I checked on him myself," Izzy said. "And he didn't leave the casita tonight." He glanced at Taylor. "It appears you have some other secret friend."

Annie stared at him suspiciously.

He raised his palms. "Don't look at me."

Annie turned, staring at Taylor.

The excuse about the popcorn. Her sister had left for at least twenty minutes. "Taylor, do you know anything about this?"

Taylor didn't answer, too busy studying the man handcuffed to the balcony. "He's got to be breaking some sort of law, being that ugly and naked in a public place."

The branches of an oleander rattled in the darkness behind Annie. "I'd say he deserves a prize for being dog ugly."

Annie sighed and turned around. "Sam, what are you doing in there?"

"Just enjoying the view, like everyone else."

The uniformed officer was on the balcony now, speaking to Marsh, who thrashed and made muffled noises. Two more cars pulled up.

Buzz walked over, his face unreadable. "We had an anonymous phone call saying a police presence was required out here." He shook his head. "Damnedest thing I've seen in twenty-five years of police work. With any luck we'll find some drugs up there." He looked at Izzy. "Don't suppose you might have any idea where his clothes are?"

"Not me." Izzy met his look squarely. "I only heard about it when you called Annie. How did he get out on bail?"

"Powerful friends," Buzz said tightly. "I told him not to come back here before the trial or I'd pick him up personally. Apparently he didn't listen." He turned, staring behind Annie. "Is someone hiding in those trees?"

"Must be the wind." Annie fought an urge to look back at Sam.

"Right." Buzz sounded resigned. "The wind. Why didn't I think of that?"

He walked across the lawn, passing Coco and Nikki Jerome, along with Mr. Harkowitz. All were wearing bathrobes.

"Someone said a naked man was chained to the balcony," Coco panted.

Taylor pointed upward. "Dead ahead at twelve o'clock high."

"*Ewwwww*," the two women said in unison.

"I didn't know men could get cellulite." Coco sounded thoughtful. "Maybe we're witnessing a medical marvel." Her brow furrowed. "Or maybe it's not a man."

Marsh turned sharply, jerking as Buzz's officer removed his blindfold, gag, and handcuffs.

"Definitely a man," Nikki Jerome murmured. "Even if he is pretty unimpressive. What's that thing on his head?"

"It looks like a woman's wig." Taylor shifted to get a better view. "And he appears to have a California state flag draped over one shoulder. Isn't that illegal, some kind of desecration of the flag?"

Annie took her arm and pulled her aside. "Taylor, did you do this?"

"Me?" Taylor's face was all innocence.

"He could sue us for millions. He could ruin Summerwind."

Gravel churned in the parking lot. A mobile news TV van raced into the lot, followed closely by a red truck sporting the logo of a major San Francisco channel. People jumped out, shouldering big cameras and racing over the lawn.

Up on the balcony, Buzz was covering Marsh with a sheet while reading him his rights.

Annie closed her eyes. Marsh deserved to be punished, but not this way. Now Taylor was in serious trouble and so was the resort.

"You could be arrested for this, Taylor."

"He was smashed. He doesn't know it was me up there."

"Then he'll go after me."

"How?"

Annie watched another news van pull up.

"How? The man's a legal shark and he's bound to sue. He may even get off for what he did to me if he shows there was a prior effort to harass him here."

Taylor's voice faltered. "But there wasn't. *He* was doing all the harassment. Your staff can testify to that."

"It might not be enough." Annie had a sudden, horrifying realization as more gravel churned in the parking lot. The Navy had gone to immense effort to shield Sam from scrutiny while he recovered, knowing that reporters all over the country would be trying to track him down. Now thanks to Taylor, he was standing right in the path of a media tidal wave, and that was the very last place he should be.

There was no other choice, Annie realized. Everything had changed. Sam would have to leave.

And she'd have to let him go.

Again.

Chapter Thirty-six

"TELL ME THIS IS A BAD DREAM." ANNIE SAT STIFFLY IN TAYLOR'S high-tech kitchen.

"Afraid I can't."

Annie closed her eyes. "Are those news teams still out there?"

Taylor checked the window and nodded.

Annie had spoken to her lawyer, who was now doing damage control. What next? She shuddered at a vision of the cover of *Spa Monthly* with Tucker Marsh, naked and dead center. "What's happening?"

Taylor passed over a cup of steaming ginger chamomile tea. "When Buzz's officers checked out the parking lot to run off the camera crews, they found a cement truck parked on the service road. Two goons were running a video camera, getting shots of Marsh. They admitted Marsh had hired them to trash the resort."

"Trash?"

"You know, pour cement in the new whirlpool, tar the sauna, rip out your irrigation system. They were also supposed to set fire to your office."

Annie felt a spasm in her chest.

"Don't worry, Marsh paid them less than he promised, so they didn't do much harm."

"*How* much?"

"Only a little tar near the new whirlpool." Taylor frowned. "It's going to take some scrubbing and you might have to replace one or two boulders and some landscaping, but that's it."

"Where's Marsh now?"

"In custody with Buzz. This time, no bail." Taylor smiled

smugly. "Turns out the Doofus Twins are more than happy to testify. Buzz says Marsh will be living courtesy of the state of California for a while."

"I still don't understand how he got up to the balcony."

Taylor gave a tight smile. "I saw him on the grounds, looking pretty smashed, and I decided to give him what he'd been asking for. I told him if he'd come up to one of the empty rooms with me, I'd make sure he had the experience of a lifetime."

"He *believed* you?"

"I flashed a pair of handcuffs." Taylor smiled smugly. "I hinted that some kinky sex might be involved."

"You didn't!"

"Hey, the man couldn't keep his hands off me after that. When we got upstairs, I told him to undress and get comfortable. Then I said I needed a little help with my zipper. While he was trying to find the zipper, I maneuvered him out onto the balcony and used the cuffs. The rest is history."

Annie shook her head. "Your trick could ruin us."

"Why? It was consensual. It's not *my* fault he got so excited that he handcuffed himself to the balcony. And after what he did to you, the man deserved to be punished."

Annie felt a stab of anger. Taylor had never really cared about Summerwind. She still didn't understand how much harm her thoughtless prank had caused. "This time you did yourself proud, Taylor."

"What? I planned it just right."

"You never plan ahead," Annie said stiffly.

"I didn't mean for things to backfire like this. I didn't think you would be hurt, only Marsh."

"That's right, you *never* think." Annie regretted the words the instant they were out, when she saw Taylor's face go pale. "No, that's not what I meant to say. It's just that there's so much at stake, Taylor. It's not about Marsh now. This affects all of us."

Her sister turned away. "You're absolutely right, as usual.

There is a lot at stake and I don't think things through. Obviously I've screwed up yet again." She took a long breath. "I think it would be best for both of us if I leave now, before I cause any more damage."

❖ ❖ ❖

BY AFTERNOON THE ROAD TO SUMMERWIND WAS CRAWLING WITH reporters. Annie had called her office twice for updates, but Megan had told her to stay out of sight or the media people would go berserk. Buzz had sent down a few more deputies to keep order, but his available personnel was limited. He was counting on things being quieter in the morning.

Annie wasn't so sure. The reporters looked prepared for a long-term siege. Meanwhile, she had hurt her sister with her angry comments, and Annie was determined to talk things through as soon as Taylor started answering her phone. Until then, she had responsibilities to Sam. She couldn't let her own problems overshadow his rehab.

She found him with Izzy hunched over Izzy's laptop. The two men appeared to be looking at a map of Washington, D.C., but Izzy cleared the screen when Annie bent for a closer look.

"More secret documents?"

Neither man spoke, and their silence was an eloquent reminder that Annie's world would never be Sam's world. There were secrets she could never know. But she had accepted that already, hadn't she?

She crooked her finger at Sam. "Come on, ace. Let's go see how good you really are."

❖ ❖ ❖

AFTER AN HOUR OF EXERCISE, SAM WAS COVERED WITH SWEAT, his muscles pumped and zinging. He could have gone on for another hour, but Annie called a halt when she saw him wince after a sudden move.

"So what's your diagnosis?"

She ticked off words on her fingers. "Arrogant. Pushy. Manipulative—"

His brow rose. "Medically speaking."

"I'm pretty sure you'll live." She shifted a barbell back and forth between her hands. "In another week I probably won't be able to do much more for you. You know the drills and the proper form. The rest of the work will be up to you."

"So you'll be glad to get rid of me?"

Annie stacked the barbell neatly in its holder, avoiding his eyes. "Did I say that?"

"Not quite, but it feels pretty close."

She took a step away, feeling a sudden need for distance. With Sam solidly on his way to recovery, it was time for her to make some decisions about their future. For that, Annie needed a clear head. "I'm going outside."

"Not alone, you aren't."

"Don't growl, McKade. I'm only going to my patio."

Sam started to stand up, but Annie stopped him. "I'd rather you didn't come with me. I—I need to be alone."

"Taylor told me you could be like this. She said you shut people out and refused to ask for help. It makes her furious, and I'm starting to understand how she feels."

"Let's leave Taylor out of this," Annie said stiffly.

"Granted, what she did was crazy and thoughtless, but she did it out of raw instinct to get back at someone who hurt you, and I know *exactly* how she feels."

Because his words chipped at her thin veneer of control, Annie turned away. She was exhausted from the emotional storms of the last two days and she had no strength for an argument. "Don't, Sam. I can't talk about this now."

"When?" He touched her shoulder.

"I don't know." She stiffened.

"Why do you pull away like that? Why are you so afraid to ask for help? Let me *in*, Annie. Is that so hard?"

Annie's fingers locked. Hard? No, it was far too easy.

She was white-knuckle terrified of how easy it would be to rely on this strong, decent man for support. In a matter of days or weeks, he would be gone without an explanation, exactly like last time. It came with the job he did, and nothing Annie said could change that.

He's the one, she thought. Exactly the kind of man she'd never hoped to find.

And he was the one man with no future to offer any woman, not as long as the job came first.

For Sam it always would, macho idiot hero that he was. There would always be another busload of children to rescue or a kidnapped American to free. Sam was too highly trained to be wasted on average, everyday Navy duties, that much was clear.

Real-life heroes didn't work eight to five, then head home to the wife and kids for a quiet night of touch football and barbecuing on the patio. For Sam, risking his life in dangerous places was standard operating procedure.

Annie had no place in that dangerous, unpredictable life. The sooner she accepted that, the less she would be hurt. She had bled inside when he'd left. Day after day she had hoped for a call or a fax or a letter, even though he'd made no promises.

She couldn't go through that again.

"You've already helped me," she said, cool and distant in the face of his anger. "I thought I'd thanked you."

"Thanked me? You mean shake hands and exchange air kisses?"

"Sam, don't."

"Don't *what*? Don't be furious that your face is white and you act like I'm a damned stranger? Maybe I should introduce myself, Annie. I'm the man you bit and clawed through sweaty, moaning sex. Want to see your nail marks?" He yanked up his gray T-shirt. "They're right here where you put them."

Annie saw the pale red marks, just as he'd said. But now she saw that they framed darker wounds, along with the faint silver traces of much older scars from bullets, knives, and ropes.

Because Sam McKade was a warrior. Fighting was his life, just as healing was hers. How could she have forgotten something so important and so irrevocable?

Annie closed her eyes. She hadn't expected him to fight dirty, which was almost funny, considering that fighting dirty was what he was trained to do best. She'd seen his performance aboard that skidding bus. He was tough and focused, and he'd been taught to survey hostile terrain, assess the enemy precisely, then fight hard, using every dirty trick and tool at his disposal.

Annie didn't have a hope of standing up to that.

So she wouldn't try.

She stared at his chest. "I'm sorry I hurt you like that."

"It's not the marks that hurt, Annie." His jaw moved once. "It's being shut out this way like a stranger."

"It was just sex, Sam."

"Like *hell* it was." He pulled a towel from the table and tossed it over her shoulder. "It was a whole lot more. We both know that."

"No." Somehow Annie kept her voice very calm. "What we did changed nothing."

"You're wrong. You don't just walk away from an experience like that."

"Why? Men do it all the time." She was tired and frightened and confused, and she needed to get away before she unraveled. It was too easy to lean, too easy to hide from making hard choices. "I'm going outside."

"Fine. Just remember this isn't finished between us."

"I'm tired, Sam."

"Of course you are." He looked as if he would touch her, but his hand fell. "You've been through hell. Maybe we both have." He smoothed the towel over her shoulder, then took a step back. "I'm not running away from this. I'm not letting you run either."

"Maybe the decision has already been made."

"What do you mean?"

Annie straightened her shoulders. If he wanted to fight dirty, she'd match him now. It was actually a relief to stop pretending she didn't know what was coming. "I know you'll have to leave soon, Sam. When the orders come, you'll vanish. You probably won't even be able to say good-bye."

He didn't move, didn't speak.

"That's what I thought you'd have to say."

"Annie, I—"

"You *are* leaving soon, right?"

His jaw worked hard. Then he nodded.

"And you won't be able to tell me when or where, because that's standard operating procedure. One day I'll wake up and you'll be gone."

He took a hard breath. "I can't apologize for doing my job."

"And I can't apologize for doing mine. Which brings us to good-bye, no matter how you look at it."

Annie closed her eyes. When they opened, she was more tired than before. Maybe some part of her had hoped she was wrong. "That leaves us right back where we ended last time. But I'm tired, Sam. I'm tired of painting pretty pictures and pretending I don't care. Since it's going to be over, I'd rather we start now." She gripped the towel tightly before her chest, almost like a shield. "Now I'm going outside. I'd appreciate it if you didn't follow me."

❖ ❖ ❖

SHE MANAGED A PASSABLE EXIT. LATER, ANNIE WOULD BE PROUD of that.

There had been no spilled tears, no wobbly knees. No panic and no second thoughts.

But it had been harder than she'd dreamed possible, because the tears had threatened, blocking off her throat. Down the hill she heard the sharp slam of a car door. Probably another guest leaving in haste.

She winced at the thought, hit by a crushing sense of failure. She'd mishandled Marsh, misreading his intentions completely. She'd been too slow to take precautions and now everything she valued was in jeopardy, and she was to blame.

The buck stops here.

The simple truth was that she should have seen where things were heading and tossed Marsh out at the first sign of trouble. Being frightened of litigation and distracted by Sam was no excuse, she told herself bitterly.

Down the hill another car door slammed. Annie did some quick math and sighed. At this rate, she'd have only five guests left by morning.

Maybe she'd have none.

Mist curled around her as she cranked up the whirlpool heater, then switched the motor to high. With a sigh she sank into the hot, churning water and closed her eyes. Her head hurt and her ribs were bruised. But what hurt most was the knowledge that she'd failed. A good reputation was hard to achieve and even harder to maintain. Surrounded by luxury hotel chains bankrolled by international resources, she had to rely on impeccable service, discretion, and word-of-mouth recommendations to survive. Customer satisfaction had always been her hallmark, and her clientele demanded privacy and peace.

Now that sense of peace and privacy was threatened by the media zoo in progress and rumors of sabotage at the resort. Two huge hotel chains had already phoned, offering to buy the resort, and even Annie's local bank had expressed concerns about how the publicity would affect her future bookings.

If the attention continued, she would lose most of her clientele, people with hectic, high-power lives who came to the beautiful, isolated beach to escape from the rat race, instead of finding it right on their doorstep.

Marsh might have the last laugh after all.

She kept her eyes from the windows, from the shadowed

figure pacing inside. In the midst of this chaos, there was Sam, distracting her, confusing her, making her want things she'd never wanted before.

But he would be leaving soon. They both knew his job demanded it. Why did he have this ridiculous idea that they had a future, something that could outlast a few torrid encounters?

Forget about the sex, Annie told herself.

Forget about Sam, too.

She traced the churning water with her hand, watching steam rise in slow spirals. At least she would always have Summerwind.

◆ ◆ ◆

SHE WAS WALKING RIGHT AT THE EDGE, SAM THOUGHT.

She was pale and strained. Even then, she wouldn't give an inch.

He stared out the window, hating the slump to her shoulders and the weary way she sank onto the deck. Tucker Marsh was to blame for some of it, but Sam knew a major part of the blame was his. It was his arrival that had thrown her life into chaos, eating into her work time and distracting her from the heavy demands of running the resort.

Taylor had told him glumly that guests were checking out at a record clip. Though they'd kept the details from Annie, she was too smart not to guess how bad things were.

He looked up as Izzy emerged from the courtyard. "How is it out there?"

"Worse than a tied Army-Navy game. There are media people everywhere. The minute Buzz's officers run them off, new ones appear."

"What about the guests?"

"Most of them have left. Taylor's down there handling things like a pro, but who can blame people for leaving? Finding a TV cameraman crouched on your balcony isn't exactly restful."

Sam prowled the room restlessly. "I've got to do something.

If Annie hadn't gone back for my wallet, none of this would have happened. Hell, if I hadn't *come* here this wouldn't have happened."

"If you show your face, they'll go berserk."

Sam knew it was true, but his inability to help only made him angrier. "Can't Buzz block the road?"

"He already has. They just go around by the back roads. Every hour or so a few manage to dodge his men and sneak onto the grounds anyway. It's not like he can put a dozen deputies here full-time. He doesn't have the personnel."

Sam stared toward the beach. "Annie needs more protection."

"Don't worry, I've got someone inside the spa."

Sam's brow rose. "If Annie didn't notice, your contact must be pretty slick."

"Only the best."

"You won't tell me who?"

Izzy shrugged. "Afraid not."

"Things aren't going to get any better, not with this circus going full tilt. If she closes, the curiosity might fade."

"Taylor agrees. She suggested you try to convince Annie."

"She won't give in without a fight. This place means too much to her." Sam stood up. "I'll still give it a shot."

"One more thing."

"Do I want to hear this?"

Izzy cleared his throat. "Probably not."

Sam waited, nerves on edge. "Let's have it."

"The admiral just phoned. They've caught some of the TV coverage back in D.C."

"So?"

Izzy seemed to steel himself for what he had to say next. "New orders. You're being pulled out as of midnight tonight."

Chapter Thirty-seven

SAM SLASHED AT THE AIR. "I'M NOT LEAVING ANNIE IN THE MIDdle of a mess like this."

Izzy said nothing, his face impassive.

"She's been through too damned much already."

"She's strong, Sam."

"I didn't say she wasn't." Sam's fingers formed a fist. "But she needs moral support. Thanks to me, her life's turned into a nightmare."

"Taylor can give her moral support."

"Right now, Taylor's part of the problem," Sam said grimly. "Annie and I were just starting to work things out. I can't leave now."

"I don't think you have a choice, my friend."

Sam slammed his palms against the kitchen counter. "Like hell I don't."

"Are you ready to chuck a distinguished career?" Izzy asked quietly.

Sam stared out the window. Steam was rising above the hollyhocks, gray streaks between a riot of pink and fuchsia. The rich, hot colors reminded him of Annie's laugh, her eye for beauty, and her passionate skill at healing.

Didn't it figure that he'd fall in love with a woman who knew how to cure everyone else's stress and pain but her own?

Whoa.

Love?

Swallowing hard, Sam sank into the nearest chair. Love was an emotion he'd managed to avoid for nearly three decades.

Love was messy and confusing and changed everything. Love was a distraction that a SEAL *couldn't* afford.

In spite of all that, he loved her.

Damn it, he'd loved her from the first moment he'd seen her running along the beach carrying a weather-beaten straw hat and a bunch of straggly wildflowers, laughing full tilt.

His head sank onto his hands.

"Something wrong?"

Sam closed his eyes. "You could say that."

"Bad?"

"Beyond bad."

Izzy studied him curiously. "Want some coffee?"

"It would take a lot more than caffeine to fix this problem," Sam said grimly. He took a long, harsh breath. "I love her," he said quietly. "I don't want a day or two, I want forever."

"So this is serious."

Sam nodded.

"For both of you?"

Sam smiled thinly. "I was working on that part."

"A wife is a definite liability in your line of work."

Sam moved restlessly, rubbing his shoulder. "Tell me something I haven't already told myself. The thing is, the problems don't matter."

"You know what happens to marriages put under the kind of stress you face."

"They nose-dive fast. I've seen the scorecard, Izzy. The odds are against us. But I don't care. I'm not running out on Annie again."

Izzy's eyes narrowed. "Again?"

"You heard me, *again*. I know what happened before. I remembered most of it yesterday."

Izzy shot to his feet. "Damn it, Sam, you should have told me."

"Relax. Nothing official has come back or I would have let

you know. What I remembered was personal, scattered details about the last time I was here." Sam shifted one shoulder restlessly, his eyes focused on the beach. Something was bothering him, but he couldn't pin it down.

Hell, he should make a *list* of all the things that were bothering him.

"I remember I told her she looked like Meg Ryan. She gave that amazing laugh and told me I didn't look much like Russell Crowe, so we were probably safe." He closed his eyes. "I hurt her when I left, Izzy. She still can't hide it. How can I walk out and cut her to shreds like that again?"

"Because you have to. Last time I checked, the Navy didn't let you pick which orders to obey and which ones to ignore. If you stay here any longer, someone will pick up your scent, and that becomes a serious security matter."

Sam cursed. He'd already realized the same thing. "When are they coming?"

"We're to expect a car and driver at oh-three-thirty hours."

"Call D.C. with some story about a final set of tests you and Annie need to run." Sam stared at the steam rising above the flowers. "I want tonight with her, Izzy. If it's going to be the last one we have, I need that."

Izzy rubbed his jaw. "It's not going to be easy."

"If it were easy, you wouldn't be getting the big bucks."

Izzy's brow rose. "How do you know what I'm getting?"

"Friends in low places. You're top of the line, and the Navy knows it. I heard about that episode down in the Caribbean last year."

Izzy's face was expressionless. "Don't know what you mean."

"The cruise ship assignment. Ford McKay happens to be an old friend of mine."

"I don't think I know the name," Izzy murmured.

Sam snorted. "Like hell you don't, but I'll forget I brought it up. Just buy us some time."

Izzy smiled faintly. "You're on."

"I won't forget it." Sam started for the back door. "Meanwhile, why don't you go keep an eye on Taylor and the media hordes?"

"Meaning you'd like some privacy?"

"Meaning I'd like some privacy."

Izzy was smiling broadly as he sauntered to the door. "Roger that. Radio silence until oh-five-hundred hours." But he turned, giving Sam a serious look. "I can't hold them off beyond that. At dawn I'm afraid all the coaches will turn back into pumpkins."

❖ ❖ ❖

ANNIE WAS STRETCHED AGAINST THE ROCKY EDGE OF THE FREE-form saltwater spa, her eyes closed as steam danced around her. A book lay forgotten at her elbow.

She would have looked the picture of serenity except for the black eye and the bruises along the inside of her elbow.

Sam still felt sick at how close she had come to serious harm at Marsh's hands, but he wasn't going to waste their last night thinking about Marsh. If there was any justice, the man would be practicing jailhouse law on surly cell mates for the next few years.

Annie opened one eye as Sam sat on the edge of the spa. She watched him heft a twenty-five-pound dumbbell with his good arm.

"Don't you ever rest?"

"No." Sam smiled. "I guess that makes us just alike." He finished ten repetitions, then started another set. "I figure I'll relax when I'm a hundred."

"You push the limits whenever you can, don't you?"

Sam shrugged. "Another thing we have in common. Face it, Annie, we're meant to be together, and you already know I can't resist a woman in red lace." Sam studied the churning water. "By the way, what *are* you wearing in there?"

"None of your business."

His mouth moved a little. "I could make it my business."

She crossed her arms stiffly. "I wanted to be alone out here."

"Just ignore me," Sam said.

"Fine." As she spoke, Annie slid the book under her towel.

"What are you reading?"

"Nothing special." She spoke quickly, trying to block Sam's hand as he reached under the towel, but he was too fast.

"*Thirty Days to a Stress-Free Sex Life?*" His smile widened. "Sounds useful." He flipped through several pages and stopped at random. "Take this idea, here on page fifty-six. The one with the whipped cream and the bowl of fruit." He skimmed the page, one brow raised. "I'll never think of avocados and strawberries in the same way again." He studied Annie. "Wanna try it?"

There was just a moment of hesitation before she shook her head.

"How about adapting this one for the blue exercise ball?" He pointed to a diagram. "Just think what this would do for my lower-body strength. You can write it all up in your final report for the Navy, complete with your own therapeutic diagrams."

He saw her lips twitch.

A good sign.

"Maybe we should try chapter six. I suggest putting pillows on the wooden bench on your porch. I'll go round up the candles."

"Are you biologically unable to hear the word no?"

"No." Sam was grinning. "I say it all the time to other people and mean it."

He did a final rep with the barbell, then winced.

"Sam, what happened?"

"Nothing."

"Of course something happened. You were twisting to the right, then you froze."

"Look, it was nothing. Just a twinge, okay?"

"Get over here and let me see."

"There's no need."

Annie shot out of the water. "Now."

Sam watched in fascination, barely aware of the throbbing at his right shoulder. Today she was wearing some kind of leopardskin-print bodysuit with little hooks down the front. The water left it glistening and translucent against her.

"Sam?"

He had to swallow to talk. "What?"

"You're staring."

"Me?" In another minute he was going to feel his eyes roll back in his head. "Oh. Your suit. It's—interesting."

"Forget the suit."

He shook his head slowly. "Not possible, Doc. Not with you in it, looking good enough to nibble slowly from stem to stern."

She drew a sharp breath. "I need to look at your shoulder."

His gaze hardened. "Fine." He unsnapped his jeans and shucked them with no wasted movement. "This way you can see better." He stepped into the water beside her, trying not to watch that unbelievable body showcased in see-through leopard print or want her long legs wrapped around him.

"You're sweating, Sam."

"Probably."

"You look really done in." She leaned against his side, her breasts skimming his chest as she gently palpated his shoulder. "Where does it hurt?"

All over, he thought grimly. But especially where she touched him. "About the same."

Annie slid over his thigh, fingering pressure points along his neck and back. "Better?"

He shook his head. Begging was a real possibility if he opened his mouth.

Annie straddled his other thigh. "How about this?"

He caught her waist, holding her still. "You don't want to know, honey."

Her eyes narrowed. "If this is some kind of macho ploy to trick me into having sex—"

"Stop calling it sex," Sam said tightly. "And it isn't a trick. My shoulder happens to hurt like hell. Problem is, the rest of me hurts even more."

The water churned around them. Steam drifted past Annie's face. Sam saw something move in her eyes, but he couldn't say what.

"So you're in pain."

He nodded.

She rested a palm against his chest. "Starting here?"

And shooting straight south, Sam thought wryly. It wasn't the sort of thing you could conceal in a pair of briefs, either. "Roughly, yes."

Annie traced the dark curve of a recent scar at his shoulder. "This must hurt, too."

Her touch was killing him, actually. "Sometimes. Did I tell you I love your hair?"

She studied him gravely. "Why do you always have to push so hard?"

"Because it's what I do."

After a long time she nodded. "So I've been told. You don't ever make things easy, do you?"

"Easy was never on my agenda." Sam bit back a groan as her body rocked against him in the water. He moved back, closer to the waterfall. He wasn't going to push Annie if she didn't want him.

But when he moved, she followed.

Sam frowned. "What are you doing?"

"Something stupid, probably. You see, I was trying to do the right thing before. The practical thing."

"Tear off my clothes and have your way with me in a night of wild, abandoned sex?" he said hopefully.

"No." The swirl of emotions was back in her eyes. Sam realized it was tenderness laced with regret. "I was trying to say good-bye, ace. Fast and painless, the way good-byes work best. We both know we don't have any kind of future together."

Sam's hands tightened. "Says who?"

"Says just about anyone with eyes."

He was getting damned tired of people telling him about the future he didn't have. "Then a lot of people are idiots. They have eyes but they still manage to be blind." He coaxed a damp curl off her shoulder as hot, frothy waves lapped at his skin.

The sudden narrowing of Annie's eyes told him she felt it too.

"So what do we do next?" Her voice was grave. Sam heard the unspoken questions that neither was able to face yet.

He felt his muscles tighten as he pulled her onto his lap. "We make tonight count." He traced her hip slowly.

"When your orders come and you have to go—"

Sam touched her lips. "Not tonight." He tilted her face up to his. "Did you know your eyes are the color of the windward clouds when a man sails into Kauai after a storm."

She took a shaky breath. "No, I didn't."

"Stay with me tonight," he said urgently. "Trust me, Annie. Trust me while we make a future together."

Drops of water shimmered in her hair. "Don't make any promises, Sam. It hurts too much later."

"I'll make all the damned promises I want," he said fiercely. "I'm thinking long-term."

She closed her eyes. "Tonight I don't want to think at all."

"That can be arranged," he said darkly. "We'll talk about the rest later."

"You don't have to do this Sam. I'd already decided to say yes to whatever you wanted from me tonight."

His voice was rough. "What I want is the next fifty years, not one night."

Annie slid a hand along his chest. "That's . . . a long time."

She took a slow breath. "Can't I interest you in a one-night stand?"

Desire sledgehammered through his chest. "Only if it's the first of about a million."

"We'll talk about *that* later." Her hand glided along his thigh, slipping beneath white cotton to find him fully aroused.

He was going to beg any bloody moment, Sam thought, fighting a haze of lust. He swallowed hard as her hands moved down his full length. But he wanted a future, damn it. Not just a night.

The wet spandex fell. Sam realized he was staring at her lovely, aroused breasts through the churning water.

Hell, two could play this game. His hand slid under her bodysuit and he watched her eyes go dark.

His fingers moved against warm, yielding skin, making her eyes go even darker. "I want all your nights, Annie. Not just one."

"Why?" She was staring at his mouth, cheeks flushed, looking distracted. Sam moved his hand so that she looked even more distracted. She was making little panting sounds, that slim, strong body moving against his, wanting him. "I still don't understand you. I try to, but I don't."

"You don't have to understand." The leopardskin suit slid open and floated away on the water. "Just enjoy it."

"How do you do this to me?" she whispered.

"Because I love touching you. I love hearing you, talking with you. Because I'm dead certain I love you," he said roughly.

Annie gave a shocked sigh as her body tightened against his hands and pleasure streaked through her.

When her breathing finally steadied, she leaned against him, trembling. "Don't call it love. Love is too big, too dangerous. I'll settle for a night of great sex."

He bit her lower lip very gently. "Stop calling it sex, Annie."

She stared at him for a long time. "I've always been a pushover for a man in a uniform."

"You never saw me in uniform."

Her hand moved over his taut stomach. "On TV, ace." Her voice tightened. "Along with about twenty million other women, I fell in love with a man in a white uniform."

As she spoke, Sam felt a memory rattle loose and skitter around in his head.

Noise and crowds. Screams and red lights. He'd been climbing something that was swinging hard, skidding under him.

A bus.

It was coming back to him now. With a vengeance.

He was shaking, couldn't stop shaking.

"Sam?"

"It's here, Annie. I remember a bus. There were children inside, all of them screaming."

She gripped his arm. "Go on."

"I couldn't get through the window. The driver was out cold, so I used something wooden." He frowned, searching for the exact image. "A hockey stick."

"That's it!"

Sam felt his body tighten as the memories came faster. "I shoved the stick down against the brake pedal and the bus kicked hard. We fishtailed some, the tires screaming. I smelled the rubber burn and—"

And then he remembered the rest, being tossed high, the wind shrill and the ground blurring, feeling terrified and light-headed, fighting to control the fall. Knowing at the last that he couldn't.

"I remember," he said tightly. "All of it."

Annie gripped his shoulder, her face wet with tears. "I knew you could do it."

"You saw that on television?"

"You were on every channel."

He thought about that for a long time. "I wasn't supposed to be there. I had something else to do that was important." He frowned, running his hand through his hair. "Then I saw the bus, the way it shook and swerved. I saw it was in trouble and I just jumped on without thinking."

"You're good at jumping without thinking." She touched his cheek gently, as if afraid to distract him. "Anything else?"

He was so damned close, Sam thought. Something heavy drifted just out of reach.

Something that hurt in a way that felt personal. Was that why he couldn't remember?

"Sam?"

He frowned, sitting up straight in the hot water.

So close. Why didn't he see it?

"Hey, you can try again later." When he didn't answer, Annie turned his face around to hers. "Anyone listening in there?"

"I'm trying." Sam forced himself to stop pushing, to let the drifting strands go. He'd remembered enough for one night. "So that's how I ended up on your doorstep at midnight, strapped onto a gurney. Hell of a thing. I don't feel like a hero."

"Maybe that's why you are." There was something soft and proud in her voice. "You were so brave even with all the pain."

He kissed her hand. "And you were so cool, so absolutely professional. Then you reached down to me and did that thing with your hands and it felt like you were slipping right inside my skin." His grip tightened. "You put me back together again, Annie."

"You did the work. I just watched and offered advice here and there."

"Good lie, but I don't buy it. You're the best. And I wanted you bad, Doc." He ran his fingers slowly over her waist, then lower still, so that her legs parted and her body cradled his. "I still do."

"You might want to do something about that," Annie murmured. "Right now."

His hands were making her brain short-circuit and the steam was leaving her giddy. She didn't want to think tonight, didn't want to be practical. Being practical made her head hurt.

She just wanted to float, to close her eyes and let the steam enfold her while Sam ran his fingers into her hair and rocked her to that place where the world winked, then fell away in a sigh.

He was slow, careful, so gentle that she felt the press of tears.

"Okay?" he whispered raggedly. "I'm not hurting you, am I?"

She looked at his face, rugged, veiled by steam in the moonlight. As she felt the deep weight of his concern, her knees opened and he slid slowly inside her as if they'd always been this way, born in one piece but had only rediscovered the truth of it.

She smiled. "Not a bit."

"Is it working yet?"

"What?"

"Everything. Moonlight, heat, and me. I want everything to work for us tonight, Annie." He found her with his fingers as he spoke, slow and clever and irresistible so that she closed her eyes and came in a soft whoosh of surprise.

When her eyes opened, he was smiling, too. She rose in the swirling water, kissing his chin, his jaw, feeling as linked as she'd ever been with another person.

Feeling gloriously *alive*.

"It's definitely working," she said, pressing into him until his eyes darkened, and he brought them together so that the water rocked hard and the heat turned them inside out while they fell and fell and fell into each other's eyes.

Chapter Thirty-eight

ANNIE WAS ASLEEP WHEN SAM SLID OUT OF BED.

The power of having her had left him stunned and exhilarated. He didn't have words for the way they'd felt together. He wasn't sure that the words existed. He ran a hand through his hair and found himself smiling like a fool.

And he didn't care a bit. But the setting moon reminded him of time and duties that wouldn't wait. So instead of kissing Annie slowly awake, he moved silently to the kitchen, cell phone in hand.

Admiral Howe answered on the third ring. Sam wondered if the man ever slept.

"Sorry to bother you so late, sir."

"No problem. Just let me finish with another call." Sounding distracted, the admiral returned in a moment. "My son was checking to be sure I'm not drinking my way into an early grave with my cache of Glenlivet. Good thing he didn't ask about the cigar." Sam heard a hissing sound and imagined the crusty old fighter with a cigar between his lips. "What's been happening out there, McKade?"

Sam was pretty sure the admiral didn't want to hear about the stupendous, brain-softening sex he'd just had. "No one knows I'm here, if that's what you mean," he said cautiously.

"First good news I've had all day. I've got three damned senators and a presidential aide holding my feet to the fire demanding answers, and these people have friends all over the Hill." There was a puffing noise, then he continued. "So what's this call about?"

Sam felt bitter for some reason, and angry at himself for being angry. "I was undercover, wasn't I, sir?"

"You tell me."

"I was," Sam said tightly. "I went undercover wherever things were messy. Colombia. Trincomalee." Blood-bright images flashed even as he spoke. "It's what I was doing just before the accident, but I can't remember where."

"Tell me exactly what you remember."

"Only that I was someplace important, sir."

There was more puffing. "You were tracking a traitor," the admiral admitted. "I'd tell you all about it, but it's a long story. The fact is, we already have one of the people involved."

"Who?"

"George Regent."

Sam's fingers tightened. "The Assistant Secretary of Defense? What does he have to say about it?"

"Nothing. Regent is dead. He spun out of control on the Potomac Parkway last night and his car exploded."

Sam imagined the inferno, his mind racing. "Was it an accident?"

"I doubt it. I think someone is getting nervous. I'd lay odds there are going to be more accidents." The admiral sounded tired and angry. "I need your memory back, Commander. Get ready to move. You'll be met at oh-five-hundred hours."

Sam managed to stifle an automatic protest.

"I don't need to remind you that your orders are to be carried out in absolute secrecy. You pack and you leave, understood?"

Sam's mouth hardened. "Understood, sir."

❖ ❖ ❖

IT WAS NEARLY DAWN. OUT TO SEA THE FIRST PALE STREAMERS OF light brushed against gray waves.

So little time, Sam thought.

Beside him, Annie slept on, murmuring as he ran one hand gently over her hair. When he looked up, the luminous dial of the clock glowed with malignant energy from the bureau.

Time to go.

He smelled her scent, lemon and lavender. He felt the brush of her skin against him and accepted that a delay wouldn't dim the pain.

His face like stone, he slipped from the bed and slid his few clothes into a regulation duffel bag. In the filtered gray light Sam thought of all the other times he'd stood this way in a chill dawn, coldly tying off loose ends before heading to an unknown mission and possible death. As he stood unmoving, images came in a flood.

Men he'd killed. Men who'd tried to kill him.

Two who'd almost succeeded.

Time to go.

He closed his eyes, knowing that he'd never wanted to stay as much as he did now. Before there'd never been a woman like Annie to hold him. Before he'd never believed in love.

But orders were orders.

As if sensing the intensity of his thoughts, Annie turned, snuggled into his pillow, one arm flung out in search of his warmth. Every muscle screamed for him to go to her, to pull her close.

He did neither.

Because orders were orders.

Izzy tapped softly at the door. *Time to go.*

He took one last look at Annie, her lashes shadowed in the dim light, her face pale and calm and deceptively fragile.

He hoarded the precious images, one by one, as his hand rose. But how could he change what he had to do? And what did he have to give her when he came back? A job that could pull him away at any second? A heart full of dreams?

Dreams didn't count for much.

Silent and grim, he turned to the door. A man in a black flight suit took his bag, waiting impatiently. Dawn was a blood-red streak above the sea when they crossed the courtyard toward a waiting car.

Chapter Thirty-nine

ANNIE FELT IT THE SECOND SHE OPENED HER EYES.

There was a stillness to the house that hadn't been there before.

Suddenly cold, she ran one hand over the far side of the bed, tracing its chill. Gone, she thought.

Sam was gone.

She closed her eyes. A moment later she was crouched on the bed gasping hard, fighting for breath.

He'd gone without a word, just like the last time, and the pain was past bearing.

She looked at the beach and beyond, where the sea was fading from flat pewter to cool, dimpled green. As she watched, dolphins crested the cove, their grace and energy leaving a sense of awe. She could almost hear their unearthly, high-pitched chatter. Did they share their worries the way humans did? Did they agonize over offspring and weather?

As the last tears leaked out, Annie rubbed her face slowly. Silent, she sat up, hugging her knees and staring out at the cove. A small boat drifted exactly where Sam had moored long weeks before.

The same place she'd lost her heart to a man with a rugged face, a calm laugh, and too many dark memories in his eyes.

Annie hadn't asked about his past although it had drifted around him like smoke, a clear warning that they had nothing, absolutely nothing in common.

One week later she'd given herself to him without fear, without limits. He'd answered her with gentle hands and a fierce hunger, and later with something like regret.

Both of them had been very careful not to speak of love. Neither had made any promises.

And now?

Now he had orders, she told herself. She was in love with a hero, and for a hero, duty always came first.

She rose slowly and began to dress. Sam had asked her to trust him and she was going to try.

❖   ❖   ❖

SHE FOUND IZZY IN THE GUESTHOUSE HUNCHED OVER A LAPTOP computer with two exterior disk drives. At least that's what they looked like to her. "When did he leave?"

Izzy looked up, his eyes narrowed. "It wasn't his choice, Annie."

She nodded, hearing the words as if from a distance. "He told me he'd have to go. I knew it was coming." She looked away and took a sharp breath. "We both knew, but we hoped it would be later."

"If Sam had his choice, it would have been."

"I believe that." Annie filled a cup with coffee and held it out to Izzy. "I suppose this fiasco with Marsh hasn't helped the situation."

"It was just a question of time. Sam's a valuable asset now that he's recuperated."

"Recuperated?" Annie glared at Izzy. "Sam's knee is still shaky and his shoulder is barely usable. He's going to need that brace off and on for at least another week. If he gets shipped out on a mission now—" She ran one hand across her eyes. "Tell me to shut up anytime you want."

"He won't push himself unless he has to, Annie."

"Unless he's in danger, you mean."

Izzy nodded. "He told me he was serious. Leaving was the last thing he wanted. Maybe that helps."

It did, just a little.

Trust him, Annie told herself.

Izzy closed his laptop and rose slowly. "How about we go out for some ice cream?"

Annie had never felt less like eating. "A little early, isn't it?"

"Never too early for the good stuff."

She managed a smile. "Only if it's truly sinful. Chocolate chocolate mocha chip."

Izzy studied her thoughtfully. "Sinful can probably be arranged."

◆ ◆ ◆

WHEN THEY PULLED OFF THE COAST HIGHWAY TWENTY MINUTES later, Annie was disoriented. "This isn't the way to town."

Izzy drove on, his eyes unreadable.

She frowned as the minutes passed and they drove inland along a pitted fire road, mountains rising before them. "I might also point out that this is a long way to go for ice cream."

"But they get the really good stuff here." Izzy turned onto a twisting dirt lane. "You'll see."

"See what?" Annie stared as they stopped before a house with weathered stone walls and a sloping blue roof. "I don't understand."

"I'll get your bags out of the back."

"What bags?"

Izzy pointed up the hill. "Go get your chocolate chocolate mocha chip."

The door on the big stone porch opened and a white dog rocketed down the hill. Behind him a man appeared, wearing worn blue jeans and the faintest of smiles.

Annie drew a sharp breath. "He's here?"

"In the flesh. You should know that somebody bent a lot of rules for this."

"Bless that somebody." Annie kissed Izzy swiftly, then swung open the door and flew over the lawn.

Right into Sam's arms.

Neither heard the sound of gravel when Izzy pulled away.

❖ ❖ ❖

THE WIND WAS GENTLE ON ANNIE'S FACE. "HOW LONG DO WE have?"

"I don't know, Annie."

No lies, no evasion. This way was best, she told herself.

Sam's fingers tightened in her hair. "Can you accept that?"

"I'll have to." She frowned. "I need to phone Taylor. It may be a while before I get back."

Sam ran his hands over her cheeks, as if memorizing every bone. "Izzy will set up a secure line. Just keep the details vague."

Annie felt a sudden kick of fear. "Sam, has something happened?" She gripped his arm. "Are you in danger?"

For long moments he didn't speak. His eyes shifted, focused over her shoulder. "I believe that's the assumption."

"You're not going to tell me any more than that?"

"I can't. You need to trust me on this, Annie."

"I can't walk around in the dark, Sam, and I'm no help to you if I don't know what to watch for."

After a long time he nodded. "Security's involved, Annie. I've got to restore those missing days, and the clock is ticking."

"You can't *make* yourself remember," she said sharply.

"Tell that to the doctors. They say I might be fighting something."

"Then you need to relax. How about a nice massage in front of the fire?"

Sam's eyes narrowed. "I can think of something that would relax me more."

"That could be arranged, too," Annie murmured. She turned as the big white dog bounded up the hill, tail swinging. "Who's your gorgeous friend?"

"His name's Donegal. Be careful, he's a real charmer."

The dog sniffed Annie's legs, then sat alertly at Sam's feet.

"Is he waiting for something?"

"For me to tell him if you're friend or foe." Sam looked down into the dark, intelligent eyes and smiled. "It's okay, Donegal. She's a friend."

In a shot, the dog was at Annie's side, pressing against her hand and barking excitedly. "He's lovely, Sam. What breed is he?"

"Irish wolfhound. But Donegal's more than another pretty face, trust me. I trained him myself."

Annie's brow rose. "You mean he's a show dog?"

Sam laughed dryly. "Not that kind of training, honey." He whistled once, and Donegal trotted to his side. "Down," he said firmly.

Instantly the dog went flat against the ground, head down, all motion ceased.

"Scout," Sam ordered.

Keeping his body low, the wolfhound moved off through the grass, ears pricked forward and body tense.

Annie stared. "You mean he's some kind of guard dog?"

"Way beyond a guard dog. Donegal's saved my hide three times now. His nose is a hundred times better than any man's, he can guard a perimeter like Rambo, and he doesn't need C-rations."

"So you actually take him on missions?"

"When conditions are right." A muscle moved at his jaw. "Donegal, heel."

In a blur of pale fur, the dog shot over the grass and stopped smoothly at Sam's side, his eyes watchful.

Sam scratched the dog's neck. "Good boy. You've charmed her already."

"You're worried, aren't you? Things have gotten worse."

Sam surveyed the hillside behind her. "I remembered something important yesterday, at least part of it. Because of what I remembered, we're looking for someone, and things could get nasty until we find him. I want you close where Izzy and I can protect you. That's all I can say for now."

Annie sensed he was revealing more to her than most civilians would have been told, though it made little sense. She tilted her head, resting her palm against his chest. "Izzy said a lot of rules were bent for me to come here. Is that true?"

"Izzy talks too damned much."

"Funny, I think he's just about perfect." Her lips pursed. "Except for a friend of his. The man's totally arrogant, of course. Stubborn and irritating—"

Sam lifted her palm and laced his fingers through hers. "I just hope you can't live without him."

"Well, I like his dog. I'll tell you the rest in a few hours." Annie shivered. "It's freezing out here."

"Must be a storm coming." Sam's voice was low, and Donegal instinctively edged closer, waiting for an order.

Looking at Sam's eyes, Annie had the feeling he was talking about more than the weather. "Where's Izzy?"

A bank of clouds was moving in from the west as Sam glanced up the hill. "He'll be around."

"I don't see anything."

"That's the general idea, honey." He slid an arm around her shoulders and turned toward the big stone porch. "Let's go inside. I've got a fire going and a bottle of merlot just waiting to pour." He rubbed Donegal's head, then pointed down to the road. "Scout."

The big dog barked twice, then vanished into the trees.

❖ ❖ ❖

SAM GAVE ANNIE A TOUR OF THE HOUSE FROM THE HIGH-TECH kitchen to the open living room with its immense granite fireplace. Upstairs the sprawling master bedroom opened onto a balcony overlooking twenty miles of mountains. There was a fully equipped gym on the second floor and an indoor pool in the back, Sam explained.

"I still can't believe this." Annie's head was spinning as she ran a hand along a leather couch the size of Fisherman's Wharf. "It seems so strange. I haven't taken a vacation in five years."

"We're going to have to do something about that problem of yours."

"What problem?"

"You're a certified workaholic, which means I'll have to find a way to make you relax."

Her head tilted. "What did you have in mind, hypnotism or biofeedback?"

Sam pulled her into his arms. "I was thinking about something more physical. Something with lots of cross training. Maybe we should have a trial run after dinner." His smile faded. "I wanted to tell you before I left, but I had my orders. We couldn't take any chance on a leak."

"I guessed it was something like that." She closed her eyes as Sam kissed her slowly. "Is this part of your relaxation program?"

"Just setting the mood. The good stuff takes place upstairs. There's a whirlpool big enough for ten, and I have definite plans on how to use it. I'm praying there's some red lace in those bags you brought."

"Taylor left a whole collection yesterday after an emergency run to Carmel. Izzy packed all the bags without telling me." Annie bit gently at his lower lip. "We could forget about dinner and take a look."

Sam looked sorely tempted. "Most of it's red?"

Annie smiled.

"You are a very dangerous woman." He brushed her mouth lightly, but somewhere in the middle her fingers ended up in his hair and his hands found their way under her sweater. By then they were both horizontal on the couch, and she felt so good beneath him that it took Sam a minute to realize he'd pushed up her skirt and eased his leg between hers.

He bit back a curse. "Since I'm planning to have you in my

bed for hours, you'd better call Taylor right now. I take it you're speaking to each other again."

"More or less." Annie looked a little giddy. She was so dazed that something squeezed hard inside Sam's chest, and it took all his control not to forget about everything else and kiss her into oblivion again.

Instead he took a breath and stood up. "The phone's right there. I'll go check on dinner while you make your call to Taylor."

"You can *cook*?"

Sam had to laugh at the shock in her voice. "I know my way around a kitchen. It isn't the Four Seasons, but I think you'll like what I've got planned."

"Don't tell me." Her brow rose. "Steak rare. Steak on the side. And steak, very rare, for dessert."

"Oh, ye of little faith." Sam crossed his arms. "Endive and walnut salad. Three-alarm Cajun chicken with pan-fried potatoes. Chocolate macadamia cheesecake for dessert."

"No steak?"

"Very cheeky." He handed Annie the phone. "Make your call before I scrap the idea of dinner entirely so we can check out that red lace."

Chapter Forty

TAYLOR GRABBED THE PHONE THE SECOND IT RANG. "SUMMER-wind," she said breathlessly.

"Taylor, it's me."

"Thank God. Where *are* you?"

"Can't go into details. Besides, I don't have long to talk. Give me the bad news first. How many have we lost?"

Taylor looked out at the empty parking lot, trying to be diplomatic. "A few. The Olympic fencer left a few hours ago, but old Mr. Harkowitz is holding firm. He gave the TV people a nice thrill a few minutes ago, jogging past in his flesh-colored swimsuit."

"Nice to know some things haven't changed." Annie's voice tightened. "Now give me the truth, Taylor. How many guests are left?"

"Three." Taylor didn't add that another guest was leaving in ten minutes. "Forget about Summerwind for once, Annie. How are you doing?"

"Fine. But no details, okay?"

Taylor looked up as the door opened and Buzz walked in. "Hold on a minute." She covered the phone. "Another problem, Buzz?"

The sheriff pointed up the hill. "Something's wrong with that new whirlpool on the terrace."

"You're kidding. The whirlpool's overflowing again," Taylor told Annie. "I'll call the company—"

"No, try this number. His name is Dooley and he handles pool maintenance." Annie read out a number. "He swore he'd come out anytime I had a problem."

"Will do."

"Is Buzz still there?"

Taylor smiled at the sheriff, who was looking more tired than usual. "Sure is."

Annie hesitated. "No details, okay?"

"Got it. Have fun. Remember, I'll want an extensive report later. I owe you for causing this mess," she said softly.

"I didn't mean what I said, Taylor."

"You should have. I'm to blame, however you look at it. Now, stop apologizing and go enjoy your vacation." Taylor hung up and propped her chin on one hand. "Annie finally took a vacation, and as of today I'm in charge." She looked at the number on her notepad. "I'd better call about that whirlpool right away."

As she was dialing the door opened. A man walked in, shaking rain off his jacket. His gray uniform said Sunset Pools, and he was smiling, a big aluminum toolbox balanced on one hip. "Saw the storm. Figured I'd make a final check before I headed north."

Taylor glanced at the notepad. "Are you Dooley?"

"Dooley's the name, water's my game."

"You really must be good. My sister said to call you if there were any problems, and now we've got one."

"Overflow again?"

"Bingo. The new whirlpool."

"I'll get right to it." The repairman fingered his toolbox, glancing at the sky. "Not much time, judging by those clouds. I'd better go."

After he left, Taylor offered Buzz a cup of coffee and straightened a pile of phone messages. "I can do this," she said. "Annie does it, and so can I. All it takes is a little focus and organization." Taylor frowned. That sounded defensive, even to her.

"No one said you couldn't do it," Buzz said calmly.

"But you were thinking it. Everybody here is thinking it. I'm the screwup O'Toole, remember?"

"You're imagining things, Taylor."

"That's what I do for a living." She closed her eyes and drew a raw breath. "I *can't* do this. I hate doing this. I hate being cheerful, calm, and conciliating to strangers and I abhor people in expensive exercise clothes."

Buzz was fighting a smile. "If you need to murder anyone, give me a call and I'll mediate. Beyond that, you're on your own. I'm sure you'll handle things perfectly."

"Says you. All *you* have to do is issue APBs and catch escaped convicts," Taylor said grumpily. "But thanks for extending moral support."

"No problem." Buzz turned his coffee cup slowly. "So Annie's gone on a vacation. Any idea where?"

"She didn't give me the details. Spur-of-the-moment thing, I guess."

Buzz looked thoughtful. "Not like her to take off without careful planning." He glanced at the remaining news vans parked up the road. "Probably this business with Tucker Marsh did her in." He stood up and straightened his belt. "Be sure to let me know if you have any more problems, Taylor. And next time you're in town, the coffee's on me."

◇ ◇ ◇

THE GROUNDS OF SUMMERWIND WERE DESERTED BECAUSE OF THE storm.

It took only a few minutes for him to lay out his tools and filter hose beside the broken whirlpool.

The rest of the time he spent setting up his equipment so no one could see the highly sensitive microphone leveled on the house at the far end of the gardens.

He swept the slope three times just to be sure.

Not a sound. Not a hiccup or a breath.

They'd gone, all three of them.

After sabotaging the new whirlpool and the smoke alarms, he had easy access to the grounds to set up his surveillance.

Being so close was a risk, of course, but an acceptable one. He was just another anonymous worker here.

He'd been all set to make his move when he was interrupted by that damned lawyer getting arrested. After that, the resort had been crawling with police.

Now his target was gone.

He packed up his microphone, slipped it beneath some PVC tubing, and rearranged the toolbox so a layer of drill bits hid his custom-made German sniper rifle with night scope.

"All done?"

He looked up and saw the big, red-faced sheriff ambling toward him. Had he seen the rifle?

No, the eyes were too placid.

Probably the man hadn't seen a real criminal in years.

He closed the lid of his toolbox and flipped the catches until they locked. "Just about. The filter was jammed again. Lots of leaves and vegetation up here." He stood up, dusting off his jacket. "They'll have to be more careful with their maintenance schedule or next time this pump will have to be replaced, and that's gonna cost a few g's."

The big sheriff looked down, studying the pile of wet debris on the grass.

Good thing he'd thought to dump some wet leaves there, just in case. But of course he never left anything to chance.

Except once down in Mexico, he reminded himself grimly. Thanks to that slipup, Sam McKade had ghosted past all of them.

Which was why he was here now, tying up loose ends.

"Glad to see it's fixed," the sheriff said amiably. "They've had enough trouble up here."

"You mean that stuff with the lawyer?"

The police officer nodded.

"Tough break. I saw it on the news. Well, your people caught him, that's what counts." The man called Dooley stood up and gave a pleasant smile. "This baby's fixed. No more problems, I guarantee it. But they gotta keep those filters clean."

"Annie will be glad to hear that," the officer said, almost to himself.

"Sure." The repairman checked his watch and made a conscientious frown. "Man, I'm late. Gotta run."

He gave a little wave, hefted the toolbox, and ambled over Summerwind's perfectly manicured grass toward his van, stolen from a schoolyard in Nevada three days before. There was no anxiety, no urgency about him.

This time there weren't going to be any more mistakes.

Chapter Forty-one

THE DOG WAS JUMPY.

So was Sam.

He stood on the big stone porch, trying to remember, trying to twist the mental threads until they made some kind of sense. But this time it wasn't working.

Annie touched his arm lightly. "Your Cajun chicken is ready, and the salad is served."

"They are?" Sam rubbed his neck, frowning. "I was going to finish doing that."

"In that case, we would have eaten around midnight, ace."

Thunder rumbled in the distance. Sam nodded, trying not to be distracted. "I'll be right there. Just one more call to make."

"Anyone ever tell you that you worry too much?"

Something was worrying him now. Why couldn't he put his finger on it?

He stared up at the tree-covered ridge where clouds swirled like smoke. Was it the storm that had him spooked? With a bad rain, the whole hillside could disappear in a wall of mud.

Not the storm.

Something else. Something he knew—but had forgotten.

"Sam?"

Hell, he'd forgotten about Annie, too busy worrying about shadows. "Sorry." He frowned as the lights flickered briefly. "I'll be right in. This time I promise."

"Take your time." There was tension her eyes, but she hid it well. "Tell lzzy I said hi."

◆ ◆ ◆

Izzy answered immediately. "Joe's Pizza."

"Very funny." Sam watched lightning claw at the tree line. "What do you have for me?"

"Nothing but rain and wind, with more to come. Could be some major gusting up here." Izzy sounded focused but not unduly worried.

"That's what I figured. I'll check the backup generator." Sam squinted as the rain resolved into solid sheets. "Anything else I need to know?"

"A man died in jail today," Izzy said tersely. "The same man who broke into your apartment in Virginia. The admiral thought you should know."

Sam stared into the darkness, considering the news. "How's your team?"

"Dug in like Georgia ticks. All major vantage points covered while we ride out this storm. And your dog just trotted up."

"Give him a rub behind the ears, then send him out. Donegal can handle point better than any of us." As he spoke, Sam continued to survey the dark slope behind the house through his night-vision goggles, though the lightning wasn't making the process an easy one. Satisfied, he pocketed the goggles and glanced at his watch. "All quiet up here. I'll check in at nineteen-hundred hours."

"Roger."

Sam pocketed his phone. But the pricking was still there, halfway between his shoulders, when he turned away from the darkness in search of Annie.

◆ ◆ ◆

After a restless meal, Sam prowled the house again. The storm growled and rain made a solid drumming on the roof, punctuated by flares of angry lightning.

He returned to find Annie sitting by the fire, wearing a red silk dress, a cup of tea beside her. Firelight touched her face as she slid in a bookmark, closed her book carefully, and made room for him on the big leather couch.

Sam stopped in the doorway, drinking in the sight of her.

Feeling that same amazing kick in his chest.

"Reading something good?"

"Taylor's latest mystery. She's been nagging me for weeks and now I've got the time. It's very good." She gripped the book, studying his face. "Something's wrong, isn't it?"

"This storm could be a big one. The generator's all set, but we might lose power briefly. I put out flashlights in the kitchen, just in case."

"You didn't touch your wine at dinner."

"Not thirsty," Sam lied. He wouldn't drink when he felt edgy like this.

Annie was still studying his face. "You didn't eat much either."

Sam shrugged. "Not very hungry." He stared out the window, watching water race off the broad porch. "We could be in for some mudslides if the storm continues. I'm going for a walk to check on things."

"Sam."

"Don't worry, I left some candles, too," he said tightly. "Waterproof matches, if you need them. But it probably won't come to that."

"Sam," she repeated patiently.

"And if there's any real problem, Donegal will let me know. And Izzy."

"*Sam.*" This time Annie took his hand.

"Something wrong?"

"You."

"What about me?"

"You can't stay wired up like this. Even a tough guy like you needs downtime."

He sat on the couch, edgy and not quite sure why. Not quite touching her and not sure why.

He looked into the dancing flames. "Hard to relax with that storm howling over the mountain."

"Forget about the storm. Let somebody else worry for a change. Izzy's there, right?"

"Yeah, but—"

"Think about something else."

"Like what?"

She leaned closer and pushed him slowly back onto the couch. "Like amazing, spontaneous sex."

His lips curved slightly. "You couldn't come up with anything better?"

"How about stupendous, mind-destroying sex?"

"Got anyone in particular in mind?"

"Unfortunately, Sharon Stone was busy." She moved gracefully, straddling his body. "I said I'd stand in. Although stand probably isn't the operative word for what I had in mind." Sam looked down and felt his brain circuits scramble when her skirt hiked up and he realized she was naked under that red dress, completely naked.

She moved to find a better fit. "See? That's better already."

He tried to talk and coughed out air. "Not exactly," he said hoarsely. She was working at his belt, opening his zipper, and Sam felt all the blood in his body race down where her fingers were moving with excruciating care.

"No?" She gave a dazzling smile. "Maybe this will be better." She eased down his pants with graceful precision, then ran her hands down his chest, rising in a whisper of red silk. Her slim thighs flexed as she moved above him, taking him slowly inside her while a cloud of lust left him rock hard and brain dead.

Every time she touched him it got better. This had to be some kind of biological impossibility, he thought dimly.

Not that he was going to question the miracle.

Lightning cracked overhead, filling the room with hot, white light and an afterimage that looked almost like smoke.

Or maybe he only imagined it. Maybe it was just the sight of her body above him and the slow, erotic clench of her thighs as she came down to meet him with a sigh, while his brain shattered into a million little pieces.

"How are we doing?" she asked sweetly.

"I'm still trying to recover from what you're wearing under that dress."

"I guess you mean this." She gave him an enigmatic smile and opened the top three buttons, revealing skin brushed golden by the firelight.

He could see the outline of her nipples pressed against the fine silk and it left his throat dry. "If this is a new fashion trend, it gets my vote."

"Maybe I'll start one."

"Maybe I'll help you." He opened the last two buttons on her dress so the silk slid over her shoulders and pooled onto the floor. "You are something to look at," he whispered, forgetting everything but how she felt as he rolled his palms over her beautiful, flushed breasts and how her eyes darkened when he explored the heat at the center of her thighs.

She smelled like cinnamon and strawberries, and Sam told her how he was going to taste her with his tongue just to be sure where one taste stopped and the other tastes started.

She looked a little unfocused at that, which made Sam smile. She looked even more unfocused when he moved his hand lower, tracing circles that grew smaller and smaller until she shuddered and pushed against him, her whole body taut and quivering.

"You are the most beautiful woman I have ever seen," he whispered, making the circles even tighter, finding the small knot of nerves that made her shudder and close her eyes, made her pant his name and dig her nails into his chest and rock against his body, making her come and come and loving every incredible second of it.

After a few centuries passed, she took a long breath. "My body feels like cotton candy."

"I bet you'll taste like cotton candy, too. Why don't I find out?"

"When did *you* take control of this fantasy, McKade?"

"I believe in a full participatory democracy. Since you mentioned fantasies," he said, lifting her hips with his hands, "I think it's time for another one."

"Will I like it?" she asked huskily.

Sam smiled, lifting her, then lowering her slowly, drawing out the lush pleasure of belonging to her, in her. "That's up to you," he said, his voice unsteady. "Let's see how we fit, Annie."

She made a restless sound, her body wet and hot and open where they slid together deeply. "Pretty good, I'd say."

"Then you'll like this, too."

He pushed deeper, let her slide back, pushed deeper still, every stroke driving him closer toward some edge he couldn't see.

"Do it more so I can be sure," she said raggedly.

Her hands tightened, braced on his chest, and he couldn't stop looking at her as he drove up, filling her openness completely, her body slick against his. Her eyes got that dark, unfocused look again and she said his name, rising up and gripping him tightly inside her.

How did she do that? Sam wondered dimly, but his mind didn't answer because he was harder than he'd ever been, his vision a hot red haze as he looked at Annie, strong and wise and sexy and beautiful above him as she fell into the pleasure of having him completely.

Sam stiffened with the sudden realization that he wasn't just having good sex or even great sex. No, this was stupendous, mind-destroying sex, exactly the way she'd promised, and he wanted it with her every day of his life.

He also wanted her wearing that red lace and the silk dress. He wanted her wearing nothing but a flush and a smile. "God," he whispered, lost at the thought, and she might have said his name as she clutched at his neck and rocked against him harder, her body tight and beautifully wet around him.

Then the heat was there, clawing away all sanity while he pushed to be closer, deeper, buried completely inside her as she moaned out his name in a climax that tore through both of them like the lightning that ripped through the heavy, rain-swollen darkness.

This is real, he thought dimly, riding the edge of oblivion down into her shuddering body.

This is amazing.

This is mine.

◇ ◇ ◇

"SO, DID YOU MANAGE TO FORGET THE STORM?"

Thunder grumbled as Sam traced the curve of her shoulder. "The storm, my name, and what we had for dinner."

"Me, too." She took a slow breath. "Must be something about the color red."

Sam shook his head. "Must be something about the way we fit together."

"Maybe." Annie's voice was husky and warm and a little tired. "I like how your mind works, McKade."

He pulled her slick, sated body down against his chest and smiled. "Ditto, Doc."

"Thank God for participatory democracy," she murmured sleepily.

Chapter Forty-two

"WHY ARE YOU DRESSED?"

Annie blinked as she sat up on the couch.

"I'm going out for a few minutes." Sam pulled a blanket over her, his fingers lingering at her face. "Donegal's here, right by the window."

"Still raining?" she asked sleepily.

"Afraid so. Go back to sleep."

"I'll wait up," she insisted. Her eyes drifted closed. "Just hurry." She curled into the pillows on the couch, slipping back to sleep.

"Donegal, stay." Sam turned, forcing his thoughts to the darkness outside and the small, stabbing awareness that wouldn't leave him.

❖ ❖ ❖

HE WAS LOOKING AT HIS MAP, CURSING LOUDLY, WHEN HE SAW the flashing red light. He shoved his Browning out of sight beneath the seat and slowed, then pulled to the side of the road.

Had he been speeding?

Impossible. He couldn't have been that careless.

The cruiser sat for a long time. Probably checking the DMV computer, scanning for a possible theft. They wouldn't find any, since this particular van had never been reported lost. No, he was an exemplary employee of Sunset Pools. All his customers were happy with his work.

Particularly Ms. O'Toole.

His eyes narrowed as a big man stepped out of the cruiser. He recognized that chapped face and the stocky body.

"Evening." The sheriff bent down to the window. "May I see your driver's license?"

"Sure, officer." The man who called himself Dooley handed over the fake, secure in the knowledge that it would pass scrutiny. All of his driver's licenses were excellent. "Wasn't speeding, was I?"

Cool eyes ran over the plastic ID, then checked out the interior of the van.

"Not speeding." The burly sheriff handed back his license. "I'm afraid we've got a problem with the road up ahead. You were up at the O'Toole place fixing the whirlpool, weren't you?"

He nodded. "Problem with the intake filter. Happens a lot."

The sheriff leaned closer, pointing to the north. "The bridge is out. You'll need to take another route."

"Heck." He rubbed his neck, glad that irritation would be expected under the circumstances.

"Where are you headed?"

It was a friendly question, and he made his lie equally friendly. "Lost Meadow. A warranty customer up there just blew out a master pump. The man swore he'll have my job if I'm not there before dark."

The sheriff nodded slowly. "In that case you'll need to head back south and take a left at the first light. That will take you to the freeway."

"South. First light, take a left. Got it. Thanks a lot. Better watch out for that storm." He smiled innocently. "It looks like a killer."

"Sure will." The sheriff stepped away from the car and waved calmly, unaware of how close he had come to dying.

❖ ❖ ❖

BUZZ WATCHED THE VAN BACK UP, THEN TURN AROUND. NICE fellow. He seemed to know his job, too.

Only thing was, he said he was headed south, but the map on the seat beside him was open to the rugged terrain along the national forest, which was nowhere near Lost Meadow.

Probably just a coincidence.

He was getting too old for this work, Buzz thought. His knee ached and his back was stiff again. What he needed was a Thermos full of hot coffee and a few egg salad sandwiches.

He watched the red lights of the van fade down the road into the streaming rain. Maybe he was too old and too paranoid, but the memory of the map was bothering him.

Frowning, he picked up his radio.

◊ ◊ ◊

THE MAN IN THE GRAY UNIFORM WAS SWEATING. HE KEPT HIS eyes on the rearview mirror as he gripped his Browning just out of sight on his lap.

Always prepared.

But the sheriff didn't follow, and that was good.

His breath came easier as he rolled south, obeying all the traffic signs, careful to creep just under the speed limit. With every mile his excitement grew.

He'd always liked tests, always liked being better and faster and smarter than anyone around him.

He rubbed his wrist, which was hurting again. Hell of a thing to get lit up by lightning. Years ago, but he remembered the storm like yesterday. Sometimes he thought the lightning had changed him, opening his eyes to how easy it was to get what you wanted if you were willing to hurt a few people. He'd been sick for three months afterward, half of them spent in the hospital. His father hadn't been around, but that was nothing new.

He frowned, trying to remember how he'd been before the lightning, but all he could think about was getting the job done. As rain sluiced down, he remembered the sharp smell of ozone and the sudden explosive crack that had made his hair stand on end just before he'd been struck to the ground, more dead than alive.

His hands tightened on the steering wheel and sweat trickled under his shirt. No nerves, he thought. Nerves weren't allowed. This was business, old business.

He'd missed McKade once, down in Mexico. He'd missed him again in D.C. when the SEAL had sprinted out of his crosshairs and jumped on that out-of-control bus. McKade wasn't going to get lucky a third time.

Not tonight.

Once McKade was lying in a pool of blood, the program could continue, moving to even bigger targets.

Meanwhile, he would have a substantial account well hidden under the name of a dummy corporation in the Caymans.

He was sweating more now. It made him angry so he took out his gun again because it felt solid and cool and calmed him down.

Up ahead, a black Jeep came into view, idling beneath an oak tree. He cruised to the shoulder and cut off his lights.

Game over, he thought as thunder growled like an old friend. There in the hammering rain he cradled his gun and waited for the rest of his team.

Chapter Forty-three

SAM SCANNED THE DARKNESS TENSELY. EVEN WITH HIS NIGHT-vision goggles he saw nothing on the move.

Lightning jumped coldly through the sky as he fingered his cell phone. "Izzy, are you there?"

Static snapped, then Izzy's voice came through. "Some serious gusting up here. The good news is that nothing's moving. The bad news is, I almost got hit by lightning a few minutes ago."

"Keep your powder dry and your head down."

"I'm trying. Annie okay?"

"Just fine. Donegal's with her." Another bolt of lightning hammered the trees at the top of the hill, filling the line with hellish static.

"Izzy, you there?"

"—check them first to see—"

"Izzy, do you read me?"

"—could be only—"

More static snarled over the line. "Hello?" When he heard no answer, Sam flipped off the phone in disgust. Light filtered through the windows, casting pale squares of silver over the porch as he scanned the rocky slope beyond the lawn.

Inch by inch he scanned the slope again. There might have been something out beneath the branches of the third oak tree. Probably it was foliage tossing in the wind.

Sam fingered his cell phone again. "Izzy, are you there?"

There was nothing but wild crackling.

Sam cursed softly. The last thing they needed was to be cut off from each other. Thunder rumbled in the distance, and he felt a sharp pricking at his neck.

A second later lightning hit a tree, snapping a branch not thirty feet from where he stood.

The pools of silver on the porch blinked, then vanished, and Sam turned to see the house plunged into darkness.

He forced himself to relax, knowing it would take a few seconds for the backup generator to kick in. Over the howl of the wind he saw a movement through the study windows as Annie emerged from the kitchen, carrying a flashlight.

Abruptly the power returned, bathing the house in light.

One problem solved.

Sam tried to raise Izzy again, but with no success. Irritated, he glanced at the luminous dial of his watch.

Three minutes. If he hadn't raised Izzy by then, he was going out to find him.

He was raising his night goggles when he heard a sound behind him.

◇ ◇ ◇

ANNIE SAT HUDDLED IN A BLANKET WITH DONEGAL PERCHED alertly beside her. Firelight warmed the Chinese carpet and fieldstone mantel, but any sense of peace was shattered by the next angry crack of lightning.

When Sam didn't return, she went upstairs and tugged on jeans and a thick sweater, then returned to pace uneasily before the windows. Donegal prowled right beside her, looking up expectantly, as if waiting for some command.

As rain battered at the big porch the chill grew, creeping through her heavy clothes. For distraction she went to the kitchen for a strong cup of tea. When she returned, Donegal was standing at the front door, ears pricked, body tense.

Thunder boomed, rolling heavily over the house. In the flare of a distant bolt of lightning, Annie saw movement down the hillside.

A tree bent beneath the wind?

Suddenly Donegal's muzzle rose. Growling softly, he looked up at Annie, then scratched at the door.

"Out?"

He barked twice, then resumed his scratching.

"You want to go out to Sam, don't you? Is that it, Donegal?"

The big dog raced to her side, caught the bottom of her sweater in his teeth, and tugged her toward the door.

"Message received." Annie pushed open the heavy door, squinting into a sheet of rain. "Go on."

Donegal shot out onto the porch, and in seconds he was swallowed up by the darkness. As the wind hurled rain at Annie's face, she tried not to shiver.

◇ ◇ ◇

SAM'S WEAPON WAS DRAWN BEFORE HE CROUCHED.

"Commander, don't shoot. Izzy sent me to find you."

Sam straightened slowly, recognizing one of Izzy's hand-picked support team. He had studied the pictures of the six men scattered over the mountain, but with communications out, there was no way to tell where they were now.

"You're Weaver, aren't you?"

"Yes, sir. Izzy sent me up to check the house. The storm's playing havoc with our communications."

"Same up here."

"Izzy said—" The big man waited for a roll of thunder to pass before continuing. "Izzy said I should plan to check in with you visually every half hour until the phones are operational."

It was a good plan, even if it was cumbersome, and a lot could happen between one check-in and the next. The storm definitely limited their options.

Sam stood just out of the wind at the edge of the porch, scanning the dense upper slope of the mountain. If an infiltration was planned, it would most likely come through there, where the groundcover was thickest.

Seeing a movement near the top of the hill, he drew back under the porch and swept the area with his goggles. This time all he could make out was branches skittering in the greenish glow of the background.

It reminded him of another place and time.

Mexico.

Waiting for a meeting that turned sour.

More memories flashed.

Riding at anchor in darkness, then two short bursts of a flashlight. Money trading hands. A computer disk. A man's face he couldn't recognize.

Frowning, Sam focused on the present. "I'll check in with Izzy, Weaver. Until I get back, your orders are to stay here and keep an eye on Ms. O'Toole."

"Understood, sir."

In the afterimage of another bolt of lightning, the mountain blurred. Fighting his uneasiness, Sam swung over the porch and headed through the rain to the spot where Izzy would be hunkered down, maintaining perimeter surveillance and cursing every drop of rain.

◊ ◊ ◊

IZZY MOVED OUT OF A TARP-COVERED CRACK BETWEEN TWO rocks as Sam approached. "You saw Weaver?"

"He told me the plan." Rain drummed on the ground, and more thunder roared in the distance. "What's the prediction for the storm?"

"Another six hours minimum," Izzy said. "Heavy winds until morning. With all this lightning, I doubt we'll have communications back before dawn. All we get is static soup."

Sam squinted into the rain, knowing the prediction was accurate and hating it. "I'll send Donegal down. Meanwhile why don't you—"

Sam stopped, registering movement up the slope. He

turned, sweeping the area with his peripheral vision, and saw a pale shape beneath the wind-lashed trees. "Did you see that?"

"I saw," Izzy said grimly. "Let me get a better look." He scanned the slope with his high-tech binoculars, then without a word handed them to Sam.

It took a moment to adjust to the pale green backlighting. Sam saw shaking branches, waving foliage, and a clumsy shape near two rocks. As he strained for a better view, he heard three sharp barks, followed by silence.

Three meant danger. They'd worked out the basic code through months of training.

"That was Donegal," Sam snapped. "Something's wrong. Find your team and then pull back toward the house."

❖ ❖ ❖

SAM LURCHED UP THE SLOPE, CURSING HIS WEAK LEG. BUT HE forgot about his clumsiness when he saw Donegal on the ground behind a boulder. The dog's body was limp, his head still. His eyes opened when Sam bent close, cradling his head gently.

"What happened to you, buddy?"

The wolfhound's tail beat weakly. He tried to bark, but the sound was faint.

Cursing, Sam cradled the dog and ran up the slope toward the darkened house.

❖ ❖ ❖

THE ELECTRICITY WAS OUT, THE HOUSE COMPLETELY DARK AS SAM swept the porch with his scope. What had happened to the generator?

He didn't climb the front steps, instead making his way through the lashing rain to a storage shed just off the driveway. He tried the door, relieved to see it was still locked.

He opened the padlock and slipped inside. After setting

Donegal on the floor, he shifted several heavy wooden shelves full of garden tools, revealing a solid metal door. Beyond the door a steep stairway led down to the basement of the house. The air was chill and musty as he made his way downward, Donegal now unmoving in his arms. The dog still had a pulse, and there were no signs of blood, which left Sam certain he'd been drugged or poisoned.

"Hang on, buddy," he said softly as he placed the dog on a soft piece of carpet outside the entrance to the basement. "I'll be back as soon as I can."

Donegal was too weak to move his tail in response.

Sam reined in his fury, focusing on an unseen enemy who was one step in front of him. War was war, and you played by any rules that let you win. But whoever had hurt Donegal was going to pay. He pulled out his Glock and began a silent climb up the basement steps, ignoring the throb in his leg, prepared for what might be waiting at the top of the stairs. If not for the storm, he would have radioed Izzy and the team, but now he had to work solo.

Where in the hell was Weaver?

At the top of the stairs he paused, ear to the wooden door.

No muted voices, no faint footsteps.

Even then he didn't move, waiting for six minutes by the luminous dial of his watch. Only then did he turn the knob carefully and enter the pantry just off the kitchen.

Lightning reflected eerily off the polished black granite work surfaces as Sam entered at a crouch, gun leveled.

Still no sign of Weaver.

Light was glowing from the corridor outside the living room. Sam saw the fire and wondered why there had been no noise. He tried not to think of Annie lying hurt and bleeding.

Ingrained habits kicked in, making him slow his breath and calculate every move. Down the corridor an elaborate breakfront filled with crystal glowed icily in the flare of distant lightning as Sam passed at a crouch, following the wall and working his way behind the big leather sofa that faced the fireplace.

The couch was empty, Annie's blankets fallen to the ground. There was no sign of her.

A book lay open on the side table. Taylor's last mystery, Sam recalled. He had watched Annie reading earlier that day, struck by her care in using a bookmark to avoid folding down the pages. Annie didn't press books facedown.

Maybe she hadn't touched this book.

Lightning flared briefly, then the house fell back into darkness. Sam crossed the rug, headed for the main staircase, his heart pounding.

Gun drawn, body low, he swung inside the next room and saw Annie sitting in a leather wing chair, her face greenish in the dim light of a banker's lamp.

She didn't move, didn't speak.

Warning bells clanged in Sam's head as he swept the room with the muzzle of his gun; he worked his way slowly toward her, his back to the wall.

"Annie, are you okay?"

There was no sign of blood. She had a book in her hands, and this one, too, was turned facedown, clutched against her knees.

Another sign, Sam thought. "Annie, where's Weaver?"

Her eyes were almost black, her lips pressed in a tight line. Her eyes flickered to the window seat bordered by velvet curtains.

Sam swung around, catching the faint smell of cigar smoke as the curtains parted. "Admiral Howe?"

A tall, uniformed figure loomed into the room. "I got your message," he said, sounding tired. "I came as fast as I could." Rain glistened on his hat and regulation raincoat.

"I didn't send any message." Sam's fingers tightened on his gun. "All the phones are out in the storm."

The admiral drew noisily on his cigar. "I sure as hell had a message to get up here. Damned bumpy ride it was, too." Cigar smoke swirled, growing stronger. "Maybe it was from Izzy."

The admiral patted the pocket of his raincoat. "Now I can't find my glasses. Next thing they'll be telling me I need a hearing aid."

This complaining was familiar at least. "I doubt it, sir."

"We need to talk about that day in Washington, McKade. Who did you see and where did you go?"

"Sir, I don't think—"

The admiral plunged on as if he hadn't heard. "Your apartment's been entered, and our China Lake research program is at risk. I need answers."

Sam heard Annie's clothes rustling on the leather chair. Her book fell to the floor.

"Sir, I—"

Again the admiral went right on, as if he hadn't heard. "Time's run out, McKade." Slowly, as if exhausted, he moved behind Annie's chair. "I need to know what you remember."

Sam shot a glance at Annie, who was fidgeting now, her face strained. "Ms. O'Toole needs to rest, sir. Why don't I take her upstairs, then we can go to work?"

"No more time." The admiral's voice was hollow as he looked at Sam. His cigar fell to the expensive Tianjin carpet and smoldered.

Thunder rumbled over the mountains.

Sam's hand was coming up when the admiral dropped low, his body blocked by Annie's chair, his fingers at her throat.

"Drop the weapon, Commander." His voice was muffled. "Otherwise your friend is going to die very badly."

Chapter Forty-four

"AT LEAST SHE'S SMART." ANNIE'S CAPTOR WAS STILL BEHIND HER chair. "I told her to keep quiet or I'd have to shoot you."

Now Sam understood Annie's tense, unnatural silence, and he was starting to understand her captor's muffled voice.

Thunder rumbled in the distance as he turned into profile, making a harder target. "Why?" he asked softly, betrayal an acid taste in his mouth. "*Why*, Peter?"

"Forget about why, McKade. My time's run out. I need to know exactly what you did in Washington and who you saw before you decided to become a hero."

"And then you'll kill us."

Admiral Howe's son shrugged. "We all have to go sometime."

Sam sidestepped to the left. "I don't know what I did. But I figured out something else in the last week. The man I was trying to remember was someone close to me. Maybe that's why I kept blocking your name." Sam's hands tightened as he stared into remorseless gray eyes starkly similar to those of his commanding officer. "Did you bug his office at home?" Sam asked his old friend. He tried not to think about the gun Peter now had wedged against Annie's throat. "Is that how you found out everything your father knew?"

"Easy enough with superior equipment and manpower. I had both." With one hand, Peter removed a small tape recorder from a strap around his neck. "Nice sound quality, wasn't it? New Japanese technology. Splicing together a sample conversation for my father wasn't difficult, since his choice of topics is always limited. National security, Washington politics, and *you*. Too bad impersonating my father didn't finesse any new information out of you." His face was hard as he dropped the tape recorder into his pocket. "Empty your pockets, Commander. Everything, including that knife in your boot."

Peter would remember that. "I don't think so. This way we're even."

"Except that I've got the girl."

Sam didn't want to think about that. "Someone said that you had a broken arm."

"X-rays can be substituted when you have helpful friends. They bought me all the time I needed."

"Nice." Sam stared at the traitor before him. "But I still want to know why you sold out."

"For the game. For the challenge and because I know I'll win." The admiral's son shrugged. "Remember how you taught me to snap a football? Remember those muddy games on the lawn? Hell, I idolized you, McKade. When I had that losing streak in college, you talked me back into one piece and made me a winner again."

"Number sixty-one," Sam said quietly. He'd come so close to remembering.

But not close enough. Now Annie was a target.

"You sold out your country, Howe. That wasn't a game, that was a *sickness*."

"I've always wanted to win. Our family doctor told my father I had an overdeveloped competitive instinct, even at six."

Sam had seen that part of Peter when they'd been roommates in college, but he'd managed to explain it away. Football was football, after all. Winning was what they trained you to do.

"Stop moving," Peter snapped, the gun jerking against Annie's pale throat.

Sam went still, calculating angles and distance and hating the conclusion. He'd never be fast enough to save her. Not from here.

He gave his old friend a cool stare. "They sent me to check

out the China Lake research team, I remember that much. I also know that I didn't like what I saw. There were a few too many projects being scrapped as over budget or structurally flawed."

"The Navy's loss was our gain." Peter smiled grimly. "Thanks to China Lake we've got some amazing technology in our private pipeline now. It's a damned shame my father can't appreciate how good I am, but he was always too busy trying to pound the rules into me and talk about you." Peter shrugged. "He always considered you superior son material, especially when you made the cut for the SEALs and I didn't."

"You're crazy," Sam snapped. "No one could be more proud of you than your father."

"What does it matter? Emotions just get in the way of doing the job. As a big, bad SEAL, you know that, McKade. I remember the first time I stole information. It felt amazing. Almost as good as that time I was hit by lightning during practice in college. Remember that?"

Sam nodded. The freak accident had put his roommate out of the game for a year, but made him a college hero. "You milked it for all it was worth."

"Something I also learned from my father. You were lucky down in Mexico," Peter continued irritably. "If my people had done their job right and contacted me sooner, I'd have stopped you then and there. Whose idea was it to put you undercover as a prospective buyer for our newest gadgets?"

"Your father's, of course. Maybe he suspected it was you even then. Maybe he hoped I would go easy on you." It was a risk, but Sam had to take Peter's attention off Annie.

"The old man never wants anyone to go easy. He knows how to play the game, I'll give him that. He taught me more than he knows." Peter's voice was icy. "By the time I checked out our newest 'buyer' and realized who it was, you were almost at the yacht."

Sam nodded slowly.

Gunshots in the darkness.

The voice, horrifyingly familiar. A man Sam had always trusted.

He remembered his blinding sense of shock when he'd realized that Peter Howe was part of a chain that stretched from Washington to several of the Navy's most advanced research programs. He remembered how hard he'd denied it at first, how he'd refused to say a word to Admiral Howe until he had all his proof.

He was on his way to turn over that proof to the admiral in Washington, only he'd jumped aboard a runaway bus instead.

The past was coming back to Sam in pieces now, his months of undercover work that had revealed long-term tampering with Navy research. Once a project was scrapped by the Navy, the technology made its way into the private sector, where the problems were eventually corrected.

Peter Howe was part of a new wave of industrial espionage, Sam thought grimly. His people didn't steal weapons and sell them to the enemy. Instead they tampered with military records, manipulated research, then sold the "defective" technology to carefully screened businesses. For the insiders who knew what was coming, the purchase became wildly lucrative, and Peter Howe's group had spread their successes over dozens of companies worldwide to make the pattern harder to trace.

The Navy had footed the bill, corporate and government backers had profited obscenely, and good men had died trying to stop it.

"Smart of you to duck into the Metro in D.C. We had three men in place to take you out when you arrived for your meeting at the Pentagon. We were taking no chances." As he spoke, Peter Howe pulled Annie to her feet. "Then you jumped that damned school bus. Being a hero saved your life, McKade. We could hardly shoot a man surrounded by police cars and news choppers."

"What happens now?"

Howe moved toward the door, holding Annie in front of him. "For me, more of the same. Our group has a long and lucrative future. For you, I can't be so optimistic."

Out of the corner of his eye, Sam saw Annie's finger slant down toward the big blue exercise ball he'd left there before dinner.

"Logistics dictate speed, Howe. She's bound to slow you down, and my people will be here any minute."

Howe pulled Annie closer toward the door. "She's the price, McKade. You want me, you've got to take her out first. Remember what you told me that day after my fourth losing game? If you want to win, there's always a price."

❖ ❖ ❖

ADMIRAL HOWE SAT IN HIS STUDY, WREATHED IN CIGAR SMOKE.

Strangely uneasy, he stared at the photos on his desk, stopping at the faces of Sam and his son, grinning and muddy after a rough game of tackle football. Nearby was a college photo of Peter taken during his junior year losing streak.

His jersey read sixty-one.

Howe stiffened.

Sixty-one.

Sam had remembered the number sixteen.

Was there a connection?

Howe couldn't think any further than that. He felt poised on the brink of an abyss . . .

He sat up, suddenly overwhelmed with the feeling that things were going wrong on that mountain. He had to find out what was happening.

He punched in a string of numbers on his cell phone and grabbed his coat. He was already at the door, waving curtly to his driver, when the line clicked in.

❖ ❖ ❖

"I BELIEVE MY RIDE IS WAITING." LT. PETER HOWE REACHED INTO the inner pocket of his raincoat. "Recognize this Smith and Wesson?"

"It used to be mine. I lost it right after I went into the SEALs."

The cool eyes turned even cooler. "Exactly. And everyone knows that covert operations can drive men over the edge."

"So you'll make this look like a suicide."

Peter Howe nodded. "A messy one, I'm afraid."

Sam heard a sound down the hall. He prayed it was Weaver or Izzy. "You won't have time to get the ballistics right, Peter. Besides, your father will never believe it. He knows I wouldn't wimp out."

"My father might not believe it, but he won't be able to prove anything else. Not when I've finished torching the house," Peter added icily.

He gripped Annie's waist. "Time to go, Ms. O'Toole. We don't want to miss that chopper."

"Bastard." Annie wrenched vainly at his arm.

In that same instant, a pale shape flashed across the floor. Teeth bared, Donegal leaped at Annie's captor, gripping his hand. Howe cursed as Annie shoved him back against the blue exercise hall, then dropped out of sight behind the sofa.

Howe staggered as Sam got one shot off. Howe knocked Donegal to the floor as he fell.

He fired wildly, splintering the parquet floor. Outside the window came the chatter of automatic weapon fire, followed by the flare of headlights.

A helicopter roared out of the darkness.

Howe's ride. As Sam crawled toward the door the wind gusted hard and a branch hit the huge picture window, shattering the glass. In the moment of confusion that followed, Sam charged forward, tackling his enemy.

There was an odd quality to his movements in the darkness, a sense of time both compressed and infinitely stretched out as he grappled for Howe's gun. A second blow to the shoulder knocked him backward, and when he staggered upright, Howe was running toward the corridor.

Sam blocked out the agony at his shoulder. *Annie*, he thought fleetingly, but there was no time to find out how badly she was hurt.

He came across Weaver's body slumped on the floor, blood matting his face and neck. Grimly he forged ahead, hesitating outside the kitchen.

A knife hissed past his head and sank into the doorframe. His instinct for caution had been dead on.

He felt his shoulder bleeding again, thanks to Howe's last carefully aimed kick. Howe had exploited every weakness in the system and he had played to win, every step of the way.

Wounded or not, Sam was going to stop him.

Crouched low, he made his way along a row of wooden cabinets. He saw that Donegal was right beside him, weak but mobile. Before they could cross the room, bullets struck the breakfront, shattering the glass.

The back door banged open.

Howe, moving fast.

Sam ran for the basement. The kitchen door would take him out into a killing zone.

As he emerged at the storage shed, he saw a helicopter hovering above the hillside, with Howe struggling against the wind barely twenty yards away. Ignoring the agony it caused him, Sam tugged away a wallboard and took down the rifle concealed inside. Time seemed to stretch out as he crawled outside, taking cover behind a low stone wall.

The helicopter's rotors kicked into high speed.

"Circle," Sam ordered Donegal, and the dog slipped away, heading up the slope above the chopper, sent out as backup in case Howe tried a last-minute retreat toward the cars parked in the upper driveway.

The chopper began to lift, barely a meter off the ground,

and Howe sprinted closer. Sam took a breath and sighted, watching Howe's arms pump as he leaped aboard the chopper. The big blades chattered, beginning a swift ascent.

Sam fired.

The fuel tanks ignited, bathing the chopper in flames. Three dark figures struggled for an instant inside the orange-red fireball before the chopper exploded.

Chapter Forty-five

ANNIE HEARD THE SOUND OF A GUNSHOT, FOLLOWED BY AN EAR-splitting explosion. Izzy reached the window before her, clutching his right arm tightly, his face grim.

Through the glass came the furious glow of a fire, all that remained of the helicopter they had heard near the lower slope. Black-clad men ran up the hillside and car lights flashed from the road.

Annie tried not to consider the possibility that Sam had been near that helicopter when it had exploded.

"Get to cover," Izzy said.

As they moved through the kitchen, Annie grabbed the heaviest iron frying pan she could hold. Not that it would be much use against an assault rifle, but it made her feel safer.

Looking at Izzy's harsh features, she realized that no one would be getting past this warrior alive. Moving swiftly, he pulled a tall display of crystal glasses away from the wall outside the pantry. Amazingly, not a single piece shifted.

"They're glued on." Izzy stood back, revealing a staircase leading down into darkness. "There's a bunker down there where we'll be safe."

"I don't know who your architect is, but I'm glad he has a good imagination."

There was a sound behind them in the kitchen. Instantly, Izzy swung in front of Annie, weapon raised. The door opened, and in the hellish glow of the burning helicopter, Annie saw a all silhouette.

She bit back a cry.

Sam's field jacket was streaked with dirt and drying blood.

He struggled to hold Donegal in his good arm, while the dog licked his face weakly.

"The area is secure," Sam said, trying to avoid Donegal's tongue.

"About time. Get over here and let me look at that shoulder." Izzy pulled a high-beam flashlight from his jacket pocket. Annie closed her eyes as she saw how much blood darkened Sam's jacket.

"You first." Sam sank awkwardly into a chair at the counter, Donegal wriggling against his chest.

"No way." Izzy managed a cocky grin. "Age before beauty, pal."

"Will you two stop being idiot macho heroes," Annie hissed. "Fix yourselves up. You're both bleeding like pigs. Even Donegal has more sense than you do." Hearing its name, the big dog barked excitedly and pushed up to lick Annie's face.

All efficiency, Izzy cut off Sam's jacket and rolled back the blood-soaked sweater. When she saw Sam's wound, Annie had to bite her lip to keep from throwing up right there.

Glad of a distraction, she patted Donegal. "They're idiots, aren't they, Donegal? Both of them are so full of testosterone that they can't see beyond their own stubborn pride."

Donegal's tail banged against her ribs, and Annie winced, feeling her own bruises, courtesy of Peter Howe's gun.

Izzy frowned. "You next. Just let me finish with this hard case."

"Your next job is to look after your own elbow," Annie said tightly.

"Just a scratch." Izzy probed Sam's wound gently. "It looks clean, ace. Everything's ripped apart again, but there's no sign of foreign matter. I'll shoot you with something for the pain and give you an antibiotic until we get you cleaned up in a real hospital."

"Forget about a hospital." Sam's face was pale, streaked with dirt and blood.

Annie crossed her arms. "Let's see your elbow, Izzy," she ordered. "Then you're *both* going to the hospital. Right, Donegal?"

Donegal barked twice.

"Two means yes," Sam muttered, just before he passed out on the kitchen table.

❖ ❖ ❖

"I WANT A STEAK."

Sam was propped up in bed, his shoulder covered by a heavy bandage.

Sunlight streamed through Annie's big windows above the coast, and Izzy watched from the doorway, a smile on his handsome face. His right arm was in a sling, but he bore no other scars of their desperate night on the mountain. After a week of recuperation, things were finally settling back to normal.

As normal as things could be with two government operatives in residence.

Donegal was in dog heaven, running from one man to the other, punctuating his trips with visits to Annie for lavish petting and vast praise.

"That dog's going to be spoiled beyond any hope of recovery," Sam muttered. But his eyes glinted with pride. "Not that you don't deserve it, Donegal."

The wolfhound barked twice.

"You did a great job, didn't you, pal?"

Donegal barked twice again.

"Come to think of it, this could be some kind of program. What do you think, Izzy? Maybe we should set up a canine support team."

Izzy looked thoughtful. "Could be a real asset, if you had the right animals."

"Enough shop talk," Annie said. "You're both supposed to rest." She gave a slow grin. "After that I have exercise programs planned for both of you."

Sam looked tired, but he managed a crooked grin. "I love it when you talk tough. Are you going to get out the leather and handcuffs?"

"Just keep any exfoliating masks away from me," Izzy muttered.

"Did someone mention exfoliating masks?" Taylor bustled in with her big leather purse draped over one shoulder. Mouth-watering smells emanated from the hamper in her other hand. "I figured you two macho men would be tired of oatmeal. Since I know Annie and her health regimens too well, I decided some real food was in order."

"Steak?" Sam asked hopefully.

"You got it." Taylor set her hamper on the table, pulled back the cover, and began removing dishes. "Skewered steak with mushrooms in sesame-jalapeno sauce. Mashed potatoes and gravy. Fresh corn and black bean salsa. For dessert we have chocolate tacos filled with hazelnut-mocha mousse. They're to die for, believe me. Zoe's been working like a wild woman." Taylor held up the last bowl. "And for my special friend, I have steak tartare and a nice big bone."

"That dog is definitely going to be useless," Sam muttered.

"If he is, you can loan him to me." Taylor patted Donegal's head. "I think I'm going to put him in a book. In fact, I might put all of you in a book," she said thoughtfully.

Sam stiffened. "This is sensitive information, Taylor. I can't let you do that."

"Oh, don't worry. I've changed most of the details—not that you've told me anything significant. No, my story revolves around stolen biotechnology. And of course, I'll have an incredibly handsome and rugged male lead. I'm thinking he's probably a SEAL."

Sam looked somewhat mollified, but Annie glowered. "Taylor, if you write so much as a *word* about this—"

"So sue me." Her sister waved a hand, reaching for the silverware. "Now, since I'm in the mood for dessert first, who wants a chocolate taco?"

Chapter Forty-six

Washington, D.C.

Sam pulled stiffly at the cuffs of his white dress uniform as a black limousine cruised toward him.

A gorilla came around the corner. Two witches with pointed hats crossed the street, escorted by a leering pirate with a peg leg.

Halloween was Sam's favorite time of year. Every time a horde of tiny goblins and pirates thronged to the door, he turned into a kid again, tossing out candy and pretending to be terrified.

Right now he wasn't pretending. He really *was* terrified.

He tugged stiffly at his collar. Beside him, Izzy crossed his arms, handsome in an Italian silk jacket custom-made to fit his broad shoulders. As they stood in the October sunshine, the rugged men drew stares from a dozen women.

Neither noticed.

"Something wrong, McKade? You look like you just saw your own ghost."

"Maybe I did," Sam muttered. He frowned, watching the limousine slow. "Why couldn't they send a *normal* car?"

"Face it, pal. You're a hero. In D.C., heroes get limousines, not Ford Escorts."

"Says who?"

"Says just about every official in the District of Columbia. Word is, they're fighting over who gets to have their picture taken with you."

Sam shrugged. Photo opportunities and handshakes left him cold. "What about Annie?"

"She's our first stop. We'll swing by the Four Seasons and

pick her up. You can give her the news about Marsh. He should be behind bars for at least five years."

"Not long enough," Sam growled. "Where's Admiral Howe?"

"We pick him up right after Annie."

Sam rubbed the back of his neck. "How's he doing?"

"About as bad as you predicted, not that he shows much. The man's spent his whole adult life in the service of his country. How can he forgive himself for a son who so completely sold out, who made a mockery of everything he holds dear?" Izzy shook his head. "Their network was amazing. And at the same time, the admiral is grieving the loss of a son."

Sam's face hardened. "Peter Howe had money, education, and a career that was on the fast track, but he spit on all of that, along with his country. Now his father is left to sort through the wreckage. That's got to be painful as hell for a man like Admiral Howe. And I've got to carry the memory of firing the shot that killed his son."

"There was no choice. Never doubt it."

"I don't." But Sam knew the memory would continue to haunt him. He put away the anger and focused on the future. Having memories could hurt as well as heal, he'd discovered.

Izzy studied Sam. "You're sweating, McKade. You didn't look this upset when you went to have dinner at the White House."

"That was business. This is personal."

The limousine stopped. The door opened, held by an expressionless chauffeur.

"Let's get this show on the road," Izzy muttered, sliding across the spacious leather seat and making himself at home.

Sam shook his head. "What am I doing in a limousine?"

"Getting honored, pal." Izzy grinned. "Better get used to it."

◊ ◊ ◊

SAM DIDN'T THINK SHE COULD BE MORE BEAUTIFUL THAN HE remembered.

He was wrong.

Sunlight dusted Annie's hair with gold as she stood in the lobby of the Four Seasons. She was wearing some kind of soft blue sweater and matching skirt with a single strand of pearls that faded before the radiance in her eyes.

Get your heart out of your throat, he thought grimly. *You're not supposed to let her see you sweat, remember?* Her eyes widened as he approached, and he was glad that her look was appreciative.

"You look wonderful," he said gruffly. "That blue reminds me of your cove at Summerwind."

Annie touched his collar. "You look pretty amazing yourself. At least four women turned to stare when you walked in."

"They must have been looking at Izzy," Sam muttered. "I'm guessing that's Armani."

Annie straightened her pearls. "I, on the other hand, had no idea what to wear. You still won't tell me what's planned?"

"Not yet. I want it to be a surprise." As Sam studied the gently clinging knit, his eyes narrowed. "Wearing any red lace under there?"

"I guess you'll have to wait and see, won't you?"

Sam took her hand and raised it slowly to his lips. "Finding out is going to be half the pleasure."

"Very impressive, Commander." Annie's head tilted. "Something tells me you're going to have a long line of swooning women wherever you go."

"I'm only concerned with one woman, even though she's as stubborn as they come." His fingers tightened on her hand. "Annie, we've got to talk. I want to marry you. I've given you time. Lord knows, we both needed time after what happened up in the mountains, but—"

Izzy appeared behind them, clearing his throat. "Time to go, folks."

Annie gave him a quick kiss. "You're looking as handsome as ever."

"We aim to please, ma'am." There was a twinkle in Izzy's eyes. "Your limousine awaits."

"So where are we going? Sam won't say a word."

"In that case, it will have to stay secret a little longer. But I can tell you this. It's someplace that you'll never forget."

"Important? As in—" Annie's voice wavered. "Don't tell me we're going to the White House?"

"Like I said, it will just have to stay a secret." Izzy glanced at his watch. "Better make tracks. The traffic's murder out there."

As Sam guided Annie out to the limousine, people in the lobby turned to stare, their eyes widening in pleased surprise.

Everyone knew Sam's face, Annie realized. In his uniform covered with medals, he was handsome and utterly confident.

She hadn't realized she could love him more, but she did, her heart jittering every time he looked at her.

But *marriage*.

That meant finding a house and picking out silverware. It meant *babies*.

Right now they couldn't even figure out which coast they should live on, and Annie simply couldn't walk away from the resort that was her parents' legacy.

Not that Sam had ever suggested it. But the differences between them were huge.

"I know there will be some problems," Sam said quietly. "But we can handle problems."

Annie looked down, assaulted by a familiar blend of desire, excitement, and raw fear. How could this possibly work? Their lives were too different. Sometimes it felt as if they lived on two different planets.

And because she loved Sam as much as she did, Annie refused to give him anything but the best.

"We'll talk," she said. "I promise we will. Soon, Sam."

"Tonight."

As he helped her into the limousine, a mummy strolled

past, walking stiff legged with three witches. "Taylor's with me on this," Sam said grimly. "So is Buzz."

"You spoke to Buzz?"

"Damned right I did. He said you should marry me, even though I'm not a Marine. I'm marshaling all my support, I warn you." Ignoring Izzy, Sam pulled a long box from his pocket. "Starting with this."

Annie opened the box, gasping when she saw a bracelet covered with silver charms. She smiled as she touched a tiny Jaguar, an Eiffel tower, a set of beach chairs, and a tiny pair of spa slippers, all the things that were part of her dreams. Then she saw the last charm. "I recognize this one."

"You should. It's in all the guide books." Sam slid the bracelet gently into place on her wrist. "And you've got your private tour of the White House whenever you want. You've also got this." He pressed an envelope into her hands.

"Sam, I can't—"

"Two tickets to Paris. The hitch is that I get to go with you."

"You're pushing. You promised that—"

"To hell with what I promised. We've had enough time to think about this, Annie. Speaking for myself, I'm crazy in love and I'd marry you tomorrow. If we were going to back out, we'd have done it by now."

He pulled her against him and kissed her hard. When Annie was cross-eyed and breathless he pulled away. "Stop worrying about problems that may never happen. There are better ways to spend your time."

She took a jerky breath, trying to clear her head. "I'm trying to protect both of us, don't you see?"

"I see perfectly. You're good at taking care of other people, but it's time you took care of yourself."

"We can discuss it tonight." Maybe then her heart wouldn't be climbing into her throat. "How's your leg?"

"I've got full range of motion back. They're going to put me through a few more weeks of testing at Bethesda to check the partial knee replacement, and they want to do something to my shoulder. Thermal capsular shrinkage, they called it."

"Must be a new technique."

"Brand-new. They heat the ligaments surgically, then tighten them so my shoulder won't go out of place again." Sam ran his thumb gently over her cheek. "Except for that, I'm tough as nails. The truth is, I've never felt so strong, and I owe that all to you."

He looked strong, she thought. In fact he looked over-whelming. And if he kept doing that thing to her cheek, she'd forget how to breathe. Right now she had to keep her head and do what was right for both of them.

Even if it hurt terribly.

She turned away as the Renwick Gallery and the Old Executive Office Building flashed by. They passed a sweeping lawn, a fountain, dignified white columns, and then the limousine slowed.

Annie's breath caught.

She whirled, staring at Sam. "The White House? You wouldn't *possibly* arrange that without telling me."

"Not the White House. He was there last month." Izzy didn't bother to conceal his pride. "I hear he made quite an impression."

"You *were*?"

The SEAL shrugged, looking uncomfortable. "It was no big deal. I wasn't going to make a fuss about it. A lot of people were there."

Behind him Izzy raised five fingers.

Annie tried to digest this new piece of information as the Ellipse faded behind them. "So where *are* we going?"

"You'll see. It's right around the corner."

Annie watched ghouls and goblins race along the sidewalks, waving bags that would soon be heavy with treats. If they weren't headed to the White House, then where? What could be more important than an official reception at 1600 Pennsylvania Avenue?

A Navy function? A press conference?

She knew Sam hated protocol and formality almost as much as he hated trying to take things easy. He'd never look forward to an evening of fuss and forced politeness.

She frowned as the limo slowed. The chauffeur opened the door.

Taylor was waiting, flanked by a distinguished, white-haired man in a uniform with even more medals than Sam had.

Leave it to Taylor to arrive on the arm of an admiral.

Taylor swung her omnipresent Louis Vuitton bag across the seat, then slid in, elegant as ever in spike heels and a little black suit. "I hope we didn't keep you waiting," she said breathlessly. "Admiral Howe was just pointing out a possible plot complication for my next book, and we totally forgot the time." She studied Annie with a critical eye, then nodded. "You look just right."

"Just right for *what*?" Annie muttered. "Sam won't tell me a thing."

Taylor smiled faintly. "You'll see." She flicked the glittering silver charms, slanting a glance at Sam. "What did she say?"

Sam's frown was answer enough.

"I was just speaking with Admiral Howe about how nice it would be for you to have the ceremony at the White House."

Annie felt her face go pale.

On the other side of the spacious interior, the admiral took a seat and looked at Sam, raising an eyebrow.

"Annie, I'd like you to meet my commanding officer, Admiral Ulysses Howe. Admiral, I'm pleased to introduce Annie O'Toole."

The admiral took Annie's hand in a firm grip. "I feel like I know you already. Your sister told me about that prank you played on the senior girls' gym class."

"What prank?" Sam looked interested.

Annie ignored the question. "Maybe you can tell me where we're going, Admiral Howe. It seems to be top secret."

"I'm afraid my lips are sealed. This is Sam's event, and he's calling the shots."

The limousine cruised into a turn, passing Buffy the Vampire Slayer, Napoleon, and an adult in a gorilla suit. "Washington as usual," Admiral Howe murmured. "Evil, egotism, and monkey business wherever you look." He smiled at Annie. "But we won't talk about that. I hope you're enjoying your accommodations, Ms. O'Toole."

"Everything is lovely. If the hotel keeps sending me roses, I might never leave."

Izzy cleared his throat.

Admiral Howe fought a smile.

"What?" Annie looked from one man to the other.

"The roses aren't from the hotel," the admiral said carefully.

"But I thought—" Annie glanced at Sam. "Why didn't you tell me?"

Sam looked at her, his heart in his eyes. "I was getting around to it, but we kept getting interrupted."

"You sweet idiot," she said lovingly.

"Macho idiot hero," Izzy corrected as Annie touched Sam's cheek tenderly.

Admiral Howe nodded. "Did you ask her yet?"

Sam looked up, blinking. "I, uh—"

"Speak up, son."

"I was trying to," Sam said grimly. "Then things started getting crowded in here."

The admiral's eyes narrowed. "Why wait until you were in the car?"

"Only way I could be sure she wouldn't run away."

Annie felt her face flush. Did *everyone* know that Sam was pushing her to marry him—and that she couldn't come up with an answer?

"Forgive me, Ms. O'Toole," the admiral said gruffly. "I'm old, rude, and stubborn. Sometimes I forget that people need to live their own lives." His gaze drifted for a moment, fixed through the windows on a place that seemed far away from Washington and their polished limousine.

Thanks to Sam and Izzy, Annie now knew something about the events leading up to the attack at the Navy's safe house in the mountains. That explained the sadness she saw in the admiral's eyes.

After a long silence, he seemed to pull himself back. "It's good to have you back, Commander."

"Thank you, sir."

"Have you given any thought to that matter we discussed?"

"I'm considering it, sir."

"Take as long as you need." The admiral's eyes narrowed. "Which means you have three more days to make up your mind."

"I'll keep the matter in mind, sir."

Annie frowned. Why did Sam look so thoughtful?

The limousine slowed in front of an old three-story brick building. Beyond the small circular drive, Annie saw broad steps packed with children in navy uniforms.

"I don't understand." She leaned closer to the window. "This looks like a school. Who are those children smiling and waving?"

"They're *my* kids," Sam said gruffly.

As the children rushed toward the car, Annie's amazement grew. She watched Sam's whole face light up, wreathed in the broadest of smiles. These were the children whose lives he'd saved on the school bus, she realized. They were more important than a Navy press conference or a private dinner at the White House.

His kids.

Emotion left her throat knotted as she stared at him, fiercely proud.

She trusted this man completely. But how could she trust herself? The things she felt were too new, full of racing highs and jittery lows. Annie's life had always been scheduled, planned, with her resort taking all her focus. Now Sam had turned that careful core inside out.

Annie stifled a sigh.

Every time she looked at Sam, her heart skittered painfully.

Giving him up was going to be the hardest thing she'd ever done.

❖ ❖ ❖

Surrounded by screaming children, Sam escorted Annie up the steps. He stopped often to grip a hand or press a shoulder. Twice he stopped to wipe away tears of a crying, overwrought child.

Annie felt her own eyes start to blur. He could be a politician, she thought, except campaigning would be sheer torture for him.

Inside the school more children surged out of classrooms, followed by their beaming teachers. The building was old, with high ceilings and small windows, but every inch was scrubbed and gleaming. Sam's discomfort seemed to vanish as he moved purposefully through the rows of clapping schoolchildren.

Admiral Howe chuckled as he moved beside Annie. "I do believe that man could be president if he wanted. I've been told his appeal to female audiences has gone right through the roof."

Annie frowned.

"Of course, we both know that running for political office is the *last* thing Commander McKade would ever consider."

Annie's frown eased just a little.

"I think he'd prefer having a few broken bones." The admiral paused. "Of course, with an attractive physiotherapist like *you* to keep him in line . . ." He stepped in front of Annie, bringing her to a halt. "So are you going to marry the man or not?"

Annie felt her face fill with heat. "I haven't—that is, we both need more time. It's not something to rush into."

"Don't take too long, my dear. I know you've got two careers to deal with, and no, it won't be easy. You're two smart, stubborn people and there are bound to be sparks." He looked off into the sunlight for a long time. "When you lose someone close, you understand how precious time is and why it's a crime to waste it. So do us all a favor and marry the man. If you don't put him out of his misery, he'll be no use to me," he said gruffly. "You'll laugh and you'll fight. You'll hurt when he's gone and you'll worry that he's in danger." His voice hardened. "But that man over there will make it worthwhile, Ms. O'Toole. Men just don't come any finer than that."

Annie turned, following his eyes. Sam was on one knee, gravely accepting a bouquet of misshapen paper roses from a little girl with gapped teeth and crooked pigtails.

The children began to clap. Through a blur of sound, Annie heard the admiral's echoing words.

Do us all a favor and marry the man.

Heaven knows, part of her wanted to.

But another part of her was huddled weak-kneed in a corner, frozen with fear. Marriages didn't last today, not even those with perfect odds. And Annie didn't want to fail, not with something as precious as Sam's love.

Why couldn't they just go on as they had, exchanging silly notes, talking too long on the phone, meeting whenever they could? That way was safer. That way no one could get hurt.

Marriage was too big, too permanent, and a good way to get hurt.

The clapping grew thunderous as the school principal escorted Sam into a classroom where pictures covered every available surface.

In crayons, paint, and markers, the children had captured the SEAL as he'd looked when he'd been publicly released from the hospital in Bethesda. Other pictures showed Sam receiving a medal from Admiral Howe, Sam on *Good Morning America*, Sam on *Oprah*.

Annie swallowed hard, trying to get rid of the lump in her throat. *Put him out of his misery or he'll be no use to me.*

She watched Sam sit down in the middle of a big rug, ringed with children who stared up at him in awed silence. He blinked, just a little, as a teacher handed him the pile of get-well cards they had made right after the accident but been unable to send, not knowing where he was.

"They're still frightened, you know."

Annie looked up at Izzy. "Why? He's fine. Thanks to the surgery, he might even be stronger than he was before the accident."

"You and I know that, but these kids still aren't sure. He almost died saving them and they saw every brutal second. Their teacher tells me they thought he was dead, and nothing anyone said would change that. They thought the grown-ups were hiding the truth to protect them, so now they just want to see him up close, to touch him and be sure he's really okay." His mouth worked for a moment. "Lots of them still have nightmares about that bus ride."

Annie understood that. She still had some nightmares of her own after that firefight on the mountain. How much worse for a child who didn't understand. Fair or not, these kids felt responsible for Sam's injuries and needed to know he was safe.

Her throat tightened as Sam bent down and tugged a small boy with untied sneakers onto his lap. Another boy wriggled up beside them, pressing a stuffed lion into Sam's hands. They were joined by two little girls with a plateful of homemade cookies.

"He's as good as they get," Annie whispered. "Those kids know that." *So do I.*

"But you meet everyone in your line of work." Izzy shrugged.

"Real A-list people. Football heroes. Movie stars. Plastic surgeons and billionaires. Compared to them, Sam's just a regular, average—"

"There's nothing regular or average about Sam," Annie said fiercely. "Money can't make a man a hero. Those kids know that, too."

Izzy didn't answer. He was grinning when she turned to glare at him. "You said it, not me."

"Stop grinning. Just because I like him doesn't mean I'm going to *marry* him."

"Like?"

Annie took a deep breath. "Okay, love. Fine, I admit it. But that doesn't change my mind. We need to be careful, to be certain we're not making a mistake."

"You can't be sure." Izzy watched Sam take a cookie from a girl with adoring eyes, smiling when another child reached up to hug him tightly. "The only way to know where life's taking you is by living it, Annie."

"How? This is all too new. I don't know what to think, how to act. I don't even recognize my own feelings anymore."

"It's called feeling alive. You almost died, so you're bound to go through some changes after that."

Annie sighed. "I've never been confused in my life, and now suddenly I'm confused by everything."

"Give it time, Doc."

There were children all over Sam now, two on his lap, a half dozen at his feet, one on each arm. He had a chalk stripe down the sleeve of his uniform and a battered Teenage Mutant Ninja Turtle shoved in his face. A juice box was tilted toward his chest, perilously close to spilling. Annie's heart skittered as Sam gently removed the Turtle, straightened the juice box, and eased the boy off his shoulder and settled him on his leg, never losing a single beat of the conversation.

Air whooshed out of her chest and all her resistance vanished. She couldn't fight the truth any longer. It would be criminal to lose what she had by worrying about what she might not have.

She knew there would be sleepless nights and juggling of schedules. There would be fights—but there would be lots of making up.

If Sam wanted her, she was his.

In sickness and in health. She'd put him back together again if he needed it, too. She wanted the whole nine yards, with a dozen kids and a few stray dogs and cats thrown in for general chaos.

The thought was still a little frightening, but she couldn't think of any better way to spend the next fifty years.

There was a stir as the door opened. A furry body streaked over the floor, pushing his way onto Sam's already crowded lap.

"I thought Donegal was down in a training program in Virginia."

"All finished," Izzy explained. "He'll be with Sam from now on. Admiral Howe likes the idea of a canine program."

Tail wagging, Donegal settled against Sam and took a bite of a cookie offered by a boy with thick glasses.

Izzy crossed his arms. "So are you going to marry him?"

Annie straightened her dress, then slowly smiled. "Just as soon as I get over being terrified."

"Terrified of what? It's only your whole future, your commitment to your resort, and the welfare and happiness of your unborn children at stake." He touched her arm. "Relax. You're going to have an amazing time, I guarantee it. Not easy, not ordinary, but definitely amazing."

Annie thought about it. Amazing was probably right. Suddenly she couldn't wait to get started.

She crossed the crowded room as the children jumped up to perform a rehearsed musical salute to their hero. Transfixed, Annie listened to drums bang out of rhythm and violins play flat. When the music ended and the children left to put away their instruments, Annie sank down beside Sam.

Leaning close, one hand on his shoulder, she whispered in his ear. "I've thought about it."

"Annie, you don't have to—"

"The answer is yes."

"I think you should take more time to—" He blinked. "Yes? You mean—"

"I mean no more worrying or bracing for imagined problems. We're going to make this work," she said fiercely.

His eyes were intent, his focus almost palpable. "I don't want to rush you."

"I want to marry you, Sam. I couldn't possibly love you more."

"You're sure? Because if you need more time—"

Annie pulled a tall witch's hat from the nearby table. Holding it in front of them, she leaned down and brushed his lips with her finger. "Stop arguing for once, McKade. Just kiss me, will you?"

"I thought you'd never ask," Sam muttered hoarsely.

Around her the room, the noise, the whole world faded. His arms tightened, the kiss enveloping her. Beside them, Donegal looked on with interest, tail wagging.

Admiral Howe pulled a cigar from his pocket and smiled, looking immensely satisfied.

Izzy looked smug.

Taylor beamed.

In one corner of the room, a little boy in a crooked bow tie nudged his neighbor. "There he goes again." He made a sound of disgust. "Heck, he's not going to be good for *anything* now." His voice fell. "Next thing you know, they're having sex."

His friend frowned. "They are?"

"Sure. Last week the kindergarten teacher was kissing the coach and she kept brushing his cheek like he had something on it. Then he kept clearing his throat like he had food stuck. The boy nodded importantly. "So sex has got something to do with food."

"Probably chocolate," his friend said morosely. "No way I would kiss a girl, not for all the chocolate in the world."

Fortunately, Sam didn't seem to agree. He pulled Annie beside him, locking her hand in his. Even with three squirming children in his lap, he didn't let go of her hand, his eyes intent with promises.

This is as good as it gets, Annie thought, giddily.

"I might be relocating to Monterey," Sam said quietly. "If this canine unit gets the green light, we'll be working with a breeder out there." He grinned at Donegal. "I know one dog who can't wait to show his stuff."

Annie could barely speak. "Monterey? But that's only—"

"Forty minutes away. Funny how it worked, isn't it?"

"But how—"

Sam shook his head. "My lips are sealed."

"Commander?" the boy in his lap asked solemnly. "Are you going to kiss her some more, then have some babies?"

Sam looked at Annie. "I don't know, are we?"

"Probably a dozen." Annie wasn't frightened anymore. Admiral Howe was right. They'd laugh and they'd fight and she'd hurt when he was gone. But they'd be just fine. Annie knew without question.

Now their only problem was Taylor slipping them into her next book, red lace and all. Annie tilted her head thoughtfully. Maybe Taylor needed a little distraction to keep her occupied. No, make that six feet four inches of distraction. Sam would probably know someone up to the task. She'd have to ask him tonight.

But Annie forgot all about her newest scheme as the door opened with an explosion of flashbulbs. Reporters jostled for space at the doorway. Five men in dark suits entered the room and scanned it thoroughly. One touched his ear, his lips moving.

"Someone wants to meet you." Sam leaned closer, his hard body brushing hers. "You can discuss the details of that private tour of the White House you wanted."

Annie was still leaning against him when she heard the piano creak. She stood up straight as the music teacher launched into the opening chords of "Hail to the Chief."

"You didn't. You *wouldn't*." Annie swallowed hard. "I'm going to get you for not telling me about this, McKade."

"I'm sure you'll think of something truly inventive." His eyes glinted as he leaned closer. "Just make sure that red lace is involved."

With one sentence he left her pulse jolting and her throat dry, wondering how soon they could be alone. Amazing, she thought. It was turning out just the way Izzy had predicted.

Then an entourage burst through the door to the wild clapping of children and teachers. Her eyes aglow, Annie faced the future with the man she loved.

Here we go.

Taylor's Toning Masque

    1 medium cucumber (organic, preferably)
    1 cup yogurt (substitute sour cream if your skin is
      very dry)
    1/2 papaya, peeled and seeded
    3 egg whites
    3 drops lime essential oil

Scrub cucumber, removing wax. Dice, then process in a blender until a smooth paste is formed. Add all other ingredients and blend until smooth.

Store excess in a glass jar in the refrigerator.

Always use on clean face. Apply generously, avoiding eyes, and relax for ten minutes. Wash off gently with cool water for a lovely tightening and toning action.

Taylor likes to use this while she's dreaming up devious plot twists.

Annie's Special Salt Glow

2 cups sea salt (with no additives)
1/2 cup extra virgin olive oil
1/2 cup almond oil
12 drops lavender essential oil
6 drops rose geranium oil

Mix all ingredients in a glass bowl.

Store in an airtight jar in the refrigerator.

After a warm bath (or during a shower), work gently over the skin with a soft washcloth until your skin glows with health. Rinse thoroughly. Great for exfoliation, but not for use on the face.

Annie swears by it.

Sam just likes how it smells.

Author's Note

HAVE YOU TRIED OUT YOUR SPA TREATMENTS YET? IF SO, I HOPE they brought you a taste of the peace and beauty of Summerwind. In fact, something tells me that Sam is going to be learning a lot more about exfoliating techniques and facial gel than this SEAL wants to know! But for Annie, he'll go the distance.

If you enjoyed Summerwind and its gorgeous seaside locale, look for *Monterey Bay Shoreline Guide* by Jerry Emory (Berkeley and Los Angeles: University of California Press, 1999). This wonderful guide is full of maps and local history along with great sidebars on everything from why shorebirds bathe to dune restoration. The pictures alone will make you feel as if you just took a vacation.

If you yearn for the pampering of a spa (and who doesn't), you'll find a great overview in *Spa Guide U.S.A.* by John Segesta and Anne Stein (Cold Spring Harbor, New York: Open Road Publishing, 2000). There's something for everyone here, from the exotic combination of an Asian-influenced spa set in an adobe resort nestled in the piñons above Santa Fe to the full-scale luxury of destination spas like La Costa and Golden Door.

Interested in massage? Look for *The Complete Illustrated Guide to Massage* by Stewart Mitchell (New York: Barnes and Noble, 1999). This is a great introduction, with subjects that range from specific massage techniques to massage treatments for common injuries. There are even case studies.

Want to whip up more home spa recipes? Try *Natural Beauty at Home* by Janice Cox (New York: Henry Holt and Company, 1995). Oils, rubs, masks, and scrubs—this book has them all. You can even find recipes for mouthwash and lip balm! Take a weekend off and create your own spa at home.

And if Izzy seems familiar, he should be! He first charmed his way onto the page in my 1999 book, *The Perfect Gift*. If you're interested in the secret cruise ship mission mentioned in *My Spy*, you can get behind-the-scenes details in *Going Overboard*, published in 2001.

Be sure to visit me online at *www.christinaskye.com*. The recipes are hot and the excerpts are even hotter! Make yourself at home while you read about earlier books, new stories, writing tips, and home spa treatments. I'd love to hear from you, so drop me a note online at *talktochristina@christinaskye.com*. I will be putting links to some of the most beautiful spa resorts at my Web site, so you can take a mini-vacation right at your computer. Be sure to drop by.

What's next?

Don't be surprised if Taylor commandeers a book all for herself! It's only fair that the screwup O'Toole sister gets her own shot at happiness. Problem is, she's got a whole lot to learn about love—and trust. Taylor knows how to shop till she drops, but it will take a special man, a hero with an iron-clad code of honor, to teach her that some gifts come with no strings attached and they are given forever.

Lucky for him, our hero doesn't realize that trouble is Taylor's middle name!

Stay tuned to my Web site for all the scandalous details.

Until then, happy reading.

Christina

Christina Skye

About the Author

Christina Skye lives on the western slopes of the McDowell Mountains in Arizona. *My Spy* is her sixteenth novel, her first set at a resort and spa. "Need I say that I loved every minute of every day of my exacting research! Just check out my collection of exfoliating gloves."

Be sure to visit Christina online at *www.christinaskye.com* for updates and more fun spa recipes. Watch for her new book, *Code Name: Princess*, coming in October 2004.

There was a naked man in her shower.

Six-feet four inches of man, judging by the brief glimpse she had from the living room.

Granted, she had just staggered off a twenty-two-hour flight, and her eyes were bloodshot, burning with exhaustion, but Summer clearly could see the outline of a male body down the corridor. She was pretty sure that ringing sound was water running, and that other sound, low and rumbling, was a dark male groan of satisfaction.

Her stomach clenched. Okay, she was out of here. Either there was a huge mistake about her room assignment or this was another trick. There had been constant hazing in the last year, little things like papers missing from her desk back at work and coffee spilled inside her locker. This could be someone's warped idea of funny. It would have taken only a few phone calls to arrange it.

See what it takes to rattle the new kid. See if she'll stick or if she'll run. Summer shook her head, swung up her suitcase, and opened the front door of the guesthouse.

The brass plaque on the shadowed porch still read "Blue Suite." Beneath that, her name was still written in small, elegant letters.

Her room. Her name.

Something moved out in the darkness, and she froze.

Then Summer realized it was just her taxi, pulling away in a hiss of gravel. Completely exhausted, grimy from hours of travel, she stared longingly at the cozy room with the fruit basket on the black lacquered dresser and the huge vase of tulips framed by the front window.

Heavenly. *No way* was she leaving.

She kicked off her shoes, padded across the room, and shoved her suitcase behind the couch. Her heavy coat went flying onto a sleek leather sofa along with her briefcase. Nursing a glass of water from the small refrigerator, she wandered through the plush living area. There were no signs of anyone living here, no dirty socks on the floor or clean shirts hanging in the closet. The bed was made, and there were no dents in the pillows.

Summer couldn't wait to sink down into that soft bed and sleep for a year.

Beyond the living area, water struck the glass walls of the shower, and the towel hanging over the door slid free, giving Summer an unobstructed view of broad shoulders and a world-class naked body.

A little voice hissed out a warning.

Punchy with exhaustion and anger, Summer ignored it. She crossed her arms and sat down grimly in a velvet chair, where she had a full view of the airy bathroom and the shower enclosure.

He was singing an old Beatles song—low and very off-key—when the water hissed off, and the glass door slid open.

An odd tingle shot through Summer's stomach. Definitely a world-class body, with the sculpted shoulders of an athlete in superb condition and a chest to make a grown woman cry. Drops of warm water clung to the dark hair on his chest, then traveled lower.

She swallowed hard. She hadn't planned to look, but somehow she was doing it anyway.

When the stranger turned and saw her, he went still, muscles locking hard. The part of Summer's mind that was still functioning noted that the man had truly *excellent* muscles. As she sat rigid, he made no move to go for the towel angled across the floor.

A smile played across his mouth. "Maid?" He had the hint of an accent she couldn't trace. Something smoky and rough.

"Guest," she countered flatly. "And unless you talk real fast, pal, you're going to be telling your story to the local police."

His smile didn't waver. "Now you're terrifying me." The roughness was there, but there wasn't a hint of anxiety in his cool smile or the slow way he scooped up his towel and tossed it over his shoulder.

Concealing nothing.

Obviously, modesty was a foreign concept to the man.

Summer prayed to the patron saint of travelers to stay cool under his unrelenting stare, but the prayer wasn't working. Heat climbed up her body in a dozen sensitive locations. No doubt it was the result of the industrial-strength Dramamine she'd taken on the plane, dulling her edge.

"Get out," she said tightly.

"You look tired. Sorry about this." He anchored the towel low around his waist and shook his head. "Things were just starting to get interesting, too." He didn't turn, giving a two-finger wave as he crossed the living area. "I'll talk to the kids about this tomorrow. Meanwhile, enjoy the shower, now that I got things all warmed up for you."

The front door opened.

"Night, Ms. Mulcahey."

Summer saw the towel slide lower on his lean hips. She was pretty sure her mouth was hanging open. She closed her eyes and sank back in the velvet chair, feeling the steam of his shower brush her face like a warm caress.

She'd had aggravating assignments before, but something told her *this* one was going to take the cake.

Don't miss out on enthralling romances from

Christina Skye

❧

__0440-20929-3	THE BLACK ROSE	$5.99/$7.99 in Canada
__0440-20864-5	THE RUBY	$6.50/$9.99
__0440-21644-3	COME THE NIGHT	$6.99/$10.99
__0440-21647-8	COME THE DAWN	$5.99/$7.99
__0440-23571-5	2000 KISSES	$6.99/$9.99
__0440-23575-8	GOING OVERBOARD	$6.99/$9.99
__0440-23578-2	MY SPY	$6.99/$9.99
__0440-23759-9	HOT PURSUIT	$6.99/$10.99
__0440-23760-2	CODE NAME: NANNY	$6.99/$10.99

The Very Best in Contemporary Women's Fiction

SANDRA BROWN

___28951-9 Texas! Lucky $7.50/$10.99
___28990-X Texas! Chase $7.50/$10.99
___29500-4 Texas! Sage $7.50/$10.99
___29085-1 22 Indigo Place $6.99/$9.99
___29783-X A Whole New Light $7.50/$10.99
___57158-3 Breakfast In Bed $7.50/$10.99
___57600-3 Tidings of Great Joy $6.99/$9.99
___57602-X In a Class by Itself $6.99/$9.99
___57603-8 Thursday's Child $7.50/$10.99

___56768-3 Adam's Fall $6.99/$9.99
___56045-X Temperatures Rising $6.99/$9.99
___56274-6 Fanta C $7.50/$10.99
___56278-9 Long Time Coming $7.50/$10.99
___57157-5 Heaven's Price $6.99/$9.99
___29751-1 Hawk O'Toole's Hostage $6.50/$8.99
___57601-1 Send No Flowers $7.50/$10.99
___57604-6 Riley in the Morning $7.50/$10.99
___57605-4 The Rana Look $7.50/$10.99

TAMI HOAG

___29534-9 Lucky's Lady $7.99/$11.99
___29053-3 Magic $7.99/$11.99
___56050-6 Sarah's Sin $7.50/$10.99
___56451-x Night Sins $7.99/$11.99
___57188-5 A Thin Dark Line $7.99/$11.99
___58252-6 Dust to Dust $7.99/$11.99

___29272-2 Still Waters $7.99/$11.99
___56160-X Cry Wolf $7.99/$11.99
___56161-8 Dark Paradise $7.99/$11.99
___56452-8 Guilty As Sin $7.99/$11.99
___57960-6 Ashes to Ashes $7.99/$11.99
___58357-3 Dark Horse $7.99/$11.99

NORA ROBERTS

___29078-9 Genuine Lies $7.99/$11.99
___28578-5 Public Secrets $7.50/$10.99
___26461-3 Hot Ice $7.99/$11.99
___26574-1 Sacred Sins $7.99/$11.99

___27859-2 Sweet Revenge $7.99/$11.99
___27283-7 Brazen Virtue $7.99/$11.99
___29597-7 Carnal Innocence $7.99/$11.99
___80326-3 Divine Evil $22.00/$32.00

Please enclose check or money order only, no cash or CODs. Shipping & handling costs: $5.50 U.S. mail, $7.50 UPS. New York and Tennessee residents must remit applicable sales tax. Canadian residents must remit applicable GST and provincial taxes. Please allow 4 – 6 weeks for delivery. All orders are subject to availability. This offer subject to change without notice. Please call 1–800–726–0600 for further information.

Bantam Dell Publishing Group, Inc.		
Attn: Customer Service	TOTAL AMT	$_____
400 Hahn Road	SHIPPING & HANDLING	$_____
Westminster, MD 21157	SALES TAX (NY, TN)	$_____
	TOTAL ENCLOSED	$_____

Name _____

Address _____

City/State/Zip _____

Daytime Phone (_____) _____

with # Marilyn Pappano

sometimes miracles do happen . . . .

Don't miss any of these extraordinary novels from

Jean Stone

Places by the Sea
____57424-8 $5.99/$7.99

Tides of the Heart
____57786-7 $5.99/$7.99

The Summer House
____58083-3 $5.99/$8.99

Off Season
____58086-8 $6.99/$10.99

Trust Fund Babies
____58411-1 $5.99/$8.99

Beach Roses
____58412-X $6.50/$9.99

Don't miss any of these delightful romances from

Emily Carmichael

Finding Mr. Right
___57874-X $6.99/$10.99 Canada

A Ghost for Maggie
__57875-8 $5.50/$8.50

Diamond in the Ruff
__58283-6 $5.50/$8.99

The Good, the Bad, and the Sexy
__58284-4 $6.99/$10.99

Gone to the Dogs
__58633-5 $6.50/$9.99